Tom Fox's storytelling emerges out of many years spent in academia, working on the history of the Christian Church. A respected authority on that subject, he has recently turned his attentions towards exploring the new stories that can be drawn out of its mysterious dimensions. *The Seventh Commandment* is Tom's second novel.

Praise for Tom Fox's novels:

'With *The Seventh Commandment*, Tom Fox has produced another fine mystery thriller that is both well-written and as intriguing as it is exciting, and its Rome setting is excellent. I look forward to the next!'
For Winter Nights

'Head and shoulders above the usual Church themed thrillers with an intelligent plot and thoughtful characters'
For Reading Addicts

'Fox takes the reader through a fast-pace exploration of the inner workings of the Holy See and attempts to place faith and proof under the proverbial microscope. A fascinating thriller that will pull readers in from the opening pages, Fox delivers and shows his potential as a first-rate writer in the genre'
Pechey Ponderings

'A twisting, turning thriller with an intriguing mystery at its heart, pits good against evil, faith against cynicism, truth against lies . . . and is guaranteed to keep the pages turning from the knockout opening sequence to a shocking and nail-biting conclusion'
Wigan Today

By Tom Fox and available from Headline

Dominus
The Seventh Commandment

Digital Short Stories

Genesis (*prequel to* Dominus)
Exodus (*sequel to* Dominus)

TOM FOX

THE
SEVENTH
COMMANDMENT

HEADLINE

First published in paperback in Great Britain 2017 by
HEADLINE PUBLISHING GROUP

1

Cataloguing in Publication Data is available from the British Library

ISBN 978 1 4722 4242 6

Typeset in Meridien by Palimpsest Book Production Ltd, Falkirk, Stirlingshire

Printed and bound in Great Britain by Clays Ltd, St Ives plc

MIX
Paper from
responsible sources
FSC® C104740
www.fsc.org

Headline's policy is to use papers that are natural, renewable and recyclable
products and made from wood grown in well-managed forests and other
controlled sources. The logging and manufacturing processes are expected to
conform to the environmental regulations of the country of origin.

HEADLINE PUBLISHING GROUP
An Hachette UK Company
Carmelite House
50 Victoria Embankment
London EC4Y 0DZ

www.headline.co.uk
www.hachette.co.uk

To Katie,
who always believes;
And to John,
who tries to.

Prophecy possesses a power unlike any other over human consciousness. However secular the race might become, however agnostic to religious belief, the thought that the future might be surely, perfectly *known* captivates and frightens in equal measure.

It is the greatest form of mind control, for if what is to come is already known, written in stone, it cannot be escaped. And if the future cannot be escaped, what sense is there in anything other than despair?

From the personal diary of Emil Durré

'The old pharaoh's heart was hard, but the new pharaoh's heart is harder.

I shall lay my hand upon him anew, and all his people, and my signs and wonders shall be multiplied.

I shall stretch out my hands against them, that they may know my great judgements – as I will upon the one who discovers these things, whose terrible death shall come most swiftly.

It shall come to pass in the seventeenth year of the second millennium after the coming of the Sun, when the great star is at her peak over the Eternal City.

And the first sign shall be that the river shall run with blood . . .'

PART ONE

Discovery

1

The present – morning

It happened during the night, or during the earliest morning. At least, so would go the official stories, to emerge in due course from the confusion generated by the discovery and the chaos of the days to follow.

The discovery itself took place at 4.15 a.m., according to the most reliable reports. Later legend would have it that it was spotted first by a jogger, eyes adapting to the changing light of morning; but with an event so large, that swept through a city of so many millions, such a tale could amount only to wishful thinking. The media, as the world had long known, always craves a point of initial contact, a voice to speak as 'the first on the scene'. And too often they will create what they cannot find.

As to when it truly began, such speculations could only be guesswork. They ranged from a few minutes before the first crowds began to gather, there in the morning light, to perhaps several hours earlier. The receding darkness of the Roman night, illuminated only by the false blues and oranges of so much electric light, made it all but impossible to tell the river's true colour until the first rays of dawn started to creep over the rooftops.

But when the sun finally rose and those rays came, there was no guessing any more.

Something had happened.

In the rising brightness of morning, the great Tiber River sparkled like a time-worn ribbon streaking through the unsuspecting city. For how many millennia she had carved her way through that landscape could never be known, but as a landmark she was as ancient as written history. And though she flowed that day in the same direction she always had, charting no different a course than she'd woven through Rome's seven hills since the city first rose out of myth and legend, the light of this day saw her appear as never before in the whole of her storied history.

The river flowed red, thick and crimson and opaque.

Between her banks, the pulsing artery swept like an angry brushstroke through the Eternal City. It lapped at the large boulders that lined the Tiber's course here and there, at the concrete barriers that cemented its path in the most central regions. And the city woke, and saw the wonder, and flocked in droves to the riverside.

The scent remained as noxious as always. The Tiber had been polluted to the point of muted ecological crisis for years, and while it retained its visual appeal, few sought out its banks for invigorating strolls or breaths of air that even vaguely resembled fresh. But this morning the elderly exited their apartments alongside children, businesswomen alongside hastily parked taxi drivers, all to bear the burden of pinching their noses at the river's shores in order to stare as a vein of blood cut through the heart of their venerable home.

They watched – a whole population, crowded along its embankments, gazing down from riverside windows or catching live feeds on televisions and browsers. Mystified. Confused. Some laughed, some took snaps and began new trends on social media as curiosity swept across the Internet and memes guessing at hows and whys blazed through online forums and filled Twitter timelines. Other observers tried to conceal their worry. Yet others openly shouted foul. Protested. Complained. Blamed.

Some stayed away, afraid.

But the river ignored them all. As blood pulses through arteries whether witnessed or not, the old river simply flowed, steadily, calmly, ominously, with redness pouring from her eyes.

One month earlier
Central Rome, near the Basilica di San Clemente al Laterano

The object that would change everything was not of impressive proportions. It was neither massive nor ornate, and in appearance it was not visually captivating. As Manuel Herrero held it in his hands, his fingers curled gently around its rough edges, it felt almost ordinary. And yet, somehow, majestic.

Manuel was himself covered in dust and grime, red nicks marking his flesh from the labours of the dig. He wore his usual coveralls, ragged and dirty from years of service, and his face was smeared with sweat that bore muddy tracks from the backs of his hands. He had never been a man to stand on formality or care about appearance, but in this instant he suddenly felt unworthy. Moments such as this were the preserve of greater men than he. Men of refinement, of authority, and with decent clothes.

Nevertheless, it was he and no one else who bore the object in his grip, and Manuel's eyes glistened. It was all but surreal that he should be holding it – that something like this could actually be nestled between his tired fingers. *A discovery.*

The stone, he imagined, must have lain at rest beneath the soil for untold generations. Silent, waiting. The earth above it had perhaps at first been only dust, maybe a thin layer. The physical residue of the sky – innocuous particles that float on the breeze, gently accumulated as they settled from heaven over the span of so many years. Gradually the dust would have become a layer of new earth, the former specks of sky transformed into ground and loam, layer over layer, shielding the stone's flat surface from view until it was secreted wholly away, hidden from the eyes of history.

Or perhaps the stone – maybe he should call it a tablet, it was really more tablet-like than stone – had been intentionally buried. It would have been a dark night, that seemed only appropriate: either devoid of or overwhelmingly filled with stars. Either would have fit the occasion. A man, likely in loose-fitting robes and probably with a hood concealing gaunt features, slicing the razor edge of his spade into the stony earth. *Would it have been a deep burial?* Certainly nowhere near as deep as it lay now, so many metres beneath the noise of the surface streets above, a whole world having arisen over it as the centuries passed. But perhaps an arm's depth, back when it was first concealed. Enough to vanish from the scrutiny of the world's inhabitants, as intentionally as any other burial, though likely far more secretive.

Or it might not have been buried at all. Perhaps it had been enshrined, right here, in this place. Not dropped into a pit dug in the clandestine night-time, but mounted in glory. Venerated, committed to eternal memory and the protection of whatever divine force had inspired its creation.

Requiem æternam dona ei, Domine . . .

There would have been songs and ceremony, surely, with chants like those offered for a departing soul, preserving that

6

which was meant to bear the light of influence upon the future.

Lux perpetua luceat ei . . .

Manuel glanced around him. The routine dig, mandated by the city, was hardly ceremonious now. Mud and dust were caked into fierce lines left over from the industrial digger, slanting at incongruous angles through layers of carved tarmac and paver stones. The tablet had been situated atop a slab of limestone that was likely once beige, before the sweat of subterranean minerals seeped in and changed its colour to a strange hodgepodge of greys and greens. Ugly, unartistic and wholly inconsequential. But it could have, just could have, once been something more. A table. A shrine. An altar.

Introibo ad altare Dei, ad Deum qui laetificat iuventutem meam . . .

Yes, Manuel thought, *I will go unto the altar of God*. The old psalm verse sprang unbidden to mind, years of pious Catholic upbringing never failing to push at the shape of his conscious thoughts. *To God, my exceeding joy*. Those were the kinds of words that would have been sung – and there would have been chanters somewhere, almost certainly, tucked away in a recessed alcove long since collapsed to rubble. What tongue would they have spoken? He didn't know enough about ancient languages to be certain of what he was looking at on the tablet's surface, but even such knowledge wouldn't provide a sure answer. The tablet could be far older than whatever society had left, buried, enshrined it in this place. Far older.

All Manuel knew for certain was that somehow, in some

way, this little discovery in his hands was going to change his life. He would not be the same, and the world would never again look as it had before.

Beneath the surface of his skin, in the nutrient-rich layer of subcutaneous fat that buffered it from flesh, tendon and bone, a host of foreign molecules hydrated and latched on to the vibrant blood cells pulsing through Manuel Herrero's capillaries. Through them the tiny forces had access to his deeper arteries and veins, into which they moved with rhythmic speed. The fact that his heartbeat was racing at a rate far higher than usual only served to push things along.

It may have been biological in form, molecular and therefore without intelligence to plot or scheme, yet the compound in his flesh was a pathogen and worked true to its foreboding name. The *pathos*, that fittingly ancient term for suffering, would come quickly enough. In anticipation, the substance raced through him, seeking the man's vital organs, latching on with a ferocity and permanence that could almost have amounted to fervour or zeal.

Outside the shell of his flesh and skin, the man still held the tablet in his hands, face flushed with the joy of discovery and his mind overwhelmed with thoughts of a life about to change. Inside, within only minutes, his organs were already beginning to decay.

By the time he learned that his life was ending, rather than changing, it would be too late. The tablet, the prophecy, and the discoverer's death – they were never meant to be separated.

And they never would be.

2

The present
Central Rome

Bodies flowed across the Piazza della Rotonda in wavelike motion, brilliant in a bewildering array of colours and fashions. They emitted the constant hum of a dozen languages and a hundred conversations – the painted, noisy backdrop of modern Rome, scented by espresso shots and cigarettes, humming in all its vibrant complexity and chaotic normalcy.

Angelina Calla observed them all, as she had so many times before.

Bodies moving like the tide. The thought was automatic, an interior voice that was a familiar rattle in her head, though its words at this moment were too poetic. She reflected, her shoulders sagging, seeking an alternative. *Like beetles. Unstoppable beetles.* A slight nod, only to herself. It was the right image, and Angelina Calla rejoiced, even as she lamented.

The tourist trade, she had long ago learned, has no down season in Rome. There are high points in the year, there are lows, but there is no moment when calm overtakes the city as eternal in its bustle as in its legend. It was the first lesson

Angelina had taken in as she'd been swept into her unwilling role and trade. She'd admired Rome all her life. Loved it. She could recount its history and mythology with the best of them, and perhaps better than most. But it was only when she'd taken to the streets and stepped out into the fray – propelled there rather than wandering the path by choice – that she had learned that ancient Roma was the true definition of a city that never sleeps or slows.

But how I wish it would all slow down, even for just a moment. Just long enough for the world to be set right.

The tourist waves came in undulating cycles. Their movements at first had seemed just as random as the beetles now imaged in Angelina's mind, just as unpredictable, and only after a season of careful observation did it become clear that there was a pattern to their frenetic behaviour. Apparently aimless bouncing from fountain to church to corners of particular squares concealed a widespread, consistently focused desire: to stand in just the right position before just the right landmarks, to take a selfie – *the absurdity of the word!* – that would make tourists X, Y and Z look precisely like tourists A, B and C, and every other gawper who'd ever bought summer tickets to the Italian Mecca.

Beetles. Maybe they're lemmings?

Shit.

She knew she had to foster a different mindset. *It's a necessity, at this point in my life.* She ruminated, not without a hint of bitterness, on her reality. *There's no other way.*

She drew her white leatherette handbag more squarely on to her lap, the knock-off gold of the cheap Versace Aurora clasp glimmering in the Italian sunlight and reflecting its rays into her brick-red hair. At the same time, she straightened herself to a less deflated posture at the metal coffee table. Beyond, framed into cramped place by surrounding buildings that had gone up over the centuries but no less impressive for it, the round hulk of the Pantheon marked the periphery of her present urban landscape.

For a woman whose livelihood came from the insatiable appetites of those wide-eyed visitors, at least a thousand of whom were currently milling about just beyond her table, filtering in great queues between the columns of the ancient temple to all the gods of Rome, now dedicated to the martyrs of the Christians, their constant presence was tantamount to job security. *No tourists, no tours.* And for a tour guide, no tours meant no cash, which meant no ability to buy over-priced espresso and sit at an outdoor café lamenting that she hadn't found a better lot in life.

But it wasn't easy to accept a reality that went against everything in her bones. Angelina Calla had brought herself up to be a scholar. She'd trained her mind, surrounded herself with wisdom and antiquity and history, certain since her afternoons as a small girl wandering through the cultural history museum in Lanciano that one day she would call those kinds of surroundings her own. Dedicating herself to the study of Classical Akkadian at university – a language tied to a culture that had flourished in Babylon and Mesopotamia almost five millennia before she had been born, long predating the Christians – Angelina had set herself on the knife-edge of a scholarly field undertaken by very few. The language itself had appealed to her linguistic interests: its characteristically angular, rune-like appearance had been one of the features that had attracted her to it when, as a teenage girl, she'd chanced upon a copy of Pritchard's classic *Ancient Near Eastern Texts* and found herself entranced in the stories of Gilgamesh's deluge and the Enuma Elish, of the goddess Astarte and the Code of Hammurabi, all of which had opened up to her in the splendour of ancient wonder and fantasy. Other people had religion and revelled in the myths of Abraham and Noah, but Angelina – conscientious humanist and, by association, convinced atheist – had never scraped after such fables or the faiths that went with them. She had ancient Babylon, the spiritual rush of human history without the burden of religious ideology, and that was more than enough for her.

By the time she'd finished her masters degree in Akkadian language and culture, Angelina was one of only a few people in the world who could consider themselves genuinely proficient in the long-dead script, and her PhD had led her into even narrower circles of expertise. It had been more than simply her academic field or the aim of her future career. It was her passion.

In the end, it had amounted to little else. A hoped-for career had been forcibly relegated to a hobby, Angelina's dreams of academic loftiness shattered by a scholarly world that just didn't seem to want her. A long string of unsuccessful job applications and discouraging interviews had left her to take whatever employment she could find – currently, as the most overqualified tour guide in Rome.

'Is that the place where Caesar got his water?' Angelina dragged a bent wooden stirrer through her coffee as her general malaise coalesced into concrete memories of the two tours she'd given that morning – stock-in-trade hour-long walks through 'The Rome of Ancient History' that were the staple nourishment of her present existence. The bizarre question had come from a particularly inquisitive member of her second group, just before lunch, as the woman had posed in a floral muumuu for a stream of photographs her trigger-happy husband never stopped taking. She'd asked it while pointing to a marble fountain with a massive depiction of the Graeco-Roman god Triton at its centre, whose date of construction, 'AD 1643', was clearly carved into its central spire.

'No, my dear. Close, and a very good guess, but not quite.'

THE SEVENTH COMMANDMENT

The reply that came out of Angelina's mildly chapped lips had been gentle, friendly and understanding – characteristics that had come with practice. 'This is the *Fontana del Tritone*, and came slightly later than that, as a gift to Pope Urban VIII by one of our most famous Renaissance sculptors and architects, Gian Lorenzo Bernini, who also designed much of St Peter's Square. Though Julius Caesar did live in this part of the city.' *Twenty centuries before.* She'd smiled, which had taken tremendous effort.

The tourist had nodded knowingly, as if this had been what she'd suspected all along. A plastic sun visor protruding from her forehead like a duck's bill cast a purple glow over her features, through which her expression suggested that it was sheer politeness by which she condescended to be corrected by a tour guide. Angelina could see the computation of her tip decreasing in the other woman's sour expression.

This was a common phenomenon, to which Angelina had grown accustomed over the past thirteen months of this strange but necessary employment. The average tourist came to Rome 'knowing' only two things about the ancient city: that Julius Caesar lived and died here, and that gladiators – who in their minds all spoke with dispassionate, monotone Australian accents and looked unsurprisingly like Russell Crowe – fought their way through the streets on a more or less daily basis. Every spot such people passed was assumed to be the locus of one or the other of these events, until forcibly persuaded otherwise; and then, the corrections were only grudgingly received.

That had been her morning. Just like yesterday. And the day before. Just like tomorrow.

And so there was a sigh, and another espresso, and another interior lamentation, and Angelina's day proceeded like all the rest.

*   *   *

The weight of her thoughts was almost enough to keep Angelina distracted from the strange movements of the crowds around her. *Thoughts can be like an anchor, the more discouraging ones forged of a heavy iron that roots us in our own spot in the sea, oblivious to the swells of the world around us, stuck and immobile*, her interior monologue had lamented more than once. But though Angelina's anchor was heavy at that moment, her ship going nowhere, she could see over the waves just enough to notice that something about the course of the bodies in the ancient square was – unusual.

Yes, many still queued at the pillars of the Pantheon, waiting to stand atop the classical marble floor and gaze up at the square-recessed dome whose bronze and gold had been stripped away in the sixteenth century to be melted down for the artistic decoration of St Peter's Basilica. And yes, many continued to sit at small tables in front of coffee shops all around the square, just like her.

But there was a motion away from the square that was entirely out of the ordinary. Hordes of bodies pushed to make their way out of its arteries – the picturesque Via della Rotonda to the south and the Salita de' Crescenzi to the west – as well as the smaller streets that broke away to the north. Normally every avenue of access to the Pantheon was a way in, but at this moment, they all appeared to be exits. All except those directed eastward, which remained almost empty.

A curiosity, Angelina mused. *The only direction that doesn't point towards the river.*

Something was drawing them, like a magnet pulling them away from the landmark site.

Because Angelina Calla had nothing better to do, she rose from her table, dropped a few euros into the glass dish she hadn't used as an ashtray, and followed the crowds towards the water.

3

Staff offices
Archivum Secretum Apostolicum Vaticanum
Vatican City

Dr Ben Verdyx sat at his office in complete silence. No earbuds dangled from his ears, and he tended never to power up his computer unless there was an immediate need to use it. Apart from the gentle whisper of the ventilation system flushing fresh air into the enclosed basement space, Ben's surroundings were pristinely silent, just as he liked them.

He was also alone, which was, again, exactly the situation Ben Verdyx preferred. One of the great perks of his position was that it, unlike so many others in the world, was decidedly not people-centred.

Ironically, gaining a post in the Vatican's 'Secret Archives', as the old Latin *archivum secretum* was generally and erroneously translated, had involved the same sort of public advertisement and interview process as any other. All those years ago – it would be five in a few months' time – encountering the phrase 'Enjoys working well with others' on the job description had sent Ben into spasms of anxiety, nearly sufficient to forgo applying altogether. But he'd held his resolve, only too relieved to learn in due course that it was merely Human Resources verbiage and had little to do with the actual expectations of the job. A senior archivist for the venerable Archives needed to be in love with books and manuscripts, with brown-edged folios and historical memoirs, not with the sound of his own, or anyone else's, voice. Ben Verdyx loved the former things as much as he detested the latter, which had made him essentially perfect for the position.

His family had of course urged Ben on to far greater and higher things. His parents, God rest their immortal souls, had never ceased pushing Ben towards higher-profile, and consequently higher-income, professions from his youth through to their deaths – both within eight months of each other through the predictable, if unpleasant, ravages of age. It had been hard to lose them both so closely together, but that was the way of God, Ben had reminded himself at the time. Always mysterious, rarely explicable, but generally in control of the broader sweep of life.

Ben had always been clever, perhaps even brilliant, and so his mother had wanted him to be a lawyer, his father a politician; but Ben's profoundly introverted personality had more or less ruled out such suggestions. The mere thought of the interpersonal contexts those positions entailed was enough to bring a physical pain into his chest, two great hands squeezing out his breath and constricting his heart. Even the little photo of him on the left-hand wall of the entrance to the Vatican Secret Archives bore witness to his general social discomfort. For the past five years Ben's visage had been a part of the small collection of staff member portraits presented there, caught frozen on film with his brow covered in sweat and his eyes appearing to point in two different, equally uncomfortable directions, looking for all the world like a man nailed for a mugshot on his way to the local jail.

But at least Ben himself didn't have to look at the photograph. He could walk straight past it on his way in each morning, moving through security and down the stairs into the Archives' second sub-level, into an office that was his oasis from the present and portal into the past. There, the only voices that spoke to him came through the long-silent words of the dead, and the only sounds that disturbed his peace were those his historically minded imagination crafted – the sounds of horse hooves along well-trod trade routes between Asia and Europe in the fourteenth century, or the ominous clanking of metal sounding from six hundred swords in a Roman phalanx in the third, or the stolid, serene voice of a poet speaking Attic verse into an amphitheatre of enrapt Greek hearers a half millennium before that. These were the sounds of life that Ben could handle. The sounds he loved.

Though occasionally this peace was shattered, and when it was, it never boded well. As the small telephone on his office desk suddenly lurched to life, dancing on the panelled surface as its shrill ring echoed through the recycled air, Ben could feel his insides constrict and his peace race from him like a charioteer from too long ago, fleeing the grounds of battle.

Five minutes later, Ben was standing outside the entrance to the Archives, surrounded by the ancient stonework of the courtyard that nestled it cosily into the heart of Vatican City. It lay beyond the Porta di Santa Anna, inside one of the three open squares of the immense structure located due north of the Sistine Chapel, known by most simply as Vatican Palace. To Ben's chagrin, the courtyard outside the Secret Archives was the only one of the three that had been, out of necessity, converted into a car park. All the glory and splendour of man's best approximation of the City of God, and his office opened on to tarmac.

He desperately wanted a cigarette, but Father Alberto had told him it was ungodlike to smoke, and Ben's devotion drove him to obey. Ben had been trying his best to give it up for months. He'd followed the teenagers he saw everywhere by taking up 'vaping', which as near as Ben could tell was all the hassle and display of smoking without the fun of a legitimate nicotine rush, but it was better than nothing. The little red light indicated his e-cig was powered on, and as Ben drew in a long inhale, the cloud that resulted removed any doubt.

The telephone call had disturbed him deeply. He didn't like calls in general, but he disliked the anonymous sort even less, and this was the second one that he'd received within a month. It was not a pattern he wanted to become established.

Especially if they were going to bear only on nonsense. Ben had always been a man of a deeper faith than most. His parents had loathed his inclinations towards the mystical bents within Catholicism, and it was only by grace that they were both with their Maker by the time Ben had discovered the Catholic Charismatic Movement and its sidelined, Pentecostally minded commune of devotees in the eastern reaches of the city. Hands raised in praise and rushes of prophetic tongues would have mortified his conservative mother beyond salvage, despite the stirring effect it had on Ben's soul. Simply mentioning prophetic ecstasy would have likely given his father a bigger stroke than the one that had killed him.

But even Ben's mystic bent knew the realm of prayer and hope was different from the realm of everyday experience and encounter. There were avenues for faith and vision in church, and there was the way the world worked, day by day, outside its doors.

But, the phone call . . .

He puffed another digital drag and walked across the car park, through two interconnected archways that led to the maze of passages linking the Apostolic Palace to the Sistine Chapel and ultimately St Peter's. Emerging on to the grand circular piazza that was among the most famous public squares in the world, he prepared to suck another dose of chemical into his lungs.

Instead, Ben stopped, his feet and his breath suddenly frozen.

Before him, the motion of the world appeared . . . Ben struggled a moment for the right word. *Backwards*.

Every day of his working life here, Ben had crossed at some point into St Peter's Square, and every time the landscape was the same. Tourists and faithful flocked to the holy site and stared at the grandiose edifice of the basilica, or at the overwhelming statuary of Bernini's twin-armed Tuscan colonnades, its four rows of columns gargantuan around them. Like sunflowers turning towards the sun, they always faced the same way, their eyes always on the same sights.

At this moment, however, they faced the opposite direction. Never before had Ben seen anything like it: hundreds of bodies, all turned away from the capital of the Catholic world, facing out of its confines and moving towards a vision beyond.

Then Ben glanced further in the same direction, and saw something even stranger.

A moment later, his feet were moving in the same direction as theirs.

4

'You cannot send this kind of information on to the Swiss Guard without bringing us in, Giotto.'

The reprimand aimed at Giotto Forte, Cardinal Prefect of the Congregation for the Causes of the Saints, came from his fellow Cardinal Dylan Camaugh, the Irish-born prelate who had spent the past forty years cloistered within the walls of the city, once serving as Cardinal Secretary of State and now, years past the Church's formal retirement age, ranking as one of the highest advisory members in the Curia. His voice bore the unique tinge of displeasure only the Irish can effectively accomplish: dismissive and disinterested, yet somehow personally invested enough to be fiercely annoyed.

'This is the kind of material that concerns all of us.'

'I'm not sure it really needs to *concern* anyone,' Cardinal Forte answered. He kept calm at his desk, though his rising irritation was in evidence. 'It's likely nothing. Certainly nothing that concerns the Curia directly. I contacted the Guard only as a matter of protocol. If events are taking place

20

that others might consider to have religious significance, it's always best for the Guard to be informed. Mobs form quickly, and act sporadically.'

'You think there will be mobs?'

'There already are,' came another voice. Archbishop Jovan Wycola sat in one of the red chairs at the far corner of Giotto's office. He'd been party to meetings such as these for almost as long as Cardinal Camaugh, though his robes were still purple instead of crimson. 'Along the river, even now. What would you call those?'

'I'd call those *crowds*, Your Excellency,' Cardinal Forte answered, 'curious crowds eager to see something which, while it is certainly out of the ordinary, is hardly miraculous.'

'Still,' Camaugh returned to his initial point, keeping his formal stance at the centre of the room, 'this body is the second-highest organ of the Curia, and should be kept abreast of everything. It is we who inform the Cardinal Secretary of State, and in turn the Pontiff, if matters – *any* matters – escalate.'

'Agreed, agreed,' Giotto relented. 'My apologies, brothers. I still do not feel this particular matter warrants our own interest beyond ensuring the Guard are aware of potential crowd activities today, but I accept this correction and agree I should have consulted with you sooner.'

The show of self-abasement seemed to satisfy Cardinal Camaugh.

'With that said,' the Cardinal responded, 'what's the actual substance of the material your people have unearthed?' The question came with a turn on his heels, coming once again to face Giotto.

'It has to do with the river, of course,' his fellow Cardinal replied, 'but with more than just that. And as of today, with two individuals who've suddenly become more than objects of mere interest.'

Outside, the Tiber River

Since the river had begun to run red in the morning, no one had been able to identify the source of the change. By the time those with curiosities for measurements and investigations had started in on their tasks, the Tiber's colour had changed from the Settebagni in the north of the city to Tor di Valle in the south, and the only thing that could be known with certainty was that it had become the biggest news of the Roman day.

Speculation was rampant over its cause and meaning. Few in a city of such significant religious history could fail to note the symbolism of the red colour. Italy wasn't Egypt, but the stories of the Nile's transformation into a canal of blood in the days of Moses were part of a common history.

Yet this wasn't blood – a fact that had become apparent as soon as the first suitably curious reporter stepped down the concrete banks and drew up a handful for a basic smell test. Among the scientifically minded there was suspicion of minerals from a suddenly unsettled deposit somewhere on the river bottom, or of an algae or other plant that might have undergone a rapid process of oxidation overnight.

Among other groups the speculations were of a different flavour. The government feared potential terrorism and suspected the colouring to be a poison, issuing a city-wide alert to avoid anything but bottled water until a full investigation could be mounted – though the water that flowed through pipes and taps appeared unaffected, coming out as close to clear as was ever the case in Rome. Ecologists immediately shouted pollution, wagging the finger at some as-yet-unidentified corporation who must have dumped something before dawn, reinforcing their long-held convictions that big companies would gladly kill off a whole river if it meant saving a few euros in chemical disposal costs.

There were other explanations, too. Religious zealots saw a sign, troublemakers saw a prank, and the Internet saw conspiracy, as it always tended to do.

All the while the river flowed, red as blood, through the heart of a city that could not know what it meant, whence it came, or what it ultimately would mean. Until, at a fore-ordained time that she held as a secret unto herself, the colour would begin to fade. She would retreat to normalcy before the day was done. It was meant to be like that. But the world around her would not go back to the way it was before.

That, too, had been etched out in the solid surety of stone.

5

Ponte Sisto
Crossing the Tiber River

It was when Angelina Calla arrived at the banks of the river that her world began to fall apart.

The crowds marching away from the Pantheon had led in an ever-increasing crush towards the riverbanks that wound themselves in a great arc through the centre of the city. By the time Angelina had emerged from the Vicolo del Polverone and made her way to the water's edge, she could barely move through the bodies. Whatever was drawing their attention, it was doing a remarkable job of it. Normally crowds like this only attended Papal audiences or major civic events, and none of those were planned for today.

She reached the bridge – the east end of the famous fifteenth-century Ponte Sisto – moments later.

Below, the Tiber flowed an incomprehensible red.

She hadn't been able to see it until she was almost on top of it. The high stonework banks that lined the river within the city centre kept the waters hidden from view, and Angelina required a few steps out on to the pedestrian-only bridge that had been rebuilt for the city by Pope Sixtus IV, before she could adequately see.

What she was actually seeing, though, she simply couldn't comprehend.

Piazza Pia
Near Castel Sant'Angelo

Ben followed the crowds as far as the distant end of the Via della Conciliazione, which ran in a straight line from St Peter's Square towards the famous, round papal fortress on the water's edge, which had originally served as a mausoleum for the Emperor Hadrian. He only caught glimmers of their ultimate goal over the swell of moving heads and intermittent traffic, but it beckoned with a strange, uncommon draw.

When he arrived there, one amongst hundreds, he finally saw it plainly.

The river ran red with blood.

The voice on the telephone had been correct. It wasn't merely mystic-speak or excitable expectation. The Tiber really was crimson as the flow from an opened vein.

Or an open wound in the side of Christ.

Ben's body was rigid, his understanding overwhelmed. Around him, tourists mumbled in bemused wonder, most speculating whether this was some summer tradition in Rome, to match Illinois dyeing the Chicago River green in the USA for St Patrick's Day. Cameras clicked almost constantly. Selfie-sticks rose in the air to catch couples' portraits over tooth-baring grins in front of the unusual waters.

But Ben felt only the trepidation of confused religious zeal, and an odd fear that came from the fact that he'd been told, by a voice on a phone call he couldn't identify, that this was coming.

Ponte Sisto

Angelina shuffled for a better view over the side of the ancient bridge. She'd been annoyed all day with crowds, and this one bore infuriating traits all its own. Mumblings of 'rivers of blood' and 'signs from above' seemed to Angelina's ideologically athe-istic background as absurd as suggestions that Caesar drew his water from medieval fountains, yet such comments blundered their way out of lips all around her. *So little knowledge. Such a flood of ungrounded belief.* A people too foolish to know the Forum from a hole in the ground could only be expected to confuse something which clearly had a scientific explanation with something descending from a mystical realm beyond.

Finally, she pushed her way through to the stone railings that ran along the bridge. From her new vantage point she could lean out over the edge and stare straight down at the water.

For the briefest instant, Angelina was tempted towards something more ethereal than her usual academic worldview. The strange flow of the crimson river was mesmerising, otherworldly. She saw her face vaguely reflected back at her, though her hair, almost the same colour as the water, seemed to disappear into its currents.

But she brought herself back to reality quickly enough. *There is an explanation for everything under the sun.* And in Angelina's experience it rarely had anything to do with forces coming from anywhere else.

She was about to begin mulling through the possibilities in her head, the comforting swell of scholarly analysis a welcome diversion from the odd tenor of the crowd – but Angelina never had the chance. Her thoughts were replaced by the exploding sound of gunfire and the pain of impact as stone shards flew into her stomach from the wall of the bridge which blew apart beside her.

6

Ponte Sisto

The duo of .380 calibre bullets that slammed into the bridge's stone siding caused it to explode in a cloud of angular granite fragments and dust. The pain of the coin-sized stone chips flying into Angelina's stomach and legs was compounded by grit blowing into her eyes, her lids scraping over their lenses as she tried to blink away the sudden blindness and comprehend what was happening.

Before vision had wholly returned, another explosive sound echoed from somewhere behind her. A millisecond later stone was shattering again, this time from only a centimetre or two to her left.

The first impact had been only centimetres to her right.

The gathered crowd burst into an instantaneous fit of screams and motion, some dropping on to the pavement in an impulsive, self-defensive posture that offered no real protection against arms fire but was a strong human impulse all the same. Others ran in any direction, every direction, confused and terrified.

Angelina's thoughts were as frantic as the bodies around

her. Her catalogue of life experiences included nothing like this, and her mind froze, flashing to blank in shock. Yet something within her moved on impulse with those who chose to run. Without pausing to debate other actions, she bolted back in the direction from which she'd come.

Beyond two lanes of traffic on the broad Lungotevere dei Vallati, which ran alongside the eastern bank of the Tiber and was lined by parked cars on either side, was the entrance to the much smaller Via dei Pettinari – a cross street that seemed like the only protective cover to hand, tall buildings lining each side and the spaces between them less open. Safety, or as much as Angelina's mind could make of it.

She fired all the energy she could muster into her legs and ran.

Piazza Pia

Ben Verdyx had never heard gunfire except in films, so when the report of actual arms tore through the lulled wonder of the crowd around him, his brain didn't know how to interpret what he was hearing.

The answer came in a spray of blood that erupted in front of his face. A man had been standing no more than two metres ahead of him, gazing out over the same red river with a shiny Samsung Galaxy held up to film the moment. A millisecond after the strange explosion sounded in the distance, his head simply disintegrated. Fragments of bone and gore sprayed on to Ben's beige jacket, and as he watched the body in front of him teeter and fall, his stomach rioted and turned over.

The only explanation his mind could formulate burst through his senses.

A murder. I've just witnessed a—

But then the explosive sound came again, and Ben realised the shooting wasn't done.

To his left, a woman suddenly spun around in a blur of motion. Ben yanked his head towards her, just in time to see a spray of blood emerging from her shoulder. *No, this is impossible* . . . Crowd shootings were hardly uncommon any more, but they were things he read about in the news. Things that happened abroad. Mass shootings didn't happen in Rome. It couldn't be real, not here.

The woman at his side had fared better than the man in front of him, the bullet shattering her shoulder but missing her head or vital organs. A companion at her side now had her in her arms, pulling her in the opposite direction from the river.

The crowd as a whole had transformed into a roaring mass of bodies fleeing in every direction, but Ben was stunned in place. Before him, the crumpled frame of the dead man lay at his feet, sickeningly lifeless amidst an expanding pool of blood that almost perfectly matched the colour of the river beyond.

When the report of the gun sounded again, Ben leapt into the air. Not on the same impulse to flee that had overtaken everyone around him, but because the paver stone beneath his feet exploded with such shattering force that he felt himself all but propelled upwards.

And Ben Verdyx's mind finally comprehended his predicament. The man in front of him had been shot. The woman beside him had taken a bullet. And now, with the crowd scrambling away and Ben left solitary in his spot, a bullet had landed centimetres from his feet.

Whoever was shooting, was shooting at him.

Ponte Sisto

During her first adrenaline-powered steps, the panic finally burst wholly into Angelina's consciousness. All the sudden realities hit home together, the voice of her racing thoughts shouting at full bore. *We're all targets, every one of us on this bridge. Everyone who'd gathered by the river. We're all—*

Another blast tore through the afternoon light as she ran, and the kerbstone beneath Angelina's right foot blew apart. Her balance faltered and almost gave way as her ankle strained to compensate, but momentum propelled her forward and she regained her step, her thighs pushing her yet faster into the main street.

Another shot. Another fantastically narrow miss.

A car swerved sharply to avoid running her down as she plunged into traffic, its driver leaning on a tinny, receding horn. In an instant sweat had flooded Angelina's whole body, drawn out of her skin by equal doses of fear and sudden exertion.

That was four shots. She'd been in the line of fire for them all.

The fifth round missed her left toe by less than a millimetre, and it was then that, through the chaos of her terrified realisations, Angelina knew the shots weren't random. She hadn't been caught out in a crowd as a gunman trained his firearm at random. She was a target.

That impossible reality propelled her forward with a new flurry of panic and speed.

Across the street
Along the Lungotevere dei Tebaldi

'For Christ's sake, take the woman out!' the man called Ridolfo snapped at his partner, irritation ripe and volatile in his voice.

'I'll get her.' The skinnier man, his handsome face distorted in an expression of frustration and focus, answered testily. 'Just . . . hold the fuck on.'

The second man, André, the younger of the duo by three years, had his pistol at eye level. It moved slowly as he attempted to track the woman in her race across the crowded street.

Hold on. Ridolfo couldn't believe André hadn't taken her out with the first shot. He was now up to his sixth, and still the woman was running, obviously unscathed – hardly what they wanted. By this stage she had to realise she was the target, which Ridolfo wanted even less.

André should never have permitted her to last that long. People who knew they were being hunted tended to try to protect themselves, just as she was now doing. The woman was clearly no expert in evasion, yet she was running for the side streets. Moving for cover. A good, laudable instinct.

André pulled his gun's trigger again, but just as he'd done with each previous shot, he pulled back far too hard on the sensitive mechanics of a fine piece of combat craftsmanship. The 102mm barrel of the Glock 25 followed the motion of his grip and the shot flew wide and high, the bullet slamming into the side of a parked car a metre ahead of the woman's course.

'Damn it, you told me you knew what you were doing!'

The other man didn't look back at him, but Ridolfo knew the remark would piss off his partner. *Let it.* André had assured him that, despite the fact that neither of them were hit men by trade, he was capable of firing a gun.

Ridolfo had assumed that skill also included aiming it.

'Aim at the centre of her chest, then a few centimetres ahead of her to compensate for the movement,' he instructed tersely, aware that they had only seconds with the woman still in sight. She was approaching the opposite side of the busy street as fast as she could make it through the dart-and-dodge game she was forced to play with oncoming traffic. 'Then squeeze the trigger, don't fucking yank on it.'

An instant later, André's Glock burst to life again. On the far end of his sights the bullet reached its mark, but once more it was brickwork that blew apart, rather than the chest of his target.

'Fuck!' he shouted, spittle flying from his lips. André didn't need Ridolfo to chastise him. He was pissed with himself, his neck swelling with indignation.

By the time he'd aligned his gaze through the sights once more, it was all too late. The woman with the red hair had slipped between buildings on the far side of the street.

His target was gone.

7

Piazza Pia

Ben couldn't see who was shooting at him, but harboured no impulse to search his surroundings. He turned from the body crumpled and bloody before his feet, spinning 180 degrees on his leather soles, and charged off in the direction of the fleeing crowd.

On the far side of the street was the Auditorium Conciliazione, a massive structure beyond which lay the cover of a denser mass of buildings. But in the frenzy of his run, Ben's main thought was not on the whole, but on one smaller building he knew was situated just on the other side of the elevated corridor, called the *Passetto di Borgo*, that ran behind the auditorium and connected Castel Sant'Angelo to the Vatican. The Carabinieri, one of the three police forces that oversaw public safety in Italy, had their small St Peter's Bureau in the little edifice around the corner, and Ben couldn't think of any place he'd rather be in this moment than in the safety and security of a police station.

He pointed himself towards the connecting street and tried

to increase his speed beyond the full sprint he was already at, but his legs could do no more.

The report of the next gunshot arrived with new terror. Certain he was now a target, the sound came replete with a series of visions – bright and horrifyingly vivid in his imagination – of a bullet slamming into his spine, or into the back of his head, causing the same kind of explosion of skull and skin he'd seen moments ago with the man standing in front of him.

Ben's world threatened to go white with the overwhelming blindness of panic. But the shot didn't hit him, and he simply uttered a frantic prayer, *Lord, help me!*

And he ran.

Inland from the Ponte Sisto

At last making it through the flurry of traffic and across the main thoroughfare at the Tiber's edge, Angelina then bolted into the first small lane she came to with every ounce of energy her body could muster. With gunshots landing within a few centimetres of her feet, her only hope was to escape line of sight. Get out of view.

Get away.

The narrower lane led away from the riverside street and was less than a third its width. Rather than trees and a river marking its embankment, it was lined with brick buildings that suddenly felt like friends. Angelina sprinted between them with a speed of which she hadn't been aware she was capable. Each second, each footstep, was one she was certain would end with the next explosive sound and – and whatever it felt like to have a bullet tear through your body.

Yet somehow she made it into the small Via dei Pettinari in a single piece. Though the sound of gunfire ceased as she entered the narrow lane, she didn't allow her feet to slow down.

Keep going. Run!

The voice inside her head commanded, and Angelina obeyed. She'd never heard her conscience or her thoughts speak like this before – never been close to a circumstance where her inner self could contemplate commanding such things. But the voice was speaking sense. She had to get far, far from here.

And the only way to get there, to get anywhere other than this spot, was to keep in motion.

A few streets behind

'Get moving, you jackass!' Ridolfo was already leaping out from behind the green saloon car he and André had used as a perch for what had been meant to be a simple execution. He should have shot the woman himself, he shouldn't have trusted his companion with the task. There was a reason André's father looked down on him as overtly as he did.

But it was a mistake Ridolfo could remedy. Once they caught up with the woman, he would make sure he took her down with his own gun. He could only hope that the other team, located a few kilometres away at another point near the river, was having better luck with their target.

'She's gone down the side street,' he shouted at André as both men tore into the road. Horns blared and cars swerved as they had moments before for Calla, and as they continued to do for the other terrified pedestrians trying to get away from the scene.

'I'll follow her there,' he continued. 'You go a street or two up and cut across.' He swung an arm in a direction further along the riverbank, then shot the fiercest look he could muster at André.

'Don't let the bitch get away.'

*   *   *

As Angelina ran, terrified that these might be her last moments, she was surprised to discover that the scenes of life really do flash before a person's eyes in the moments before the end comes. She saw her parents, gathered around her and her younger brother at a Christmas party when they were children, gifts wrapped in bright colours all around them. She saw a rope swing hanging from a tree, on which she'd swung for hours in her youth. She saw her first student accommodation room, spartan and plain, which had inspired and excited her.

The scenes were heavy, joyful yet simultaneously mournful. The flashing of her life had a weight to it she didn't expect.

She'd lost track of how many times she'd turned corners and altered her path now, though her pace was slowing as the rush of fear and its associated chemicals, which had powered her through her initial bolt away from the gunshots, began to recede and tear through her muscles with the fire of pain rather than strength. The clamminess of shock had given way to the genuine sweat of her sprint, and as a new wave of apprehension turned her skin cold again, her clothes stuck to her chest and back with a sickening, oppressive grip.

She'd only started glancing behind her a few corner-turns ago, terrified that she might see a gun barrel aimed straight at her eyes when she did, but she'd seen only the milling of the crowds through which she'd come, some glancing at her in surprise or bemusement, unsure whether to take her high-speed course through their streets as something fearful on which to exercise compassion, or simply another mani-festation of the all-too-frequent craziness exhibited by strangers in their cosmopolitan melting pot.

But her feet were growing heavier. Her legs felt as if they truly were on fire, each step increasing the temperature, until the pain became so intense that tears began to flow down her cheeks.

And that, more than anything else that had happened so far, pissed Angelina off.

She had no idea who was behind her, or why they were shooting. She'd only caught flashing glimpses of men, blurred into visions on which she didn't have time to linger. She had no idea if she would survive this unexpected, unwanted moment in her life. But she knew one thing about her pursuers. They'd made her cry. And damn it, Angelina Calla was not a cryer.

8

Minutes earlier
Governatore building, Vatican City

High above the crowds that were gathered along the water's edge, from a window looking down on the whole of Rome from a unique, ivory height, Cardinal Giotto Forte stared out across the dazzling cityscape. It never ceased to thrill him, this strange world into which he had been drawn as he had ascended the ranks from seminarian to priest, to Monsignor serving in the Congregation for the Doctrine of the Faith and eventually to the rank of bishop and archbishop. When, some years later, the Pope had informed him that he'd been selected as a prince of the Church and would be incardinated the following March, Giotto's chest had swelled with pride. Of course, pride was nominally a vice. He was supposed to aim for humility. But how could a man who, since he'd first decided that the desire within his teenage bones was a calling from God and dedicated his life to the Holy Mother Church, not feel a little pride at being handed the crimson fascia and zucchetto of a cardinal?

These days, as Prefect of the Congregation for the Causes

of the Saints, he had one of the nicest offices in the Vatican, with one of the finest views in the whole of the city. It was a fact that had been confirmed for him by none other than the Supreme Pontiff himself, who on a visit to Cardinal Giotto's offices, shortly after the latter's investiture, had opened the patio doors and gazed out over the city with an audible intake of delighted breath. 'My dear Giotto,' the Pope had said, with all the cheerful humour in his voice for which the current pontiff was known, 'this is the finest view in all of Rome. And that,' he'd added, turning towards the Cardinal with a wink to his eye, 'that's infallible.'

Giotto Forte smiled at the memory. The Pope was a good man, humble yet strong, able to govern well without losing his humour or simplicity of character. Giotto could only hope that his own life of service to the Church would leave him equally as good a person.

He stepped away from the window, and with the motion his smile fell. The business of the afternoon had been far less inspiring than his memories.

He did not enjoy being reprimanded by his fellow members of the Curia. It was unpleasant, as well as worrying, whenever it happened to occur. A man could ascend to great heights, but the threshold back to the very bottom was one over which many men had fallen. Usually without much notice.

Should he really have informed them earlier about the dossier his office had received a fortnight ago? Had declining to bring it before them really been a mistake?

One of the responsibilities of the Congregation for the Causes of the Saints, apart from the obvious and well-known role it played in investigating individuals proposed for canonisation by the Church, was the gathering of information on the unusual and out-of-the-ordinary in Catholic life, both within Vatican City and across the Roman Catholic world, which tended to be viewed in conjunction with manifestations of particular holiness and came under the same scrutiny. In this role they were often thought of as the Church's 'miracle investigators', and there was more mythology about their work than just about any other sector of Catholic administration.

Investigating miracles had an obvious public appeal, but Giotto's teams did more than simply deal with the miraculous. It was his same office that responded to more or less any event or episode that strayed outside the customary flow of the Church's life. If new congregations with a particular social agenda, following particularly notable leaders, began to appear – such as the rebellious 'Liberation Theology' devotees had done in South America in the fifties and sixties – it was Giotto's offices that would first explore the trend, often in conjunction with his former colleagues in the Congregation for the Doctrine of the Faith. If rumours came in that, following a particularly 'inspiring' individual's influence, a whole nation's Catholics were converting to bagpipe Masses with jazz liturgical dance, it would be Giotto's office, again, that would look into it. *Not that a bagpipe Mass sounds so bad*, the Cardinal murmured to himself. His Perugian name notwithstanding, he had Scottish ancestry on his mother's side, and had always liked the pipes.

It was this scope to his work that had brought the file in question to Cardinal Giotto's attention. A clay tablet had been unearthed a month ago. It had been of no interest to anyone in the Vatican, beyond perhaps a few scholars. It was written in Akkadian, which as best as Giotto could remember from seminary was a language of the Ancient Near East that had only tangential connections to Christian patrimony.

Yet something about the tablet's find had disturbed him. Not the bulk of its text, which he had to admit he hadn't read, but one passage in particular. At the front, the initial lines, which he'd sent away for translation, had predicted of the tablet's discoverer that 'his terrible death shall come most swiftly'.

And the man who had discovered it was dead. His death, moreover, had come swiftly, and it had been terrible.

An acidic bubble churned in Giotto Forte's stomach. Outside, police sirens sounded, as they so often did in the city, though at this moment they seemed designed to emphasise his angst.

He'd been right to contact the Swiss Guard. Surely. The discovery of an artefact on Church property that was linked to a death – they had every right and reason to know about it.

But such a crime, if it even was a crime, hardly warranted the involvement of higher-ups in the Curia more broadly. Old things were regularly dug up in Rome. And people died, even gruesomely. Life went on.

Besides, how seriously could a tablet of old predictions and prophecies really be?

It was a question that had sounded far more compelling prior to this morning. Prior to the infallibly perfect view from his office changing.

Because after the prediction of its discoverer's death, the first 'plague' the tablet described was that the river would flow red.

And that prediction, like the curse upon its finder, had inexplicably come true.

9

The neighbourhood of Campo de' Fiori

By her best estimation, Angelina had been running, twisting her way in as convoluted a path as she could orchestrate on the fly, for at least ten minutes. Though there had been no further gunshots, and though she'd seen no sign of pursuers since she'd made her way into the tighter quarters of the neighbourhood, she hadn't stopped. *Rome is big. It's possible, sensible, to get much, much further away.*

It was her body, however, that ultimately demanded that she halt. Angelina's legs would move no more. Her chest had heaved and her heart had pulsed at this rate as long as it could.

Praying that the decision wouldn't be her last, Angelina slowed, picked out two cars parked perpendicularly to the side of the road, and lunged between them. She crouched down, trying to bring herself out of the sightline of the pavements, then leaned her back against the yellow Fiat behind her, sliding down its passenger door until her bottom bounced against the harsh tarmac of the road.

For at least five minutes Angelina did nothing, thought

almost nothing. She simply allowed her heart rate to slow and her breathing to come under control, waiting in silence in the fear that her pursuers would round the row of cars and spot her and it would all suddenly, terribly, be over. But as the minutes passed and the noises beyond remained only the usual stirrings of evening pedestrians out on the stroll, she finally allowed her mental block to give way, permitting her rational mind out of its sidelined cage. It burst immediately into a chaos of thought.

What the hell is going on? What do I do? Where do I go?

She commanded herself to breathe, then forced her mind to order her thoughts into categories, into clear groups of questions. It was the same process she took with an academic puzzle, and it brought her a small degree of calm to approach this shock in her life with a familiar pattern of mental action.

She wasn't hurt, at least not significantly. Her torso was still smarting with pain from the rock shards that had flown against her from the bridge's shattering stonework, but as she quickly scanned over her body, it was clear that none had pierced her flesh, and nothing felt broken.

She strove to piece together the structure of her afternoon. What could possibly have led to this? But there was nothing – no cause that fit the result. She might have got on the wrong side of a tour member or two, but she'd done that before and it had never resulted in gunfire.

And the water of the river . . . she didn't know what the hell to make of that.

Her stomach stirred with panic again. She had to get further away. It wasn't safe here. She needed to find her way to a metro station, get underground, and then get as far from this spot as she possibly could.

Taking her wits into her two hands as best as she could, Angelina stood.

No bullet tore through her flesh. No men leapt out from

behind cars or awnings to renew their chase. So Angelina turned, stepped on to the pavement, and inserted herself into the crowd of pedestrians. Then, as best she could, she disappeared.

A few streets away

Ridolfo didn't appreciate that he was being made to race at this pace through the side streets of Rome. The span from late afternoon into evening was social hour for urban Romans, which meant that crowds lined the neighbourhood lanes – especially of such an urban stalwart as the region around Campo de' Fiori, with its tightly interwoven ancient lanes and squares lined with flower sellers, cafés and small local shops. The strange change in the waters of the Tiber had them out in even thicker droves than normal, spilling foot traffic into narrow roadways that barely ran a car's-width across when they were empty. Not only was Ridolfo being made to run and sweat his way through his clothes, which had been perfectly clean when the day began; he was being made to do so in the midst of crowds whose gazes were drawn to his face like a magnet.

Ridolfo had had his whole life to come to terms with the fact that not only was he – unlike his partner – no gem of masculine attractiveness; he was outright ugly by just about any standard of measure. He remembered visits to the doctor as a young boy, where his family physician had spoken to his parents – always when he'd thought he'd been out of young Ridolfo's earshot – in terms of 'birth defects' and 'physical deformities', though his parents had always been careful to shield him from such language. He was 'special', in his mother's caring tones, and 'unique' in his stepfather's.

For a time, in his childhood, the kinds of 'special' and 'unique' that required tall collars and knitted scarves to cover

44

up the splotched, potted mess that was his neck – these were things he could have done without. He'd been ashamed of, then resented, the strange grooves that ran along his cheeks and created folds of flesh and skin where no human face should have them. And he'd resented, then hated, his fellow children who had done what, he later understood, was only standard for children to do. They'd mocked him mercilessly, ostracised him from their little cliques as thoroughly as they could, and ensured that he always knew he was different, unwelcome and unwanted.

As Ridolfo had grown, he'd learned to live with his looks. Some part of him even uttered a little prayer of gratitude, now and then, for the course they'd forced his life to take. He'd had to learn to be self-contented. To be fierce, to learn to deal with whatever came his way, and to care fuck-all about what anyone else thought of him. They were traits that had served him nicely.

But the looks Ridolfo got from strangers still grated on him. As politically correct as the world had become over the past few years, no cultural force on earth seemed strong enough to stop the open gaping that people exhibited when-ever he walked among them.

Which is why he so rarely did, and why he resented that André's incompetence with a handgun meant he had to be jogging through the midst of so many now. The stares came from every angle, and given the crowds, they came from up close. He could almost feel the breath of the leering bystanders, withering their stares at him as he pushed through them.

He did his best to ignore it all, but the back of his neck still warmed with anger and resentment.

Killing Dr Angelina Calla had now become something more than just the heeding of an instruction from his boss. Ridolfo would make the bitch pay for his humiliation.

*　　*　　*

Angelina turned yet another corner, trying to keep her pace below the panicked sprint her nerves wanted to repeat from before. She was walking amongst the crowds now, getting further and further away from the site of her attack. Blending in was better than standing out as a racer among passers-by. She forced deep, long breaths, walking toe to heel and holding down her speed.

She'd fished her mobile out of her handbag a few streets ago and called up Google Maps for a quick view of her location and a route to the nearest metro station. It was only a few turns ahead, and Angelina could feel her pace increasing as she drew closer to it. Would she be safer there, underground and whisked away at high speed from the centre of the city? Or would the men follow her there as well – trapping her in a steel box within a concrete tube beneath the city: a mobile grave from which they would never let her emerge?

The two possibilities duelled within her consciousness as she kept her steps deliberate. It was a risk, going into the metro system. It couldn't be denied. But she couldn't think of any better option. She felt far too exposed here. It seemed her best hope.

A few steps ahead, her present street intersected with the massive Corso Vittorio Emanuele II, one of the largest thoroughfares through the centre of Rome. The metro station was only a few dozen metres to her right. She was almost there.

As she rounded the corner, it was Angelina's focused gaze ahead – scanning for the traditional signage and stairway that led into the metro system – that prevented her from seeing the glossy black Transit van that pulled up alongside her. Its windows were tinted as black as the paint job, so she wouldn't have been able to see inside even if she had been looking. As the van matched her speed and spotted her position, its side door slid open and the bodies of four black-clad men inside came into view.

Her abduction happened so quickly that she was off her feet before she knew she was being taken. Two of the men leapt out of the van, one reaching down to grab her legs and the other wrapping thick, solid arms around her chest, a huge hand covering her mouth. The two propelled her towards the van with skilled coordination, the men inside receiving her and pulling her in.

A second later, the two outside had leapt back into the vehicle, the door was slid shut with a slam, and a hood was drawn over Angelina's face as her world went black.

Piazza Pia

The abduction of Ben Verdyx took place within sight of the Stazione Carabinieri San Pietro at which he had been aiming in his flurried escape from the gunfire by the river. It was a mark of his abductors' confident boldness that they took him on an open street, only metres from the police station, apparently without fear.

A black van of similar make and appearance to that which had taken Angelina Calla swerved into Ben's path as he ran. Unlike her, he saw the door open, saw the men emerge, but he was no more equipped to prevent what came next than she had been. The hands that grabbed him were of a strength far beyond his own, and before his mouth could utter a protest or a cry, it was all over. He was in the van, the door was shut, and his hands were being bound behind his back as a hood was pulled over his head, blocking out all vision.

The last thing Ben Verdyx heard before he passed out from fear was the roar of the van's engine.

The men who had abducted him didn't make a sound.

10

'Sit down and be quiet.' The first words out of Emil Durré's mouth were typically severe, emerging through their customary thick accent. The Belgian expatriate motioned towards two leather chairs covered in crackled burgundy leather, brass studs sparkling in the light of a simple fixture that hung from the ceiling of an otherwise unremarkable office. The chairs and the immense mahogany desk between them were the only signs of excess and looked wholly out of place in their otherwise cheap surroundings. But they were an extravagance that Emil more than deserved. One day, he would deck out the rest of his paltry surroundings to match the set.

The two men who had walked into the room a moment before took their seats, uncomfortable in the oddly old-fashioned glamour the misplaced furniture strove inadequately to represent. However, given the events of less than an hour ago, they were more uncomfortable still in the presence of the man who had called them there.

Emil drew in a deep, long breath. Behind him, a broad window opened out on to the cityscape of a less than fully posh section of the Roman skyline. The buildings in view in the dying afternoon light were mostly industrial, some residential, without the domes and towers of the city centre that everyone the world over associated with the city.

And there was, most regrettably, no view of the river.

Still, the office window faced west and provided him with striking sunset views on an almost nightly basis. And night would come at the end of this day, despite its setbacks.

The two men opposite him squirmed in their seats. Emil had always liked that word. *Squirm.* So slavish, so demeaning. Utterly delightful. His native Belgian French didn't have a satisfactory equivalent. *Se tortiller* sounded too polite, and *se contorsionner* was both too long and too literal. Some words simply worked better in translation.

Emil's temper, however, was not prepared to let them continue *squirming* in silence.

'It should go without saying that I am displeased.' He peered across his desk at the two men. Both straightened. They'd known this was the direction the conversation would go, but neither of them liked it.

'We're sorry, Pops,' the younger and handsomer of the two said quickly in response. 'Things just got a little out of hand.'

It took effort for Emil to restrain a disgusted outburst. That the stupider of the pair was his son was a fact of nature that couldn't be helped, though the boy could have at least done his father the courtesy of not opening his mouth in order to sing his familiar song of ineptitude.

Emil had hesitated to bring André into the project, given that the boy had so little to offer to it. Circumstances, however, would hardly allow him to be kept in the dark. One cannot go from pauper to prince, from insignificance to storied fame, without one's kin noticing the change. Short of cutting André out of his life completely, which would have meant Emil himself relocating physically out of his son's life once everything was over – an option that he nonetheless hadn't dismissed without careful consideration – there was no other option but to bring him into the fray. And at the end of the day, Emil supposed he did, in fact, harbour a touch of familial sentiment, something that might even qualify as paternal loyalty. He would have preferred a smarter child, of course, one with more business sense and drive, but the genetic dice had rolled where they willed. Emil's first wife had been a looker but an airhead, so the sole fruit of their union could hardly be blamed for his lot in life.

Yet, he'd failed. In this, one of his first important tasks.

'You had only a single aim,' Emil said, 'quite literally. Take out the woman. One lady on the street, and an academic to boot. Hardly the most capable of opponents. And you're telling me you couldn't do it?'

'Pops, it's just that—'

'Don't speak,' Emil cut off the boy's pitiful attempt at a reply. 'And don't fucking call me that.' He hated the affectionate slang his son used, and André knew it, though the fact never seemed to influence his behaviour. It was just possible that Emil didn't intimidate his son the way he hoped he did.

He turned to the man in the other chair. 'You, you should have prevented this.'

'I'm sorry about that, boss.' The man said nothing more, but held his gaze up to Emil's without flinching. Something the latter man respected.

Ridolfo Passerini, who was only three years the elder of Emil's son, yet in ability far more substantially his superior, had once been described to Emil as 'ugly as a whore's back end', and the fact that the description had come from his own mother had given it a certain merit. Emil had never been able to muster up convincing disagreement. In private moments, when he and Ridolfo had first met, Emil had joked behind his back that if he ever walked into a bar fight without a weapon he would simply thrust Ridolfo between himself and his attacker – 'The sheer force of such undiluted ugliness would be enough to shock a man into retreat.' Then, after Emil had got to know him better, he'd joked in this way to Ridolfo's face. He was a young man who assessed himself accurately, dispassionately, and therefore took little offence in the knowledge that he was ugly as sin, being perfectly aware that he made up for it in a brilliance that was just as pronounced. It was Ridolfo's emerging ruthlessness that had raised him to the level of a prize in Emil's eyes. The man had a coldness about him, and that coldness signalled a willingness to do, uncompromisingly, what was asked of him.

'Not only did you not kill the woman,' Emil continued, 'you let her get away. Unacceptable. Though, it has to be said, your counterparts fared little better with the man.' He would have his discussion with the other team later. 'And now there are police everywhere, reports of the attacks on every television station. Sections of the city are on lockdown.'

'She didn't get away,' Ridolfo answered calmly, 'she was taken.'

'Taken?'

'She was headed for the metro, as near as we could tell. Once we figured that out, we were holding back, waiting for the chance to catch her underground. A closed environment, easier to capture.'

'Get to the point.'

'Just before she got to the entrance, a van pulled up along the street. Four men in the back, and a driver.'

'They were professionals, Pops,' André butted in. The look Emil shot him silenced André instantly.

'Whoever they were, they knew what they were doing,' Ridolfo confirmed. 'The van was unmarked, I couldn't catch the plates. But the abduction was . . . perfectly orchestrated.' He said the words with unfeigned respect for whoever had pulled off the abduction.

Emil rattled his fingers over the surface of his desk.

'The same thing happened with Verdyx,' he finally admitted. Ridolfo's eyebrows rose. 'The team I had on him reported exactly the same set of circumstances. Caught them entirely off guard.'

A tense silence. 'What does it mean, that they were both taken right out from under our noses?' Ridolfo finally asked.

Fingers rattled again. 'I honestly don't know, but it can't be anything good.' Finally, Emil looked up and stared intently at both men.

'I need the two of you to take care of this. Bartolomeo's team has different work to be doing now. I'm going to need you to take care of both these – problems.' He let his gaze linger on Ridolfo. 'Can I count on you?'

Ridolfo firmed up his posture, nodded in the affirmative.

'Because,' Emil continued, now turning to face his son, 'the point of no return on this whole project was passed the moment the water went red this morning.' André nodded in return, though there was little sign of deeper comprehension on his features. 'There can be no turning back,' his father continued, 'and there can be no room for being tripped up by the involvement of others. Prophecy is something that cannot be controlled.'

There was a delightful irony to the statement, but Emil made it convincingly. 'It will run where it will. It will run amok. And we will delight in the running.'

It seemed so incongruous to hear Emil Durré, bygone scholar and loathed exile of the establishment, speak of prophecy. His atheistic antagonism was as well known among his friends as his dislike of his former colleagues, and prophecy was just the sort of 'culturally antiquated nonsense' he'd inveighed against for years.

But then, both André and Ridolfo knew that prophecy was what this was all about. And they both knew, with the certainty of a surprising faith, that all around them visions were about to become reality.

PART TWO

Prophecy

11

Beneath the Apostolic Palace

The hood was pulled from Angelina's head with force, but not briskly. She was seated on a chair that felt wooden, hard, her hands bound and positioned behind the chair's back to keep her fixed in place.

From the moment of her abduction till now, no one but Angelina herself had made a sound. Frantic cries of 'Who the hell are you?' and 'What the fuck are you doing?' were met only with silence, and eventually Angelina had given them up, out of breath and exhausted. She'd been raced from her abduction point to God knows where – a drive that took perhaps fifteen minutes in the starts and stops of what she assumed was traffic – and was eventually unloaded with the hood over her head still on, shuffled into the interior of some building, somewhere.

The certainties of Angelina's life had all but disappeared. The only one that remained was fear.

As the hood finally came off, she squinted at the sudden arrival of brightness. For a few seconds she could make out only blurs and splotches of bright, amorphous colour in a well-lit space; but as her eyes adjusted the colours began to solidify into definite shapes.

A room, rectangular. Concrete walls. Plain, unpainted. No windows. Fluorescent lights sunk into low ceilings. A few plain tables, and not much else, over a poured concrete floor. Fear tightened Angelina's chest. This was no office, and her gut told her nothing good happened in this sort of room.

Men were in various positions around her. Two stood directly in front of her chair, dark suits matching, dominant and tall. Another sat in a chair to her left, just at the periphery of her vision.

'Dr Calla,' one of the standing men said in a measured, businesslike tone, 'I would like to do you the courtesy of unbinding your hands. That is, if you can assure me you will remain calm, and seated.'

Her terror choked at her throat, but Angelina suddenly wanted to explode. At this man's condescending words her fear was overwhelmed by anger.

'The *courtesy*?' The words were darts shooting out from between her teeth. 'You chase me down with guns, you kidnap me off the street, and you have the gall to talk to me about *courtesy*?'

At least they didn't shoot me, she heard her interior voice affirm over her rage. They'd fired so many times, but each time they'd missed. *Reassurance.*

Then, a realisation. Maybe that had been her pursuers' aim all along, from the bridge and throughout the chase. Not to kill her there on the street, but to lead her to a spot where she could be taken. Like a sheep in a pasture, fleeing from the sheepdog only to run straight into a waiting corral. She'd thought she'd been so clever in her convoluted course, but she'd been led, rather than leading herself. Into a concrete room, with no windows . . .

'I'm sorry about the manner in which we had to bring

you here,' the man's steady voice continued, sounding anything but sorry, 'but given the circumstances, there was little option.'

'Go to hell,' was all Angelina could muster. It didn't sound convincing, but it felt good.

'I'm sure that, once your circumstances have been explained to you, you'll feel less hostile towards our activities.' The man's tone was difficult to read, and Angelina squinted to get a better look at him. He was tall, perhaps just under two metres, with cropped brown hair that took on an odd halo from the fluorescent tubes above. His whole body looked . . . Angelina struggled for the right word. *Sturdy.* He was solid, a thick tree trunk planted firmly in the earth, sure of his footing and hard to sway.

'There's nothing you could possibly "explain" to me that would justify what you've done. Those were bullets you shot at me, you bastards!' The *fuck you's* kept creeping towards the tip of Angelina's tongue, but somehow she managed to hold them back. 'And you did it in a public place – in a crowd! God knows how many people you could have hurt!' Then it occurred to her that she had no idea if others had, in fact, fared worse than she. 'For Christ's sake, how many bodies back there caught your bullets?'

'Dr Calla,' the stoic man added, moving for the first time to take a small step in her direction, 'you need to calm yourself down. Breathe.' Then, impossibly, 'We did not shoot at you.'

'Fuck you!' the words finally exploded from Angelina's lips. The man might be imposing, but she wasn't going to just sit and take his lies.

'That language is not appropriate in this place,' he answered. For the first time, Angelina could see a flash of something other than force in his eyes. The vulgarity had apparently genuinely offended him. His nearly reverent 'this place' echoed in her ears.

The concrete walls around them hardly looked hallowed.

'Take a breath,' he continued. 'If you'll give me a chance to explain, you'll realise we've brought you both here for your protection.'

Angelina's anger momentarily halted. Instantly confused, she peered into the tall man's eyes. 'Both?'

He didn't answer. Instead, he merely gave a nod towards Angelina's left.

She slowly turned, following the line of his glance. She remembered that another of her captors was seated off to the side, and soon found herself looking in his direction.

What she saw, however, was not another well-suited man in command of his situation. On a hard chair that looked identical to her own, a man in a beige coat sat stiffly, his arms tied behind his back, pale as the white light that illumined them. Brown stains of blood marked his coat and stained his face.

The man glanced at her, eyes bulging with fear, and for the briefest instant Angelina felt all her other emotions – the fear, the anxiety, the terror – slip away. Where moments ago nothing in her present experience had seemed certain, now one thing did.

She had seen this man's face before.

12

Beneath the Apostolic Palace

The plastic tie that had bound her hands together for nearly the past half-hour snapped apart as one of her captors clipped it off. Angelina's sudden shock at seeing a familiar face in this unexpected place had silenced her stream of angry protests, and the man in charge had apparently felt satisfied that she wouldn't shoot out of the chair in hysterics.

Angelina brought her hands on to her lap and began rubbing the red stripes that now encircled both wrists. Her shoulders and forearms ached from the strain of the awkward position in which they'd been bound, and her legs, she suddenly acknowledged, still burned from the race that had come to such a sudden and unexpected end.

'Allow me to introduce myself properly,' said the tall figure who was quite evidently in charge. He stiffened into what approximated military straightness. 'My name is Hans Heinrich, a Major of the Papal Swiss Guard. Behind you is my sergeant, *Wachtmeister* Jonas Wüthrich, and just beyond the door,' he motioned behind him to a steel door that was firmly closed on the far side of the room, 'is

Korporal Max Yoder, who has joined us to ensure we're not interrupted.'

Angelina heard the words, but processing them was temporarily beyond her. *The Swiss Guard?* The fabled corps of bodyguards was, as far as she remembered, the private security staff of the Roman Catholic Pope – but Angelina The Atheist hardly had dealings with pontifical clergy. Besides, these men didn't look anything like the guardsmen she'd seen within Vatican City on her frequent visits there with tour groups. They always appeared traditionally clad in ceremonial attire befitting a religious vision of a dancing clown, as she'd interpreted their outfits: bright, contrasting primary colours with overly inflated trouser billows and ridiculously outsized collars. The men in this room, by contrast, were dressed slickly: grey suits over black shirts that clung to what were visibly muscular bodies.

Swiss Guard, my academic ass.

None of it made sense. *Not these men, and not . . .*

The man continued to explain himself – or lie about himself, as the case might be – but Angelina involuntarily let his voice fade into the background. Her mind was drawn more powerfully to the face of the man who sat bound in the chair next to her. She knew she didn't know her captors, whoever they might actually be, but from the first instant she'd set her eyes on this other man, she'd known she'd met him before. As she lingered on his features, terrified as they were, she gradually remembered where.

Nineteen months ago

Despite all the setbacks she had faced in her life, Angelina had never wholly given up hope in her future. Though, after forty-three job applications since the conclusion of her PhD, the need to acknowledge failure was starting to weigh upon her. Forty fucking three. *She let profanities swirl through her thoughts with a bluntness she generally managed to prevent in her speech. Twenty-seven interviews. No results. Angelina Calla the professor of ancient history, or even the assistant researcher in ancient history – hell, she'd have taken junior typist in a university office that dealt with anything remotely related to ancient history – they were dreams that simply weren't transforming into reality.*

Her fellow man was trying his best to strip her hope from her. Or, in a much more direct sense, not her fellow man, but males. There was no point in glossing over the fact. A round face with just the right number of fashionable freckles, accompanied by good tits and a perky backside – Angelina had been well equipped from birth for just about anything in life except a career that demanded the respect of men rather than their condescending fancy. And the one field she'd always desired, academia, was as male-dominated in Italy as could continue to be the case in the modern world. It was a realm that still managed to remain more or less closed off to those Italian human beings who failed to pass the 'your penis must be this long to go on this ride' mark.

Angelina had faced the other sex's domination of her field gallantly, despite the challenges. Each time she was ready to give up, she reminded herself that she hadn't hit rock bottom yet. She wasn't homeless, hadn't yet spent a night in a gutter. But then, Angelina never really thought such lows were realistic pitfalls on her horizon. It was mediocrity she had always feared slipping into, not oblivion. An excess of success, or of failure, had the ring of merit to it – one had to be terrifically good or terrifically bad to get to either extreme. But to be stuck in the middle required nothing and offered nothing. And there Angelina was, squarely between two poles, which as the days passed felt more and more like nowhere. Like nothing at all.

Only one experience in her litany of frustrations had been in any way inspiring. A month and a half ago she'd applied for an entry-level research position in the Vatican Archives. Junior. Archival.

Assistant. *Bile re-entered Angelina's mouth as she remembered the demeaningly low rank of the post, for which she'd been vastly overqualified and yet for which she'd 'somehow' still managed to be rejected. But by then she'd been at the point of applying for anything and everything in the field, however debasing its rank on paper, without discrimination. She could always work her way up. Could always take the basest of starting points and make it the launching pad to greatness. Or, that had been the plan. In the end, things had gone rather differently.*

'We've all been deeply impressed with your work, Ms Calla.' The head of the interview panel, the well-known senior Cardinal Archivist, Edoardo Oberti – who, Angelina noted, went through the entire day's proceedings without ever using the title 'Doctor' to which he knew full well she was entitled – had spoken with polite formality and pomp.

'You seem to have an adept mind, and every recommendation we've received indicates you've a powerful intellect inside a commanding personality.' That remark had come from another member of the panel, Angelina could no longer remember precisely who. They were all the same, clones of each other's senior-looking faces, greying hair and wrinkled suits. And all male, of course. 'This is the kind of job that rewards such qualifications,' one of the lookalike copies had uttered. 'There's only one way a junior scholar can go in this kind of post, and that's up.'

The words had been delivered with a kind of grandfatherly encouragement that Angelina would have found intolerably condescending if she hadn't been so used to it by then. Instead, she simply smiled, inclining her head slightly, feigning gratitude at what amounted to little more than veiled insults gift-wrapped in arrogance.

By then she had lost faith in all of them. All, save one. A senior archivist called Ben Verdyx had been assigned as her liaison for the day-long visit, showing her around the Archives, describing the work the various internal teams undertook on a day-to-day basis and the key projects currently ongoing. He had struck Angelina as a genuinely nice man, perhaps seven or eight years her senior but with a quality that made him seem both older in wisdom and, paradoxically, younger in character than his years should allow. He was a man absorbed in his work, entirely at home in library stacks and rooms filled with filing boxes, at his most vibrant and alive when walking slightly in front of her – presumably to make him less aware of her presence, as he seemed overwhelmingly shy – describing random pieces of historical data. Angelina loved to see that familiar quality in another person. And there had seemed to be something genuinely kind about Ben's words to Angelina throughout the day. 'Let me tell you, you'd love this work,' didn't sound condescending when it came from his lips, and his 'I really wish you the best,' didn't feel duplicitous.

But in the end the interview process had gone just like all the others. Polite smiles and handshakes ended the day with promises of a decision being sent in short order – promises that belied the fact that no one in the room actually believed Angelina had any chance of being offered the post. That had been confirmed two days later by a letter which had probably been printed before she'd ever walked into the interview. Another rejection to add to the stack.

That was it. The last straw, the wisp of chaff to snap the camel's spine – whatever cliché worked. She'd had enough. It was time to admit defeat, and start to look for something else.

As the man in the chair to her left had the ties around his wrists cut free, Angelina knew for certain that his pale, frightened features belonged to the same Ben Verdyx she'd met those long months before. He'd appeared kind then; he looked terrified now.

'I presume you recognise each other,' the monotone voice of the one who'd called himself Major Hans Heinrich broke through her thoughts. 'Our records show you've met.'

Angelina returned her attention to him. 'Your records . . . your ranks . . . kidnapping for our "protection".' She shook her head in angry disbelief, then pointed at Ben. 'Yes, I've met that man before, but I'm not going to sit here and discuss the pleasantries of my past until you explain what the hell is *actually* going on. And no more nonsense about the Swiss Guard or "necessary circumstances". Either kill us and get it over with, or start telling the goddamned truth.'

The last comment took all the boldness Angelina could muster, and the words had barely left her lips before the terror of what she'd possibly just asked for shifted her back into mute silence.

Damn it, woman, do you really need to speak every single thought that comes into your head?

Once again, Heinrich responded to the vulgarity – this time what religious folk would call blasphemy – with a look of genuine discomfort.

'Dr Calla, I have not lied to you yet, and I don't plan to do so in the future,' he said, reclaiming his form. 'I have every intention of explaining this situation to you, for my own interests as well as yours. Because though Dr Verdyx knows more about our present circumstances than you do, neither of you, it seems, knows as much about it as we previously thought.'

Angelina looked again to Ben, whose features, still pallid, were now screwed up in confusion. He glanced involuntarily in her direction, their eyes meeting for the first time. She saw only bewilderment.

'If you're going to explain, explain,' Angelina spat, turning back to the Major.

He pulled up a chair and sat stiffly in front of her.

'It begins with how much you know about a certain tablet.'

13

Quartiere Prenestino-Labicano, eastern Rome
Church of St Paul of the Cross
Charismatic Catholic community headquarters

The sanctuary was almost empty. The young man noticed that first of all. He normally didn't come here apart from the services, though he made almost all of those, and thus he had never seen the broad, modern space other than filled with people. The angled rows of pews seemed strangely barren with only a few individuals scattered here and there, sparse inhabitants calling in off the streets for a moment of private comfort in the midst of the day. They looked out of place, eyes closed, kneeling in ancient postures of prayer in a sanctuary that was utterly contemporary and designed for crowds rather than casual visitors.

It was enough to be unsettling, and he was unsettled already.

The parish church of St Paul of the Cross, one of the few parishes of the Roman Catholic Church's relatively little-known charismatic movement to exist in a city that was far more comfortable with liturgical rites that were still formal and ritualised, even if they were no longer Tridentine or Latin, was an aberration in style as much as in tradition. Its exterior was boxy, red-brick and plain, and its interior bore more in common with Baptist or Evangelical houses of worship than the Catholic churches to be found everywhere else in the city. Its walls were unadorned, white plasterboard with matt paint, floors carpeted in a commercial-grade soft maroon rather than marbled. There were no pillars or carved altarpieces, and the high windows were of a clear glass rather than stained. Only an oblong, wooden altar at the far end, covered in a plain green cloth, together with row after row of identical pews, marked the interior space out as a church at all, though this stark appearance did not stop throngs of faithful from coming each Wednesday, Saturday and Sunday to seek out a glorious refuge from the world and the enlightenment of spirit. St Paul's worship services always packed the building to capacity.

On any other day, the plain interior would have inspired the young man who now moved hastily down the carpeted central aisle – the simplicity of style drawing out the joy within his heart rather than crowding it out with overbearing pomp and display. This building was all but his second home.

Today, however, even home wasn't comforting. Outside, sirens hadn't stopped sounding throughout the city since reports of gunfire were lodged in two separate locations, and the whole of Rome was on edge.

But that wasn't the main reason for his discomfort.

As he reached the front of the aisle he made a rushed genuflection before the simple altar, which stood separated from the main space of the church by a low communion rail. He should pause, he knew. Should stop and comport himself. He should say a prayer and take the time to open his heart to God as he entered into his holy house. All this was second nature to him – but he couldn't follow nature now, either. The news he bore within him was too monumental. He ignored it all, sweat glistening on his brow, his heavy breathing echoing in the otherwise quiet space.

He approached an elderly custodian pushing a mechanical sweeper across the carpeting behind the altar.

'I need to see Father Alberto.' The statement came out between deep breaths, his shoulders rising and dropping in metre with his clipped speech.

'Father is resting.' Denial. The janitor paused, gave his old shoulders a shrug. The two men knew each other well. Most members of the parish did, unusual as the community was. The janitor, whose name was Laurence, was a newer recruit to their number, but it never took long to integrate once it became clear that a seeker's intentions were genuine.

'I'm aware this is his time for personal retreat,' the young man persisted, perhaps too testily, 'but I must see him all the same. Please.' Pleading strained his voice. 'Go to his room, Laurence. Tell him I'm here. He'll understand.'

He has to understand.

The custodian's expression changed, and at last he looked up from his sweeping. Deep lines of age grooved his face and made canyons of his fading eyes, but even the trails of so many years couldn't conceal a look of surprise.

Thomás didn't normally behave like this.

'Is everything all right, young man?'

He considered answering. He could say so many things – things that resonated with the deep faith both of them had. With their expectations, with all their experiences. His lips parted, he was so tempted; but after a moment's contemplation he clamped his jaw closed again and shook his head.

'Just . . . go, tell Father.' Thomás nodded towards the sanctuary's side door. 'Please.'

The janitor held his gaze a moment longer, then set the

sweeper aside. He walked out of the sanctuary without another word.

To speak with Father Alberto Alvarez was always a spiritual experience. Just to be in the man's presence was enough to change a person's soul, Thomás had often reflected, and men and women were attracted from all over the city and beyond for precisely that reason. To stand in his company, to experience something wholly different from the usual encounters of their day-to-day lives. To be inspired, changed.

In the four years of his discipleship at the Charismatic Catholic Church of St Paul of the Cross, Thomás Nascimbeni had never once been in a room with the holy priest, whether it be this sanctuary or any other, without feeling the same sense of overwhelming awe that had first drawn him to the parish and its sidelined traditions. On his first visit, walking through the strange glass doors that felt more like the entrance to a shopping mall than to a church, into a room he'd have sworn was a Presbyterian prayer hall if a tiny plaque outside hadn't indicated the place was, at least formally, part of the Roman Catholic communion, Thomás had felt something. Deep within him, far beyond the confines of intellectual faith or the rational consolation of belief he'd associated within his religion throughout his twenty-two years of life, he'd felt . . . it had been hard to put it into words, then. Even now, it remained difficult to describe. He'd experienced the immanence, and closeness, of the divine. Unlike any other church he'd ever visited, this one was lacking madonnas and pietás, it had only the plainest and most basic of crosses mounted on a single wall. There was no glorious organ lining the apse and the customary clerical chasubles and copes were nowhere to be seen, the clergy robed in simple white with an unadorned stole around their necks. And yet Thomás had felt, in the midst of all this, this *plainness*, that his heart had suddenly surged into life. He'd sensed, in a way that surpassed anything he could have intellectually determined, that there was nothing worldly here for him to see, and so he'd closed his eyes and seen the face of God.

He'd never gone to another church since.

In the years that had passed since then, he'd become a devoted disciple of the Catholic Charismatic Movement. He'd known nothing about that group before his first visit, nothing about the way its similarities to Evangelical Pentecostalism – with its emphases on mystical experience, charismatic gifts and personal inspiration – had led to its being marginalised by mainstream Catholics the world over, especially here in the capital city of its religious empire. Gradually, the pieces of its history had become known to him, including the barely concealed disdain in evidence in the faces of his pious family and friends when he mentioned his new-found affiliation. But for Thomás, the movement's dismissal by so many rank-and-file religious only reinforced the truth of its message. Since childhood he'd known only dry services mired in formulaic ritual and the institutionalised shape of church governance. At last he'd found a place where the living, beating heart of faith was still alive. Where hope would speak, and God could move.

And Thomás had never known him to move more forcefully, and yet more gracefully and tenderly, than in the person of Father Alberto. In a world where priests had become businessmen and bishops politicians, he had found a good pastor who was a true mystic. Father Alberto had no ulterior motives. He wanted only to be, in his typically poetic words, 'clay in the hands of a loving God, ready to be shaped by him according to his will'. And so he had been. And was.

He was a man worthy of being followed, and a man who absolutely needed to know what Thomás had seen.

* * *

Only the slightest of creaks, wood rubbing against wood, announced motion from the side door. All Thomás's emotion halted at the sound. He realised that he was holding his breath, that he could hear his pulse pounding through his ears. If the kindly but stern janitor reappeared and said anything other than 'Father is ready to see you,' Thomás thought his soul might burst.

He turned towards the sound, but the janitor was not there – and then Thomás's heart went from thrashing to what felt like a dead halt. Before him stood Father Alberto himself.

Thomás's emotions swelled back into life. He was elated that the priest had come out at his request – this was more than he had expected. Father Alberto's curling hair, once a dark black but now spiced with bold locks of grey that were almost white, was trimmed short but otherwise untended, and his greyer beard reached down to his upper chest. His face was not so much wrinkled as pockmarked by age, with caverns and hills that made smooth places rough and gave him the natural appearance of an outcast, of one who'd been scarred by the world. And yet, it was a face of serenity. Thomás had gazed into it so many times before, into Father Alberto's alarmingly blue eyes, and felt that there was something far more than just the priest staring back at him.

At this moment, however, those eyes were different. Within them was something Thomás had rarely seen there.

Concern.

'What is it, Thomás?' he asked. 'Your heart . . . it is deeply upset.'

Thomás swallowed. 'Yes, Father, I am disturbed.'

'Try to calm yourself.' The priest laid a hand on his shoulder. A disarming warmth descended through the fabric and eased into his bones. 'Tell me what's troubling you.'

Rumours of gun attacks came to Thomás's mind again.

The police barricades he'd passed on his way here. But he shoved them aside.

'It's the prophecy, Father,' Thomás blurted out. He felt that his eyes had gone glassy. Perhaps there were tears welling within them. They may have been tears of joy. 'The prophecy . . . the hand of God. All the things that have been revealed to us in bits and pieces over the past months, they've all come together. Just like you said.'

He could feel Father Alberto's grip tighten on his shoulder. 'My son, calm yourself. You're overcome.'

'They've found it!' Thomás exclaimed. 'The whole of it!'

'You're speaking in riddles, Thomás. Tell me what you mean.'

Thomás reached into his trouser pocket and dug out his phone. He slid his finger effortlessly across its screen and brought it to life. A web browser was already open, an image centred on the screen.

'They've found it!' he exclaimed again, handing the phone to the priest. 'A tablet, written in some ancient script. Apparently it was unearthed a month ago, but they've just announced it today, with parts of it translated. Father, it's a tablet of prophecy, and it confirms everything you've been telling us would come!'

Father Alberto stared at the small screen of Thomás's phone. As he scrolled through the news article his features grew tighter, his eyes narrower.

'You know what's been going on outside today,' Thomás added, his words finally delivered more softly, filled with wonder. 'It's the first of the miracles.'

'This text calls them plagues,' Father Alberto countered, reading.

'Its translators can call them whatever they want,' Thomás answered. 'The first was revealed to us months ago, and now we find it's written right there,' he pointed towards the display, 'on a tablet produced who knows how many centuries ago. And it's *happened*. Right here, outside.'

Thomás beamed. This was reality, and it was overwhelming.

'That tablet,' he added, 'confirms what we already know.' He reached forward and gently wrapped his fingers in an embrace around the priest's hands.

'The Lord has begun to act. And this wonder is only the first.'

14

Beneath the Apostolic Palace

'The tablet was discovered one month ago, almost to the day,' Major Hans Heinrich said, presenting the details in as dry and concise a manner as any report Angelina had ever heard. He was a man who cut to the chase, approaching the present topic with professional detachment. 'The discoverer was a civil archaeologist by the name of Manuel Herrera, of Spanish origin, who'd been working on the HSBC building site near San Clemente.'

Angelina knew the site, chiefly through the roadworks that had been causing traffic delays in the neighbourhood for months.

'As is usual in central Rome, the government requires a survey to be performed whenever new building works are approved. This is land where every square metre of earth has history beneath it, and it's a matter of routine to investigate what ruins and artefacts might lie underneath a plot of soil before foundations are laid and concrete poured.'

'There's always something.' The interruption startled Heinrich as well as Angelina. It was the first time Ben Verdyx had spoken since they'd arrived in the room. 'You shouldn't belittle the need.'

'I had no intention to belittle—'

'Those digs reveal all sorts of things. We've found pottery, libraries, the foundations of houses, even whole churches, buried under our feet. The Vatican Museums are filled with things "found beneath the streets".'

Despite her circumstances, Angelina felt a surprising comfort at Ben's words. It was reassuring to hear an historian revel in history, even when he'd just been abducted at gunpoint.

'Dr Verdyx, you misunderstand,' the Swiss Guardsman continued. 'That these digs find things is precisely the point. While the bulk of what is unearthed is usually inconsequential to all but the hyper-enthusiasts – generally it's simply surveyed, itemised and catalogued and the sites are approved for building – on this particular occasion something was found that has proven entirely . . . consequential.'

'A tablet.' The words came from Angelina's mouth, echoing the Guardsman's announcement from a moment before. She was anxious to know what kind of object had prompted all this. The shock of how she'd arrived here was giving way to her own historical draw.

'Precisely,' Major Heinrich affirmed. 'Mr Herrero discovered a small tablet buried at a depth of approximately two metres beneath the current topsoil level. It is manmade, of a reddish clay common – as I'm sure you will soon agree is of the utmost relevance – to the whole of what is today southern Iraq.'

Angelina felt something within her swell: an interest and excitement that rarely any more had occasion to emerge. To her left, her peripheral vision caught a new straightness in Ben's posture as well.

'I say it's called Iraq *today*,' Heinrich continued, 'because in the ancient world it was known as—'

'Mesopotamia.' Ben cut him off.

'Babylon,' Angelina added. Their faces turned towards each other and once again their eyes met. This time, fear had given way to wonder.

'Both answers are correct,' Heinrich confirmed. 'The lands of ancient Babylon, the heart of the kingdom of Mesopotamia, one of the greatest realms of the ancient world – the fabricators of legend, of laws, and of their own unique language. Which is of the utmost relevance, as impressed upon the tablet are twenty-seven lines of slightly decayed, but by and large well-preserved, ancient Akkadian script.'

Fire now shot fully through Angelina's system.

'Akkadian?' The word burst out of her in tones of excited disbelief. 'You discovered a new Akkadian document?' The irony of referring to anything in the long-dead language as 'new' was not lost on her. Akkadian, old even by the time it had become the principal language of Mesopotamian society, was linked to a culture that died out almost three thousand years ago. Even if limited examples of ritualised Akkadian continued to be crafted after the Babylonian language's decline in the eighth century BC, the most modern of its texts dated to no later than AD 105, which meant that *anything* written in its uniquely captivating script was at the very least over 1,900 years old.

'So it would seem,' the Swiss Guardsman answered.

'Can . . . can we see it?' Ben asked the question with such hesitancy it was almost inaudible.

'Of course you can,' Heinrich answered, nodding towards his colleague who immediately walked towards a table at the back of the room, on which a briefcase lay open.

'For you, Dr Calla,' Heinrich continued, gesturing towards Angelina, 'this will be something entirely new. But for you, Dr Verdyx, I believe you're about to discover you've seen part of our mysterious tablet before.'

*   *   *

A glossy A4-sized photo-printout was handed to Angelina by *Wachtmeister* Wüthrich, and she gazed at it with abject wonder. Her day thus far had been inexplicable. Now, it seemed all but impossible.

In the course of her years of study, Angelina had read every Akkadian text that existed. She'd always taken pride in that fact, though the catalogue of materials wasn't precisely vast. This wasn't Latin or Greek, or even Aramaic or classical Hebrew, all of which had veritable libraries of volumes that could consume even the most adept scholar's entire life. The assembled Akkadian collective could fit on a reasonably sized bookshelf, which amounted to a rather different scenario. She'd been able to go through the whole received history of Akkadian literature, multiple times. She'd been exhaustive.

But Angelina had never seen this text before.

Printed at the bottom of the page, beneath the photograph, were a few of its pertinent details. The tablet was oblong, twice as tall as it was wide at approximately forty-eight centimetres by twenty-four. The twenty-seven lines of text ran from what looked like approximately a centimetre from its left edge in neat, though slightly downward-slanting lines, to a margin roughly the same distance from the right side. Its rough-hewn edges suggested it may have come from a larger panel, though the text appeared to be self-contained.

'This is a photo of just one side,' Angelina said, looking up to Major Heinrich. 'Do you have others?'

'There is nothing inscribed on the back,' he answered, 'and no other tablets were found along with this one. The search was thorough. It appears to be a complete document.'

She acknowledged his response with only a nod, returning her attention to the vivid photograph. Whoever had cared for the tablet after its discovery had been careful and thorough. Its surface was cleaned, each runic impression clear and visible. The lighting was similarly well composed, rendering the impressions vividly offset against the surface.

Angelina's lexical memory was already speeding back to life. She hadn't had occasion actually to translate Akkadian in – hell, it felt like far longer than it probably actually was. *Years.* It wasn't like new documents just popped up every day. Still, despite the fact that she no longer had regular cause to delve into ancient linguistics, some skills never really left a person. Hers hadn't completely atrophied, and they returned with a thrill that momentarily overpowered her perplexity at everything else about her day. For an instant, Angelina was no longer in an underground room with papal guards, but was instead back in the Sapienza University library, an ambitious graduate student brimming with enthusiastic curiosity. Now, as then, she watched as each phrase and clumping together of runes gradually formed into meaningful phrases that in her mind were forever linked to the mythology of the cultures that had produced the language. She could feel the flood waters of Gilgamesh's great deluge sweeping over the legendary Mesopotamian landscape. The great walls and ziggurats of Ur, the pillars and gardens of Babylon in Sumeria. All the worlds of which this language was the witness, the legends of which it was the only remaining voice – though those myths and legends had worked their way across cultures and into other traditions as well – they all came rushing through her consciousness as she was swept into the task of translating.

But as with so much else in this day, things quickly began to feel uncomfortable.

A few lines down, one set of triangles and dashes filtered its way through her storeroom of lexical memory and became a clear word: 'river'. It could refer to the Tigris, of course, or the Euphrates – the traditional rivers of Mesopotamian lore, the latter so much the standard in Akkadian literature that it could regularly be referred to without mentioning its name, in the same way that citizens of Washington, DC could refer to 'the Hill' without needing to specify Capitol Hill, or financiers in London could refer to 'the City' without further qualification.

But another river was more vivid in Angelina's mind today.

Then another rune, with its lines arrayed more perpendicularly and without as many cross-hatches, resonating with action: *'run'*. Though, even as Angelina found herself whispering its meaning aloud, she realised it was set into the future. 'Will run.'

The river will run . . .

A prophecy. Trembling once again, she somehow knew that the next rune would speak of blood, even before she looked at it.

Ben Verdyx's examination of the photograph was undertaken amidst a wholly different interior atmosphere than Angelina's. He was only a few metres away from her, still sitting on the chair to which he'd formerly been bound, but his thoughts had him in entirely another world.

I've seen this tablet before.

The thought was impossible. Clearly he'd never seen it in his life. The artefact was entirely new to him – not only its contents and shape, but even its very existence. This was the first moment he'd heard such a treasure from the distant past had been so recently unearthed.

But he *had* seen it before. Or, properly speaking, part of it.

'These four lines, here at the top,' he finally blurted out, pointing to the upper edge of the image and leaning towards Heinrich, 'I know this text.'

The Major said nothing, but a slight nod of a shining forehead confirmed he'd expected this recognition.

'You knew about this?' Angelina demanded, Ben's surprising statement perhaps the only thing in the world that could have drawn her focus away from the image in her hands.

'Not the actual tablet. But these lines . . . I've read them before. Transcribed, in the absence of any context.'

'How is that possible?'

'Because I gave them to you,' a new voice announced. It came as the door on the far side of the room slid open and a man in flowing black robes, offset at the waist by a sash of vivid crimson, stepped towards them.

'I gave them to you, and with that act, things began to fall apart.'

15

Outside – central Rome

The alteration of the waters had started the change in the atmosphere of the ancient city, but it had been the gunfire that had transformed strange into fearful. The waters ran red and people were curious, confused. But then gunshots sounded in the city's streets, not in one location but two, almost simultaneously, and the people became afraid.

There was nothing obvious to connect the events. The most prevalent theory for the water's altered colour had gradually settled on some freak contamination: a spill or a burst pipe. But it didn't take overly creative minds to link together the 'blood' of the river, as purely coincidental as that colour might be, with the very real blood that had been spilled in the streets.

The waters had changed, and people had started dying.

One had been killed along the Tiber at the Piazza Pia. Another had been wounded and died en route to the hospital. A second barrage of gunfire had erupted at the Ponte Sisto. No deaths there, but three members of the expanded crowd had received injuries that had them in intensive care. The casualty count still had the opportunity to rise.

But the fear already was. The city was growing edgy. And the waters were still red.

16

Beneath the Apostolic Palace

Cardinal Giotto Forte's diminutive, slightly rotund figure did not approach the height of the two Swiss Guards, but there was an immediate deference in their demeanour which suggested he was, without question, the man in authority.

'The lines of text at the top of the tablet were sent to you at my specific instruction, less than two days after it was unearthed.' He spoke directly to Ben, who gazed back in obvious recognition of the figure who was speaking, but equally obvious confusion over his words.

'Cardinal Forte, I, I . . .' Ben stuttered for clarity. 'I don't understand. What would something like this have to do with your office? Or, moreover, with me?'

'The second question might be the easiest to answer.' Giotto Forte gave a nod towards Major Heinrich, who in acknowledgement of the unspoken command brought the Cardinal a chair. The encrimsoned man sat with a grunt, his frame too wide for the small wooden seat.

'The text was provided to you because you're the only resident expert within Vatican City on Akkadian script. It took us a bit of phoning around the various colleges and halls to find you – but it turned out you were, literally, right beneath our noses.' The wit of his reference to the underground expanse of the Vatican Secret Archives, whose precise extent was unknown but was estimated to include more than eighty kilometres of underground tunnels and storage stacks, seemed to please Cardinal Forte. No one else in the room joined in with his smile.

'The long and the short of it,' he continued, bringing seriousness back on to his features, 'was that we wanted to know what it meant, and you were the man for the job.'

Ben's gaze had slipped gradually away as the Cardinal offered his explanation. His eyes settled on a point buried somewhere in the floor, memories more vivid than vision.

'I remember translating it,' he muttered. 'The text was given to me as a scan of a hand-penned copy.'

'At the time, we didn't feel it pertinent to disclose any more details to you,' Forte continued. 'Usual practice around here. When we don't know what we're dealing with, caution is the ruling principle.'

'Over an ancient tablet?' Angelina protested.

'A presumption!' Cardinal Forte answered back, energetic and commanding. 'You *presume* it's old, just as we did. But one can never know. There have been plenty of recent discoveries of "ancient" documents, scrolls, fragments of papyrus and the like, which have turned out to be forgeries. Antiquity can be faked, though these days it's immensely difficult to do. The Vatican has no interest in making a fool of itself by announcing an ancient find until we're absolutely sure that's what we've got. Have to look into the text. Into the materials, that sort of thing.'

Angelina sat back, her head offering only the slightest nod of acknowledgement. The Cardinal might be a pudgy cleric with an overbearing attitude, but he wasn't wrong. The past years had seen too many cases of fraudulent 'discoveries' coming into the mainstream, the most famous being the so-called 'Gospel of Jesus's Wife Fragment' published, to immense worldwide fanfare, by one of the most eminent scholars in religious studies. It had been lauded as the find of the century, had made scholarly journals and public media; but in the end it had been a reporter who had chased down its provenance and discovered it to be a hoax. It had cost the scholar her reputation, and the venerable institution that had tenured her slipped dramatically down the rankings of international scholarly respect as a result. Angelina could understand why the Vatican would be anxious not to follow suit.

'But there was nothing terribly unusual about the four lines I translated,' Ben said, sitting a little taller. 'I remember working over the glyphs. They appeared to be the introduction to some sort of prophetic oracle – a series of predictions, woes, that sort of thing. Hardly out of the ordinary for an ancient document emerging from a myth-laden culture.'

'Once you sent back your translation of those initial lines,' Cardinal Forte said, his jowls bobbing as he nodded his head, 'we came to the same conclusion. A newly discovered collection of prophetic utterances, from a quarter of antiquity that produced them like snow from heaven. Interesting for the scholars in due course, but hardly something cataclysmic to the reputation of the Church or the broad understanding of history. And your lack of criticism of the text,' he added, 'led us to believe it was authentic Akkadian. I'm told it's a difficult language to forge.'

'Extremely,' Ben confirmed, 'since so few people know it well enough to use it creatively, and since the whole corpus of Akkadian literature is essentially known.'

'Your work reassured us. We released the full imagery to our various scholarly offices, to let the tablet go through the normal process of cataloguing and registering, then be released to the scholarly world in due course.' He paused. 'I only wish we'd sat on it a little longer, now. Once that process starts, so many hands get involved that it's hard to stop. I'm told the imagery was published on some scholarly website earlier today.'

'Why call it off?' Angelina asked. The Cardinal, however, did not look at her. Instead, he kept his eyes bolted on to Ben's.

'Dr Verdyx, do you remember what those first lines you translated were?'

Ben pondered only a second, his memory refreshed by the photograph in his hands. 'Something about a plague of death coming upon whoever would discover the prophecy. That sort of thing. Typical introductory remarks to this kind of document.'

'Correct,' the Cardinal confirmed. 'More precisely, your translation read . . .' He reached into a deep pocket in his cassock and pulled out a folded piece of paper which he opened and held at eye level. '"He who lays claim and discovers these words shall die swiftly and most terribly." Does that sound familiar?'

Ben nodded in the affirmative, and Angelina peered down at the photograph as the Cardinal read. Translating Akkadian on the fly wasn't really a skill that any scholar possessed, but as the words were read they appeared to match the impressions she could see in the clay's first lines.

'Those were the words that ultimately brought all this to my attention,' Major Hans Heinrich reintroduced himself into the conversation.

'I . . . I don't understand,' Ben confessed, passing his gaze back and forth between the Cardinal and the Guardsman.

'The words may have felt standard when you translated them,' Heinrich continued, 'but three days later, the prediction, or prophecy, or call it whatever you want, that you interpreted from that tablet – it came true.'

Neither Ben nor Angelina had the faintest idea how to respond. Too much new information was passing through their minds to process it all, and for a few seconds they simply gaped in silence.

It was Angelina who finally burst the bubble.

'What on earth is that supposed to mean?' she asked. She found she felt more comfortable addressing Heinrich than Forte. Her antipathy towards religion harboured a more refined dislike of the male-centric clergy that ruled it, and though the Cardinal had been nothing other than respectful and businesslike since he'd entered the room, he was still an embodiment of so much that Angelina despised. 'Prophecies on ancient clay tablets don't just "come true".'

'That is precisely what Cardinal Forte thought,' Heinrich answered with an incline of deference towards his superior, 'and why he passed the text to us.'

'I may be a believer,' Forte inserted, 'but I consider scepticism a healthy dimension of faith. Questions should come before accepting answers.'

'And when a man dies,' Heinrich continued, 'we all become sceptics. The man who discovered the tablet, the Manuel Herrero I spoke about before, died four days and eleven hours after he first found the tablet underground. The precise cause of death, some sort of virulent pathogen, is still undetermined. But suffice it to say that it was, in the words of your translation, Dr Verdyx, both "swift" and "most terrible".'

Ben sat fixed in his chair, his face immobile.

'You're right, of course,' Heinrich continued, 'and His Excellency is also right: prophecies from the ancient world are like water in the sea. They're everywhere you look. But when one is unearthed and its first foretelling "comes true", to my mind that smacks of fraud, not history. All the more so when it amounts to a prediction of what very well may be murder.'

Heinrich allowed his pace to slow slightly. His gaze arced sternly between Ben and Angelina.

'It was the moment that we found out about Herrero's death that the two of you became suspects.'

17

Twenty-six days earlier
Hospital Fatebenefratelli
Central Rome

'Is he gone?'

The question sounded surprisingly cautious, almost hesitant. For a moment the tenor surprised the man called Bartolomeo, as Emil Durré always seemed in eminent control. Yet Bartolomeo had to remind himself that in all the years of Emil's time on this planet, his boss had never taken the life of another, even by proxy. He could be forgiven for suffering a pause at the realisation that the three words of his question – assuming they were answered the way he expected – would forever change that.

'So I've been told.' Bartolomeo replied calmly through the tinny telephone line, his voice redolent with a practised, grief-tinged sobriety.

It was the message his boss was waiting for. Unambiguous. Arranged in advance.

'I'm very sorry to hear that,' Emil answered, continuing the scripted dialogue. Whether it was relief in his voice, or anxiety, was difficult to determine. 'I hear he was a good fellow.'

Bartolomeo knew that Emil desperately wanted to say more. He was a man of theatrical ideals, who routinely had to be talked down from the ledge of far too showy and revealing extravagances. He'd been plotting the course that led to this moment, and to everything that was to come, for months, and he wanted the actual events to have – magnitude.

This was the day it all started to come together.

But a moment later, the line went dead at Bartolomeo's ear. They had finished their script. There was nothing more to say. There would certainly be no pleasantries or small talk. Bartolomeo's own name had never been uttered over a phone line between them, and he would never dream of using his employer's given name, even in person. There was a trust that emerged from that dependability, a trust Bartolomeo had no intention of diminishing.

Emil had given him one of the most important tasks in the whole of the operation. There were many players, all with significant parts to call their own. But Emil had trusted Bartolomeo with ensuring that the tablet was discovered at the right time, and that its discoverer would not survive.

For two weeks prior to its 'unearthing', Bartolomeo had lodged himself in the necessary surroundings, enrolling as a temporary labourer with Manuel Herrero's civic excavation and survey unit. He'd had a background in building works before he'd gone illegitimate, so it hadn't been a difficult role to secure, and with his credentials firmed up he'd been able to be present on the work site with Herrero day after day. Perfectly placed to slip the necessary quantity of the white, tasteless powder into his disposable coffee cup on the morning that had been set as discovery day. To take the crumpled cup with him after its contents had been drunk, shoved into a pocket and removed from the site so that it would never be found.

The pathogen, they had been told, would take only days to destroy the man's body, and the effects would start to become apparent almost immediately. Both elements – its prompt uptake as well as the arduous torture – were part of the appeal.

Curses, after all, are never meant to be gentle.

At Emil's direction, Bartolomeo had watched over the unfortunate man, discreetly, over the four days since. He'd 'found' the tablet, which had been placed at just the right point in the dig to ensure it would be located, and all had gone according to plan after. It was a rather miserable thing to have to do to another human being, yes. The pathogen ate away at his organs with fierce efficiency, causing blood to drip from his eyes and ears and foamy spittle to flow from his mouth. Cinematic really, and dreadful.

But that which was coming was so immeasurably greater than the value of his singular life, so incomprehensibly wonderful, that there could be no hesitation. The tablet had, as they'd ensured, been found. It predicted the death of its discoverer – and so there had been no other choice.

Besides, hadn't it long ago been said that it was, from time to time, expedient that one man should die for the people?

Emil had quoted the saying to him as they'd concocted this segment of their plan. Attributed it to Jesus, or Pilate, or someone from the Bible. Bartolomeo, despite his biblical name, had never been a churchgoer and so couldn't be sure. But he liked the saying.

He doubted it would be the last time he used it.

18

'What's that supposed to mean, we're suspects?' Angelina was incredulous. Nothing about her day had made sense thus far – from the shootings to the chase, to her capture or to the revelation of the tablet and its discoverer's sorry fate. But the idea that she or Ben Verdyx could be suspects in the man's death was the most preposterous thing she'd heard yet.

'It was a natural conclusion to draw,' Major Heinrich answered calmly. 'We weren't about to take the line that Herrero's death was the result of some prophetically induced plague, however convenient the text's prediction might make it. Which means that his death was orchestrated, somehow, with the discovery of that tablet.' He wagged an accusing finger towards the photograph that was still in Angelina's grip.

'And apart from Dr Verdyx here,' Cardinal Forte interjected, 'you, Dr Calla, are the only other person in Rome with expertise in the language of the hour.'

'Akkadian,' Angelina whispered out her beloved word.

It suddenly had an unpleasant flavour, and sounded self-condemning.

Sometimes the things we love turn around to bite us.

The implication wasn't unreasonable. How could someone orchestrate the death of another man – if, indeed, that's what had happened – and tie it into a prophecy in the ancient script, without knowing the script itself? The fact that the tablet was a new discovery meant there were no existing translations that could be looked up in dusty library collections. Whoever had tied Manuel Herrero's death to the prophecy of the tablet had to have known about its discovery, and known the language in which it was written.

'So, you think we're forgers.' Even as the words came out of her mouth, Angelina wasn't sure whether they were an accusation or an appeal. The thought was absurd. Repugnant.

'That was our suspicion,' Heinrich affirmed. For the first time, his military bearing struck Angelina as sharply as the angles of his face. In their usual dress the Swiss Guard looked like fluffy playthings of Renaissance memory, but if they were all cut like this beneath their costumes, they would be a decent human force indeed.

'You keep using the past tense,' Ben finally spoke. He'd remained distant to the exchange between Angelina and the others, interjecting only occasionally, and even this comment was spoken more to the air than to either Forte or Heinrich in particular. 'Why is that?'

'Things . . . things have changed,' the Cardinal answered. He followed his words with a huff, and a nod to Heinrich, instructing the Guardsman to explain.

'We thought we had you for sure this morning, once we saw the water go red,' the Major continued. 'We'd sent the remaining lines of the tablet's text off to a linguistics expert at Tufts in the USA, so we knew the next prophecy it contained – the first in a series of plagues.'

Angelina looked back at the image. The runes she'd already translated glowed on the page. *The river . . . will flow . . . with blood . . .*

'When that "prediction" came true, we knew we had concrete manipulation on our hands, and that one of the two of you – or perhaps both – had to be behind it. I assigned a team to each of you, covertly.'

'You had us followed?'

'Followed, tapped, and electronically surveilled, yes,' Heinrich answered, plainly and with no suggestion that he felt any remorse whatsoever for what amounted to a massive invasion of their privacy. 'Since the moment the water changed colour, our men have been with you.'

'You couldn't have, I don't know, picked up a phone and called us?' Now Angelina's voice was deliberately harsh. 'It's not like I wouldn't have been willing to talk to you.'

'We didn't want to let on that we knew anything about you. If you were plotting something, which it seemed clear you were, we wanted to learn as much about your actions and intentions as we could before revealing ourselves.'

The *fuck you* was back at the tip of Angelina's tongue, but with immense effort she bit it into silence.

'In the end, you can be grateful we were there,' Heinrich said, noting her increasingly red colour. 'It's only because we were following you that we were there to see the attacks.'

With that, all Angelina's interior protests halted. For an instant, she could hear the gunfire at the Ponte Sisto afresh, exploding in her ears. She could feel the shards of shattered stonework flying into her skin.

To her left, Ben looked equally pale.

'You and Dr Verdyx were attacked almost simultaneously,' Heinrich continued. His tone was now a shade gentler, broaching compassionate. 'The gunshots came only seconds apart, in two parts of the city. A coordinated attack.'

'The man in front of me . . . his head . . .' Ben's words blurted out the fragmentary anxieties of memory. 'I've never seen a person die.' His eyes rose to meet the Major's. 'There was a woman next to me when it started. She was shot, in the arm or shoulder, I think. Did she survive?'

'I'm afraid the welfare of others was not my men's priority,' Heinrich answered, his voice back to cold efficiency. 'They were there to watch you. The local police will have dealt with other casualties.'

Ben sagged in his chair, his gaze sinking into the floor.

Angelina eyed Heinrich, then the Cardinal. Both men were quiet, and where moments ago she'd felt only anger towards them – and to the cleric with special fervency – she realised she now felt the first flowerings of something different. Gratitude. It was, in a direct way, because of these two men and their suspicions of her, that Angelina was still alive.

'But why would anyone have been shooting at us?' she suddenly asked. 'I'm just a tour guide. Dr Verdyx is an archivist.'

'That's simple,' Heinrich answered. 'It seems we're not the only ones in Rome to know you're the only two experts in Akkadian.'

19

Beneath the Apostolic Palace

For the first time since their capture, Angelina stood.

'You're going to have to do more than just hint that others know about us,' she spoke accusingly to the Swiss Guardsman. 'If others feel our scholarly interests for some reason give them cause to shoot at us, then I for one want more than a vague idea of who they are.'

'I'm afraid that's information we don't know,' Heinrich said flatly. 'Until an hour or two ago, we were looking into you, not anyone else.'

'Well, that's a fucking comfort.'

The profanity escaped the stolid fetters of her usual propriety, and Angelina felt a sudden embarrassment, compounded by the fact that it had done so in the presence of a member of the Pope's guard, steps away from a cardinal. She scolded herself. *You might not like the clergy, but rude is rude.*

'I'm sorry, I'm just— '

'Don't apologise, Dr Calla,' Major Heinrich answered. 'We're as eager to find out who was after you as you are.'

'I doubt that.'

'We'll have CCTV footage from the two regions of your attacks advanced to us from the Carabinieri within an hour or two. Something's bound to show up on one of the cameras, and that will give us a starting point as far as the assaults go.' Angelina noticed that when Heinrich talked about operations like this his demeanour became confident, at ease, as if this were the environment in which the man was the most comfortable. 'We'll start cross-referencing your phone records with any known third parties, which might give us another lead.'

Angelina looked to Ben, to see if he showed any signs of this all being as absurd to him as it felt to her, but he sat motionless on his chair, eyes once more fixed afar.

'It would be helpful if you could liaise with my men,' Heinrich continued, 'to let them know whether you've had any contact with—'

The rest of his sentence never came. Instead, Heinrich halted abruptly, mid-phrase, his mouth still hanging open but his head suddenly tilting slightly aside. Only at that moment did Angelina notice the small wire dangling out of his left ear, barely visible along his neckline as it disappeared beneath his collar.

Heinrich remained motionless as he listened to the voice in his earpiece, then suddenly straightened and started moving towards Cardinal Giotto Forte.

'Your Excellency, if you would please come with us, we need to get you to a meeting to which you've suddenly been called.'

Forte rose and Heinrich gently urged him towards Sergeant Wüthrich on the far side of the room. The Cardinal nodded politely first to Ben and then to Angelina, and without a further word turned and left the room with the other guard.

Heinrich swivelled back to them.

'I'm sorry, but I must take my leave of you for the time being. If you will kindly remain here, *Korporal* Yoder just outside the door will look after you until I'm able to return.'

He didn't wait for a response before marching towards the exit.

'Hold on a minute!' Angelina protested. 'What's all this about? What's happened?'

Major Heinrich paused, considering whether or not to answer, but at last spoke without turning back to face her.

'The river's gone back to its normal colour.' He resumed his course towards the door, which slid open for him. Before Angelina could even ask the question, Heinrich answered it.

'The first "plague" is over. But there's going to be another.'

20

Outside, throughout central Rome

It was 5.16 p.m. when the first observer noted the change. The water that had flowed red since earliest morning had kept its mysterious colour strong throughout the day, but as the sun began to set over Rome it was a young girl, fingers clenched through her grandfather's protective grasp, who pointed with her other hand towards the river and said innocently, 'Look, Grandad, I can see the bottom!'

Her glee had attracted the attention of others, though the numbers along the riverside had dwindled dramatically after reports of the two gun attacks earlier in the day had spread. But those who remained noticed that they, too, could begin to see through the waters as they lapped at the shore – though not in their depths, where the Tiber had not run clear for a long time – and gradually the redness of the water had faded before their eyes, until blood became rust, and rust became bark, and finally the Tiber's flow was the same off-brown that it had been before the start of the day.

By then the bystanders had newspapers in their hands, and those that didn't have papers had mobile phones open to web sites and apps that all reported the same story. A seemingly routine dig at an archaeological site a month ago had unearthed a stone, written in some obscure language, which spoke of a series of strange events. Most of the commentators, like most of the spectators, didn't care what culture had produced it, or what language it had been written in, or really what the whole archaeological affair was all about. They were interested only in the fact that on one of the tablet's lines was written, 'the river shall run with blood', and all day long they'd been able to snap photos of their river doing just that.

Church of St Paul of the Cross
Charismatic Catholic community headquarters

In a back room of the structure that housed both their sanctuary and offices, Thomás and two others were assembled together for what he considered one of the most important works of his life. The room was normally used for Sunday school – instructing the youngest of their members into the living faith the Charismatics knew fuelled every breath of their lives – and now he was using it for something that would fuel faith for countless others. Thousands. Maybe millions.

When God spoke, he spoke to the whole world.

'Is the camera ready?' Thomás was impatient. It seemed to take an inordinately long amount of time for his two associates to configure the tripod and small digital device. They were younger even than he, barely more than teenagers. This sort of thing was supposed to come as second nature to them.

'Just another second, I want to make sure the resolution settings are right. This is an HD camera, but we don't want the resolution too high or it'll take us ages to upload. Seven hundred and twenty pixels will be more than enough.'

Thomás was in no mood to be concerned about such things, but he trusted they knew what they were doing.

Just as he trusted that God would help him with what Father Alberto had charged him to do.

Today, Thomás would be the messenger.

'Okay,' his cameraman finally announced. 'All good to go. You ready?'

For all his eagerness, Thomás suddenly wasn't sure whether he was. He slicked back his hair with two open palms – an act more ceremonial than functional, given the short cut he always sported – and ruffled the billows out of his shirt. He was as presentable as he could be. Yet he was terrified, and unsure whether he'd ever before shaken quite like this.

Remember, my child, the words of his beloved priest came back to him, spoken only a few hours before as Father Alberto had delivered Thomás his charge, *be at peace with yourself. The words are not yours, but God's. It is the Lord himself who will work his wonders.*

Thomás closed his eyes and breathed in a long breath. The words soothed him, and the exhale seemed to waft away his anxiety.

'Okay,' he looked up to the camera, 'let's do this.'

A moment later, a small red light indicated that recording had begun.

'My beloved brothers and sisters,' Thomás announced solemnly into the digital lens, 'the time of wonders is upon us.'

The words felt monumental, as if the whole world might shake in awe as he spoke them. But when silence reigned and the young cameraman waved his arms in a frantic *keep talking* gesture, Thomás continued.

'The Holy Spirit has never ceased to talk to humanity through the centuries,' he said, the words carefully measured, 'and he has not ceased in our day. We have received prophetic utterances in the divine glory of prayer. We have been told of signs and wonders.'

The thrill shot through him again.

'Today, the world saw a sign of the glory of God. The ancient river ran with blood, like the Nile of old, that God's power might be known.' He drew in another long breath. '*We* knew this would come. We had been prepared.'

Thomás leaned towards the camera. 'But as for you, my brothers and sisters – were you ready? Had you heard the voice of the Lord, announcing he would come?'

He sat back, his face solemn.

'Because what happened this morning is only the beginning.'

21

Torre Maura district
Eastern Rome

'Did it come off as planned?' Emil asked the question with urgency, not because he didn't know perfectly well that the Tiber had run red for thirteen solid hours, just as had been intended, but because he wanted to know the details that really mattered to him. Those that fitted this day into the grander picture of what was yet to come.

'There weren't any problems,' Bartolomeo answered. There was no look of satisfaction on his face, though there could easily have been. He was all business on this matter, just as he had been with that of Herrero's execution.

'It was fucking great,' his partner added. Yiannis was almost precisely the same age as Bartolomeo – their birthdays fell within two days of each other – and though a man of equal skill in his own area of expertise, he was of a decidedly different temperament from the other man. Where Bartolomeo was calm, monosyllabic when possible, and formal in almost all his words and gestures, Yiannis was a typically demonstrative Greek with bushy eyebrows over an olive-skinned face that contorted into expressions of every emotion in a catalogue through which he seemed to cycle on a minute-by-minute basis.

Yet despite his tendency to disfavour emotional displays in men, Emil couldn't fault the more boisterous of the pair his enthusiasm for their work. They'd done well, and once again Emil was reassured of his own wisdom in organising his teams into partnerships of complementary skill sets, specialised for just the areas of focus his project required.

'I can't imagine anyone in a hundred-mile radius missed it,' Yiannis continued. 'And hell, for hundreds of miles beyond. It was on the news, on the Internet, everywhere.' While Bartolomeo had been chiefly responsible for working out the technical where-and-how of the event, Yiannis had had his hands in the orchestration from the outset. He was clearly delighted at the effectiveness of his work.

Emil kept his expression unreadable. He was pleased, yet everything had to be held in proper perspective.

'Don't gloat,' he said simply. 'Of course people noticed. It wasn't meant to be subtle.'

Yiannis kept his smile, but sat back in his seat. He didn't expect warm or glowing words from his boss, but he sensed Emil was satisfied.

'More important than what the general public noticed,' Emil added, 'is what they didn't.' He turned his gaze towards Bartolomeo. 'Are there any reports out yet on the nature of the . . . incident?' He put extra emphasis into the final word, a particularly pleasing descriptor he'd read in a blog post a few hours ago. The term was being used by most reporters, none of whom knew quite what to call a river changing colour.

'None that are accurate. The Net's awash with theories – a complete mayhem of guesswork and ideas – but none have been on the mark. Best they've been able to do is rule out iron or other mineral deposits on the bottom of the river, which was the reigning hypothesis for the first few hours.'

'Their reason?'

'Minerals like that are easy enough to test for, and the iron level in the red water wasn't any higher than before or after.'

Emil nodded, satisfied. 'And?'

'The general trend now is to suspect some type of biochemical agent.'

This brought up one of Emil's immaculately groomed eyebrows. It was precisely in this sort of detail that things could quickly go wrong. 'Biochemical? Are there concerns of terrorism?' It was what he wanted least of all.

'There are always concerns of terrorism,' Bartolomeo answered with a shrug of his shoulders, a little too flippantly for Emil's liking.

Yiannis quickly took over. 'This is the twenty-first century, boss. A handbag left on a park bench makes people scream terrorism. This was the transformation of an entire goddamned river.'

Emil glowered at him but said nothing.

'The prevailing scientific response is that a terrorist act is unlikely, since the affected water is benign,' Bartolomeo continued calmly. 'No radioactive signatures, no toxins, no poisons. "Perfectly drinkable" was how one guy on the television put it.'

Emil's features softened fractionally. 'Good. God forbid it gets written off to a band of fanatics.'

A tremendous amount of effort had gone into finding a chemical compound that would change the water's colour effectively without posing any health risks. A key to the whole charade was its harmlessness. Only that could allow for the response Emil wanted.

That, and no one being able to rip apart the tablet's contents too thoroughly before they had a chance to reach their goal, which would risk throwing the whole project upside down. Dramatic events in Rome were either the work of miracles or of men, and so long as hype and superstition tended towards the former rather than the latter, he would have the time to get where he wanted to go.

It was the very reason they'd chosen to work with Akkadian. Other classical and ancient languages had far too many specialists out there. Latin might as well be a second language to half the clergy in Italy, and nobody made it into the academic world without at least a passing knowledge of ancient Greek – so both of those had obviously been ruled out. Hebrew would have been fitting, but it wasn't just the Jews who spent time learning that ancient Semitic script. They shared their love of it with every two-bit biblical theologian in the world, so it, too, couldn't possibly work.

But Akkadian. Hell, even with his own background, Emil knew no more than two or three symbols in the dead language. Which more or less made it perfect.

His attention fell back to the matter at hand. 'Our first endeavour went well, but it's important not to get cocky. This was the easy one. The next plague will be much more difficult, and will require more of you.'

'Yes, sir,' Bartolomeo answered for them both, standing and dragging up Yiannis by the shoulder.

Emil signalled them out of the room without another word, then listened as the door clicked closed behind them.

The next plague. He'd brought in an industrial engineer for this stage, and Emil was as confident as he could be that their preparations had been undertaken properly. But he was still nervous.

A river, after all, was one thing. Night and day were quite another.

22

Beneath the Apostolic Palace

The sudden silence that followed Major Hans Heinrich's departure from the concrete room, only moments after Cardinal Forte had been escorted out by his colleague, hung heavy in the well-lit subterranean space. Neither Angelina nor Ben seemed to know what to make of the spontaneous departure, any more than they were able to make sense of the strange discussion that had preceded it.

Eventually, Angelina wandered over to Ben's chair. He still hadn't risen, and apart from his hands being unbound and on his lap, folded over the photograph they'd been given rather than tied behind his back, he was in an identical position to that Angelina had first seen him in when their hoods were removed. Bloodstains still marked his coat and face.

For a moment, she was drawn back to her impressions of him when they'd first met. His kindness had been matched by his shyness, and Angelina imagined his reclusive social skills left him particularly ill prepared for the type of confrontation this day had brought them both.

'I always feel more comfortable alone,' he'd confessed to her then, as he'd led her through a few of the public stacks of the Vatican Secret Archives on her interview tour of the facility, *'here where it's just history I have to deal with. Always found it easier than with . . . real people.'*

And he'd hesitated, even then, recognising that it was a 'real person' to whom he was speaking. *'Sorry,'* he'd added, *'it's not that you're particularly hard to deal with. It's just that I, as a general rule, I—'*

'It's okay,' Angelina had interrupted, *'I know how you feel, Dr Verdyx. I can relate to it.'* Angelina had never been shy, never been even marginally reclusive. A girl wanting to make her own way in a world of boys learned, even at a young age, how to be bold and confident. But she could entirely relate to the draw of slipping away into the world of the past, finding comfort in stories that were written in stone, reassuringly constant and knowable. A world like Ben had in the Archives, in which an ordinary morning didn't suddenly change into something with gunfire, kidnap and revelations of murder suspicions.

It was that thought that wove a new spark of electricity through Angelina's body.

'Listen,' she said to Ben, taking another step towards him and kneeling down to his eye level, 'I have an idea.'

His gaze remained distant, stuck somewhere in memory.

'Ben,' she said again, and reached forward a hand to lay it on his. She felt a tremble in his fingers, and wondered for a moment whether this all had simply thrown him over the edge.

If she could keep him from falling off it, she would.

'Ben, do you want to get out of here?'

The words finally drew him out of his reverie. 'Out?' A shift of colour returned to his features. His eyes met hers. 'How?'

Angelina smiled tensely. 'Leave that to me. But I do have one condition.' Ben screwed up his face in curiosity.

'Once we're out,' Angelina said, 'you have to take me where I want to go.'

Moments later, Angelina had taken Ben by the hand and led them both to the door on the far side of the concrete room. She'd observed before that it appeared to be automatic, and was relieved as it began to slide open at their approach. But as she'd been equally certain would be the case, the third guardsman immediately became visible beyond it. He began to turn towards them even before the door had completed its motion.

'I'm sorry, ma'am, sir,' he nodded politely at both in turn as he swivelled his step to gently block the exit, 'I'm afraid I'll have to ask you to remain here until Major Heinrich returns.'

The man was enormous, far bigger in both height and bulk than his superior, and seemed to stretch the fabric of his suit nearly to its seam-bursting point. For an instant, Angelina wondered whether this was as wise a plan as she'd first thought, but they were here, and she wasn't about to let the moment pass.

'We politely decline,' she said, as courteously as she could. She even mustered a smile, which brought a rush of satisfaction.

It seemed to be just about the only response the guard had not been expecting. *You see*, spoke her inner monologue, *much more effective than your insults.*

'Excuse me?'

'We. Politely. Decline,' Angelina repeated.

'Decline?'

'To remain,' she answered. 'Here.' She motioned to the space behind them. 'We were brought here, we heard what your colleague had to say, and now we would like to leave.'

The enormous guard shifted his weight in his boots. 'I'm afraid that's not possible. Now, if you would please return to your seats and— '

'Are we under arrest?' Angelina persisted. The man squirmed again.

'Well, no, I don't suppose that you technically are, but—'

'If we're not under arrest, then we're leaving,' Angelina repeated, matter-of-factly. 'I'm quite certain that you'll be able to find us again if you need us.' She wasn't sure if the guard caught her sarcasm, but she heard a muffled snort from Ben that indicated her fellow spied-upon captive had.

'I'm going to have to phone up and ask about this,' the guardsman finally said, but Angelina sensed the time for movement had come.

'Call whom you wish,' she replied, stepping forward and gently brushing him aside as she led Ben through the door, 'but we're under no obligation to remain here, and we're going.'

Ben followed, and Angelina walked as boldly as she could towards a staircase beyond. There was motion behind them – presumably the guard moving for a phone or radio – but Angelina didn't allow herself to look back. Just one foot on to the steps, then the next, and the assumption that up meant out.

Outside the Apostolic Palace

Angelina and Ben emerged from the Swiss Guard's command centre beneath the Apostolic Palace fewer than five minutes after they'd departed from their interrogation room. Apart from the Guardsman who had attempted to stop them at the initial door, they'd encountered no additional resistance as they'd made their way up through the two levels that led to the surface. None of the other officers of the Guard seemed to know about them, much less have instructions to hinder their movement, and apart from the occasional side glances that Angelina associated more with her being a woman than anything else, the officials they had passed had gone about their business without accosting them.

Outside, the glow of daytime had almost entirely faded. The lights of Vatican City had come on, bathing the ancient buildings in golden illumination as a navy blue canvas gradually repainted itself into black high above.

'I can't believe we just did that,' Ben said after they had fully emerged into the open. 'All my years here, I've never even been in there. I can't believe we just marched our own way out.'

'Sometimes it just takes a little boldness,' Angelina answered. In honesty, her limbs were shaking. Walking determinedly out of the captivity of the Swiss Guard was as brash a thing as she'd ever done, and until this precise moment she hadn't been sure it would work.

But they were free now, and Ben owed her.

'You promised me you'd take me where I wanted to go?'

'Did I?'

Angelina nearly started, not wanting to face denial and frustration from another man, but in the electric light of the square she saw gentle wrinkles forming around Ben's eyes as he lifted his cheeks in a smile.

Something of his confidence was returning, and a touch of wit along with it.

'Very funny,' she answered, trying to sound annoyed, but her own smile had made its return appearance, too.

The light had also reminded her of something else. She reached into her handbag and fished out a wet wipe.

'You need to wipe off your face.' She unwrapped it and handed it to Ben. 'And you'll probably want to take off that coat.'

He looked down and saw the dried red stains on his jacket. Seriousness marched back across his face, and he unzipped it and pulled it off, tossing it into a nearby rubbish bin in revulsion. He took the wet wipe from Angelina and cleaned his cheeks and brow.

'So, where is it, then,' he finally asked, 'that you'd like to go?'

Angelina had become serious as well. She drew the folded piece of glossy photo paper out of her pocket. 'I don't know about you, Dr Verdyx, but this photograph isn't quite enough to cut it for me. If people are shooting at us because of this tablet, then I want to see the real thing.'

Ben peered at her a moment, and then his smile returned.

'It so happens,' he said, 'that I know where items like this are kept once they come into the possession of the Vatican.'

Angelina met his gaze. 'I thought you might.'

Ben began to move, signalling her to follow. 'But I have to swear you to silence before I take you there,' he added.

'To silence?'

When he looked back, his expression was genuinely warm. 'They don't call them the Secret Archives for nothing.'

23

Throughout Rome

As evening had fallen on the Eternal City, as the river had returned to its normal colour and the day moved towards its end, the citizens of Rome had left the edges of the Tiber which had captivated them since morning. Tension was thick in the popular conscience now. Details of the two gun pursuits earlier in the day had been reported on widely, small clips of mobile phone video from passers-by released to the press and cycling through the news. When, only hours later, the water had changed again, it had not calmed the city's nerves. There was nothing left to see, but sections of Rome had been shut down, combed for any clues as to either the attacks or the changes in the Tiber, and they were only beginning to be reopened. Perpetrators were being hunted for, but none had been found. Fear escalated, then escalated further.

Humanity at its finest, taking advantage of any opportunity to find a new low to which it might sink. And in a world too familiar with how quickly situations could escalate, there were more Roman doors locked on a double bolt this evening than there had been in months.

But behind those bolted doors and drawn curtains, the city's discomfort did not equate to inaction. It led Rome's inhabitants through smartphones and laptops, home computers and Internet cafés, towards the twisting web of the Internet and whatever truths it might disclose about the events that had taunted them. They were shocked, increasingly afraid and wanted answers.

Instagram was as red as the Tiber had been, tens of thousands of photos transforming its feeds into shared emotions about the oddity of the transformation. Facebook emoted every emotion its enhanced features would allow, permitting droves to offer explanations, reactions and general commentary.

And dotted amongst it all, the video clips of hundreds who had something to say, vocally, about the day that had overtaken them.

One video, in particular, was already taking on a life of its own.

A young man with short hair and a plain shirt, perhaps no more than twenty-five, sat before a camera in a small and unremarkable room, cropped to a bust in the frame. He had a look about him that some would call possession, others madness, yet others inspiration. But he spoke with purpose and zeal to whatever audience would find him, on a new YouTube channel for a religious group most had never heard of, and which had never ventured into Internet video before.

'My beloved brothers and sisters,' his voice began, 'the time of wonders is upon us.' The religious verbiage that followed was rich, filled with talk of revelation and divine encounter. '. . . Today, the world saw a sign of the glory of God. The ancient river ran with blood, like the Nile of old, that God's power might be known.'

But it was his next words that would capture the public interest.

'*We* knew this would come.'

A few hits of the 'like' button had initiated the response to the short clip. Then it was shared, embedded, reposted – and spread like a virus across the web that spanned city, country and world. The 'likes' ran into the thousands, then the tens of thousands.

'. . . What happened this morning,' the speaker continued, his voice filled with foreboding, 'is only the beginning.'

And then he had lifted up a sheet of paper, and had begun to read.

'The old pharaoh's heart was hard, but the new pharaoh's heart is harder.

I shall lay my hand upon him anew, and all his people, and my signs and wonders shall be multiplied.

I shall stretch out my hands against them, that they may know my great judgements – as I will upon the one who discovers these things, whose terrible death shall come most swiftly.

It shall come to pass in the seventeenth year of the second millennium after the coming of the Sun, when the great star is at her peak over the Eternal City.

And the first sign shall be that the river shall run with blood.

The next shall be like it in power, as the bright places become dark in a city filled with light.

Then shall come the fog, which clouds the minds of the children of fallen men;

And in the fourth place, a cross of fire shall consume their holy things, the seat of the Mighty See at its head.

And then shall come the moment, at the hour of first light on the third day after these things have begun, when above the resting place of the Rock dawn itself shall be stopped and the sun shall be blotted out of the sky.

THE SEVENTH COMMANDMENT

And then the earth shall quake,
And the firstborn son shall die as he stands,
They shall come, one by one,
Until all the world shall know the power of the Lord.'

PART THREE

Deception

24

Eighteen months earlier
Rome

Emil Durré had never contemplated a move like this in his life. He was no criminal – at least, he never had been. Until now. He was a professional man, a scholarly mind in a capable body. His were the circles of the educated elite, and his measure of excitement had always been purely intellectual, scaled in terms of expanding awareness and new levels of mental comprehension.

Yet if he were to venture into the territory he was now contemplating, Emil's life would be traced out by entirely new contours. He would certainly be a criminal. That much was understatement. He was entertaining a life of purest and most perfectly contemplated crime. And of danger. *Risk.* Elements Emil had never known before, but which shot new thrills through him, body and spirit. Excitement, he realised, was a term that was going to take on entirely new dimensions.

Emil's life would change. That was, in the end, the whole point.

Nobody does something for nothing, he reminded himself constantly, *save the petty self-sacrificers and the self-destructive philanthropists.*

God, he loved Ayn Rand. A furious pity the woman wasn't still alive – *there* was someone who knew the true difference between power and weakness. And Emil was still in the market for a second wife.

His first, back in Belgium, had been a bombshell – a far higher grade of beauty than he'd deserved, especially since at the time he'd met her he'd been a scrawny postgraduate student with a monthly income barely capable of covering his food and board expenses at the University of Leuven, and with little to commend him other than the possibility that one day, somewhere down the line, he might be able to make a name for himself in a field that, at its finest, would provide him with a salary that would only slightly outdo his current circumstances. But Theresa Laclerq, feisty bombshell of the neighbouring accommodation block, had said she'd loved him anyway, chirping out sentiments about being 'in love with your mind, babe', that had drawn Emil in. However imbalanced the visual relationship had seemed to be – her with a curvaceous, silken figure flowing under shoulder-length blond hair and emerald eyes that glowed like gems set in a face of perfectly made-up skin; him with brownish, curly hair that always tried to stick to his oily forehead, capstoning a frame that might have looked decent done up in a suit and tie but for which he could only afford casual trousers and button-down shirts that made him look gangly and awkward – something between them had clicked.

And unclicked almost as quickly. The woman, Emil lamented, had proven herself a complete airhead. 'I love you for your mind' had, he eventually decided, been the confession of a woman craving what she herself didn't possess. A year into their hasty marriage, he'd had as much as he could take. Emil was an historian. He'd completed his PhD eight months after their wedding and he craved learned conversations about antiquity, about the human condition, about the plight of man and the saga of social enlightenment. Instead he spent his evenings chit-chatting about new Italian fashion trends and music releases – topics about which he couldn't conceivably care less. It was all more than he could bear, and Emil hadn't been able to find his way to the local court office to pick up the divorce papers fast enough.

Theresa had already been pregnant by the time he'd left her, but Emil had decided that subdividing his paltry pay cheque between his personal maintenance and support for a son was better than sticking around. So he'd faithfully posted off a cheque each month as he'd left Belgium for Italy, where the Roma Tre University had offered him a junior lectureship in Mediterranean Antiquity following a year's postdoctoral research. He had a stable salary, such as it was. He had a career.

He'd interviewed for a visiting curatorship at the Vatican Secret Archives three years later – a post for which he considered himself perfectly qualified – and the interview panel had apparently agreed. Thus it was that he'd moved into slightly more comfortable digs in the massive city, continuing to correspond with his son back in Belgium, and took up the job that should have made him.

Memories of the Vatican Archives brought bile into Emil's throat. Fourteen years of his life he'd dedicated to that godforsaken place. *Fourteen years!* His curatorship had become a permanent residency with the institution, and that had been followed in due course by a promotion to senior researcher. There were few positions higher in the ancient environs of what was properly the private papal library, at least for those unwilling to give up sex and everything Emil considered part and parcel of a normal life. The clerical ranks of a Monsignor or cardinal were unwritten requirements for the Archives' highest posts. Yet Emil's pay had gone up with his newer position, and while no academic was ever going to make it rich on an institutional salary, even within the Vatican, Emil took home a pay packet that allowed him to live comfortably, if modestly.

Then the troubles had begun. Emil had never considered his actions anything like sufficient to arouse the ire of his colleagues. They worked in the Vatican's *Secret* Archives after all – why should a little secrecy be frowned upon? A little undisclosed dealing, all in the name of the greater cause of learning and progress? Emil hadn't done anything dramatic like try to steal artefacts or smuggle out documents for quick sale on the black market. All he'd done was take a few photos with a tiny digital camera – and not even of the collection's items themselves. Shit, it had basically been nothing. He'd quietly gone into the Leone XIII reading room when no one else was there, taking advantage of his staff access to the facility outside the hours it was open each day to hordes of academic researchers, and photographed a few pages from the bound indices of the Archives' contents.

Content listings, nothing more. Indices. It had been before much of the catalogue had been digitised for internal reference – Emil imagined he would have just cut-and-pasted the data from his computer had those resources been complete when he was there – but the same rules were in effect then as still technically applied to the bound indices today: no photography, no scanning, no reproduction of any kind.

Emil supposed he could understand, in principle, why the Vatican didn't want the whole inventory of their collection out in the public sphere. The treasures contained in the Secret Archives were almost incomprehensibly vast, and what was known to be located on a certain shelf in a certain basement might easily become intoxicating prey for relic hunters, 'traders' and petty thieves. So, security first – it was a policy that made sense. But Emil saw no real harm in sharing a few pages of content listings with researchers from a foreign institution when they'd asked for them. They were men of a common mind, engaged in a common work, not treasure hunters or fame-seekers. Emil hadn't even accepted payment for his assistance. He'd just done it as what had felt like a professional favour.

A few pages, from a catalogue. And they'd sacked him as if he'd tried to deface the Papal Apartments or give away the keys of St Peter.

One of the professors to whom Emil had sent the photographed indices eventually contacted the Admissions Secretariat with a request for a research entry licence, citing his knowledge of specific contents he wanted to review, about which he had been made aware 'through the kind cooperation of your senior staff member who sent me photos of the relevant index pages'. The letter had been Emil's professional death warrant. After a brief investigation, yielding the discovery that the culprit had been him, the ranking supervisors of the Archives had unceremoniously terminated Emil's employment and placed a black mark on his academic reputation – the status of 'a man of questionable professional ethics' – which had meant he couldn't get academic work anywhere once the Vatican's doors had been slammed closed behind him.

Bastards. It was the biggest overreaction Emil could have contemplated. *Asinine curates too concerned to preserve their secrets to know real talent when they had it in their employ.*

The irony was that they didn't even know what secrets they were really guarding.

Emil could feel his molars grating against each other, the muscles in his cheeks sore from the tension. The memories always did this to him. He scolded himself, forced his jaw apart, then took a series of long, calming breaths. Life had not been entirely intolerable since he'd been sacked from the Archives. He'd had to work blue-collar jobs for a time, which was grating, but an aunt back in Belgium had had the good courtesy to die only eighteen months later, leaving him the settlement of her small estate. It was enough to live off without needing extra income. And it gave him the means to plan for . . . greater things.

It was time to let go of all this. The past was done. It was unpleasant, but it was over. The time had come to cease being gripped by it.

The time had come, too, to acknowledge that he was far past 'contemplating' or 'entertaining' the course his life was going to take in the months ahead. He was certain of it. He had been, he knew, since the first day the idea had occurred to him.

At first it had felt too grandiose, too impossible; but as time had worn on and the burgeoning thought refused to flee his attention, its impressive dimensions and apparent impossibilities had come more carefully under his diligent scrutiny. They had started to become – lesser. Manageable. Not insignificant, but surmountable.

The goal was simply too great not to take the risks the operation would involve.

For an instant, the past again encroached on his present, but Emil allowed this particular intrusion.

The goal. *His goal*. The bastards he'd worked for had been so damned keen to guard their secrets and treasures, that they'd led him to something far greater.

Something he would rip away from them.

25

Emil's home office

The only way Emil's plan would succeed would be through intense preparation. Success or failure would reside entirely in the work done beforehand. The actual act – reaching out and taking what he wanted most of all – was the easy part. It was getting the whole world's attention, manipulating it, directing it, that required artistry.

Artistry, and assistance. Though the thought of the renegade masked man going it alone held a certain appeal to Emil Durré, he recognised from the outset it wasn't a realistic possibility. Men who tried those sorts of feats always ended up caught, and they were rarely after as big a prize as Emil intended to claim. No, for his plan to work, he would need a team, perhaps several. He would need men with skills he did not possess, ready to work for a fragmentary share in what they would claim together. For even the smallest portion of it was worth whatever risk they would be taking on.

So he had begun to formulate his designs, from their broad scope down to their most minute details. Four months had already been spent dedicated to the task, and with each passing day Emil was more convinced of his ultimate success. If he found the right people to help him make it a reality.

Last week, the interviews had begun.

That he would need technology specialists was a given from the outset. Emil knew little to nothing about computers and technology, though he wasn't inept with the basic devices of modern day life. He would need men who were far more capable – the kind of men who knew the ins and outs of online data, of telecommunications, of industrial grids. Things Emil understood only as concepts. So he had found a trio, a group that, he was assured, was able to do just about anything – certainly anything he would need.

The leader of the small group, Vico Esposito, had been discovered through a series of excursions into Net cafés known to be frequented by hackers, in whose community he was apparently regarded as something of a legend. It had taken some time for Emil to figure out how to approach the man, but when he'd finally arranged an interview, Vico had proven himself precisely the kind of talent Emil needed: stellar skills, coupled with a moral flexibility that led him to see criminal activity more as a decent challenge than an affront to right behaviour or order. But Vico had one non-negotiable condition to his coming on board the project: he was part of a trio, and the three men always worked together. Emil hadn't been sure whether such an expansive team was really necessary, but if it was what Vico wanted, Lord knew paying them wouldn't be a problem.

Beyond the technological, the project would require substantial interaction with civic enterprises – industrial teams, survey units, power systems, sewer infrastructures. It was another realm about which Emil knew nothing and had no personal ins, but it had been Vico himself who had recommended Bartolomeo Scarsi, 'Someone we worked with on another project a few months back. A good sort. Got things done.'

Bartolomeo's interview with Emil a few days later had gone just as well. The man was gruff, impolite, but exactly the right sort for the work Emil had in mind for him. He had a powerful build that could easily pass for that of a construction worker or dig crew member, and he knew his way around the civic circuit, having been gainfully employed as a roads engineer before a night of far too much booze and blow had ended his life of legitimate employment. He'd been scouring out a living in the greyer edges of the black market ever since.

'You'll find yourself a partner, someone you can work with,' Emil had instructed him. 'And someone you can trust. Take two weeks, find the right man, then bring him to meet me.' He'd come through on the responsibility, as Emil had expected he would.

The most troubling need was the requirement for a wet team. It was difficult for Emil even to imagine using that phrase. 'Wet team.' It felt like jargon out of a CIA action movie, utterly foreign to his former life in academia and scholarship. But there was the very real risk that, once his plan was set into action, problems could arise that required . . . adequate response. He couldn't permit his goal to slip away from him just because one or another obstacle got in his way.

So a wet team it would have to be. For this he would want the people closest to him – those he trusted most completely, and over whom he could exert the most absolute authority. Emil already had an idea who would constitute this team, though it was going to take some time to convince himself that his son was really up to the task. André had followed his father to Italy a few years ago, though he could hardly be said to have made his mark here in any significant sense. But if he could be paired with Ridolfo, one of the few close friends with whom André had ever managed to form a real bond, then the strategy could work.

But today Emil needed to keep his focus on what his calendar held for the present. The interview he'd arranged for this afternoon was, he knew, one of the most critical of them all.

The success of the entire plan resided in its religious element. It was, after all, the power of God that he aspired to call to his advantage, and while Emil felt himself perfectly capable of dealing with the historical dimensions of the religious aspect – its calling upon the past, its comparability to ancient examples – he himself wasn't a believer and understood little of what motivated the actual emotions of faithful devotees in the world around him.

Which meant he needed someone who did.

The thought was still circulating in his mind as a soft knocking sounded from his office door.

'Come in,' he announced, voice strong and firm. Slowly the door swept open. The man behind it had a wrinkled face and stood slightly hunched, bending with a surfeit of years. It was the first time Emil had ever laid eyes on him, and the man's flannel shirt and wrinkled jeans came as a surprise. He'd expected robes, or a black shirt with the traditional dog collar.

'Please,' he said, concealing his thoughts, 'take a seat.' He motioned towards one of the chairs opposite him and the man entered, closed the door behind him and sat.

'I'm Emil,' he said plainly. It was enough of a greeting for the circumstances.

'I am pleased to meet you,' the man answered. 'My name is Laurence de Luca.'

26

Emil's home office

The old man sat quietly, motionless, as Emil looked him over intently from the opposite side of the desk. This was, potentially, the individual in whom he was going to place an immense amount of trust. On whom much would rely, including Emil's own future and freedom.

And he wore such tattered clothes.

'You don't look like I expected,' Emil finally announced.

The man gazed back through expressionless eyes. 'I suppose I could say I am sorry,' he said, 'though I have no idea what you were expecting, so I'm not sure whether I in fact am.'

Emil felt the urge to smile, and did. The shrewd remark from the older man pleased him. Laurence de Luca was at least twenty years Emil's senior, if not thirty, with weathered skin that was kept close shaved, though today there was an emerging white stubble across his chin. His eyes were blue, sunk into sockets that seemed a size too large for them. His nose was hawk-like, a claw arcing down towards thin lips. But the man spoke articulately. Short breaths and raspy tones couldn't mask either his erudition or his wit.

'I take it I don't address you as Father?' Emil continued.

'Not any more.' The man answered without emotion.

'You left the priesthood, what, a couple of years ago?'

'A year and a half, if you're looking for precision.'

Emil nodded. That timeline would work well for his purposes.

'I'm interested in your reasons,' he said, shifting slightly in his seat, 'for that departure. You were a priest a long time.'

'Almost thirty-five years.'

'Though, I've been told, during that time, you weren't exactly a seminary instructor's vision of an ideal cleric.'

Finally, a change came over the hardened face of the old man now called simply Laurence. A grey eyebrow slowly rose. 'What is that supposed to mean?'

'I'm told,' Emil continued, 'that you were that unique blend of a devoutly religious man who was wholly committed to the religious life, without being burdened by . . . what shall we call it . . . the shackles of actual belief.'

The man merely blinked, but Emil could see thoughts moving across his eyes. Laurence's elevated eyebrow slowly descended.

'I'd hardly call that a rarity in the clergy,' he finally said. 'The lack of belief?'

'The ability to fulfil a calling without being overly concerned about that particular dimension of it,' Laurence countered. 'If the only priests out there were those that had unyielding faith in everything they taught, well, let's just say the current clerical shortage wouldn't seem so dire by comparison.'

'Ah, I see,' Emil replied, leaning fully back in his chair, permitting another smile to wend its way on to his lips. He folded his hands across his lap. The older man appeared unsure how to interpret Emil's change in demeanour.

'This is something laughable to you?' he asked, a hint of defensiveness charring his words. 'Is this why you've called me in here, to mock me about a lack of faith? I'm sorry if I'm not impressed. I've had plenty of time to grow accustomed to the scorn of others.'

Emil forced the smile from his face and sat forward.

'You misunderstand,' he said with genuine warmth. 'I am not in the slightest bit perturbed by your lack of faith. You can be a rock-solid atheist or a devotee of the Faery Queen for all I care.'

Laurence's expression slid towards real confusion.

'Besides,' Emil added before he could interject, 'I'm hardly in a position to judge you on these matters. Personally, I find your position . . .' He struggled for the right word. 'Enlightened.'

The other man stared at him a few moments. It was clear this meeting was not what he had expected. Emil appreciated that.

'In fact,' he continued, 'it's what interests me in you the most. The fact that you didn't believe, perhaps never really believed, yet worked for years among people who did.'

Laurence nodded, a simple affirmation.

'Even helping them build up their belief,' Emil continued, 'fostering it. Speaking to it.'

'I don't see what this could possibly have to do with anything,' Laurence finally answered. 'I coped, did what I had to do to get by. And I left the priesthood when I couldn't get by any more. I could make people believe I was pious. I could say the words they wanted to hear, go through the motions they expected. But at some point, a man has to ask himself how long he wants his life to be nothing more than an elaborate charade. I'd become a good actor, that was all.'

'You were far more than that. I'm told you were extremely popular before you walked away from it all. Beloved in your parishes.'

The man sat silently. The comment made him uncomfortable, but he was still waiting to see where all this was going.

'My question for you,' Emil said, sensing his opportunity, 'is whether you would be able to do it again.'

From that moment, the conversation between Emil and Laurence took on an entirely different tone. The older man's stoic quietude gave way to a curiosity that grew by the minute as Emil spoke. The blue eyes buried in his face seemed to catch light, glowing ever brighter as the details of Emil's plan were drawn out of secrecy and shared.

'It would be hard to pull off convincingly,' Laurence said, as Emil talked through the specific role he wanted the older ex-priest to play. 'Groups like the one you're considering are close-knit and generally suspicious of outsiders. They're used to being looked down on and have grown protective and defensive to compensate.'

'That's precisely why you'd be a perfect fit,' Emil countered. He leaned forward on his desk, resting on the fronts of his arms. 'An outcast, joining the outcasts.'

Laurence pondered the idea, shaking his head mildly. 'The analogy doesn't fit. I wasn't cast out, I left.'

'But they weren't either,' Emil answered. 'They've set up their own community on the periphery of the church. They're outcasts by choice, just like you.'

This time Laurence didn't answer, but simply soaked in the words.

'You could easily mould your story to fit their ideology,' Emil continued. 'Say, I don't know, that you left the clergy because you'd grown disillusioned with the institutionalised hierarchy of the church. The dead and soulless structuralism. You wanted something more . . . alive.'

A nod of acknowledgement from the older man. 'They're

nothing if not committed to that narrative. Faith versus the church. Spirituality versus religion.'

'Of course, it would mean concealing your own lack of interior conviction.' Emil gazed closely at Laurence as he spoke. 'Charismatics are a group ruled by the idea that faith has to be a living, breathing thing inside you. "In your heart." It's been like that in every charismatic group in Christian history, from the Montanists in the second century up to the Pentecostals in ours. The Catholic Charismatic Movement is no different.' History had taught Emil so many lessons.

Laurence's old head bobbed in affirmation, and he peered back at Emil with what looked like admiration.

'Now I see why you focused on my past as we began,' he said. 'As you rightly noted, I've had a bit of experience in feigning faith to believers.'

Emil smiled wryly back at him, the sense of conspiratorial understanding binding them together.

Suddenly, the older man's features darkened.

'What is it?' Emil asked, sensing the change of mood.

'They won't accept an outside priest, even a former one. Their leadership here in Rome is centred entirely around the spiritual leader of their congregation, a Father Aliegro, I think he's called.'

'Alberto,' Emil corrected. 'Father Alberto Alvarez.'

'Yes, him. They're totally devoted. They won't welcome any new voice of leadership.'

'Then don't try to be a leader,' Emil answered, his smile returning. He had anticipated this, already thought it through.

'I hear they're advertising for a more suitable job opening at the moment. Tell me, Laurence,' he said, now grinning broadly, 'have you ever contemplated life as a janitor?'

27

Emil's home office

A week later Emil called Ridolfo Passerini into his office, alone. In the partnership of this man and his son, it was definitely Ridolfo who was the thinker, and Emil wanted the opportunity to run his plans past him alone, to make sure the full scope of what was being asked – and expected – was fully understood.

'I get it, you want me for my brawn,' Ridolfo said after Emil had gone through as much of the plan as he felt it necessary to share with the younger man. He paused a moment, then looked into Emil's eyes. 'I guess I shouldn't have expected you'd be after me for my looks.'

Emil met his emerging grin with a smile of his own. This was the Ridolfo he knew.

'It's going to involve hard work,' he said, bringing the tone back to reality. 'And it may get messy. You'll work for me, directly and exclusively, and I'll have to be able to expect absolute loyalty. You'll be well rewarded, of course, when we're done.'

'Are there others?' Ridolfo asked. 'Other people, also working on this? I can't imagine it's just you, me and André.'

Emil nodded in the affirmative. 'There are others, but you'll only be made aware of them if needed. The less you know, the better.'

Ridolfo rubbed a hand along the deformed skin that covered his cheek, brooding.

'So, this is some sort of . . . what, a secret society? Which one am I being courted to join? Opus Dei? The Illuminati? I've read the books.'

A disgusted sigh barrelled out of Emil's chest.

'Why does everything that happens in this city automatically get assigned to the work of secret societies? For God's sake, you'd think every bloody man, woman and child in Italy belonged to P2, or the Masons, or some underground collective keen on taking down the Church.' Annoyance bled from his vowels.

'To be fair,' Ridolfo countered, 'you are talking about working in pretty deep fucking secrecy. And the Church is a target.'

'Taking down the Church is of absolutely no concern to me. The institution is irrelevant. Let it thrive or let it die, I simply don't care.' Emil pressed forward towards Ridolfo. 'Must *everything* in Rome be a religious vendetta? Can't it be enough just to be human, and to crave what every human craves, without religion entering into the discussion at all?'

Ridolfo eyed him. 'If not a move against the Church, then what? What, precisely, are you after here?'

Emil sank back into the welcoming leather behind him. Silence preceded his answer, his fingers tapping over firm armrests.

'Perhaps I spoke incorrectly,' he finally said. 'Religion isn't wholly outside my interests, I'm simply not motivated by religious ideals. I'm far more interested in claiming what I want, out from under the grip of religious ideologies.'

If Ridolfo understood Emil's words, his face didn't show it.

'Christianity has so many rules,' Emil continued. 'Do this,

don't do that. And it's not enough just to call them rules – they become commands, *commandments*, uttered from a mountaintop to tell us, you and me, what we can and cannot do.' Redness flushed his cheeks, but a series of slow, deep breaths allowed him to regain composure.

'I've never been a fan of the ten commandments, Ridolfo. The first has always seemed implausible, and the rest are just too . . . binding.'

'Mr Durré,' Ridolfo interrupted, 'I don't see where this is leading—'

'I wouldn't say I've ever felt myself on a mission to *break* the commandments,' Emil continued undeterred, 'though there's one in particular that really pisses me off.'

Ridolfo halted. 'Which?'

'The seventh,' Emil answered. He let his hands fall into his lap.

'The seventh?' Ridolfo's features scrunched in confusion. 'Can't say as I know them by number.'

Suddenly Emil rose. With fierce intention he walked over to a small bookshelf and pulled a bible out from amidst a stack of other volumes. He considered the shelf 'research materials' and gave the bible a similar significance to a dictionary or an atlas – and he knew how to use it, just as he knew how to use those.

A few seconds later he'd thumbed his way through to the page he wanted, and he set the open volume down in front of Ridolfo.

'Right there,' he said, pointing to a verse, 'that's command-ment number seven.'

Ridolfo leaned down to the page, focused on the words, and read aloud.

'Thou shalt not steal.'

When he looked up, Emil was smiling down on him.

'Care to break the law of God, my son?'

PART FOUR

Distraction

28

The present day – evening
A hilltop in Rome

The sunset over the hills of Rome had been beautiful. As the bright rays of daytime had gradually transformed into brilliant oranges and reds, then faded with their customary swiftness into blues and eventual night-time blackness, the lights of lampposts and storefront windows had gone through their traditional dance and blinked into life. Rome's daytime display of sandstone and domes had changed into the electric glow of modern Rome at night – cobblestone streets glimmering under street lamps, fluorescent blues shimmering out of glass skyscrapers, creating the supernatural and strangely beautiful brilliance of a night-time skyline only modern man could imagine.

What made it more majestic tonight than most nights, Bartolomeo reflected, was that in the flickering of an eye, in the glimmer of a single instant, it would all disappear. The brightness of man's creation would fall away, and the Eternal City would stop her shining.

Unlike the river, this plague would not arise unobserved,

flowing gently into the public consciousness. They would mark the moment the darkness came. The minute, the second. It would be beheld by young and by old, by those who knew the prophecy and by those that did not.

It would come upon them all and, God willing, it would overcome every one of them.

Bartolomeo shivered in his place. The thought, this impossible, wonderful, marvellous thought, was almost orgasmic.

Belvedere Courtyard
Vatican Palace

Angelina and Ben approached the heavy wooden door, wrapped in brick, that marked the entry into what were technically known as the Vatican Secret Archives. Their full name, the *Archivum Secretum Apostolicum Vaticanum*, was emblazoned on a brass plaque to the side of the door, a small rendition of the apostolic seal positioned immediately above it in a tarnished and blackened rotunda of unassuming metal. There was a black buzzer beneath the plaque, and nothing else – nothing to mark the grandeur and singularity of what was contained within.

As they crossed the tarmacked Belvedere Courtyard on the interior of the Vatican Palace, Angelina's mind involuntarily flashed back to the last time she'd been in this impressive, daunting space. She'd pressed the small bell, wearing a navy blue trouser suit she'd ironed into nearly regimental stiffness. Her hair had taken almost a full can of spray before finally yielding to the uber-tidy look she'd been going for the morning of her interview. She'd left her favourite white Versace handbag at home in favour of a leatherette holdall binder, which added just that extra touch of formality and professionalism.

None of it had worked.

The circumstances of her arrival today were as different as she could possibly imagine. It was nightfall, first of all, which lent the lamplit courtyard a rather different feel from the bright daylight she'd experienced there before, and she suddenly realised that she was as dishevelled as she'd ever been in public. The chase of the afternoon had left her hair in a wispy mess, and though the sweat of the run had dried over the hours since, it had left her clothes splotched and stiff. She felt like a vagabond, treading into one of the most vagabond-free locales on the planet.

Ben marched ahead of her with purpose, oblivious to surroundings that were far more familiar to him. The door was locked when at last they reached it, the opening hours of the Archives well surpassed, but Ben withdrew a security card from his wallet and slid it through a reader so slender and well concealed that Angelina hadn't even noticed it was there. A millisecond later a faint buzzing indicated it had been read successfully and Ben pulled the door towards him.

'After you,' he said politely to Angelina, motioning her towards the dimly lit interior, and with a few steps she was inside a palace of secrets she'd never thought she'd see again.

Ben watched Angelina enter the small foyer, pulling the door closed as he entered behind her. For the first time since they had been 're-acquainted' with each other through their abduction by the Swiss Guard, the memories flooded back of their earlier encounter. He'd met Angelina Calla here, in this diminutive vestibule, the day she'd arrived for her interview.

'Welcome to the Secret Archives.' He'd greeted her with a handshake. He hated being assigned the role of interviewee liaison: it was far too social a task for his liking. But the staff rotated through the responsibility when it arose, and it had been his turn.

'*Though that title is something of a mistranslation,*' he'd added, falling into the well-rehearsed speech that was always used for these first introductions. '*The Latin* secretum *doesn't really mean "secret" the way it's used today, as if it implied something hidden, or kept from public knowledge. A better translation might be "personal". The Archives began their lives as the collection of the pope's personal materials: correspondence, records, that sort of thing. Though it's expanded over the years.*'

Ben remembered that Angelina had tried hard not to look like the words were something of an insult to a woman who, though she was applying for an assistant-level post with a background in his own linguistic speciality, Akkadian, never-theless would obviously be proficient enough in Latin to know this for herself.

She'd straightened herself, returned a polite smile, and allowed him to lead on with the brief tour. There was a strength about her that he remembered well. There had been little chance she would ever be hired to the post for which she was applying, of course. He remembered that, too. It was the way the world worked. Unfair, but understood by all parties – including, he had swiftly realised, Dr Calla. He'd seen it in her eyes as he'd shown her around the corridors and reading rooms: the look of anticipated defeat and the harsh sorrow of recognising that what was being beheld would never be possessed. Yet it was coupled with a deter-mination to, if not today then someday, break through the barriers society was imposing around her.

Nothing had been able to mask her obvious love for the world that was being perpetually dangled before her like a carrot on the end of a string. Angelina positively lit up at the first signs of a genuine discussion on antiquity, and she had seemed truly rapt at the sight of the few sections of the Archives into which Ben had led her on her tour.

Ben knew that rapture well. He'd been working here

almost five years, and he still felt it every day. For some people history was dust and outdated stories, unpronounceable names and the irrelevancies of bygone eras. For others, it was the human story in all its vibrancy and life: every artefact was a point of contact between the hands that held it today – which also held smartphones and laser scanners – and the hands that had crafted it, which might have milled flour from a pestle and mended wheels on chariots. Every ancient document was the voice of someone the world had long considered dead, but who was now, in the hands of those who could read it, brought back to life and given the chance to speak again. To teach again. To be heard again.

He knew Angelina Calla felt the same way as he. He could see it now in her face as he stepped across her path and moved in front of her, guiding her through the foyer a second time.

'This way.' He motioned to a door at the back. She said nothing, but followed as Ben drew her into a small corridor that led to the staircase that pointed down into the trove of the Archive's treasures.

Angelina followed Ben down stairs that were surprisingly steep and narrow, the sound of her footsteps mixing with his and echoing off the metal-grate construction that was obviously a modern insertion into a space well over five hundred years old. *Probably to conserve space, to redesign the interior shape*, she mused as they walked, incapable of not analysing what she saw. Whatever the architect's initial thoughts might have been when he'd designed this wing of the palace so many centuries before, he couldn't possibly have considered that it would one day be used to house such an enormous collection as the Archives and Library had become – and so Angelina imagined that here, like just about everywhere else in Rome, interior 'reconfiguration' was a necessary response to space being at a premium.

Within a few steps they were on the first sub-level landing, where Angelina remembered Ben had led her on her tour. A metal door led off to the left, which in turn provided access to the Pio XI Reading Room, where scholars were allowed to read through documents called up from the stacks, which Angelina remembered were accessed through a small door yet further back.

But Ben didn't stop. He carried on past the door, turning and continuing his descent down another flight.

That room, those contents – always just out of my grasp.

'Won't the tablet be in the stacks?' Angelina asked. She watched her feet, the light dim in the staircase, trying to keep up with his pace as she grudgingly assented to follow him away from the reading room.

'It's too new,' Ben answered without stopping. 'Requisitions have to go through cataloguing and indexing, as well as digital records and conservation, before they're assigned a place in the stacks and made accessible for general research.'

They rounded another corner and headed down to a third level beneath ground.

'But even after that's done, it's unlikely something like this tablet would go into the stacks. They're mostly reserved for documents and printed volumes. Something more fragile, and less likely to be accessed regularly, will be kept in the bunker.'

Despite herself, Angelina's step halted. 'The bunker?' She'd heard of the multiple storerooms that housed some of the Archives' most significant treasures – such as the quill-penned records of the trial of Galileo Galilei and the eighth-century documents establishing the functional nature of the Roman Catholic Curia – but she'd never heard of one of them being referred to as a 'bunker'.

'It was added in the 1970s,' Ben explained, continuing their descent, 'and officially opened by Pope John Paul II in 1980. Just through here.'

They had reached another landing, which housed a metal door identical to those on the other floors they'd passed. As Ben opened it, Angelina could see it fed into a narrow corridor running in a straight line for at least twenty metres.

'The bunker is actually located under the Cortile della Pigna, part of the Vatican Museums which run through various lengths of the Palace, but it's reserved solely as a storage vault for the Archives. We call it the bunker because, well, it basically is one.'

Angelina couldn't see his face. She didn't know whether the remark came with a smile, but noticed that the pace of his step increased as they moved through the narrow space.

At the far end of the corridor, as Ben swiped his access card through a digital reader far less subtle than the one outside, Angelina saw why.

29

Twenty minutes earlier
Via Tina di Lorenzo
Residential neighbourhood, north-eastern Rome

The three-man team Emil had assembled as his technical crew sat before their computer terminals, surrounded by greasy snacks and a flow of coffee that had been constant for nearly the whole of the day. It was a day that, in their dark seclusion from the outside world, had begun dully, but which since had escalated into something entirely different.

The man called Vico, who had been the dominant personality of their trio ever since they'd met at the TechCafé coffee house in their early days of graduate school and become as inseparable as brothers, stood watching the other two tap away at their keyboards. The basement room was a jumbled collection of cheap Ikea tables and masses of wires that linked up their three computers, the enormous monitors stationed at each of their positions casting the whole room into shades of electronic greens and blues.

'You've got her?' Vico asked impatiently. The man immediately in front of him, whose name was Pietro and who was slightly pudgier around the middle than any of his imaginary girlfriends would approve of, simply nodded. He shoved a collection of empty Pepsi tins aside to make more room for his mouse, his left hand tapping his keyboard as the glow of his monitor reflected on to his face.

'Yeah, we got her,' he finally said. A hand went up, pointing to a window on the monitor. Not a map with a blinking red cross hair as was always the case in movies – it was a black window with white plain text scrolled across it. Amongst the numbers, a series of digits marking out coordinates offered a far more precise location.

Their third member, Corso, sat at the other side of the small room, his blond hair hanging down in an overgrown fringe that covered far too much of his face. But he typed with a ferocity that Vico knew meant he was at work on the same feed.

IP geolocation was no longer a difficult chore. At one point in the not-too-distant hacking past it had been an arena of speciality, something to be proud of. Nowadays geolocation was so straightforward as to be essentially automatic, and the real skill of the twenty-first century was learning how *not* to be spotted by those who wanted to know far more about you than just your physical location. Of course, there were still certain hurdles that threw themselves up in the course of the task from time to time, but most people who used the Internet were so unaware of the trail of digital breadcrumbs left behind their every keystroke that they all but invited invasive tracking.

The woman that Emil had them following was a perfect case in point.

Once he'd instructed them to seek out anyone in the region who had an expertise in whatever the hell the ancient language Emil cared about was called, things had been more or less automatic. Apart from the man in the Vatican, about whom they already knew, searches revealed only one other: this woman. It had taken a matter of minutes to link her name from social media entries to the principal IP address attached to her online activity, and then a matter of keystrokes to connect the IP to a server company. From there a few rudimentary firewalls had been easily hacked through to reveal a username and account, which in turn provided full personal details stored on an equally vulnerable customer database.

IP address 0:0:0:0:0:ffff:d191:66c, the long IPv6 form tied to the old-fashioned 209.145.6.108, belonged to an Angelina Eloisa Calla. Vico had never heard the name before this project, but then he'd hardly suspected he would have. There were over 2.5 million Internet users in central Rome, and he didn't particularly care to know any of them. Not until there was a need to do so.

When it was necessary, though, it was a matter of professional satisfaction to Vico that, through less than an hour's worth of work by their little trio, he'd been able to learn a terrific amount about the woman who had been a non-existent entity to him before that hour had begun.

Calla's Internet hosting company had her registered address as Via Antonio Cerasi 18a, which Pietro had verified by cross-referencing data from both the power and telephone companies. From those combined details he'd determined that the woman had a single computer – an abysmally out-of-date MacBook that Vico could only assume was powered chiefly by steam and memories, and which included a virus scanner as obsolete as the hardware – as well as a Samsung Galaxy smartphone operating the previous generation of Android. By the cellular and WiFi tracking logs, the phone appeared to be the woman's primary access point to the online world.

But these things were rudimentary. Any two-bit hacker

could know as much about a target in just as little time, and Vico had needed more.

From the *Agenzia delle Entrate*, the Italian Revenue Agency, he knew that Angelina Calla was unmarried and filed her taxes each year without spouse or domestic partner. A woman who lived alone. From those records he identified her bank, which he passed on to Corso, who had in turn learned that Calla's income of roughly €1,200 per month was paid out chiefly on the rent of her flat in the neighbourhood of Monteverde, utilities and surprisingly pricey subscriptions to a number of online journals normally bought into only by university and college libraries. There were no car payments, which suggested that she either owned something outright – which seemed unlikely given her overall financial portrait – or that she was one of the tens of thousands of Romans who commuted from A to B to C on their normal daily routine.

The journal subscriptions were a unique thread of character, and Vico had followed them thoroughly. Angelina Calla was apparently a woman of strong academic mind. She'd finished a BA in Classics at the University of Bologna, then moved to the capital to do both a masters degree and PhD at the Sapienza University of Rome. Apart from the keyword 'Akkadian' in her published doctoral thesis, 'Elements of Pseudepigraphic Revisionism in Middle Akkadian Cultural Mythology', he understood nothing of her subject, but it was clear that Calla was an adept in her field. And it was that field that meant she had to be found. It was the reason they had located her in the first place. They'd been commissioned to search out anyone who might know the territory of the ancient language, and the digital net that Vico and his team had laid across Italy had quickly focused in on her and the man. They knew the territory, so they became targets.

Vico had consolidated the whole of his research into a

small digital dossier and forwarded it to the boss. Most of it, he imagined, was overkill – but he prided himself on his work, and a bit of ingratiating oneself to others was never wholly off base.

All that was really needed now was the fact that the MAC address of Angelina Calla's smartphone pinged to cellular towers and open WiFi ports automatically. She had all the 'convenience features' of modern portable computing switched on, which meant she was live everywhere.

Which meant she was trackable. Everywhere.

'Where is she at, right now?' Vico asked.

'She's inside Vatican City,' Corso answered.

'Damn it, be more precise than that!' Vico wasn't as impatient as his voice suggested, but after the wet teams had lost both the woman and the male target earlier in the day, Emil's charge to find them again had come with a sufficiently threatening tone to inspire Vico to get back to him with nothing other than a pinpoint location.

'Belvedere Courtyard inside the Palace,' Corso continued, squinting through thick spectacles, 'just a second.' His fingers danced over his keyboard. 'North-western quadrant, ten metres to the right of the corner. Let me look that up.'

He began to type again, but Pietro had already cross-referenced the location.

'That's the entrance to the Secret Archives.'

Vico stared at the screen, nodding over the other two men's heads.

'That'll do.'

His phone was already open, Emil's number on the speed dial digit beneath his thumb.

30

The buzzer on the electronic security door was still going as Angelina followed Ben out of the corridor and then froze in place as she set her eyes on the 'bunker' buried beneath the Vatican Palace.

The underground vault was vast. The door at the end of the access corridor permitted entry through the solid metre of metal-reinforced concrete that constituted its walls, opening into a two-storey space that looked like a cross between an industrial warehouse and an overpacked museum. Giant vents circulated air that Angelina presumed was precisely climate controlled; security cameras pointed at almost every square metre of space; and the dual-level expanse was divided by metal-grate flooring built around a series of storage shelving on the top level and rotating stacks on the bottom. It was a vault designed to house as much as possible – and it appeared to be almost entirely full.

'Welcome to the belly of the beast,' Ben said, and Angelina could see the pleased smile on his face. Ben was obviously at home. For the moment, it felt like a sentiment she could share.

'And now,' he added, 'let's find our tablet.'

It took a matter of seconds, not minutes, for Angelina to realise that the majesty of the innermost chamber of the Secret Archives was of an entirely different sort than that she'd glimpsed in the reading rooms above.

She, like most people, had once made her presumptions based more on legend and speculation than any actual knowledge. The very name of the Archives sounded as if the whole establishment was a cloak-and-dagger institution of closely guarded secrets cut off from public access – but on Angelina's previous visit she'd been divested of some of those delusions. The Secret Archives were open for public research to anyone with suitable academic qualifications and references, and several thousand passed through it each year on various research projects, having gone through a detailed but hardly exotic procedure to secure a readership ticket.

Once inside, the Archives were hardly as cloak-and-dagger as was guessed. It wasn't filled with gaslit expanses of stone caves piled with dust-covered manuscripts, nor was it home to barometric Plexiglas chambers sealing out oxygen and light. It was, to any scholar who had spent time in some of the more famous manuscript libraries of the world – the Bodleian's Duke Humfrey's Reading Room in Oxford, or the Laurentian Medici Library in Florence – an expected space. Rows of wooden shelves housed leather-bound volumes of post-sixteenth century manuscripts in hand-labelled codices, while older parchments were kept in flat-access drawers. It was beautiful, and genuinely awe-inspiring – but hardly unusual. Angelina's own alma mater had a manuscript wing in its library that, while significantly smaller, looked and felt much the same on the inside.

But the 'bunker' was something altogether different.

'What the hell is this?'

The words, as they erupted from her mouth, surprised Angelina as much as they did Ben. He turned to face her, his features a puzzle.

'Excuse me?'

'This,' Angelina waved both arms at their white-lit surroundings. 'This is . . . not what I'd envisaged.'

Hardly a vision of splendour.

'It's a bit different from the rooms upstairs,' Ben answered, 'I'll give you that. But it's here that some of our most remarkable treasures are kept.'

Beyond them, rows of metal shelving were filled, from one end to the other and in all their height, with muted grey storage boxes, each of which was fronted by a white label of a few centimetres squared, containing nothing but a printed set of filing numbers and a bar code. The overall effect was bland, repetitious, monotonous. Beneath them was more of the same, though the shelving units were on stacked rollers that allowed them to be positioned flush against each other on tracks, cramming nearly a third more storage space into the same footprint, facing shelves only sliding apart when necessary for access.

The magnitude of the collection gradually sank in. Angelina was no expert at maths, but even basic computations of the number of filing boxes to shelves, to rows, to aisles, meant that the bunker contained tens upon tens of thousands of individual grey containers.

'Do you have any way of knowing which one of these contains the tablet?'

Ben reached confidently into his back pocket and extracted a mobile phone that looked more or less identical to Angelina's.

'I thought you didn't do technology,' she said, brows raised pointedly, remembering a detail about Ben's personality. She recalled him describing himself as something of a self-determined luddite.

'I may not enjoy it intruding its way into my life outside of work,' Ben answered, 'but it has its uses when required.' He swiped his finger across the phone's display, entering a passcode that looked far longer than the four-digit pin on Angelina's own, then spent a few seconds navigating through its contents. Finally, he held the screen back up towards her.

His finger pointed at a small icon beneath which were printed two Italian words.

ARCHIVIO SEGRETO

'You have an app . . . for the Vatican Secret Archives?' Angelina asked.

Ben's smile returned. 'Only for parts of it, and it only works within the building.'

'Okay, I'm impressed,' she conceded. 'But I'll be more so once I see it work.'

Their mutual smiles lingered a moment longer, then Ben's face became serious. He stepped across Angelina and held out his hand towards one of the boxes on a shelf at chest level. With a thumb press on his screen, the app switched into camera mode and a small set of red cross hairs positioned itself in the centre of the screen. He focused them on the bar code on the box's label, steadied his grip, then clicked the shutter button. A moment later, the camera display disappeared and the app displayed a blank screen with a pinwheel rotating at its centre.

Seconds later the pinwheel vanished and the white screen was replaced by a colour photo surmounted with descriptive text.

'MACHIAVELLI, *THE PRINCE*, PRE-PUBLICATION EDN, HANDWRITTEN CORRECTIONS BY AUTHOR IN MARGINS, 1519.'

Angelina's breath stuck in her throat.

'That's, in . . . this box?'

Ben's smile exposed all his teeth, his eyes feathering out with wrinkles that crawled towards his temples.

'Can I see that?' she asked, pointing towards Ben's phone. He nodded and passed her the device.

'Pick a box, any box.'

She freely obeyed, taking a few steps down the nearest aisle and aiming the scanner at a random bar code on another in a line of indistinguishable storage containers.

'GALILEO GALILEI, *SIDEREUS NUNCIUS*, 1ST EDN, 1610.'

Suddenly, the smile on Angelina's face was gone.

'Holy shit.'

'Excuse me?'

'I'm, sorry, I'm . . .'

Angelina had been overcome already, but in this instant she wanted to weep. *There, just there, on the other side of a piece of acid-free cardboard*, her thoughts called out to her. Galileo's 'Starry Messenger'. *A document that, in the most real way imaginable, changed the way the whole of humanity sees the universe.* A book through which the earth became a traveller, soaring through the heavens in its course around the sun, flying in symphony with sister planets and moons and stars in a concert that portended so many of the scientific advances that had come over the centuries since.

She could almost touch it.

Everything within her pulled, churned, compelled her to petition, *Please, can I see it?* Could she possibly stand so close to such a monument of history and not set her eyes upon it?

But then, in the strange light of the LED bulbs high above them, the tightening in Angelina's chest changed. It had started as awe, but as it increased it gripped differently at her heart – more ferociously, more painfully. Her breathing shortened, and in her ears her pulse became audible as anxiety turned the beats into memories of gunshots.

Panic came suddenly, without warning, and it took every ounce of Angelina's already waning strength to shove it down, somewhere deep inside her, and keep control over the moment.

She turned to face Ben directly.

'So, this app can search contents as well as reveal them, right?'

The question, with its obvious answer – the whole reason Ben had shown her the app in the first place – thrust him swiftly back into complete seriousness.

'Of course.'

'Then let's find what we came here for.'

31

'She's in there?' André turned his face to Ridolfo as his nod signalled the wooden door of the Vatican Secret Archives, next to one of the maintenance entrances to the main Vatican Library. They'd entered Vatican City as tourists, just like floods of others, though Ridolfo had realised that with the descending darkness of evening their motion towards, rather than away from, the monuments of the religious capital was beginning to make them look out of place. He'd opted for them to find their way to a discreet corner of the courtyard, and then position themselves behind a low stone wall built to conceal a collection of coloured rubbish bins.

'That's what the tech team's told us,' he answered, not taking his eyes off the entrance. He knew they couldn't get in, not at this time of day. By now its office was shut and any staff who might open the door to an enquirer had long since gone home.

'What the fuck are we supposed to do, then?' André asked. The man was still pissed off he'd let Angelina Calla slip away from them earlier in the day. He had a bloodlust on his face that Ridolfo could see through the darkness, outlined as clearly as the opulent architecture of their surroundings.

He glanced at his watch. Fake gold, but still a pleasant make. 'We wait.'

André spun at him. 'I'm not just going to stand here, twiddling my goddamned thumbs!'

God, Ridolfo wanted to smack him. André and he had become close friends over the years, but that had never hindered their ability to get on each other's nerves.

'You won't be standing for long.' He looked at his watch again then let his hand fall to his side. 'Don't you remember the second prophecy?'

André halted. A rant was on the tip of his frustrated tongue, but his friend's words silenced it. *The second prophecy.*

His tension lessened as the thought overtook him, and Ridolfo nodded at the sight of André's sudden calm.

'It will push them out,' he said, turning his attention back to the door. 'And it's only a few minutes away.'

32

The bunker

It didn't take long for Ben to locate the tablet. With a little collaborative brainstorming with Angelina over which search terms to use, the app on his phone had given up its shelving details and new location in the belly of the Archives.

'NEW ACQUISITIONS: AKKADIAN – ROME/CLEMENTE STELE 1435.2002AF.'

The results glowed on the tiny screen of Ben's phone. A moment later, they were both moving.

The location code led Ben towards a staircase nearly steep enough to be called a ladder, which led down to the bottom floor of the vault. Angelina followed him as he made his way carefully down, and then over to the control panel for one of the banks of rolling stacks. Ben entered the call number on to a digital keypad, and the whirring of an electric motor sounded the instant 'ROW 27' began to flash in response. A second later, the enormous shelving rows began to move along rails laid into the concrete floor, vast banks of them sliding to the left while a few moved to the right. When they were done and a small chime sounded, row twenty-seven was open and accessible, all the other rows compressed to a width of no more than six centimetres each.

'This way,' Ben said and started down the aisle. Angelina noticed that his words were barely more than a whisper, and the thought occurred to her that the deeper they got into the bunker, the closer they drew to the tablet, the quieter Ben became. She'd initially assumed it was merely focus, but the timidity of his words hinted at something more.

Ben walked them down the length of row twenty-seven, glancing at section markers on engraved plaques on the shelving, until they came to a section about three quarters of the way towards the aisle's end. Turning to face left, he counted up shelves from the bottom until he reached the fourth, which ran at just about his shoulder level.

'This should be the spot.' He scrutinised the call number on his phone again, then looked back at the row of indistinguishable grey storage boxes. 'And that should be the one.'

The box he indicated sat at the level of Angelina's eyes, and she silently observed as he held up his phone and scanned the bar code on its white label.

'It matches,' Ben announced, matter-of-factly. 'We've got our tablet.'

A question had been percolating in Angelina's mind since they'd started their descent from the upper floor to here. Now, with the box containing the tablet right in front of them, she could no longer keep it to herself. The design of the shelving system made it imperative.

'Ben, are we going to be able to open it?'

Ben's face registered immediate comprehension.

'All the shelves are access controlled,' he answered, motioning towards two steel bars that ran across the row of filing boxes, one descending a few centimetres from the shelf above and the other rising a few from the shelf beneath, fixed across the surface of the boxes and effectively preventing them from being removed from their spot. Angelina had spotted the bars and correctly surmised their purpose.

'You need to enter an access code to release the security bars,' Ben added. 'It allows us to keep track of which shelves are accessed, and by whom.'

Angelina's eyes were no longer on the box; they were squarely bored into Ben's face.

'I assume you have access?'

He hesitated, 'Yes, though we're not meant to use it without . . .'

But the words died in his mouth. Protocols were protocols, but they were both here for the same reason.

'Just give me a second,' he finally said, straightening himself. He squeezed past Angelina and made his way back to the head of the aisle. There he entered a few more strokes on the same keypad that had formerly shifted the rolling stacks to life, and a second later a buzz emerged from the shelf at Angelina's head.

She watched as the two metal restraint bars moved on electric hinges and freed up access to the shelf that contained their box.

'Give me just a second and I'll get us a stepladder and some equipment to—'

Ben's voice continued in the distance, but to Angelina it had become background noise.

'No more time to waste,' she whispered.

She reached out and took the grey box firmly in her grip.

The box came off the shelf more easily than she'd thought it would, weighing less than its size suggested. As there were no tables nearby, Angelina opted to lower it gently to the floor, then laid it on its side.

From the end of the aisle, Ben saw her movements. 'Wait, Angelina, what are you doing? We can't just open that here!'

He rushed towards her, and a moment later his hand was on her shoulder.

'We need to take it up to one of the reading rooms. There needs to be padding, we need gloves. For God's sake, there's history in there!'

It wasn't that Angelina didn't agree with him. But inside her, emotion had grown too strong a force to resist. *The tablet is here, and I need to see it. Now.*

A string wound around a peg held down the box's closure, and Angelina calmed her breath, focused her attention, and unwound it.

With a flick of her wrist, the lid came open.

The tablet lay encased in a custom-cut foam embrace. History it may be, but it was history in its sanitised and curated form. There was no dust to be blown away, no cobwebs to brush aside. The box was clean, its interior pristine.

But a muffled 'My God' fell from Angelina's mouth all the same. The tablet was right . . . here.

Her whole, short-lived academic life had been spent studying the culture and language of the people who wrote in this script, and she had seen photographs of just about every clay tablet and inscribed stone on which Akkadian pictographs had ever been written. They recounted the famed hanging gardens of their culture's most famous city; they spelled out legal codes that predicted the Enlightenment by millennia. They told the stories of gods and goddesses; they recounted the life of a civilisation that had once been spread across the earth, but which Greeks and Persians and other forces of history had gradually eliminated completely. All their history, from beginning to end, impressed as triangles and dashes into the runic figures in clay that Angelina had come to love.

But never in her life had she seen an Akkadian document this closely – one not hidden away behind three centimetres of museum casing next to a placard offering an inanely simplistic description of its contents. Never had she been able to reach out and . . .

'Angelina, don't!'

But she couldn't stop herself. Every careful academic instinct she had demanded that she wait, get gloves and a proper cushioned stand to examine the relic – to do everything *correctly* – but something else had overtaken her. Something was different about these circumstances, and this moment.

She pressed her fingers into the edges of the foam and lifted the tablet out of its encasement. Her hands held its smooth shape securely, though she was trembling in her core as she lifted it up towards her face. Doubts over its origins notwithstanding, everything about the tablet screamed authenticity. The cuneiform indentations of the ancient script were realities, centimetres from her eyes – the impressions in the clay becoming three dimensional as the once-soft material took in each angular groove intentionally pressed into it. The past reached forward to touch Angelina. A world lost, so vaguely known, connected stone to skin. Her heart began to sing, her eyes began to mist.

And then the world went black.

33

Across the Seven Hills of Rome

From the tallest of skyscrapers to the smallest of shopfronts and kiosks, every light in Rome blinked its way into simultaneous oblivion. The bright technicolour hue of evening vanished, and save for the headlights of cars, unaffected, which in their lengthy bonnet-to-boot queues suddenly became like luminous snakes, slithering along the paved corridors of the city, a blackness overtook all else.

There was a pause, the whole city momentarily shocked, unable to absorb the sudden change. So much had happened during the daylight; the population's nerves had not yet recovered. But then sirens began to sound, first from one quarter then another, overlapping into an auditory cacophony. The purity of surprise led swiftly to confusion. Confusion not at one neighbourhood or quadrant of the city going dark, but the whole of Rome, from one edge to the other – black like the night itself.

No one understood. But with visceral swiftness, they remembered.

The strange prophecy that had circulated on the Internet

since the river had run red in the morning churned through the memory of the city. As did the words of the small group of charismatic believers in the east of the city.

And the face of a young man, speaking into a camera after the first plague had come and gone.

'The next shall be like it in power, as the bright places become dark in a city filled with light.'

The first plague they had experienced today had been, it appeared, predicted. Now, a whole population stood in the midst of the second.

With a deepening unease, sceptics and believers alike recalled that they'd been told there would be more.

Atop the Esquiline Hill

Near the peak of one of the fabled 'Seven Hills' of Rome, Bartolomeo drove away from the insertion point with as much satisfaction as he had ever felt in his work and as much power as he had ever sensed in his person.

The choice of insertion point had been, by some measures, arbitrary. Once the work of hacking into the city's power grid had been accomplished, it was possible to initiate the necessary protocols from almost any point in the city. Bartolomeo had chosen the small hub atop the Esquiline Hill for personal reasons. The view from the call box, which was normally wired to affect the connections of only a few local streets but which had been toggled by Vico and his team to affect the entire grid, allowed him to look down over Rome from a superlative height, affording him what he knew would be a direct and unrepeatable view once the switch had been flipped.

His expectation had been amply rewarded.

He'd plugged his computer into the weather-reinforced ethernet port in the small hub, and with a few keystrokes Vico's boys had pre-recorded into a scripted macro, the system-wide shutdown had been initiated. There was just enough lag time between his initiating the script and its dramatic coming into effect for Bartolomeo to reflect on the magnitude of the work he was undertaking, and to revel in the artfulness of what he'd done.

Evidence of the machinations behind the shutdown of the city's power grid was being, even as the thought passed through his mind, eliminated from the data recording systems that normally monitored all grid activity. The usual observational protocols that allowed for the tracking of a problem's source, so that technicians could be sent and repairs could be made, had all been disabled by Emil's tech boys. It was masterful work. Artistic and, as near as Bartolomeo could tell, technically flawless.

When the power grid was switched back on – and the work they had undertaken together would ensure that switch was just as sudden as its going off – there would be no way to trace the problem's source. No single point within the city that could be isolated as its origin. Instead it would simply be the case, to all eyes and all observers, that inexplicably, unpredictably, indefensibly, Rome had gone wholly dark.

Just as they'd all been told it would.

He looked out over the city as the next millisecond ticked over on the clock, and watched with intense satisfaction as the second plague descended and took hold.

34

The bunker

The blackness that overtook the Vatican Secret Archives' bunker was immediate, complete, and overwhelming. The subterranean vault wrapped in concrete beneath the earth had no avenue for exterior light, and so the darkness that came as the power failed was of the purest, deepest black – like a night sky, without the pinpoint texture of the stars, extending from blind senses in every direction.

It was unlike anything either Angelina or Ben had ever experienced.

Her instinct was to freeze. As her most familiar sense was stripped from her, her body clenched into a mass of taut muscle, her tongue instantly tainted with the taste of pure adrenaline – a flavour with which she'd become familiar only a few hours ago. In the blackness all the terror of her experience at the Tiber bridge came coursing back: the explosions of gunfire behind her, the bursting stonework at her side. Once again her breath started to come in shallower, faster flutters. She sensed her head lightening, her balance starting to wobble.

But Angelina's rational mind wasn't ready to be wholly outdone by the anxiety of memory, however intense. She forced the panic down.

You can't see, she forced a scolding voice into her consciousness, *but that doesn't mean you're blind.* One sense might be gone, others remained. *Calm yourself down.*

Angelina could still hear, and she heard no gunshots. No footsteps charged across the metal flooring above or thudded over the concrete beneath her. No one was shooting, no one was chasing. This experience wasn't mirroring that of the afternoon.

Her grip around the tablet tightened, all the same. The fingers that clutched it were, she suddenly realised, sweaty and slippery, and in a surprising moment of intellectual clarity she realised she had to be careful or she might snap the precious object in half. Or drop it on to the solid floor. Or—

'Angelina, are you there?' Ben's hesitant voice broke the silence that had fallen upon them with the darkness. For a moment she'd almost forgotten he was only a few steps away.

'Yes, right where I was a moment ago.' She pushed down the anxiety in her throat, relieved at the sound of his voice. 'You okay?'

'I don't know what's happened,' Ben answered. 'We've never had a power outage down here before. There are supposed to be back-up systems. The emergency lighting's linked up to another part of the grid.' His voice came as a disembodied narration, but Angelina could tell his head was moving as he spoke – a vain attempt, perhaps, to scan surroundings that were impossible to see. 'Or at least, that's what they told us.'

'I'm sure it'll be back on in a minute,' Angelina replied, though in the moment it was difficult to believe her own words.

It took a few seconds for them to be proven right, at least partially. A few minuscule lights appeared, though they came from the floor rather than the blocky security light boxes she'd seen mounted on the walls as they entered. The little pinpricks of light were a muted red and ran in rows at their feet.

'Exit path lighting,' Ben muttered. The red dots beneath them barely cast a glow as far as his face, and the little light that reached it cast his features into an otherworldly pallor. 'It seems to be all that's working.'

Angelina's thoughts were not on which lighting system was managing to function.

'Ben, I don't think this is coincidence.'

From his direction, the scuffling of motion stopped abruptly and the barely illumined, Halloween-esque visage of his face turned towards her.

'What do you mean by that?'

'I'm out on the street earlier today,' she answered, 'when the river turns red and I get shot at. You're minding your own affairs, I presume, when the same thing happens to you.'

'I was following the crowd . . . towards the . . .' His voice trailed away.

'Then the Swiss Guard takes us in. Then this tablet, which it turns out you knew about, without really knowing about it.' Angelina paused, but Ben said nothing. 'Now we're here, the tablet literally in hand, and the lights go black?'

She swivelled to face him more directly, expecting a look of recognition, acknowledging that this was too strong a coincidence not to set off a few alarm bells. But not only had Ben gone silent, he had turned away from her. His head was lowered, his gaze somewhere beyond the floor, his lips mumbling words Angelina couldn't hear.

* * *

Something had changed within Ben Verdyx when Angelina had impulsively untied the filing box and revealed the tablet to both of them.

At first he'd been reactionary, shocked at a capable scholar acting so impulsively around an ancient artefact. When Angelina had gone beyond opening the box and actually reached in to extract the object with her bare hands, he'd exploded in cries to stop – to think about what she was doing, to at least let them take it to a place where they could deal with it carefully.

Then Ben had caught his first full sight of its surface, and the protestations had ceased.

It was, indeed, right there, right in front of him – this tablet which he had never seen before, yet which he had seen. But it wasn't the fact that Cardinal Giotto Forte, as he now knew, had sent him the first lines for translation, that struck such awe into Ben's soul as he saw the actual object in front of him. What filled him with a wonder capable of muting all his instinctual protests was that, in a way that defied his rational credulity, he knew exactly what the rest of the text on this stone said.

He could not translate Akkadian instantaneously any more than anyone else, including the woman next to him. Even the best experts, for which title they both qualified, required lexica and dictionaries for serious translation work. But Ben saw certain symbols he knew well. *Water. Red. Darkness. Fog.*

They were enough to convince him of something that an interior voice had already brought him to sense was true. This was not just any tablet, nor could his involvement with it be a random circumstance. This tablet – inexplicably – contained . . . *them.* The prophecies. The revelations.

The sure vision of future things.

He mumbled about the lighting as Angelina queried it, but

his head wasn't with his words and soon he felt the ability to respond slip away from him altogether.

Instead, his gaze fell to the floor as the revelations of the Lord spun their way again into his mind.

'It shall come to pass in the seventeenth year of the second millennium after the coming of the Sun . . .'

The words echoed in his ears, heard so often.

'The first sign . . . the river shall run with blood . . .'

Ben wasn't sure whether he was still in the bunker or somewhere in another world, in another realm. All he could hear were the words that he somehow knew were inscribed on the tablet held in Angelina's hands.

'The bright places shall become dark . . . in a city filled with light.'

Ben's behaviour in the new-found darkness defied Angelina's understanding. He appeared to have descended into some kind of quasi-catatonic state, crouched over his knees and staring at the floor, and neither her words nor her taps on his shoulder would snap him out of it.

Claustrophobia. The thought came to her suddenly. Ben had social . . . 'issues' would probably be the PC word these days. It wasn't out of the question that claustrophobia could be tied into them, and if it was, the world suddenly going black in a concrete-reinforced bunker metres beneath the surface of the earth wouldn't exactly settle nicely.

But he'd have to get over it. Angelina was convinced that there could be nothing coincidental about the lights going out while they were here – which meant the sooner they could be out of here, the better. Even so, she wasn't ready simply to turn on her heels and run. *Not yet.* She hadn't come this far, and neither had the catatonic Ben, just to give up with nothing to show for it.

'Does your phone have a torch function?' she asked abruptly. Ben didn't answer, but she could see where he'd slid it into his shirt pocket and she simply reached down and snatched it. Her own mobile's battery had died somewhere in the middle of the morning – she'd forgotten to connect it to the charger overnight – and so his was the only hope for the plan swiftly forming in her mind.

She clicked the home button and the device came to life. The illumination of the display transformed their surroundings from the palest red to a ghostly, bright blue.

'I need your pin number,' she said abruptly, pointing the display down at him. Ben said nothing, and Angelina's impatience flared. Perching the tablet on her knees, she grabbed his shoulder and forcibly turned him to face the phone's display.

'Snap out of whatever you're in, Ben.' She waved the device in front of him. 'Your pin.'

His eyes slowly rose and held her gaze for a second that felt far longer. Fixed, unmoving. Then he simply began to recite digits.

Angelina had been right before: his access code was longer than customary. Ben had recited twelve digits before the numbers stopped, and a second later, the system registering the right code, the display transformed to the rows of icons that marked its home screen. A few finger presses later and Angelina had activated the torch, a powerful beam of light flashing into sweeping brilliance in her moving hand.

The light was small, but in the utter blackness it might as well have been the sun.

'Let's get out of here,' Ben suddenly announced. He sprang

174

up from his crouch and Angelina instinctively turned the light towards him. It lit up a pale, frightened face. 'Right now. We have to leave.'

His sentiments had been Angelina's own only moments ago, but she had something else she wanted done before they fled this place.

'Not yet,' she answered, voice hard and filled with more resolve than she'd realised she possessed in the moment.

'We have to go right now, we have to—'

She didn't permit Ben to continue. 'Hold this,' she said abruptly, then lifted the tablet off her knees and thrust it gingerly into his hands.

Ben's eyes widened as it came into his grasp, and his tongue went silent.

'Hold it flat, just like this.' Angelina positioned it perpendicular to his chest, held out parallel to the floor like a dinner tray. 'Now, keep still.'

'Angelina,' Ben finally said, 'enough. You said yourself, no coincidences. *We have to go!*'

But her attention was on the series of icons on his phone. 'There's a camera app in here somewhere, right?'

Photographing the tablet in the utter blackness took moments neither Ben nor Angelina felt comfortable expending, but which Angelina insisted were absolutely necessary. Ben's phone was capable of torch mode or camera mode, but not both at the same time, so he and Angelina were forced to line up the shot with the torch on, then freeze in the blackness as she switched it off, opened up the camera app and prayed that when the LED flash burst into life she was still holding it in the right position over the clay surface in Ben's hands to allow for autofocus and a clear shot.

They made six attempts before they landed one Angelina felt would be sufficiently clear to allow them to examine the entire surface of the tablet once they were outside. By that time the anxiety level between them had increased dramatically.

No coincidences. Ben's approximation of her own words, together with his bizarre behaviour more generally, were beginning to rattle her. She didn't know what had come over him, but on one point they were now both agreed. It was time to leave.

Angelina took the tablet back from Ben and lowered it into its foam encasement, closed the filing box, and returned it to the shelf.

She turned to him.

'Now?' he asked simply, imploringly.

'Now, Dr Verdyx, we get the hell out of here.'

Outside

'How long do we wait for them to come out?' André fidgeted in his position behind the collection of rubbish bins on the far side of the courtyard. 'They've been in there for ages.'

'We wait until we see them come through that door,' Ridolfo answered. 'There's only one way in and out of that building. They'll show up eventually.'

Despite his measured words, Ridolfo shared André's impatience. The urge to break through the door and force their way to their targets' location was strong. It posed, however, the practical potential of losing the man and woman altogether. Inside, Ridolfo imagined that the Archives were a maze of corridors, storage rooms and vaults. Seeking out two people inside would be a tricky challenge. Far better simply to wait until they fleshed themselves out.

'Maybe there's an exit you don't know about,' André protested. 'Can we really be that sure they're even still in there?'

'For Christ's sake, André, you've got her signal on your tablet.' Ridolfo pointed at the device strung to his partner's hip. The small device was fed Angelina Calla's location in real time by Vico's team. Her phone had apparently gone into hibernation mode due to low battery sometime during the afternoon, but Vico had surprised Ridolfo by assuring him that the device being off didn't hinder their ability to track it. 'You can see her position for yourself.'

André grunted. He grabbed the tablet from his waist and switched it on. The small green dot superimposed over the Google Maps rendering of the area continued to move, but only in the most fragmentary of ticks one direction or another, then back again, movements overlapping. She was clearly still in the structure before them, probably underground, where Vico had explained their tracking couldn't monitor vertical motion, meaning that ascents and descents would look more like flutters than actual movement.

Clucking in annoyance, he switched off the device and returned it to the clasp on his belt.

Ridolfo could smell his friend's frustration.

'Calm yourself, André.' He permitted his tone to grow a little more gentle. 'They'll come out soon enough. And when they do, we'll take them down properly.'

35

It took time to ascend from the bunker back up to the ground level of the Archives. Precisely how long was something Angelina couldn't be sure of. Seconds seemed like hours and minutes could have been weeks as she once again followed Ben, this time by the beam of his phone's torch. They spoke little. His odd mood hadn't passed even after they were free of the bunker's concrete shell, and for her part, Angelina felt that silence better fit the air of apprehension that lingered palpably between them.

The whole time, however, her mind was abuzz. The questions she had about the tablet they'd just left behind consumed her. Having held it in her hands she now knew it was composite clay. The historical significance of such an artefact was enormous, but it was hardly an item of extraordinary worldly value. It wasn't inscribed on gold or precious stone or invitingly ornate. Lexical contents aside, it was a series of shallow indentations marked in a plate of what had once been mud. How much could something like that really be worth on the black market? A few hundred euros?

Maybe a few thousand? Hardly enough to try to kill someone for.

She shuddered, and her memories shifted. The bullets by the river had come within centimetres of her chest, feet and head. A different posture, a slightly repositioned stance, and she would have been left bleeding on the streets of Rome, a piece of lead torn through her flesh.

'Watch your footing here,' Ben's voice sounded. Angelina peered down as he held the beam of light on a small dip in the flooring. She was grateful for his voice as much as for the guidance. Something familiar, something to snap her out of her suddenly morbid, terrifying thoughts.

'It's only a few metres further,' Ben continued, his voice still tinged with self-reflection but stronger than before. 'One more security door, and we'll be back in the lobby.'

Fewer than two minutes later he and Angelina emerged into the small space of the Vatican Secret Archives front lobby, ground level. Normally, the foyer at night-time would have been dimly illuminated by exterior rays beaming in from two windows set high into the courtyard-side walls. Beyond stood all the glories of Vatican City in its night-time splendour: fabulously illuminated domes, stone palaces, statues and courtyards – a vision as awesome by night as by day.

But as they entered into the lobby, it was only marginally less dark than the stacks and corridors from which they'd emerged. Above them, the windows were a deep navy blue, barely a shade above blackness itself.

Ben noticed the oddity of the surroundings more than Angelina, to whom they were foreign in any case. All she saw was the door, the exit to the outside world where she desperately wanted to be. She didn't wait for Ben to guide her. With the door in sight she stepped forward and took the lead, depressing the lever on its wooden bulk and pushing.

A moment later she and Ben emerged into the Belvedere Courtyard of the Vatican Palace, smack in the heart of God's own city.

'Thank God we're out of there.' Angelina didn't stop, keeping her feet in motion towards the arched exit on the southern wall of the courtyard. 'For a place I was once desperately hoping to get into, at this moment I'm thrilled to have it behind me.'

It would have been a natural moment for Ben to smile or to offer some comforting remark or compassionate 'I can relate to that', but instead he was silent. Though his lips continued to move, something Angelina had noticed downstairs, no sound emerged.

She also noticed, at this moment, his eyes. They darted between the principal objects of the exterior landscape: the few remaining cars parked on the tarmac. The fountain at the courtyard's centre. The buildings themselves. With each, Ben's face appeared more puzzled.

It was only when Angelina turned to look in the same direction, focusing on the same sights, that she started to realise why.

All around them, the darkness they had left below seemed to be following them.

The usual courtyard lampposts were not lit, and as Angelina surveyed the windows of the other buildings lining the space, she noticed that none of them were illumined, either. Most striking of all, the immense dome of St Peter's itself was dark. The massive structure, the central feature of the Roman skyline for five centuries and a monument recognisable the world over, was normally lit in brilliant display from the moment the sun went down over Vatican City. Angelina had heard once that it cost the Holy See upwards of 250,000 euros a year just to illumine the exterior of the capital of Catholic Christianity – a figure she revelled in quoting to her tour groups. It might not speak well for the eco-mindedness of the Holy See, but as far as Angelina was concerned it was entirely worth it. The sight drew visitors from every corner of the globe.

Tonight it was a dark grey shadow on a black backdrop, haunting and silent. Angelina had never seen it like this before.

'The power outage must be for the whole of Vatican City.' She walked alongside Ben as they made their way towards the courtyard's southernmost exit. He continued to glance around them, but said nothing.

His behaviour's starting to freak me the hell out, she muttered inwardly as they moved. It was time to be rid of the whole place.

Under normal circumstances she would have vocalised her thoughts, perhaps; maybe tried to lighten her anxiety by making a jab at unpaid Vatican electricity bills. She would have said something witty. Would have said anything.

But the opportunity never came. Instead, Angelina's breath stopped abruptly in her chest as a sound so explosive it might as well have been the earth cracking in half broke through their relative silence.

A millisecond later, and for the second time that day, a stone wall beside her shattered into a cloud of dust and debris.

36

In the heart of Vatican City

The fact that the sound of gunfire was familiar to her would have struck Angelina as ironic if it weren't for the fact that it meant she knew exactly what was happening. She was being shot at, again; and just as before, the bite of fragmented stone and concrete flying into her skin shocked her system to attention. All the panic from the afternoon's attack at the bridge returned with an intensity impossible for anything other than the rush of genuine fear, and before the shards of the stone wall had fully ricocheted off her body, Angelina had tensed to full alert, adrenaline once again spiking through her system.

Her head spun towards Ben, who stood frozen where his legs had locked at the explosive sound. His face was pale, though on his features Angelina saw the signs of terrified recognition. He'd been shot at today, too, and was clearly even more traumatised than she was.

The suggestion of vomit arrived at the back of her tongue, fear reaching a new intensity. Would the brusque men who had abducted her earlier return to save them again? Had it been a mistake to flee the confines of the Swiss Guard? The thoughts swarmed in her mind with instantaneous speed. She still wasn't sure her captors and the attackers weren't one and the same, she—

Another gunshot tore through the night, and all Angelina's thoughts stopped. Her impulses sprang to life.

She lunged towards Ben and grabbed his shoulder, her eyes boring directly into his and only a single word on her tongue.

'Run!'

Ridolfo wasn't about to let André fuck this up a second time. This time around the woman would already be spooked, and a spooked target was always more unpredictable than one taken by surprise.

Ridolfo would do the shooting himself.

He'd never trained as a marksman or felt a strong draw towards weaponry, but he wasn't a complete neophyte. A target range outside Mondragone had been a popular place of retreat over the years, and Ridolfo knew his way around a gun and a target. Though they usually weren't moving, and they'd never before been human.

Still, there was a first time for everything.

His first shot had fallen wide, slamming into the wall beyond the woman in his sights. He cursed himself, and then again when his second round fared no better.

He would do better to target the man, who'd frozen in evident terror before she had pulled him back into motion. Cogently alert was not a phrase Ridolfo would use to describe the woman's petrified companion.

He took a few breaths to line up his sights anew, then fired again. The shot was perfect, the sights square. But just as his finger gently squeezed the trigger to life, the woman grabbed her companion by the shoulder and yanked him out of range. Ridolfo's third shot pursued its course, a line that would have gone straight through the man's head, just as he'd intended. Instead it found itself, too, buried in the ancient stonework beyond.

Fuck! Before the profanity had finished barrelling through his mind, Ridolfo saw his targets were on the move. *That fucking woman!* She was guiding him, as wily on her feet as she had been in the afternoon. They had to be stopped.

But they were too swift. Before Ridolfo could line up another shot, they'd reached an archway that led out of the courtyard and rounded it sharply, taking them out of sight.

Ridolfo lowered his gun and forced all his strength into his thighs as he rose from his crouch.

'Damn it!' he shouted at André, his body already in motion. 'After them!'

Behind Angelina, Ben's race to keep up was all that prevented a flood of panicked confusion from consuming him. The exertion and his need for breath limited what flowed out of his lips, but even though he knew his panicked words were heard only by himself, he couldn't stop them from coming.

'The bright places shall become dark . . .'

All around him, bullets slicing through the air with demonic intent, aimed at Angelina and himself, the prophecy was proving itself real. They were awash in blackness. The city-state that was called by Christ to be a 'lamp on a hill' had gone dark. A bleaker darkness than any he'd seen before had fallen . . . *in a city filled with light.*

He followed Angelina on impulse. She ran out of the Vatican Palace structure into one of the narrow alleyways that led between ancient buildings. Her face was terrified, yet determined.

But Ben's heart beat with some other force. His two worlds had always been separate – the professional and the personal, the historical and the faithful. His work gazed ever into the past while his faith burned always for the future.

Today, they were colliding.

With the looming hulk of the Apostolic Palace behind them, there was a momentary lapse in the cracks of gunfire that had forced Angelina and Ben into their current sprint, but she was far from satisfied that they were safe. She hadn't got a solid look at their pursuers – she was too concerned with getting away from them to stop for a careful identification – but as she'd glanced backwards in that first lunge for Ben she'd caught sight of two figures behind a low stone barrier across the internal square. She was as convinced as she needed to be that they were the same two who'd shot at her by the river.

Her skin went even colder. Vatican City wasn't like the neighbourhood she'd been in earlier – there were a few twists and turns around the sacred buildings of the Holy See, but nothing approaching the spider's web of interconnecting alleys and streets that had helped her escape before. Here she and Ben were far more exposed, contained, and Angelina sensed their pursuers would use that to their advantage.

No sooner had the thought formed in her mind than the cobblestone roadway between her and Ben burst apart and a new crack of gunfire tore through the air.

Ridolfo couldn't believe he'd actually missed them again. André was never going to let him live down the series of failed attempts, especially after the words he'd shot in the other man's direction following his poor display of marksmanship earlier that afternoon. There would be ribbing and there would be insults.

But neither of those irritations would compare to the anger of their boss, André's father, if they failed in this assignment. Ridolfo knew the stakes they were playing, and though he didn't fully understand the nature of the threat Angelina Calla and Ben Verdyx posed, he knew that Emil's crew – of which he was an integral part – was going to get only one shot at their prize, and if Emil said this pair could potentially disrupt that, then Ridolfo had as much of a reason to stop them as his boss.

Ironically, it was the current plague that was hindering him in his task. Without any electric illumination, Vatican City was a shadowland of dark lanes loomed over by hulking grey masses of stone. It was surprisingly difficult to see shape and motion in the darkness, and the duo they were chasing hadn't stopped moving.

But you take the circumstances you're given, his father had always said to him, *and make what you can of them*. The pep talk may have been aimed at helping Ridolfo overcome his physical deformity and deal with an unpleasant lot in life, but over the years it had come back to him in various ways as a help.

Today's circumstances weren't great, but he would make do.

He raised his gun again, aligned the sights, and fired.

Outside – throughout Rome

The blackness that had overtaken the city was too much. Having borne the water's strange discolouration and the attacks that had come along with it, tension and fear rising at the pairing, the population seemed unable to bear this new 'coincidence' without some degree of reaction.

It came in bodies descending into streets and squares to examine just how far the darkness had swept through their city. When they saw it reached everywhere, that the only lights in the whole of Rome were those of torches held in hands and headlamps on moving traffic, tension began to turn to outright fear.

What the hell was going on in Rome?

Without phones – the vast majority of modern Romans having long ago ditched landlines and opted for mobiles, all of which were rendered defunct with the loss of power to the city's cellular towers – and without Internet, the only way to confer and confirm their fear with others was to reach them physically.

So Rome began to take to the streets. In the blackness, the thoroughfares and lanes that criss-crossed the city began to glow like veins illuminated in black flesh. Traffic slowed to a crawl, the anxiety of drivers causing them to pound on their horns with increased frequency, raising up a great howl over the city.

Rome was losing her self-control. Fear had come with the darkness, with the guns, with the blood. And fear was a hard beast to tame.

Inside Vatican City

The bullet blew its way into masonry and stone with a crackling thud that was becoming far too familiar to Angelina. This time, though, it was accompanied by another sound, one she hadn't heard before: a yelp, something resembling an abbreviated cry, caught in an incomplete breath. It took Angelina a full second to realise that the sound had come from her, and it was as she glanced down at her moving legs that the pain accompanying it hit.

The bullet that had exploded into the wall in front of her hadn't entirely missed its intended mark. The fabric of her trousers was torn just above her left knee, and the appearance of a bloom of blood beneath the frayed material was accompanied by a fire that tore its way through the nerves of her legs. Angelina had never felt a pain like it, and the unfamiliar sensation struck her in an assault that renewed itself with each pounding of her foot on the cobblestone lane.

'Shit, you're hit!' Ben cried out, seeing the sudden change in her gait and lowering his eyes to the red patch forming above her knee. It was the first cogent thing he'd said since they'd emerged from the Archives. Angelina saw the look of horror on his face, as well as the terrified hesitation that overtook his pace.

But though Ben was right, and though a gunshot wound was something Angelina had no idea how to digest, she sensed that she had to keep them moving. She hadn't heard bone crunch, and though the wound was agonisingly painful, the blood coming from it didn't look like the kind of flow that drained the life out of a person. She might live, but they'd both be dead if they stopped.

'Don't slow down,' she shouted at Ben, forcing herself to resume her pace despite the sickening jolt that shot up her leg with each step. 'It's nothing.'

'Nothing!' Ben was incredulous, though he scrambled back to his former speed to keep up with her. 'You've just been shot! By, by . . . ' His shortness of breath overtook him.

'It only grazed me,' she shouted back. The world around her felt wobblier than before, and a surge of panic came with the thought that she'd been wrong in assessing the blood flow. Was this what it felt like to have consciousness ebb away? To enter into the gradual fade-to-black of existence?

But what wobbled didn't go entirely dark, and Angelina forced herself to remain focused on the only thing that mattered.

Ahead of them, the cobblestone route met a wall and

connected to a perpendicular walkway. Angelina had a choice – right, or left – and only a matter of seconds to make it.

The fire in her left leg seemed to spread through her hip, her side, threatening to consume her.

Left. The decision made itself. Right felt as if it led back in the direction of the interior of the walled city-state, and Angelina had no desire to get anywhere but out.

She reached out to push Ben in what she had determined was their new direction. The ninety-degree turn brought them into a narrower lane, which ended only a few metres ahead. For an instant Angelina feared she'd made the wrong choice. *Maybe right had been right, after all.*

But a second later – the rush of relief. Beyond the end of its narrow run the lane opened into a broad space. Initially its parameters were difficult to assess in the blackness, but as she and Ben raced into its expanse she instantly realised where they were.

They had emerged into the most famous public piazza in the Western World. St Peter's Square, the vast space that stood before Catholicism's chief basilica, was a circle of stone wrapped in the embrace of twin galleries that stretched out from the sides of the basilica's facade. They extended in mirror arcs to the north and south of the rounded square, almost meeting at its far end. Atop them, over a hundred statues stood silent guard over the throngs of pilgrims that normally filled the space, milling around the ancient and mysterious obelisk that stood proudly at its centre.

Right now St Peter's Square was as dark as everything else in Vatican City, and from their vantage point Angelina could see beyond to Rome itself. The absence of light in the Holy See was echoed outside, which was dark as far as the horizon, and who knew how far beyond. The power outage, it appeared, reached much further than the thick stone walls surrounding them.

The darkness had thinned the crowd that normally filled the vast piazza, even at night, rendering the space far too open. She and Ben needed another way out.

The situation seemed hopeless, but then, in the distance, Angelina spotted something she'd overlooked a moment ago. The moment she recognised what it was, her heart beat with new strength.

Beyond them, on the far side of St Peter's Square, it flashed at her like a beacon. Rows of twin eyes sparkled in the blackness, formed in a chain that slithered a numinous course.

Not all the lights in Rome, she suddenly realised, had gone out. Those that remained might be their only chance.

Ridolfo spun around the corner with so much speed that he nearly lost his balance, André emerging behind him less than a second later. Their targets were fast, but one of Ridolfo's bullets had finally hit something other than stone. The woman was wounded, if not mortally then at least significantly enough to slow them down. That would be enough. Ridolfo knew his friend was in as fit a physical condition as himself, and that a wounded tour guide and a terrified archivist were no match for them in the long run. They just needed to keep running and keep them in sight.

But as his eyes adjusted to the scene in front of him, Ridolfo felt a pang of worry. It wasn't what he expected to see.

The square.

'Shit!' The profanity barrelled its way out of Ridolfo's mouth as he planted his feet and came to a sudden halt. 'God damn it!' he shouted, not caring if he was overheard. Such a vast space, scattered bodies within it as distractions, was not something he'd factored in to this pursuit. In the darkness, the scrum of tourists was hard to distinguish. They were grey shadows, the bright colours of clothing in the daytime reduced to indistinguishable shades of grey. He didn't mind shooting into the middle of them, as long as he hit the two people he was after – but that depended on at least having some sense of where they were in the fray. Ridolfo scanned the diminished crowd, but recognised no one.

Maybe he'd just have to start shooting. Screw who else got hit. Let them drop with that bitch and her friend.

'Over there!' André's voice was energetic, his arm flying up and pointing to their left.

At first, Ridolfo didn't see anything. Bodies were gathered in various groups, the stonework structures looming behind them. But then it caught his attention.

Motion.

Halfway down the expanse of one of the covered colonnades, keeping tight to the edge of the piazza and as close to protective cover as they could, two grey bodies moved in the darkness. And moved fast.

It took mere seconds for Ridolfo to compute their aim. Beyond, outside the piazza, a twisting line of cars moved slowly beyond the eastern limit of Vatican City, their lights a strange beacon in the otherwise black landscape.

He knew he couldn't get a clean shot at Calla and Verdyx from this distance – not in the darkness and with obstacles between them. There was only one option.

'Get fucking moving!' he shouted at André as he bore slightly left and began to cut through the heart of the piazza. 'We have to get to them before they make it to the street.'

37

St Peter's Square

The pillars of the northern colonnade surrounding St Peter's Square swept by as Angelina and Ben ran between them, layered four deep and massive in their dimensions, obstructing her view in flashes that seemed to animate the scene beyond. In the distance, closing as they moved, the dark exterior world was framed by the visible gap where the two colonnades nearly met at their far ends, like two arms reaching out to embrace the space within them, beckoning to the world beyond.

Angelina knew the layout well, every Roman did. The Piazza Pio XII stood just beyond the official border of Vatican City, leading into the broad Via della Conciliazione that ran east, past the Castel Sant'Angelo and alongside the Tiber, where Ben had been shot at earlier in the day. The enormous street was home to some of the most touristy and glitzy shops in Rome, second only to the Piazza Navona, and right now it was their only hope.

Because the Via della Conciliazione was bright with the only lights visible to them. Rows of cars moved in steady, slow progression around the square and down the wide street, their headlamps a creeping illumination in the black city.

Closest to St Peter's Square was precisely what Angelina remembered was always there: a rank of taxis, eager to pick up tourists and charge them twice the going rate for a drive on to the next major sight.

'We need to get into one of those cabs,' she shouted breathlessly to Ben, pointing through the columns as they moved. 'They're our best chance to get away, as far from here as we can.'

Ben simply grunted his affirmation. He was winded from the run and clearly still in shock, but he understood perfectly well the need to put as much distance as possible between them and this place.

Yet Angelina's plan involved one element that couldn't be avoided, and that scared her to death.

Within fifteen metres they were going to reach the end of the covered colonnade. Getting to the taxi ranks was going to involve leaving the protected space. They would have to make the last distance through the piazza, then dart out into the even more exposed square beyond.

Angelina had taken note of the crowd. It was thin. It would hardly be adequate cover.

But she'd also seen their pursuers, out in the square. Two young men. Even at this distance, in the darkness, she could make out the pale shapes of their faces, one of them pitted and deformed. Her mind raced. Cutting through the circular space rather than running around its periphery as she and Ben were doing meant that they were gaining ground. If they reached the end of the colonnades before her and Ben, they'd be trapped.

Cover or not, moving out into the open was going to be their only choice.

*   *   *

Ridolfo knew that if the duo were to make it to the street, they would have an out. They could jump into any of a hundred cars within easy sight, and after that Ridolfo didn't know how he and André would catch them. They'd have to be traced, tracked, and pursued all anew.

He could feel the burning in his calves as he propelled himself forward. His younger friend and partner kept pace, even advancing a little, the fire of youth driving him like a motor.

There wasn't room to play about. They had less than seventy metres between them and the end of the northern colonnade's reach.

Angelina grabbed Ben's wrist and yanked him out from beneath the protective cover of the ancient colonnade. Open air suddenly loomed above them, starry yet still surprisingly dark.

All Angelina could see were the taxi ranks. Despite the agony of her leg, she pushed all her energy into her feet. Thirty metres, twenty . . .

She processed the scene at lightning speed. A huddle of tourists was moving towards the first car in the taxi rank, so she aimed herself and Ben towards the second. They would only have one chance at this. *And screw it if I'm going to get shot knocking on taxi cab doors trying to find an open car!*

Fifteen metres . . .

She could hear the thump of feet on stone behind them. Their pursuers were close, though Angelina dared not look back and see just how close. She shoved Ben towards the second taxi, which felt an eternity away. She tried to focus on the door, though her mind couldn't help but be over-shadowed by the panicked fear that at any instant the world would go black, or white, or whatever colour it goes when a bullet lands in your skull.

But the world stayed as it was. Less than two seconds later she slammed into the side of the waiting cab, unable to slow herself to a stop in time to avoid the bodily collision.

Ben arrived with a similar thud, and before Angelina could bark any instructions, he was already ripping at the door. *Afraid, but not inept,* she noted, grateful to have his companionship in such a terrifying moment.

Ben lunged into the car, Angelina following suit, slamming the door closed behind them. The driver was already turned back towards the rear of his cab, a young man with olive skin and a baseball cap advertising a football team, swearing profanities at the aggressive entry.

'Be careful with my fucking car!' he shouted. 'I paid for this myself, no loans!'

He looked like he would have shouted more and Angelina was preparing a desperate answer, when the side window closest to the Vatican exploded into a thousand shards of crystalline breakaway glass. She impulsively slammed Ben's body down into the seat, covering it with hers as she crouched low, protecting them both from the flying glass and whatever bullets might follow the one that had shattered it.

'If you want anything to be left of your car at all,' she shouted at the driver from the protective position, 'then drive!'

Horrified, his face instantly a sickly pale, the driver spun round and slammed his right palm hard against the gearstick. One foot powered down against the accelerator as the other flew off the clutch and the car lurched into violent motion. His hands spun the wheel to point them out of the ranks, and he tore his way out of the piazza. The profanities returned a millisecond later, their pitch higher and laden with terror.

Another gunshot boomed, so loudly that Angelina thought the shooters might have caught up with them and been standing just outside as they moved away, but no more windows exploded. Another shot, more distant. Then the only sound Angelina could hear was the car's engine revving to its full, strained power, and the beating of her own heart pounding over the obscenities flowing from the driver as he sped them away.

38

Torre Maura district
Eastern Rome

Emil was not going to be able to sleep tonight. Despite the darkness of the blackout, he'd recognised early on that emotion and anticipation meant rest wasn't a realistic option, so hadn't even bothered trying. For the past hour he'd been pacing the sitting room in his small house in Torre Maura, alternating between refreshing the email display on the laptop he'd connected to an extended battery pack and a satellite Internet connection, and compulsively checking his phone for messages from his various teams, all of whom had been equipped with satellite phones for this phase of the operation.

He paused long enough to pour himself a third tumbler of the finest Scotch he'd ever drunk. Emil wasn't a man of vast wealth – not yet – and his tastes weren't normally so exalted. But this was the dawn of . . . everything. He felt it ought to be seen in with nothing but the finest. Even in the darkness.

He didn't have ice, so by the light of a battery-powered lantern Emil topped his glass up to a respectable level and took a sip, neat. The amber liquid glided over his tongue with a hot, buttery bite. It was, in his humble estimation, worth every penny.

At this very moment, Ridolfo and André would be taking care of the only leaks the tech team had discovered. This was, Emil recognised, the only thing that genuinely had him nervous. He was pulling strings that had put the whole city on edge, enacting a plan that involved deceit and risks far greater than any he'd ever undertaken in his life, but it was this one issue that churned his stomach. Everything else was going well. Everything except . . . them.

He couldn't believe it could be so difficult to take out a pair of scholars. Emil had been a scholar himself, before his shunning by the establishment, and he would rank neither himself nor a single one of his former colleagues as particularly capable individuals in a violent situation. 'Our weapons are the pen and the book,' he remembered one of his bygone friends saying at a staff reception, years ago, 'and they're much mightier than guns.' It was the kind of romantic drivel that felt laudable and believable right up to the moment someone pointed a gun barrel at your forehead. Pens were rarely effective in convincing someone not to pull the trigger.

The frustration he felt wasn't really at the difficulty in killing them off, however, but at the fact that they were running, and that someone seemed to be helping them run. This was far, far more worrying.

Emil had been convinced his advance work was impeccable. The text was perfect. They'd brought on, used, and then 'disposed of' an Akkadian scholar abroad to ensure that. It had been checked and double-checked. It had been inscribed into a clay mixed with the powdered dust to which his men had reduced a thirteen-hundred-year-old clay urn they'd stolen at his direction, so that any rushed carbon dating would show signs of age enough to confuse interpreters. And the planting, the delivery, the discovery – all had gone exactly according to arrangement. Scrutiny would come upon the document, of course, and in due course it would be denounced. The ageing trick would eventually be discovered; the text would eventually be hyper-analysed. But those things took time. Everything Emil wanted rode on belief in its authenticity lasting just long enough to get the job done.

There were only two people who posed a threat to that. Two scholars who had come on to Emil's radar when his tech crew had chased through their web histories or Net trailings or whatever-the-hell other records those geeks had access to, and announced that they were experts in this obscure field. Experts who could expose the fraud far faster. Discovery that two such scholars lived in his city had upset Emil, but at least this was a simple problem to deal with. Elaborate shows of prophecy-led death wouldn't be needed here. A bullet to the head of each would accomplish what he needed.

But for reasons that baffled description, Emil's men were struggling to kill them.

The acids in his stomach churned, and Emil set down the whisky, worried it was only compounding his discomfort. He commanded himself to calm down. The whole show only had to last another day and a half. After that, it wouldn't matter who knew what.

He walked over to his small desk and swept a finger across his laptop's trackpad to bring it to life. A few keystrokes later his email was refreshed. Nothing new.

Damn it. He wanted to hear something. Anything. He was the kind of man who'd grown to assume the worst of tense situations. He wanted a report from one of his teams, *any* of his teams, to reassure him things were moving forward as they should.

With little else to focus his worried mind, Emil scrolled down through the old emails still in his inbox. Hundreds of messages. He rarely deleted anything.

Yet he realised his scrolling wasn't as aimless as it at first seemed, even to him. His attention was drawn like a magnet towards the lengthy message he'd received earlier in the day from Vico and his crew. It contained all the data the techie trio had gleaned on the two individuals who had attracted their attention. On the woman, they had all the pertinent details: name, address, financial portrait, locations. Everything Emil expected. And they had the same for the man – what was his name? Emil scrolled further down the message.

Dr Ben Verdyx.

A jingle of memory. Something tugging at his personal past.

He read the name again, aloud. 'Dr Ben Verdyx.'

Then, for the first time, Emil felt weak at his knees. He knew the name, and, he gradually recalled, he had known the man. Ben Verdyx had been brought on to the staff of the Vatican Secret Archives towards the end of Emil's tenure there – perhaps six or seven months before the scandal and shaming that had resulted in Emil's dismissal. He remembered Ben as socially awkward, shy, like a bat craving the solitude of a cave.

So this was the 'other Akkadian scholar' in the duo his men were after. Emil could feel the acid work its way up his oesophagus, perilously close to reaching his throat and threatening to trigger his gag reflex.

The Calla woman was risk enough, but Verdyx had worked in the same environs as Emil himself. It was too close to home. It meant he could know . . .

And as Ben and the woman had been taken by others – Vico had concluded the black vans had belonged to the Swiss Guard – it meant he could have told them.

No, no, no, Emil's thoughts raced. *I can't have them killed. Not until I know what they've said, and to whom.*

He yanked his phone from his pocket and hit the speed dial for Ridolfo's number. He had to modify his men's instructions before they carried out the orders he'd barked at them when they'd spoken forty-five minutes ago.

But the line simply rang and rang.

39

Headquarters of the Swiss Guard
Apostolic Palace, Vatican City

'What do you mean, they just walked out?' Major Heinrich glowered at Corporal Yoder. The junior officer was in fact significantly taller than Heinrich, but the Major seemed to wither down upon him all the same. 'You were supposed to keep an eye on them!'

'Keep an eye on them, sure, as long as they chose to stay put. But they weren't under arrest.'

'It took us two teams to bring them in! We barely kept them alive!'

Max Yoder stood tall. 'The Papal Swiss Guard may not detain Italian or foreign nationals within the Holy See without a writ of arrest or significant findings of criminal behaviour likely to lead to the issuance of such a writ.' He recited the code from their training manual verbatim, then looked down directly into the eyes of his superior officer. 'Major, sir.'

Heinrich kept the man's gaze, clenching his jaws and rubbing his molars together with the tension of frustration.

The Corporal was, however, correct. The relations between Vatican City and the Italian government were delicate and based on a fragile trust between what were technically the agents of two different governments, overlapping in a packed, tense territory inside the borders of a single Italian city. Overstepping the boundaries of that agreed code of conduct, even in a minor way, tended to have disproportionately vast repercussions. And this was hardly minor. Detaining two Roman citizens would lead to word of the Swiss Guard having effected their capture in the first place – outside of Vatican City, on Italian State territory, without the knowledge or cooperation of the Polizia di Stato – which would open up a can of worms that Vatican–Roman relations did not need.

He turned away from the other Guardsman. Behind him, rows of glass desks housed computers that were manned by the Investigations Division of the Papal Swiss Guard, humming with electrical whirs and the constant finger-tapping of focused computer work. The machines had only been brought back to life fifteen minutes ago, a sudden power outage having cut every trunk into the city – including their high-tech offices beneath the stone grandeur of the Apostolic Palace. The Guard's control rooms were only back in the running thanks to a bank of petrol-powered generators on reserve in a wire-mesh cage at ground level, precisely for such emergency situations.

It was the first time they'd ever had to be used.

Heinrich wasn't yet able to wrap his head around the events of the day. Cardinal Forte's suspicions over the text that had been unearthed near San Clemente had proven well founded, but it had come as a shock to learn that Calla and Verdyx were not the culprits behind it that Heinrich had suspected. They'd barely managed to sweep up the two academics in time before others – presumably the actual individuals responsible for whatever the hell was going on – succeeded in their attempt to kill them off.

Now they were out of their hands. *Fine, fend for yourselves out there*. His thoughts were hard, realistic and unemotional, yet deeper inside he knew that Verdyx and Calla might still be relevant to their work.

'Put a track on their phones,' he said, directing the words towards a desk where a young man in the informal business dress of the Guard seemed to expect such instruction, 'and whatever else you need to tap to keep an eye on them. I'd like to know where they go from here.'

Heinrich turned away without waiting for affirmation of his instruction. He knew his men would follow it diligently.

Angelina Calla and Ben Verdyx were no longer his primary subjects of interest. Having ensured that Cardinal Forte and the other senior members of the Curia were updated on the affairs of the afternoon, his chief interest was in identifying who was behind their attempted assassination. It was an elaborate and difficult process, to start from complete unknowns and work back to something solid. CCTV footage from the site of each attack could be used to try to identify assailants – hoping for a shot clear enough to run facial recognition, or perhaps a vehicle with plates that could be processed. These would lead to data trails, which would lead to identities, which Heinrich was convinced would eventually lead to concrete persons that could be called in and questioned. All they needed was time.

'Sir,' a voice suddenly broke the silence, 'outside. In the piazza.' The man who spoke was audibly alarmed, his words curt and tense. To the members of the Guard, 'the piazza' always meant St Peter's.

'Report,' Heinrich commanded.

'There's been gunfire. The public security squads on ground level are already responding.'

Heinrich's skin went cold. It wasn't with fear, but with determination.

Whoever was wreaking havoc on the city had just brought it into his own walls. And that, for a man of devotion of Heinrich's calibre, was a step too far.

40

Via della Conciliazione
Central Rome

Ben's face was completely pale. The lack of blood flow to his capillaries, his body protectively sending more to his core organs as a defence mechanism, gave him a ghostly pallor that offset his brown eyes, transforming them into deep wells that interrupted his face. It had taken several seconds of driving before Angelina had felt secure releasing her protective huddle over him, allowing them both to return to an upright position in the back of the taxi cab, the wind from the shattered right window whipping her red hair into a frenzy.

She was terrified, and wasn't yet sure when the lump in her throat – where it felt her heart had leapt and taken up permanent residence – might melt away.

But another feeling swirled in her well of over-provoked emotions. *Indignation*.

Angelina Calla was a good person. A smart person. She'd had her challenges in life and she'd always met them. She kept to herself, out of trouble. Yet in the span of a single day she'd been chased through the streets, twice. Shot at, twice. Kidnapped. And, apparently, all because the language she'd failed to make a career out of knowing was involved in events in which she played no part and about which she knew nothing.

Screw it, she thought from the back of the cab, clenching her fists, *I have had just about enough of this*. Her rising resentment overwhelmed her panic. The time had come for Angelina to push through the barriers thrust in front of her. Whatever they were.

She turned to Ben. The motion fired new shots of pain through her leg and she diverted her gaze down towards the shredded fabric above her left knee. She hadn't had a chance yet to examine the wound closely, and a new knot tightened in her stomach at the thought of what the gunshot might actually have done to her.

'Let me have a look at that.' Ben's voice emerged over the constant flow of terrified, abusive profanities emanating from the driver in front. He'd spotted Angelina's hand moving towards her wound, and he gently diverted it away and attempted to examine the injury as best as he could in the back of the fleeing car. He tore at the fabric slightly to enlarge the opening around the wound, and as he did Angelina felt angry jolts of agony course through her nerves.

'I'm sorry,' Ben muttered, 'I know that must hurt.'

'Just . . . just tell me how it looks.' Angelina had closed her eyes, sparks and explosions going off at the backs of her eyes.

'It doesn't look deep,' he answered a moment later. 'I mean, I don't know anything about gunshot wounds, but this doesn't look that bad.'

She could have smacked him. *Not that bad? It's a gunshot-fucking-wound!* But in reality she was grateful for even an amateur diagnosis. She bit her lower lip to control the pain.

'The wound's only a couple of centimetres long and, like I said, not very deep. I think it needs to be cleaned out.' Ben sat back upright. 'Maybe some sutures.'

Angelina had always hated hospitals, and especially stitches. The one time she'd had them sewn into a wound on her hand, the feeling of the needle weaving its way through her flesh – even through the anaesthetic – had made her sick. The tactile memory of the sensation threatened to overturn her stomach again.

'Let's just get it cleaned out,' she answered. 'If it's not deep, it doesn't need sutures.'

The profanities from the driver barrelled through the Plexiglas divider with new intensity. He hadn't stopped yelling since their frenzied drive had begun.

'Turn left here!' Angelina shouted back at him. The volume of his shouts increased again, but the car swerved left a moment later. Angelina sighed, relieved to be off the main street. Traffic was as bad as she had ever seen it, and the sound of horns constant in her ears. Something had provoked tension on the city's streets tonight. 'Keep changing direction every few streets.' She leaned forward, her eyes watering from the pain. 'That is, unless you want the shooters to catch up with us.'

For only an instant, the driver's face blanched in the rear-view mirror. A second later he was back at his shouting, but seemed to grasp the point.

Angelina flopped back into her seat. *The shooters.* They'd come after them like animals, and all for this stupid tabl—

She suddenly spun to her side. 'Ben, give me your phone.' He hesitated, processing, but a moment later fished his mobile out of his pocket. To the relief of them both, it hadn't been damaged in the run and dive for the car.

The taxi swerved harshly to the right as the driver altered his course yet again. His foot was pressed heavily on the accelerator.

Angelina switched on the phone and followed Ben's instructions for the access code, then navigated her way to the photo roll, scrolling through the series of images they'd taken in the bunker. The final photograph, as she remembered, was by far the clearest. She pinched and spread her fingers over the display to zoom in on the individual lines and characters imprinted on the hardened clay. The resolution was adequate if not astonishing, though the bumpy motion of the car made it almost impossible to read.

Angelina saw something else on the display, however, that registered perfectly clearly despite the jolts of motion. The battery indicator in the upper right-hand corner was at two percent, already flashing red. With her own phone already out of juice and Ben's almost to the point of giving up the ghost, Angelina was afraid they might lose the photo they'd taken, so with a few nimble keystrokes she'd attached it to an email and clicked the button to send it to herself from Ben's account. There was no reception at all from wherever they were at the instant, so the email's 'Sending' status bar simply began to rotate.

Ben glanced over his shoulder – a motion that had been compulsively repetitive since Angelina's focus had shifted to the device. There had been no further signs of pursuit since the driver had started changing directions, and as he caught sight of the image of the tablet on his phone, Ben settled back into his seat, the pallor of his face altering once again.

His lips, as before, started to move in silence.

Angelina clicked the phone closed. The email still hadn't sent, but it could work on that in the background. The device's power reading had already fallen to one percent, meaning keeping the display bright was going to threaten a shutdown before the email got delivered. She passed the phone back to Ben, thumping it against his knee to call his attention back from wherever it had wandered.

He looked ashen. Vulnerable. He'd been strong when he needed to be, focused when it was required, but Angelina recognised that here, in this moment, all his weariness showed.

And his lips were moving.

'The bright places shall become dark . . .'

She could barely make out the syllables over the engine noise and grumbles from the front.

'What was that?'

He didn't appear to notice her. His lips kept moving, his eyes locked ahead and his voice hardly a whisper.

'Then shall come the fog . . .'

The words were senseless, and Angelina felt the rising warmth of compassion. Ben was not dealing well with the situation, though she knew she was hardly coping in perfect form herself. Adrenaline, indignation and intrigue had kept her going, but she sensed she must look just as haggard as Ben, and she felt that beneath the tension she was likely as exhausted as he. The day had been physically, mentally and emotionally overwhelming. If they didn't get some rest, they were done for.

But she didn't feel safe going home. These people, whoever they were, clearly knew who she was. As Ben was just as much a target as she, going to his home was out as well.

She faced forward towards the driver, ignoring the fresh jolt of pain in her leg.

'Take us to a hotel,' she demanded, banging on the divider between them.

The driver glanced over his shoulder, incredulous. 'Which fucking hotel would madame like?' he shouted, sarcasm embedded in his anger. 'In case you hadn't noticed, Rome's a bit fucked up tonight! People on edge, everyone out on the goddamned streets! Traffic ain't exactly light!'

Angelina realised the poor man, who looked only a few

days over twenty, was probably in shock himself, but she had only so much emotional energy to expend on strangers.

'Doesn't matter,' she answered, ignoring his tone, 'take us to something out of the way. Not too big, not too small.'

'And what about my fucking car!' the man shouted again. 'You shot out my window! I just paid for this!'

'*We* did not shoot out your window,' Angelina answered. 'The men behind us did.'

'Whatever, lady. The window's still out.'

Irritated, Angelina turned to Ben. 'I'm cash-strapped,' she said matter-of-factly. 'How much do you have with you?'

Ben's mind was still elsewhere, but he fished his wallet out of his trousers and passed it to her. Angelina ran a thumb through the small collection of banknotes inside. 'Looks like about a hundred and eighty euros.' Without waiting to seek his permission, she reached forward to hand the driver the cash.

'There's a hundred and eighty. That should cover your window, and the drive. Now get us to a hotel.'

41

Across Rome

The lights in Rome had been dark since nightfall, and every hour had increased the sense of dread. There had been no explanations, only repeated claims by officials that 'this sort of event shouldn't be possible'. But it was not only possible, it had been predicted. And the people knew this. They'd been told it would happen, and it had, and as the minutes scraped along, it was beginning to terrify them.

The average Roman citizen was educated, enlightened and no more prone to superstition than a man or woman in any other modern culture. But there were few who didn't mutter the word – whether in disdainful dismissal or in an increasingly tense worry – that seemed planted on everyone's lips.

Prophecy.

The words of the tablet which had been circulated on the Internet had predicted the darkness, and it had come. Just like the river. It couldn't be denied. And guns had come with the water. And deaths. And fear.

Just what was going to come with this darkness?

But amidst the streets flooded with people taking to their

cars, not sure where they were going but content to be moving *somewhere*, the darkness came to an abrupt end.

In an instant Rome was bright again. As if at the flip of a switch – not in phases or cyclically regenerated power flows as was the case when any large-scale grid system was reinitiated. As the lights of Rome had twinkled out in the blink of an eye, so did they return. Street lamps snapped back to attention, interior fixtures of houses and flats popped back to life, even televisions and kitchen utilities which had been in use before the strange outage whirred and garbled back into electric action.

Impossible, the official line resonated in the populace's memory, *the electricity in Rome doesn't switch on and off like a lightbulb.*

But it did. And the instant it had, the city went racing for answers.

The Internet exploded with activity the moment the citizens of Rome were able to reconnect their computers to WiFi networks, cable feeds and cellular data connections. But there were no answers to be found. No official explanations. So the people had nothing else to take in but guesswork and hypothesis.

Or a video, which many had seen before.

They returned to it now with new viewers in the tens of thousands. The video clip ran only three minutes, and featured its lone man speaking directly into a camera, reading them the revelations contained on a tablet.

'You have tasted the prophecy,' he said as the video rounded into its final seconds, 'but we know the whole. We knew it before, and we know it now.'

The man on the screen coughed, and with him the whole of Rome held its breath.

'Like all prophecy, it speaks of what is to come. Next . . .' He leaned into the camera as the file ran with only six seconds to go.

'It speaks of the fog.'

42

The island of Pantelleria
100 km south-west of Sicily
305 nautical miles south of Rome

On the hillside of the Cinque Denti caldera that formed one of the two peaked features of the Pantelleria island-scape, the small research module sat on concrete foundations that had been poured more than forty years before. Its operations were largely unmanned in modern times, the last eruption to have been recorded of the semi-defunct volcanic island dating back to 1891, and that underwater and several kilometres off the coast. Still, the research module retained its importance as one of a network of geological stations that monitored the whole Mediterranean basin on a continuous basis.

The module was a metallic rectangle, half the length of a lorry trailer but in its other dimensions similar. It was mounted to the poured concrete slab on which it stood by four steel feet that lifted it twenty centimetres off the ground, and out of its belly ran a trunk of cables that divided and subdivided to traverse the distance to monitoring equipment

214

stationed all over the eighty-three square kilometres that constituted Pantelleria itself. From the height of its taller peak, called Montagna Grande and reaching 836 metres into the sky, down to the ancient Castello that was the heart of the island's small coastal town; from the minuscule airport to the huddles of hot springs scattered all across the small landscape, every dimension of Pantelleria was monitored. Each measuring unit sent its data back to the research module, where computers assessed, processed, stored and relayed it all.

The module's interior was mostly made up of computer racks and data storage units, though a small space accommodated a swivel chair and a bank of real-time equipment monitors for the occasions when scientists came to service it in person. The floor was a metal grate, and an air conditioning system worked twenty-four hours a day to keep the stock of valuable equipment from being melted by the heat of the Sicilian climate.

It was empty today, of course. The scientific teams came on a monthly rota, and there was rarely need to modify their predetermined schedule. Pantelleria was not an island of active concern. Its residents lived peacefully, grateful for the hot springs but otherwise dismissive of a geological past that was well and truly the stuff of history.

So no one was in the module, seated at the monitoring station, as the manual dials connected to the central survey equipment began to come to life for the first time since they'd been installed.

Outside, no one noticed anything at all.

PART FIVE

Decisions

43

Fourteen months ago

The document that lay on Emil's desk was longer than he'd anticipated. Not that he hadn't seen it in each of the four drafts that had preceded the current copy. He'd watched it grow beyond the proportions he'd initially anticipated, though always from afar – from the sidelines of second-hand copies fed to him as the small preparatory team headed by the ex-priest did its work.

Today's meeting was the first he'd seen of the document's final form, and the first occasion he'd had to be shown it by the author himself.

Emil took his eyes from the sheet of A4 paper on which the text was printed in neat, twelve-point Arial font. Beneath it was another sheet covered in pencil scrawls of Akkadian cuneiform symbols which Laurence's team, in conjunction with qualified helpers, had been working on for weeks.

'The translation will stand up?' he finally asked. Laurence's old features remained emotionless as he nodded slightly.

'We've had a doctoral researcher from Canada working on it since we reached a final text,' he said. 'He's a bright young thing in the field, doing his research in the language from the high period of 1000 to 1500 BCE. There's no one out there who knows the language as well as he does.' He paused, stared directly into Emil's waiting eyes. What passed unspoken between them was the knowledge that this helper could not be allowed to survive his contribution to their efforts. There could be no loose ends. Not once things went public.

'As linguistics go, it's a perfect fake.'

Emil let his eyes fall back to the pages, swapping the printout for the cuneiform draft. He had worked with a few Akkadian items during his tenure at the Vatican Archives, though the language had never been a speciality of his. He recognised a few glyphs here and there – enough to know it wasn't gibberish.

That alone put him miles ahead of ninety-nine percent of the population, who were the main targets for the writing. The average member of the Italian populace wouldn't know Akkadian from Klingon. They would believe it said what it said, because someone would tell them.

It was the other one percent that was the worry. Italy grew scholars of antiquity like a field grew weeds, only without the benefit of pesticides to eradicate the excess. The text had to be convincing enough that they would buy it, or at least to keep them occupied and working long enough to give Emil his window.

'We've ensured the English version that will get circulated contains a few minor errors,' Laurence added, sounding pleased with this particular point.

'Errors?'

'Small things,' the other man explained. 'A few variations of tense, a mixing up of insignificant vocabulary here and there. That type of stuff.'

'Why?'

Finally, the tiniest smile. The first show of emotion on the ex-cleric's face. 'Because a few errors make it more believable. We can't have a perfect translation right out of the gate – that never happens. It would be suspicious. Give the translators out there a few errors to fuss over. They'll trip over themselves to correct each other's punctuation and tense shifts. It'll keep them focused on that rather than provenance and things that really matter. Then we can release our own translation, correct, with all its "divine origin", when the time comes.'

Emil absorbed the comment, nodded. Laurence had proven himself more than capable, thinking through dimensions of the project that hadn't even occurred to Emil. He was a gem of a find.

But there was one issue that still troubled him.

'Do there really need to be so many?' Emil asked abruptly. He shuffled the pages in his hands so that the printed translation was again on top. 'It's far more than we need.'

Laurence kept his gaze level. Emil's face, rather than the papers, attracted his stare.

'It's a symbolic number. In this kind of document, symbolism is everything.'

'But there were ten plagues in Egypt,' Emil countered, meeting Laurence's stare. 'If you were going to go for overkill, why not go all the way for the traditional count?'

'Mirroring shouldn't be our aim,' he answered. 'We want allusions, not exact parallels. So we engage with the first – the water of the Nile turning to blood – but we go our own way with the second. Unless . . .' he hesitated, a wry smile on his lips, 'unless you wish somehow to concoct an infestation of frogs?'

Emil tried to smile back, though his focus wouldn't let him.

'Little twists here and there,' Laurence continued, 'to let us do what you need done.'

'But seven?' Emil asked. 'I only need three or four.'

'Seven is a good biblical number, especially for Christians. Seven days of creation, the number of cosmic and divine perfection—'

'I know the symbolism, *Father*.' Emil stressed the man's former title in annoyance.

'Then you should have no trouble seeing why it would be helpful in selling this little dream to the kind of audience you want to receive it.' Laurence leaned forward. 'Every little helps, Emil.'

He huffed. 'Understood. Still, it's more than I was anticipating. I'm not sure we'll be able to pull them all off.'

'Oh, you won't go through with all of them,' Laurence answered confidently, sitting back. 'I haven't modified your plans that much. Only carrying out the first few will be necessary. The rest are there simply to build expectation.' He paused, and when his voice returned it had a bemused air that even the conspiratorial tone of their conversation couldn't mask.

'I mean, come on, Emil. Even you couldn't blot out the sun.'

Their conversation went on for another twenty minutes, Laurence describing in detail each of the plagues that the text articulated, together with the means that he and Emil's technical crews had worked out for accomplishing those that would actually be brought to life. The longer Emil listened, the more confident he became in the preparations, and the more poetic the text began to feel.

Once there had been ten plagues, now there would be seven. And they would roll off the lips of a populace to whom he would feed, line by line, this new message from 'antiquity'.

He read the text over again, allowing its contents to resonate and slip into his memory like some sacred song.

When his eyes at last returned to Laurence, the smile had finally come.

'This is good, very good. Everything up to the fifth plague.'

Laurence leaned forward. 'You don't like the final two?'

'I think we can do better.' The words weren't a condemnation, and Emil's smile had only broadened. 'I mean, if we're going to go big, let's go big.'

'How . . . big?' Laurence asked.

Emil rose from his desk. He was growing to like this man, and suddenly felt as if the two of them needed to share a drink and enjoy these moments for the grandeur they truly represented. He walked to a small shelf, uncapped a bottle, and poured them each a neat drink.

'Join me,' he said, and handed Laurence one of the glasses. And then, back to their task, 'Let's go all the way.'

44

Emil's home office

Alone in his office when the drinks were done and plagues six and seven had been decided upon, Emil was afforded something that had become a rarity since his plans had begun to take shape in earnest: a moment of peace and solitude. He was by nature a man who favoured quiet over noise, who disliked idle chit-chat as much as he was perfectly content to run a meeting or speak his will to others. The constant stream of conversations that had been necessary over the past weeks were not idle, and so they didn't really bother him; but he was still happy with the moments of quiet that seemed like rarer and rarer gems scattered throughout his days.

All this talk of religion, of plagues, it was the worst sort of conversation. Not that he didn't enjoy his time with Laurence – the old man had a cynicism and boldness about him that Emil admired, combined with a deviousness that he hadn't expected. His departure from the priesthood had left him poor in addition to resentful, with few prospects for anything approximating a comfortable future, so when Emil had been able to promise him a complete change of circumstances, and a remainder to his life that could be lived in a kind of luxury Laurence had never known, the older man had committed whole-heartedly to the project.

Still, the theme they had to address was one neither of them cared for. Prophecy was the very heart of the plan Emil had concocted that first afternoon when the idea of the operation that would change his life had occurred to him. The key to it all. But what a foul-smelling key! The idea that grown men, seemingly intelligent by most other standards, could actually believe that God spoke to them – that a divine voice would so spend its time as to dictate things as mundane as the colour of rivers or changes in the weather – it was the height of absurdity. If a god existed at all, surely he would just fix the earth or destroy it. Those had always seemed like the only reasonable options Emil would consider, were he ever in a divinity's shoes. Make things better, or wipe them out and start over. What kind of god would be so whimsical and inefficient as to expend his voice and will to send . . . frogs? That's what it had been in Egypt. And then, bugs?

Fucking insects. Emil simply couldn't fathom people who would believe these things and then go on worshipping a god of 'power and might'. Not when what was billed as one of the fiercest shows of his power in the Old Testament was a 'plague' that could have been overcome with a good batch of insecticide.

But the fact was that there *were* people who believed these things. More than believed them: there were people who lived in the light of such ideas. Who saw the evidence of God speaking in the past, and fervently believed he did so still. Who waited for his words. Who heard them in the mouths of their teachers, in headlines in the news, in the songs of children. Christ, their god seemed to talk everywhere. Everything was a revelation, everything a prophecy.

Vacuous, stupid – and precisely what Emil needed.

All the more reason he needed to get it right. There was a way these people spoke, and a way they expected God to speak. If he was, for a moment, to play the part of the divinity, he needed to get his voice right.

Of course, Emil's interests were far less divine than theirs. God only knew what today's ranks of charismatics, Pentecostalists and revelation-ready believers thought God was actually leading them towards through his apparitions on a slice of toast and appearance in watermarks on the underside of a bridge. Spiritual enlightenment? A better world? Peace and love and . . . the notions became more sickly and annoying as he listed them in his mind.

Emil's interests were more base. The minds and hearts of the masses had never appealed to him, and Emil had never fancied himself a prophet, had never desired to play the part of a religious leader or to develop a cult of followers. Yet since his life in legitimate scholarship had been stolen from him, he had fancied himself one thing – one thing that, to his mind, stood higher than a prophet or leader or voice of the people.

A man with the power and wit to get what he deserved.

If what was deserved was not going to be given, it would be taken. And Emil would take far, far more than anyone would expect.

But as any good thief knows, the art of the heist rests in a key ingredient never to be overlooked or ignored.

Distraction.

Emil phoned Laurence at the end of a thoughtful silence. The old man didn't like to speak on his mobile, being 'of too different a generation to care for that sort of thing', but he answered when it rang.

'We forgot to discuss one thing,' Emil said abruptly. 'The next step.'

Laurence hesitated only slightly.

'Next?'

'Now that we've decided on the plagues, what's next on the to-do list?'

'Nothing,' Laurence answered. 'The planning is done. There's nothing left to be done but to turn something new into something old.'

Whether the pause that prefaced his next words was meant for dramatic impact or not, it had that effect on Emil.

'The tablet,' Laurence said, 'is ready for its inscription.'

PART SIX

Death

45

The hotel at which Ben and Angelina eventually arrived was just what she'd wanted. Nothing too big, and nicely out of the way. She didn't want to risk the exposure of staying in one of Rome's enormous tourist establishments, and she'd had enough of narrow dodges in side streets to want to avoid the economy dives that lined every alleyway in the tourist-trap city. The pompously named Hotel Majestic was ideally in-between: a boutique establishment with just over forty rooms, a plain exterior, and a nice classical air inside. It was also exorbitantly expensive, as Angelina recalled as soon as the name registered in her memory – one of the finer, more reclusive hotels of Rome. That, too, was reassuring. The higher the price, the more private the city's establishments tended to be. She didn't exactly have money to spare on such a place, but she figured that narrowly escaping being shot justified going beyond budget for the sake of security and privacy.

The hotel had looked as welcoming as home when the

swearing taxi driver had deposited them outside its front entrance. He'd offered a final barrage of profanities, to the brow-raised surprise of the genteel hotel doorman who stepped out of brass-framed doors to meet them at the kerb, but seeing that no more cash was forthcoming from his unwelcome clients, the driver eventually slammed his foot against the accelerator once again and sped away. The power outage that had affected the city had ended some time during their drive – Angelina had no idea what had been its cause or its resolution – and the hotel glowed beyond an orange-lit frontage.

Angelina had laid down her card at reception, extracted from her wallet before they'd entered so she could keep her handbag at her side, carefully laid against her leg in an attempt to conceal the tear in her trousers and the congealing blood of the wound beneath it. Fortunately, the reception counter was high, its old-fashioned oak buffed to an impossible shine, and the overly made-up receptionist uninterested in anything other than entering the new booking details into her computer, now that 'the bloody ancient thing is actually running again'. With only a few minutes of negotiation Angelina had arranged a queen room for them to share. The hotel's stock of family rooms with multiple beds was, it seemed, fully booked for the night.

'We're going to stay . . . together?' Ben had asked. His sudden shyness and visible embarrassment marked yet another shift in his oscillating demeanour. It was quaint to see him so concerned about the propriety of their lodgings, having just having survived a gun chase in the darkness. For a heartbeat Angelina wondered whether it wouldn't be more merciful to the man to go somewhere else and get them separate lodgings, but the simple fact was she felt safer together, and that outweighed any discomfort Ben might feel with the situation. She didn't give him time to argue before confirming the arrangements and accepting their key – the old-fashioned type, forged of brass, attached to a large leather tassel.

The room, situated on the fourth floor and accessed by an ancient elevator which they used despite the bellboy's concerns that the power might go out again, was spacious and comfortable. It was done out almost entirely in pure, glowing white: white bedposts and linens, white fabric chairs, white enamel desk in front of three thicknesses of white curtains over the windows. Even the doors were painted gloss white, the whole room accentuated by numerous floor-to-ceiling mirrors that made it appear larger than it was. Angelina didn't think she'd ever been in a hotel room quite so fine, though she also wasn't certain that, if these were the decorating tastes of the uber-wealthy, she'd been missing all that much.

The first fifteen minutes of their stay were dedicated to treating Angelina's wound. Terrified of staining the white bedsheets with blood and facing the interrogation that would ultimately result with the staff, she'd perched herself on the edge of the porcelain bathtub and gingerly slid off her trousers. If the thought of lodging together had caused Ben to blush, seeing her in her pants, the colour of bare flesh reflected again and again through the ricocheting angle of the mirrors, turned him almost as red as the wound in Angelina's leg.

'Take a closer look, please,' she said, ignoring his discomfort, 'now that the light's better.'

Ben did as instructed, trying to keep his eyes focused only on the injury. Gently, he treated the wound with warm water and soap, followed by a good dose of disinfectant and an antibacterial cream obtained from a first-aid kit he discovered in one of the drawers beneath the sink. As he had rightly suggested in the car, the wound was superficial. The bullet had scraped across Angelina's flesh at a downward angle from her knee, tracing a red line of blistered skin and raw flesh about three centimetres across her calf, but the heat of the bullet had mostly cauterised the wound as it was formed. As long as it didn't get infected, it would be a cause of pain but no real harm.

Fifteen minutes after he'd begun, the wound was treated, covered in gauze that Ben had taped firmly to her skin.

'Are there any waterproof plasters in there?' Angelina asked, motioning towards the first-aid kit.

'Waterproof?' Ben shuffled through the contents, finally locating two paper packets containing large, square plasters made of nylon and marked as water resistant. 'Planning on going swimming sometime soon?' She was still half nude, and without the work on her wound to distract him, the joke seemed designed to make the situation feel less awkward.

Angelina smiled, motioning him to unwrap one of the plasters and put it on.

'No swimming,' she answered, 'but I'd give my right arm for a shower.'

Minutes later, Angelina was standing in the tub beneath a hot flow of water, allowing its steady streams to wash away layers of sweat, adrenaline, dirt and fear. She cranked the lever as far towards 'Hot' as it would go, steam soaring off her body as water met skin and evaporated into the thick air.

She'd taken a double dose of paracetamol before opening the tap, and she could feel the drug begin to come to life in her blood as the water calmed her from the outside. For the first time that day, Angelina felt safe.

Getting into the shower had involved stripping out of the remainder of the clothes she'd worn all day – through both chases, her kidnap and her injury. In the bright surroundings of the bathroom, Angelina had realised how filthy she looked; but she hadn't exactly left home this morning anticipating a hotel stay or the inability to return to her wardrobe, so the only clothes she had were those on her body.

The hotel offered a six-hour wash and pressing service, advertised on a clipped hanger in the cupboard space, and as Angelina had undressed she'd funnelled all her dirty attire into the attached plastic bag. She'd taken a few moments to rinse her trousers off in the tub before she added them, to remove the blood that would surely arouse suspicion if it appeared in the downstairs laundry. The room she'd booked for her and Ben came with two plush – and, unsurprisingly, entirely white – bathrobes hanging behind the door, and she would have to do with that until her clothes came back clean.

Ben would have to do the same. No blood, in his case, but the same tensions, sweat and panic of the day.

She let the thought slip away from her as the water fell from the broad rain-style head goosenecked above her. For the first time today she allowed herself not to think, and was grateful that the inner voice that so often scolded, pondered and dwelt on the minutiae of her life was content for the moment to be silent. She wanted just to feel the heat against her flesh and the steam in her nostrils, as the tension, little by little, began to melt away.

Ben sat at the absurdly white desk, its lamp switched on, and stared down at his mobile phone. He'd connected it to the charger a few minutes ago, but it hadn't yet taken in enough juice to come back to life. In the bright room, its display seemed all the more black.

It meant he couldn't look at the photographs it contained, which had been his hope, but Ben realised even as he sat without them that the imagery was still fresh in his mind from the glances he'd caught over Angelina's shoulder in the taxi. Not precise, of course, or exact. Ben certainly didn't have a photographic memory – he'd always thought the idea more myth than reality – though his ability for recall was better than many. Yet what was truly significant in this moment was that he didn't need it.

The contents the tablet were familiar, and not from seeing its surface.

The hotel provided a small pad of notepaper and a plastic biro emblazoned with 'Hotel Majestic' in gold lettering, and Ben twisted it open and dropped its tip to the paper.

He could remember what the tablet predicted. The words were within him. What was their order?

The discoverer would die.

That was first, and as of a few hours ago he knew its message hadn't been idle. He jotted down 'discoverer's death'.

The one that came next had been obvious to the world.

The river.

He wrote it down as well, just the two words. Then, on the next line, the most recent of the plagues.

Darkness, in a city of light.

Ben's spine stiffened as the prophecies came back to him. God, they'd inspired him as they'd first come trickling in, the way they always did in a community of inspired faith: one voice revealing a truth, joined by another, and another – until the vision of things to come took flesh and form 'and the people of God begin to see with the vision of God'. The words used by Father Alberto sounded in Ben's mind. They inspired, as they always did.

His mind flashed again to the revelations. The one that came next had always been the hardest to understand.

Fog.

The single word, drawn in his own sloppy handwriting, looked strange on the page.

And fire.

God, it was too much. Ben had never prepared himself for the possibility that these things would actually . . . *happen.* How was he going to make sense of what had been spoken, and what had now been written?

And how was he going to tell Angelina?

46

Hotel Majestic

Angelina emerged from the shower after nearly twenty minutes, making it one of the longest she'd ever taken. She'd have gone on longer, letting the water sweep away more and more of the strains of the day, but even the heat and steam couldn't wholly calm her. Eventually, her mind caught up. Soothed muscles relaxed, and without the tension that had almost been crippling before, her thoughts returned with force and began to tread over everything that had happened.

Everything that was still happening. There were still people after them. The tablet was public knowledge. And she still didn't know what any of it meant.

Her mobile remained dead, and while the 'universal' charger provided by the hotel fit Ben's phone, it didn't fit hers. Her normal first call for Internet access was out. However, Angelina had noticed as they entered the hotel that a small, well-decorated lobby off the main entrance contained a number of public computer terminals. For a few euros' payment, she could have forty-five minutes of Internet access at her disposal.

She emerged from the bathroom amidst a billow of steam that flooded out through the opened door, her towel-dried body wrapped snugly in the terrycloth robe. Ben was sitting at the room's glossy writing desk, his face angled away from her and his mind, as she'd noted routinely was the case, elsewhere.

'I'm all done,' she announced, walking across the room and throwing down the plastic laundry bag on the bed. 'The water's still warm, if you want to have a go yourself.'

Ben slowly brought himself out of his reverie. 'No, it's okay, I think I'm fine without.'

Angelina turned and gave him a full, obvious once-over with her eyes, frowning. Ben's black hair was as dishevelled as hers had been an hour ago, its mid-length locks clumped together with sweat. He'd ditched his bloodstained jacket back at the Vatican, but the wet wipe she'd provided for his face had missed a few spots, now speckled by reddish-brown flakes that clung awkwardly to a full day's stubble. His shirt had escaped the spray of blood, but the marks under his arms were enormous, dark pools and a line of sweat ran down his spine.

'I really think, Dr Verdyx,' Angelina announced formally, 'that a shower would be a good idea. We're going to have to be seen in public in the morning, and, well . . .' She swivelled him to face a mirror next to the desk, allowing him to see his appearance directly. The change in his expression was acknowledgement enough that it wasn't the most inspiring of sights.

'To be honest,' Angelina continued, 'a shave wouldn't hurt you, either. There's a kit on the bathroom counter.'

He nodded, returned a faint smile. As they had all afternoon, his emotions seemed to alternate fluidly between fear, friendliness and whatever plane he slipped off to when he was in between.

Ben rose and walked towards the bathroom, beginning to unbutton his shirt.

'There's a second robe hanging behind the main room door,' Angelina instructed, pointing towards it. 'I'll add your clothes into the bag with mine. They'll be cleaned by the time we get up in the morning.'

He entered the bathroom, closing the white door behind him. But Angelina stopped it before it could click shut, pushing back.

'Now, please.' She held out her hands, pointing towards his clothes. 'I'm going down to the lobby for some Internet access. I'll drop them off on my way.'

Ben blushed again, and Angelina walked back into the centre of the room to wait.

Behind her, the bathroom door remained ajar. It took a few moments for Angelina to realise that she was staring, not at the door itself but at one of the many reflections that bounced off the multitude of mirrors in the room. The light that came from the bathroom entrance was tantalising, steam still flowing out in the wake of Angelina's shower. As it cleared, she caught a glimpse of Ben reflected in yet another mirror. His shirt was off and he was at work unbuttoning his trousers. He was partially hidden by the door, but Angelina caught enough of a view to see that he was surprisingly fit. His chest was almost hairless, but not quite, the delineation of his muscles clear. His shy demeanour and professionally drab clothes hid his body well.

Angelina caught herself, jerking her eyes away before any more of his body was exposed to her gaze. She was surprised with herself. Not because she'd caught an illicit glance at a man she'd never thought of in anything close to physical terms, but because she found herself feeling . . . almost interested.

She forced her thoughts to a halt. This was absurd. Angelina didn't feel this way. About anyone.

She glanced around the room for something to distract her from the unexpected heat rising inside her.

On the desk was a small tablet of paper, and Angelina realised it might be useful for taking down notes when she was at the computer downstairs. Walking over to the desk, she noticed Ben had scribbled a few lines on the top page, but he would hardly mind if she took the remainder while he showered. She tore off the top page and left it next to his phone, then shoved the tablet into one of the plush pockets of her robe.

'Here you go.' Ben's voice sounded from the bathroom and Angelina approached. The door opened more broadly, and Angelina saw he'd wrapped himself in a towel. He held his clothes in his hands and lifted them towards her. She grabbed the plastic bag, held it open, and let him drop them in.

'Er, thanks,' Ben said awkwardly, now standing exposed in nothing but the towel.

'The water's good and hot,' she answered, purposefully looking past him, 'and the shower gel's got mint in it, I think.' *Got mint in it? Christ!*

He smiled, she thought, because she realised she was spinning away, embarrassed.

'I'll be downstairs,' was all she said as she walked away, leaving the room with key in hand and hearing the door click closed behind her.

At reception, Angelina handed over the bag of their dirty laundry and agreed to whatever overinflated rates they would charge to have it washed and ironed by morning, then paid for forty-five minutes' Internet access in the lobby. If the woman at reception was shocked to see a guest milling through the chandelier-lit, burgundy-carpeted surroundings in a bathrobe, she didn't show it. Maybe this wasn't an entirely abnormal event in posh hotels.

Angelina situated herself at one of the small desks and entered the hotel credentials into the computer. Seconds later, a web browser automatically opened in the middle of the screen and Angelina set to work.

She spent a few minutes scouring the web for information about the circumstances of the day. There was still no explanation for the changing colour of the water, and nothing official about the power outage which she learned had taken in the entire city – a feat modern technology and something called 'auto-redundant grid layouts' was supposed to have made impossible. Yet, it seemed that there were very few people – at least, those who spent time on the Internet – who weren't speculating on both events having something to do with what site after site called 'the prophecy'.

Angelina instinctively recoiled at the title, as she always did at the human tendency to see divine, miraculous meaning behind simple events it couldn't explain. Why was ignorance so hard to acknowledge? Not to know something – it wasn't a sign of weakness, simply a sign that there is something yet to learn. Yet humanity seemed hell-bent on attributing every new corner of its lack of understanding to the supernatural, until forcibly proved otherwise. And, just like her tour groups generally receiving the correction of their misperceptions only grudgingly, the race as a whole proved singularly unwilling to accept the truth, even once it became incontrovertible.

Nevertheless, prophecy had become the word of the day. If the morning's events with the river had stirred up the ranks of the sign- and vision-happy, the evening's had fully brought out the host of the conspiracy minded. There wasn't a search phrase Angelina could enter that didn't garner a stream of blog entries and video clips offering increasingly wild theories as to just what the hell was going on in Rome.

One group's contributions, in particular, seemed to be at

the top of all results. They had posted just a single video, and Angelina could only bring herself to watch the first few seconds of it before closing the window in disgust. Charismatically minded religious nuts boasting revelation and predicting plagues and the end of the age. *God, if I haven't heard that line before.*

She had more concrete things on which to focus.

The most important was contained in the message she knew would be waiting for her. The email she'd sent herself from Ben's phone had, thank God, arrived before the device had lost power, and had managed to catch the cellular network as it came back online. Angelina switched from browsing for news to scrutinising the photograph of the tablet in her inbox. She didn't know how, but she couldn't help but feel that this tablet was a key to understanding what was going on.

She printed out two copies, one in colour and one in black-and-white for contrast, and scrutinised the text as thoroughly as her nerves and the available resources would allow. She had none of her books with her, but – God bless the Internet – she had access to a host of online lexical and morphological tools, which enabled her to search through databases and seek out guidance on the symbols. The language was far from simple. Whole sentences didn't come easily or automatically. Instead, key words, phrases, started to leap out from the scrawl of indentations.

She jotted down her notes in hotel pencil on the margins of the colour printout as she worked. Word by word, the text was starting to appear.

And through all that she still couldn't discern about it, a few things made themselves clear. It was remarkable. And unpredictable. And utterly bizarre.

Via Tina di Lorenzo, north-eastern Rome

'What do you mean, her signal's *gone*?'

'It went dead more than an hour ago. When she was just around here.' Pietro placed a greasy finger on the massive display in front of him. It landed on an intersection marked in a multi-colour map of central Rome.

Vico snorted, angry. 'You told me you could track her signal despite the power cut, even if her phone was switched off.'

'Off, yes,' Pietro answered, 'but not dead. There has to be some juice leaking into the system. It had been off before, but it was here that it lost power entirely.'

Vico wanted to slap the other man, but these were facts he already knew and for which he could hardly blame him. Mobiles continued to feed a slow trickle of power into their essential systems when asleep or even, in most cases, powered down. Those systems made it possible for them to be tracked even when they were switched off, which was what made the whole cellular infrastructure such a godsend for people like him. People could be followed anywhere. Always.

But if a phone was genuinely dead, with a battery removed or truly out of juice altogether – well, the system wasn't magic.

'Hold on.' Corso's soft voice suddenly emerged from his corner of the room, drawing Vico's attention.

'What is it?'

'Someone is . . .' He sounded unsure of himself. But then, 'Yes, yes.' He looked up at the other two men. 'Someone is searching the Net for Akkadian.'

Vico straightened, but he held back any overt enthusiasm. 'I would think everyone would be searching it, by now. The photo of the tablet is out there, in the public – it was released through Vatican channels. Even with a translation, people will still be curious about the original.'

'This is more than just browsing the news or general word searches on a theme,' Corso answered. 'These are real queries, with access to lexical databases. Scholarly resources.'

Vico slowly moved towards him.

'What sort of queries?'

'They started out as what appeared just to be casual surfing of news sites carrying stories about the tablet,' Corso said. 'There's a buzz about them now the power's back on, and our code on all the servers carrying them shoots us the IP and ping trail of everyone who visits the pages.' He didn't remove his eyes from the screen as he spoke, his hands multi-tasking during the narrative. Vico loomed over him, his daunting six-foot-seven-inch height accentuated by a pole-like frame.

'We're getting thousands of similar reads an hour,' Corso continued. 'But the algorithms Pietro coded are doing a great job of monitoring each IP to see if subsequent online activity suggests anything more than casual interest.' He nodded in the third man's direction, and the other coder simply shrugged at the recognition.

'However,' Corso added, raising a hand from his mouse to point at an IP trail he'd highlighted on his screen, 'then there's this one.'

Vico adjusted his glasses and leaned forward. A large window contained a text-based log of the web sites accessed by the flagged IP address since, and simultaneous to, viewing the various stories about the tablet.

'Shit,' he mumbled.

'Yeah, that's what I said.' Corso smiled. He'd done his work well. 'Then the same IP started accessing a morphological analysis database hosted at Tufts University in the USA.'

'Morphological analysis?'

'It's an online tool that lets you input various cuneiform symbols and it analyses grammatical forms, variant readings, comparisons with other texts, that kind of thing. Really quite advanced.'

'Fuck.' Vico's breath exhaled slowly.

'And yes, to answer your next question, it definitely allows for searches in Akkadian.'

'Fuck, fuck, fuck.' Vico began to pace the expanse of their little room. Then he spun towards Corso.

'I presume you can locate the IP source?'

'I can do you one better than that,' his friend answered, his grin now covering the whole of his pockmarked face, 'and give you something more. The IP address traces to a public terminal in a hotel, here in the city.' He picked up a tablet on which he'd already scribbled down an address.

'And the something more?' Vico asked.

'The morphological analysis database I mentioned? It requires access credentials to log in.'

Vico's face brightened as he realised what this meant.

'They were easy enough to hack,' Corso confirmed. 'The person who logged in from the IP address of a computer in that hotel, a few minutes ago, is Dr Angelina Calla.'

47

St Peter's Square
Vatican City

The whole of the famous circular piazza had been cordoned off by uniformed members of the Swiss Guard for the past two hours. A handful in their ceremonial garb still stood at their official posts with halberds and pikes in hand, guarding the main points of access to the papal quarters as they had for hundreds of years, but the mass of their fellow Guardsmen were in combat uniform: navy fabric tailored much closer to their bodies for unobstructed movement and their halberds replaced with Swiss Arms SG550s and Heckler & Koch MP5s.

They had taken up positions around the square in a formation that had been practised and rehearsed dozens of times by each of them. The moment that the general alarm was sounded and the piazza identified as the focal point of instruction – with the extra code 1187 broadcast over their earpieces, indicating active gunfire – the procedure had been automatic and efficient. Two teams swept into the Palace to encapsulate the Pope in a protective enclave three layers deep. His location was always known through a small broadcasting microchip woven into each of the three white cassocks he wore in public, as well as into his bedclothes and any other items he might wear in private settings, and there were always at least four Guardsmen within earshot of the Supreme Pontiff. At this moment, there were more than a dozen.

Outside, the three fully armed SWAT-style teams had ringed off the city-state: two taking up positions round the whole of the piazza, while another divided up and supplemented the usual presence at each of the access points to Vatican City. Until the situation was cleared, God's earthly city was closed to the world.

Filtering out the few terrified pilgrims who had remained as the Guard locked down the piazza had been made easier by the fact that the city-wide blackout, which then had still rendered the whole area dark, had greatly reduced the number of visitors in the large space. The gunshots themselves had depleted it significantly more, as everyone in earshot had run for all they were worth. By the time the Guard arrived en masse, supplementing the ten who were always in position at or near the square and who had sprung into action immediately, the piazza was almost empty.

That had been two hours ago. Since then the power across the city had come back on, each person in the square had been photographed by the Guard and interviewed prior to being permitted to leave, and pressure was mounting to reopen the 'borders' between Rome and the Vatican: the few streets, gates and public access points which were in most cases also major arteries of movement through the city.

But Hans Heinrich had no intention of recommending to his superiors that they be reopened until he had more material to work with.

The same generators that had earlier been called into service to power the Swiss Guard's operations centre hardwired electric current not only into their bunker-like underground compound, but also to certain vital security systems throughout Vatican City. These included the CCTV cameras and security equipment in the papal chambers and offices, ensuring that the Guard had access to the systems used to ensure the Pontiff's safety at all times. They also included cameras positioned along all the feasible escape routes from Vatican City, in case in some sort of attack situation the Guard would be required to secrete the Pope away to safety – permitting them to see their paths and choose the best available option.

They also included the CCTV cameras aimed around St Peter's Square.

'The gunshots were reported after the power outage, correct?' Heinrich had asked his men once their equipment had been operational on the generators.

'That's right.'

'If it was more than a few minutes after,' he'd continued, 'then that means the cameras would have been back online already.'

His colleague had immediately understood where Heinrich was going, and began to pull up the feeds from the piazza on his monitor. There were fourteen of them in total, covering every square metre of space, but only four had night-vision infrared capacity. Normally it wasn't required, even at night, as the square was always kept well lit and all the cameras were more than adequate in such settings. Tonight, however, they were the only four that mattered.

It had taken a bit of searching, zooming and filtering, but after a few hours of work, Heinrich had what he wanted.

He had video of the attackers: two men with guns drawn. And he had enlarged stills of their faces, which, taking into account the circumstances, were surprisingly clear.

They should be more than enough to run through facial recognition software.

Heinrich finally had something concrete to go on.

48

When her time on the public Internet terminal was up, Angelina returned to the hotel room. Her left leg was throbbing beneath the bandages Ben had affixed, but at least the painkillers were muting the effect a little. She tried not to demonstrate her limp as she walked across the lobby to the lift and made her way back to room 402. Behind her the few guests in the lobby were huddled together in small groups, seemingly still fazed by what had been going on throughout the day and night. *A tension*, Angelina's thoughts noted, *a tension real and concrete in the air.* Lord knew she could feel it, too.

As the brass key rotated in her grip and she pushed open the heavy door, she could immediately hear the sounds of Ben's shower coming to its end. The flow of water stopped, and the familiar sound of a towel being slid off a rack echoed from tiled floors and gloss-painted walls. As Angelina closed the door behind her, she noticed that the bathroom door across the room was still ajar, steam leaking out in softly rolling billows.

'I got the shot of the tablet,' she announced, deciding quickly that it was best to let Ben know she was back in the room in case he'd thought his surroundings a little more private than they actually were. 'Came through on the email. Decent resolution. I printed out a couple of copies.'

'That's great,' Ben answered from within his cloud of steam. She could hear the motions of a body being towelled off. 'Were you able to translate it?' he asked.

'Parts of it. You know how it goes.' Ben Verdyx was one of the few other people in the world who, indeed, did. 'It's not easy to piece together all the symbols, and many words didn't come up in the online databases. Still, I managed a fair amount. And the craziest thing of all: there's a translation already out there on the Net.'

'A translation?' Ben was audibly startled.

'Cardinal Forte told us the tablet had been released to the public,' Angelina answered. 'Apparently, so was a translation. I don't know who could have done it, but I got a copy and compared it to my notes. Seems to line up pretty well with the pieces I was able to translate myself just now. Not perfect, but you know.'

The towelling sounds resumed. 'Anything else?'

'The Internet's abuzz, of course,' Angelina answered. She sat herself down at the small writing desk, depositing her printouts and the notepad she'd used. 'All sorts of crazies out there trying to make links to prophets and revelations. Christ, the day's barely over.'

Ben said nothing. A moment later, he emerged from the bathroom with the towel now wrapped around his waist. His hair, still wet, glistened atop his head, and Angelina found herself puzzlingly unsure how to look at him without staring.

She forced her eyes to bore into his.

'Er, sorry,' Ben said uncomfortably. 'I, uh, forgot to grab the robe before I went in.' He reached to the back of the room door and grabbed the terrycloth robe still hanging there, then stepped back into the bathroom with a bit more haste than the move required.

Angelina shook her head. It was not at all helpful to find she was attracted to the body in the other room. She had texts and bullets and kidnappings to worry about; she didn't need another distraction.

Hell, woman, what's wrong with you?

She peered down at the desk, urgently seeking a distraction. The night together was going to be more challenging than she'd first thought. Maybe separate rooms *would* have been a good idea.

The printouts of the tablet lay in front of her, the notepad on top. To their left, the single sheet on which Ben had scribbled a few words earlier. Her eyes wandered towards the page, noting the angular nature of his penmanship, which would count as sloppy by even the most generous of assessments.

Yet the uneven strokes and loops eventually revealed themselves as words, and it was when Angelina read those words that her skin started to tingle again – this time, not from the steam of the shower or the rising sensations of unexpected lust.

She bolted forward in her seat, grabbed the single sheet of paper in both hands. Ben had jotted only a few words there.

Words that Angelina knew.

Words that Ben could not.

She read them again, and again, and again. As she did, her blood went cold.

Seconds later, Ben re-emerged from the bathroom, this time snugly wrapped in a robe that exactly matched Angelina's, his features clean-shaven. He looked refreshed, even something approaching confident, as he strolled from the steaming bathroom, but within an instant, his confidence was shattered and his gait frozen.

'What the hell is this?' Angelina demanded, bursting up from her seat. The sheet of paper on which Ben had written his notes was clutched in her grasp. 'What the *fucking hell* is this?'

Her face was fierce, her skin almost matching her hair's redness. The vision jolted Ben. He'd never before seen her – or anyone – in such a state.

'I'm not sure what you me—'

'How are you involved, Ben?' Her accusation cut across his faltering reply. 'In everything that's going on? *How are you involved?*'

Ben went cold from his core to his skin. Angelina had discovered something. She knew . . . something.

'I'm not going to bloody ask you again!' she nearly shouted, controlling her volume only when she remembered they were still in a hotel room and too loud a cry would be noticed by others. 'Tell me how you know these things!' she demanded, brandishing his page. 'These words that I've just translated off a tablet neither of us had seen before, but which you clearly knew beforehand!'

It was clear that Ben was going to have to face this moment.

'I'm not . . . *involved*,' he said hesitantly, repeating Angelina's accusation. 'I was just . . . just . . .' His skin paled as he fumbled for words, threatening to match the bleached palette of his robe.

'You were just *what?*' Angelina demanded.

'I was . . . forewarned.'

49

Hotel Majestic

Angelina glowered at Ben, fury and confusion blending within her into a mixture she couldn't grasp.

'What is that supposed to mean, you were "forewarned"?' Her tone telegraphed her incredulity. 'These words you've written here – "river", "darkness", "fog", "fire" – shit, Ben, they're the key words from the tablet!' Her pitch ascended as her anger unfolded. 'There's no way you could know that, Ben! Not unless you've seen a hell of a lot more of this tablet than you let on before!' With her free hand she reached down and swiped up one of the printouts she'd made down-stairs, shaking it accusingly at him.

Ben's face looked as if it might burst in a befuddled mixture of surprise, shame, anxiety and shock. He walked slowly to the centre of the room and sat down on the edge of the bed.

'Until you and I were in the bunker a few hours ago, I'd only ever seen the first four lines, just as I said when we were with the Guards.'

'Bullshit!' Angelina shot back. 'These words, these phrases, they're not contained in the opening. They're spaced out through the contents.'

'I told you, I was—'

'Yes, *forewarned*! I don't buy it, Ben. You've either seen this text before, and for some reason you're hiding that fact from me, or you were involved in . . . in . . .'

'Angelina—'

'In producing it.' Her features widened as the accusation emerged from her throat, the full meaning of her own words only gradually occurring to her. 'Of course,' she finally added, sinking back down into the swivel chair before the desk, her voice suddenly barely more than a whisper, 'Cardinal Forte and Major Heinrich said they suspected the tablet could have been forged. My God, Ben, you?' Her eyes were bewildered orbs as they peered deep into him. 'Forging ancient artefacts?'

'Angelina, I'm—'

'No, no, of course,' she said, speaking to herself as her gaze wandered into the distance, 'it makes sense. Who else could forge a text in Akkadian, apart from an Akkadian scholar?' Her eyes snapped back to his, fierce with the sudden awareness of betrayal. *The Swiss Guard had it right from the first.* 'As was pointed out to us today, Ben, there are only two of us in Italy.'

'Angelina, I haven't forged anything!'

'I don't believe you.' Her words were flat, emotionless. 'It's the only explanation.'

'You seem to be forgetting, I was shot at today, too!'

It was the one thing Ben could have said that could truly give Angelina pause. She sat silent, her face still accusing, but her features involuntarily softened as she considered what it meant.

He has a point. Had it not been for Angelina yanking him out of the way of one shot in particular, Ben wouldn't be here to protest his innocence.

'Then *how*, Ben,' she asked, a pleading now ripping through her voice, 'how can you explain knowing what that tablet says, if you aren't somehow caught up in it?'

Ben rubbed his palms over his terrycloth-covered thighs. His nervousness was ripe.

'There's something you don't know about me,' he finally confessed.

'Of that I'm bloody well certain!' Angelina snorted. Ben held up an open palm, his eyes pinched closed, signalling he wanted her to keep silent until he could get the truth off his chest.

'You know about my academic life,' he continued, 'my scholarship, the sorts of things one professor learns about another.'

She said nothing. Of course she knew Ben's background. It was nothing short of professional idiocy to walk into an interview without knowing personal data on the people who would be interviewing you, and Angelina had researched every member of the Vatican Secret Archives' staff before she'd gone in for her disappointing interview eighteen months earlier.

'But there's more to me than just a fixation on history and antiquity,' Ben said. 'I love it, I really do. But I'm also . . . I'm also . . .'

Anticipation of how Ben might finish the sentence was an acid churning at Angelina's insides. *A crook? A fraud? Christ, what could it be? A committed, practised liar?*

The only words Angelina truly did not expect were those that next came out of Ben's mouth.

'I'm also a . . . deeply religious man.'

She stared at him in utter disbelief. The wind of her accusations had gone from Angelina's proverbial sails, replaced by sheer confusion.

'You're a religious man.' She repeated the words slowly. Then, with increased vigour, 'What the *bloody hell* has that got to do with anything?'

'It has everything to do with our present circumstances,' Ben answered. He firmed up his posture, attempting to bring a backbone of resolve into the discussion. 'If you'll let me explain, I'll tell you how.'

Angelina took the subtle reprimand and said nothing more.

'I grew up religious,' Ben continued, what sounded like a familiar story taking up its first refrains, 'a good Catholic, like just about everyone else in this country. And I went to church, just like everyone else. Mass on Sunday mornings and Wednesday evenings. Confirmation, first Holy Communion, Sunday school. All the norms.'

Angelina noticed that the last word, 'norms', bore a tinge of resentment along with it.

'For my parents, this was normal, as for their parents it had been normal. And as for me, well, it became just that. *Normal.*' The resentment again. 'And nothing more.'

'Ben, I don't see what this has to do with—'

'But it never really did it for me,' he continued, ignoring the interruption. 'The scripted services, aesthetically beautiful as they were. The formalised ritual. The career clerics looking for the next leg up the religiously corporate ladder.'

Angelina watched as Ben's face flushed with the memories. This was clearly territory that touched him deeply, and the pain was visible in his eyes.

'By the time I'd found my way into the academic world, wonderfully detached from the nonsense of modern life, I'd grown completely disillusioned with it – with my religious background. I stopped going to Mass. I stopped saying my prayers, forgot about my rosary. And it didn't bother me, leaving those things behind. They were never really . . . me.'

He hesitated, gazing not so much at Angelina as through her.

'But something else gradually overtook me. Something I hadn't been expecting. A longing. A desire, somewhere inside of me. I can't explain it, Angelina. A desire for something *more*. God, I loved my work – I still do. It drives me. But as much as I gave myself to it, as much as I ascended through one scholarly circle to the next, I still felt this emptiness inside.'

An unease began to grow in Angelina's stomach. There was an emotional intimacy to Ben's self-confessed religiosity that went beyond stolen glances of bare flesh and muscle. He was laying open his interior world. It felt – uncomfortable.

But it was also beginning to grow redolent of so much religious-speak she'd heard before. Heard, and never liked.

'I was craving something,' Ben continued, 'even though I wasn't sure what it was. Something that would breathe a little *life* into me. And then, one afternoon,' his posture opened up as Ben's tone suddenly shifted, 'I was walking through the Quartiere Prenestino-Labicano and I chanced upon an unassuming red-brick building. I don't know what drew me in. It could only have been divine providence.'

Angelina groaned, failing to keep her innate revulsion from showing. *Divine providence*. It was a phrase she didn't expect and didn't want to hear from a respected academic.

'I walked into the Church of St Paul of the Cross that day, and my whole world changed.' Ben's features brightened with the memory. 'I'd never heard of the Catholic Charismatic Movement, never even really known about charismatic movements at all except by hearsay, but that afternoon I found a faith utterly unlike anything I'd experienced before.'

It was Angelina's turn to straighten her posture, suddenly

having more to focus on than just generic religious sentiment.

'The Church of St Paul of the Cross?'

Ben nodded, his features still beaming, but Angelina's
stomach squeezed again. A memory surfaced quickly, and it
set her on edge.

The video she'd partially watched online downstairs, of
the zealous young man reciting prophecy into a camera and
predicting that plagues would befall the city – he'd been
affiliated with the Charismatic Catholic Church of St Paul of
the Cross. She'd only heard of them a few times before – a
Pentecostal-style subset of Catholicism that believed in
personal inspiration, charismatic revival and all sorts of other
things Angelina couldn't stomach. They'd never been much
liked by mainstream Catholics, either; and that, at least,
Angelina could understand.

'Ben, this is absurdity. That group is insane!'

He shook his head, as if accustomed to this response to
the nature of his faith.

'Reality can appear insane to those who don't understand
it,' he answered. 'Our church is *unusual*, I'll give you that.
Especially in this day and age, and in this context.' He
motioned around them, signalling beyond the hotel walls to
the ancient religious formality of the city in which they lived.
'But what I discovered there, was a religion that is *alive*,
Angelina. Not dead words, but a living faith.'

'Enough, Ben!' She cut him off in frustration. 'I know the
spiel. I've heard it from a hundred religious fanatics before.'

'You're not a believer, then, I take it?' The question was
asked without any hint of accusation.

'I'm a firm believer in sanity over nonsense,' Angelina
answered. She normally wasn't so hostile to those who
believed in one religion or another, was usually more objec-
tive and reserved, but at this moment her emotions were

frayed. 'I'm a believer in what can actually be known, as opposed to what must be blindly believed.'

Ben stared into her. 'Some things can be known that go beyond what you might be able to explain.'

Angelina shook her head. 'This group, Ben . . . Charisma? Prophecy? I expected more of you. You're a scholar, a rational man! You know enough about history to know that religions come and go with the cultures that invent them – hardly someone I'd have expected to be an adherent to a faith that spoon-feeds you "revelations" and tells you you can talk to God.'

'It isn't like that,' he answered. 'But . . .' His voice dropped off.

'But what?'

'Because of everything that's happening, it's important that you understand what it *is*, even if you don't accept it.'

There was no chance of Angelina accepting anything that approximated what she knew of charismatic Christianity, but she wanted to know how this group was related to the tablet and the series of circumstances overtaking them.

'I'm not the right person to explain,' Ben finally added. 'It's better that you see for yourself.' Then, looking straight into her eyes, 'It's better that you talk to Father Alberto.'

Their conversation went on for a further twenty minutes before they reached a point where Angelina had no more questions that Ben could answer sufficiently, and he had no more to share than he felt he could without her seeing for herself the church to which he belonged, and learning how it was connected to the prophecies befalling them all.

Angelina, worn out and dispirited by the whole conversation, agreed to go and meet the priest at the head of Ben's church. Both of them, however, knew they couldn't make a move until morning came. The church was closed, transit at night was slow, and if nothing else their clothes wouldn't be ready before dawn, and travelling through the city in hotel bathrobes was hardly a realistic option.

Beyond that, they were both exhausted. The day had more than depleted even their adrenaline-spiked energy reserves, and their conversation had drained their emotions. They needed rest, and they were in the right place to get it.

'I'll take the right side of the bed, if you don't mind,' Angelina announced once they'd decided it was time to stop talking and sleep. She lifted up the thick duvet and slid underneath. Ben once again looked uncomfortable with the sleeping arrangement, but exhaustion beat down any protests. Saying nothing, he slipped beneath the covers of the other side of the bed. They both continued to wear the thick bathrobes, neither having any other options.

And so they lay, in a hotel room neither of them could afford, robed beneath the covers at the conclusion of a day of gunfire, kidnap and plagues, hoping that sleep would come and tomorrow would bring something different.

50

The next morning, before sunrise
Residential prayer meeting
House church, Via dei Zeno

The room was dimly lit, a traditional urban front room illuminated with two floor lamps, its furnishings unremarkable. A few extra chairs had been brought in from the dining room to add seating in addition to the sofa and rocking recliner. They were arranged, as usual, in as close to a circle as the space and furniture would allow.

It was nothing like the bright space of their public worship, but the house church setting was one that Thomás loved all the same. Like all members of the parish, he belonged not only to the main community which met for Masses and praise, but also to a small local 'stake', as they called it, which met together each weekday morning for fifteen minutes of prayer before they all went off to work. Even on days like today, when a full service would follow at the main church later in the morning for those able to attend, few ever missed the house church sessions as a start to their day.

On the coffee table in the midst of their circle lay the

whole revelation. Its various elements had been known to the community for months, but always in bits and pieces, as revelation usually came. In the midst of the ecstatic states achieved during true worship, when the Spirit moved within the hearts of men and women and stirred them to speak with the voice of angels and not of men, shouts had emerged that gave voice to the prophecy in various utterances. They came in the home sessions, they came in the community meetings. One man had spoken of the river. A woman's voice had revealed the colour would be of blood. And the other elements had come to them, too – night, fog, chaos, and all the rest – all had surfaced from prophetic lips at one point or another.

But now they had it all. It was concrete. The tablet that had been discovered had conveyed into their present a verification of their experience, engraved in a relic of the ancient past. Thomás was shaken to his depths by the realisation of what that meant. Something so ancient, which precisely matched the revelations God had been giving them in their heights of spiritual ecstasy . . . it was confirmation. Absolute confirmation of what he realised he'd long known to be true. The charismata of faith were real. Man really did commune with God. Truths as ancient as the world itself could be met and known – and the God who had spoken in the past was speaking in the present.

He was speaking of their future.

'This was received from friends.' The calming, sure voice was that of Giulio Selmone, a stock trader who owned the house and who was the appointed leader of their stake's weekday sessions. A moment ago, Thomás had helped him distribute the photocopies they'd received from the church office, with Father Alberto's blessing, the evening before. 'The full revelation of the tablet discovered in the mud,' he continued. 'The full revelation of . . . everything.'

They all began to read. The text was a translation, of course, presenting the ancient prophecy in their modern tongue.

Their faces lit the room as they took in its contents.

Giulio Selmone turned to an older man at his right. 'Has our message been received by those on the outside?'

The older man was the church's custodian – the man called Laurence who had helped Thomás yesterday when the first news of the prophecies coming true had been his to pass along to their priest. Laurence had been with them for the past few months, being assigned to Thomás's stake at the same time he took up his menial job in the church, and his kindness and gentility had quickly rendered him a beloved new recruit. In years he far surpassed most other members of the church, and his openness to revelation and the will of God was nothing short of extraordinary for a man 'of a previous generation'. An inspiration to everyone. Father Alberto, who was roughly Laurence's contemporary, had taken him closely under his wing, his fondness for the man openly showing.

'I'm told that people all through the city have heard our call to action,' Laurence answered. His old eyes surveyed the others in the room. 'It is a receptive populace, especially given the signs at work before them. Though as to exactly how many have heard, I may not be of the right generation to know those sorts of details.' He smiled, and the others did too. 'But Thomás was the one to give our message voice. I am sure he knows.' The custodian inclined his head kindly in Thomás's direction.

He felt a surge of pride and leaned forward. 'We recorded the messages as Father Alberto and Laurence directed us,' he answered, acknowledging that the older man, though technologically inept, had been one of the most receptive hearts to God's voice. 'It went live online about an hour after we recorded it. So far we have over seven hundred thousand views.'

He sat back. Pride would urge him to say more, but humility was a virtue that lent itself to silence.

'We are warning them,' Laurence continued, 'even if they do not wish to be warned.'

'The world may be blind,' their group leader announced, 'but it's eager to receive our visions of what will come.'

Silence overtook the group again.

Finally, Thomás asked the question that was on all their minds. 'And what is that? What's going to come next?'

'You've seen the prophecy as well as I,' Giulio answered calmly. He let his eyes fall back down to the paper, and seven other sets of eyes followed suit. He slid his finger down the lines of the complete translation, finally stopping at a single line.

Thomás strained to see where he had stopped, and when he had a bearing on the right spot, found it on his own copy of the text. He read, and re-read. The words were there, and he saw them clearly – but he didn't understand.

The group broke up moments later, dismissed by a nod from their stake leader and a few words of prayer for the day ahead. Thomás walked quietly down the steps outside the front door and turned down the street. He wouldn't go into work this morning. He would make his way towards their main church to participate in the Wednesday morning Mass and hymns of praise. Today, he felt like he needed it.

He kept the translation in his hands. He read the line again.

And again.

But understanding didn't dawn. What kind of plague was . . . fog?

51

Outside

It began in the belly of the city.

The early risers among the citizens of Rome had awoken in worry. Yesterday had brought fear. The night had elevated it. Now, in the silence and mist of the early morning, foreboding hung over the city.

Something was coming. They could feel it.

And it terrified them.

So they returned to the text that was making the rounds, predicting woes to come. They were looking ahead. They were looking at the impossibilities of their fears.

The one place they were not looking, was down.

Down, beneath the streets, beneath the pavements, to the rumbling steel arteries and vessels of a city continually pulsing with life.

So when those arteries began to rumble, they rumbled unobserved and unheard. Cars propelled by anxious drivers moved along the roadways; nervous feet tapped against cobblestone and concrete. Morning Masses for calm were sung in glorious cathedrals, and coffee brewed in a million half-ounce shots to provide its longed-for rush of the familiar. The normal.

All the while, the pressure of Rome's underground arteries grew – monumental, ferocious – until the plague gained its full momentum and reached the threshold that would transform prophecy into reality.

And then the third plague burst forth.

It burst through sewer grates, through manhole covers, through air vents and regulator valves. It seeped through the edges of modern plumbing and burst the rings of the older sort.

It came from everywhere, unfurled itself – everywhere.

And the words of the prophecy were fulfilled in the midst of the wary people:

'Then shall come the fog, which clouds the minds of the children of fallen men.'

52

Hotel Majestic

Angelina awoke abruptly. Sleep had hit her with an over-powering swiftness once she'd relaxed her body – if not her mind – into the plush covers and inviting mattress. It had come like possession: a force that overtook her, rather than gradually sidled up and made friends. Her sleep had been filled with dreams of prophets and rivers, bullets and the frailties of faith, until it left her as abruptly as it had come.

As she lifted her head from the pillows compressed beneath it, her hair was still wet.

'How long was I out?' she asked with a groggy voice, sensing movement from across the room. Ben was already up.

'You slept for almost four hours,' he answered, 'which isn't bad, considering.'

Angelina blinked open her eyes and let them adjust to the light. Ben stood a few metres from the foot of the bed, dressed in clothes that were crisp, clean rejuvenations of those he'd worn yesterday.

As she breathed in, Angelina's nostrils filled with a swirl of welcome scents. Coffee, eggs, toast.

'I thought we could both do with something to eat,' Ben said, taking note of her expression. 'Sit yourself up, it'll be easier.'

Surprised, but drawn in by the scents and the sudden awareness of a ravenous hunger, Angelina pulled herself forward, readjusted the pillows and sat upright on the bed. A moment later, Ben had laid a silver tray across her lap. An omelette dripping with melted cheese was on a plate at its centre, surrounded by a fan of sliced melon and berries, a rack of brown toast beside a tiny pot of jam, a bowl of purplish yoghurt, and a cup already filled with steaming black coffee.

'I hope they're things you eat,' Ben said, stepping away. 'I didn't know your diet, so I just guessed.'

'It's perfect,' she answered, going straight for the coffee. She couldn't think of the last time she'd actually had a meal – had it been breakfast the day before? – and at that moment would have eaten anything within arm's reach.

An enormous forkful of omelette was in her mouth a second later, the flavours milling on her tongue.

'Did you get some sleep, too?' she asked around the food.

'A couple of hours,' Ben answered. 'Adrenaline, you know. Didn't allow for much more.'

Angelina understood perfectly well. She dunked a corner of a slice of toast into the jam and added a bite to the other flavours merging in her mouth.

'Our laundry was hanging outside the door when room service brought up the food half an hour ago,' Ben added. 'I hung your things in the wardrobe. I hope you don't mind, I already ate without you.'

He motioned towards the desk. A second tray was there, its contents already devoured. Angelina looked up and smiled at him.

'Nice to know I'm not the only one with an appetite.' The

odd – no, inexplicable – tone of their conversation before sleep had not left her, but with the morning came a new energy, a new calm, and Ben's kindness was sufficient to let her overlook it for the moment.

He smiled back at her, then sat in silence at the desk, watching her eat. He let her get about halfway through the plate of food before he added, 'You should get dressed, quickly, once you've finished that.'

A tinge of energy. The emotions of yesterday started to flood back. Angelina peered at him over the rim of her coffee cup. 'Why the rush?'

Ben's eyes fell to his shoes. 'You don't want me to tell you.'

The tingle in her spine became a fire. 'Ben, what is it?'

He slowly faced her again. The same distant look she'd beheld multiple times the day before was back.

'The third plague,' Ben said flatly. 'It's already upon us.'

Somewhere between their interrogation beneath the Apostolic Palace and his revelation of belonging to what Angelina considered roughly the equivalent of a charismatic cult, she had thought she'd lost the ability to be shocked by anything that came out of Ben Verdyx's mouth. This proved that theory wrong.

She shoved aside the tray of breakfast and swung her legs over the side of the bed. 'What am I supposed to make of a comment like that, Ben?' She tightened the belt of her robe as she stood. '"Good morning, have some breakfast, then get dressed quick since a plague is upon us"? Christ, man!'

He didn't answer. Instead, he was already tearing the plastic wrappings from Angelina's laundered clothes and passing them to her, urgency in his eyes.

Infuriated, yet puzzled by his behaviour, Angelina grabbed

the clothes and marched crossly into the bathroom to put them on.

It was there that she heard the first explosion.

It was not the explosion of a firing gun she'd unwillingly become only too familiar with yesterday. This was an utterly different sound, and a feeling that went along with it. A rumbling that shook her feet, her core, and the whole room around her, even as a thumping *bang* followed by a rumble sounded in her ears.

She spread her feet immediately for balance, reaching forward and bracing her hands on the granite countertop. The boom still echoed in her ears, but gradually the rumbling stopped and the world regained its stability.

'What the hell was that?' She shot out of the bathroom, buttoning her blouse as she went.

'The third plague,' Ben said solemnly. His words were measured, if not entirely calm.

'No more about plagues!' Angelina's toleration had reached its limit.

He appeared to sense that no answer he could vocalise was going to convince her, so instead he walked over to one of the tall windows and drew back the layered curtains. He'd not opened them before, but he knew precisely what he would see.

He motioned Angelina closer.

She huffed as she approached, more disgruntled than ever at Ben's behaviour. Halting a step away from him, she glanced outside, then lowered her gaze to the street.

Another boom sounded, and this time Angelina watched as a manhole cover midway across the Via Veneto lifted up off the tarmac with explosive force and flew at least two metres in the air before clanking to the ground with a terrific, metallic thunk. Out of the black hole it had covered shot a geyser of steam, erupting into the early morning air.

But no, it wasn't steam. The gooseflesh on Angelina's back started to rise as she realised it was too thick, too solid a grey.

It billowed as the geyser reached nearly to the height of their fourth-storey window.

'You don't have to believe anything you don't want to,' Ben said forebodingly. 'You can call them chance coincidences, lies or anything else you like. But the prophecy on the tablet predicts plagues, and you know as well as I that the third is—'

'Fog.' Angelina finished his sentence. She gazed at it a moment longer, temporarily mesmerised by the curling tendrils spreading out across the street.

Then she turned to Ben.

'It's time you took me to your church.'

53

Hotel Majestic

Even if Angelina hadn't seen the explosion of fog from the sewer through their window, it would have been clear enough that something was seriously wrong as she and Ben made their way down the interweaving flights of feathered staircases to the hotel's lobby. Other guests milled around the corridors and landings, themselves aware something new was out of the ordinary, the next in a series of frightening events; and the further towards ground level they approached, the thicker the interior air of the hotel became. By the time they passed the bar level and reached reception, the air was a misty grey, and the few people that were there were clearly terrified.

The fog. The fog. The words repeated themselves in Angelina's consciousness as she moved with increasing speed. Another couple stood before them at the wooden reception desk, apparently prompted to check out early by fear of the events outside.

Events outside. She realised the mental phrase wasn't accurate. Across the lobby, one of the ancient pipes that had been covered with decades of matt paint to conceal its ascent up the wall had burst a connecting seam. Though the stream that hissed out of it was tiny, Angelina could already see that it was the same colour as the fog outside.

Outside, and in.

She turned to reception, ready to toss the room key on to the counter and walk away if their turn wasn't up, but the anxious couple in front of them had finished their strained dialogue with the receptionist and marched swiftly towards the door.

'Room 402, checking out,' she said briskly. She plopped the heavy brass key on to the counter, its tassel bouncing at its end.

'Calla, Angelina,' she added, hoping to shorten the conversation before it began.

The woman behind the desk tapped efficiently at her computer. 'Would the signora like to keep the room on the same card provided at check-in?' The clerk tried to remain all business, though there was worry in her eyes as well. The strange fog swirled around them in thick arms.

'Yes, fine. The room and the incidentals. We had some laundry, and some room service.'

Two nods confirmed the charges, and a moment later a whir accompanied a laser printer spitting out a receipt.

'We hope you enjoyed your stay, and—'

Her forced farewell continued, but Angelina had already turned away. Ben kept close to her side as they stepped out through the glass doors and into the fading darkness of morning.

All along the street, and indeed along every street on to which they turned, the scene mirrored what Angelina had witnessed from their window. Manhole covers were blown off, geysers of fog-like smoke shooting upwards; sewer drains had become exhaust vents for the rising mist; and buildings already flooded from interior plumbing bursts poured fog out of open doors and windows. The fog fell as it was released into the air, sinking down to street level and piling up in an ever thickening, dense layer.

It hovered at Angelina's knees as she and Ben turned off the Via Veneto on to the Piazza Barberini. By the time they'd walked to the end of Via delle Quattro Fontane it was near her waist. The bodies of other pedestrians, whose faces were marked by alarm, and some by outright fear, seemed as disembodied torsos hovering across the sea of mist.

It was only as they rounded a corner on to Via Marsala that they encountered the first cloud of fog that reached up to her face. She tried to alter their course to avoid it, but there was nowhere that the fog wasn't. It lined the street from edge to edge, mounting in height by the second.

She couldn't avoid breathing it in, and a new terror gripped her as she pulled the first draw of the thick substance through her nostrils. She could hear Ben gasp at her side as he was forced to do the same. Muffled screams came from further down the street, as others were confronted with the same terrifying need.

A second later, Angelina began to cough. The urge towards panic increased. Was this terrorism? An attack? Was this how her life was to end – not with a bullet piercing her flesh but some chemical agent choking the life out of her from within?

She coughed again, and her eyes began to water. The noises of others around them continued to grow. Coughs, wheezes. Cries.

She rubbed the back of a hand across her eyes to wipe away the moisture. Next to her, a muffled sputter escaped Ben's lips.

But then, Angelina realised, it didn't grow worse. The fog tickled the back of her throat annoyingly, but it didn't scald or burn. It caused her eyes to itch, but didn't render her blind – didn't appear to affect her vision at all, save for the physical interruption to sight the grey mist itself represented.

'What *is* this?' she asked Ben.

'I don't know,' he answered tensely, honestly, 'apart from what we were already told.' He kept them moving, attempting to maintain a brisk pace despite the decreased visibility.

Angelina coughed again, and noticed that Ben didn't seem nearly as affected by the fog as she was.

'Why isn't it bothering you?' she asked. 'Don't tell me faithful believers are immune to your "plagues".'

'Not sure why,' he answered, not entirely managing to keep annoyance at the sarcasm out of his voice. 'But I've been vaping lately, maybe it's not so different.'

'Vaping?'

'It's like smoking, but with these electronic things, and—' He cut himself short. 'You know, it doesn't really matter. This way.'

He motioned to their right, a gesture barely discernible in the mist, then gave a tug on her arm and led her forward.

Angelina continued with the small talk in spurts as they moved. It helped to break up the increasingly awkward silence that had come upon people in the street. The screams of fright had muted as it became clear the fog wasn't going to kill them, and had settled into coughs and mild wheezing, with whimpers of confusion and fright occasionally piercing through.

It was becoming harder to make light of Ben's beliefs, or sarcastically converse about the 'coincidences' of their circumstances. The fog was real. It was everywhere. And however incomprehensible Ben's faith was to her, Angelina could not deny that the group he belonged to knew *something* about what was going on.

The question was, what?

54

Torre Maura district
Eastern Rome

The third plague had settled in. The chaos it was meant to engender – practical as well as psychological – had already blossomed to life, and Emil felt an increasing confidence with every report that came through to him.

The chemical agents Yiannis had concocted for introduction into the sewer system were noxious but not harmful, and Bartolomeo's helpers had magnificently managed the over-pressurisation of the whole piping network, to ensure the bursting of only non-gas pipelines throughout the city. Maximum destruction, minimal casualties. There might be a few, here and there, but that risk could never be entirely alleviated. The time had come to cease being concerned over such things.

As for his other risk – that of exposure by Angelina Calla and Ben Verdyx – the time had also come to modify his response to that. His fear that they might have decoded his intent and shared it was obviously unwarranted. If they were able, they'd have moved to stop him by now.

By now. The last push had already begun. Verdyx and Calla were beyond the time frame of exposure. Emil had every intention of revealing himself, at the right moment. All these two could do now was discover his end game and try to stop it, and that Emil would not allow. It was time to fall back on his original desire. Get rid of them both.

He swivelled his chair towards Vico. 'You're sure they've left the hotel?'

Vico stood before him, tall and spindly. 'The hotel computer confirms their checkout a few minutes ago.'

'And you're sure where they're going?'

'Sure as I can be.' Vico started to shrug, then forced the motion down as he remembered how little his boss liked ambiguity. 'The woman watched the video during her web searching. Not the whole of it, but enough. And the Verdyx fellow, he's one of their members.'

One of Emil's artistically curated eyebrows spiked. 'He's a member? Of St Paul of the Cross?' He hadn't been aware of this. Quite frankly, the news rather surprised him. He didn't take Ben Verdyx as the type to go for such a community-centric and people-based faith. He'd always considered the man something of a recluse.

'We double-checked,' Vico affirmed. 'He's been a member for several years. Contributes a monthly tithe of forty-five euros by standing order.'

Emil nodded. He'd happily take this kind of surprise.

'This is good work, Vico,' he said, smiling at the man.

'Sir?' Vico was not accustomed to praise, nor to the look of fiendish pleasure that now possessed Emil's face.

'Now we have a way to get them both. One that doesn't involve the chance of running away, or of bullets not hitting their mark.'

'You're going to send men in there?' Vico questioned. 'Into the church?'

'No need.' Emil smiled back. He drew out his phone as he spoke, his smile beaming back at Vico.

'We already have a man inside. They're going to come straight to us.'

Church of St Paul of the Cross
Morning Mass

The charismatic mass began not entirely like any other. The faithful of St Paul's gathered in their pews as an electric organ synthesised the pipes of a not overly energetic processional. Father Alberto, robed in a simple white alb with a plain green stole around his neck, walked slowly up the central aisle, his years affecting his gait. When he'd reached the plain altar he turned and blessed his flock, then walked to a small chair reserved for him off to the side.

Music followed, not from the organ but from a small ensemble that included a woman on acoustic guitar, a dishevelled and heavily tattooed teenage boy on drums, and a man in a T-shirt who could easily have been his grandfather on an electric bass. They played with energy, their selections upbeat and rhythmic, lyrics beamed on to one of the sanctuary's white walls by a projector mounted to the ceiling. The music stirred up the congregation, who joined in the singing with more and more energy as the verses rolled along.

Eventually singing gave way to prayer – though the participants would say that they were one and the same thing – and the eucharistic canon began, culminating in the lifting up of the wafer-thin bread and plain ceramic cup of rosé wine and the repetition of the Lord's Words of Institution. Everyone spoke along with the priest. Most communed. Then, more singing, even more energetic. A tambourine was added to the band, and people started to stand as the voices became more fervent. Utterances like eastern ululations mixed in with the devotional words, jubilant arms raised in swaying praise.

Finally, the time came for the sermon. Father Alberto returned to the centre of the altar, now bare after the conclusion of the Eucharist, a lapel microphone clipped to his stole.

'The latest of the prophecies delivered from the Lord has come to pass!' he exclaimed, a strength to his voice that belied his fragile age.

The congregation cheered, hands stretched to heaven.

'We saw in a haze!' the priest exclaimed, 'through a mirror dimly, through a fog not unlike that now covering this ancient city.' Cries of joy, shouts of agreement. 'But now, now we see clearly. The *world* sees clearly!'

Voices wafted over his as full, joyous roars.

'All thus far has come to pass, just as was foretold!' Father Alberto Alvarez took a deep breath, his own eyes raised up to the clear windows at the height of their church. 'And so will all the rest!'

At the edge of the room, the janitor Laurence watched the jubilant scene with satisfaction. Outwardly, his eyes brimmed with the glossy, near-teary expression of devotion he'd cultivated for years and refined over the past months. He puffed out his chest as the priest spoke, filled with evident inspiration. He allowed one arm to rise in Pentecostal glory, then the other, stretching his fingers into open flowers as he lifted his head upwards and visibly basked in the grace of God that poured down upon them like rain.

Inwardly, he merely laughed.

Idiots. His repulsion was almost overwhelming. *Blind sheep. All this over a few lines of nonsense.*

Nonsense from a text he'd helped to fake. Not that he'd produced the tablet himself, of course. He didn't know rune

280

one of the Akkadian language. But he knew religious-speak, and he knew the kind of utterances prone to inspire faith and zeal in the right kinds of faithful. He knew it well and could craft it easily. Then it had just been a matter of using Emil's connections to find the right helpers abroad to turn his words into something 'ancient'. Something that would prove their 'authenticity'. Then craft a tablet, ensuring the clay used was from the right region, dug from a quarry of the right type and mixed with the far older stolen clay samples, and the end result weathered appropriately. Then its burial, its discovery, and then . . . this.

And these people bought it. Wholesale.

It was an affirmation of all Laurence's doubt, all his agnosticism. Moreover, it was an absolute affirmation of the gullibility of religious believers as a whole. Creatures so thick they could be led like this fully deserved their stupidity being taken advantage of.

They deserved what they would get.

So Laurence was content to help Emil. Rob the bastards of everything, for all he cared. Take their heart and their soul from them. Let them learn where faith really leads, in the end. And in the midst of it, Laurence's life would change. He would have all he could ever want. The ability to live without care, without worry and without restraint. More than he ever could have hoped for.

He kept his arms outstretched, his rapture utterly convincing.

He only lowered them when a vibration from his pocket called him to a different posture. Sliding his phone from his trousers in as unnoticeable a manner as he could, he saw the caller ID on the screen.

A second later, the church's elderly custodian slipped through a side door and out of sight.

55

Outside the Church of St Paul of the Cross

Angelina had not known what to expect of the church that had produced the video. The youth in the clip – somewhere in his mid-twenties, perhaps, cleanly kept and brimming with intensity – wore normal Italian street clothes, so at least she knew not to be expecting throngs in common robes or cultic uniforms. She'd chided herself for the thought as she and Ben had walked. *Of course they wouldn't wear such things.* Ben dressed normally, and Angelina reminded herself that as utterly bizarre as it seemed to her, and as unusual as they were in Rome, charismatics were a large percentage of the Christian population worldwide, especially in America. She wasn't exactly walking towards a cult.

She was, however, making her way towards something entirely beyond her realm of both comfort and experience. Religion was hard enough to swallow when it was simply adherence to codes of conduct and beliefs about the past that went beyond what was credible or substantiated by documentable fact. Once religion became something more . . . she wasn't sure of the right word. *Spiritual? Dynamic?* Then it became something else entirely, and that 'something' was even harder for her to relate to in anything other than baffled, dismissive terms. The idea of God existing at all was a supreme invention of human need matched with creativity; to believe one's self-crafted deity actually spoke to people, that his voice echoed down from heaven and whispered into their ears or bubbled up like a spring in their hearts – this was simply delusion.

A house of delusion, harbouring the deluded. That was what Angelina had decided she and Ben were walking towards.

Which made the plain, boxy, red-brick edifice before which they finally stopped something of a surprise. There was no great courtyard before it like there were with so many Catholic churches throughout the city. There was no dome, no steeple, nothing at all to mark it out as different from a warehouse or storefront. Only a neon cross lit above twin sets of glass doors, with metallic letters bolted to the brick between them spelling out 'St Paul of the Cross'.

'That's it?' she asked, eyeing up the building.

'This is the place,' Ben answered. He seemed to gain an inch in height as they drew closer to the entrance. 'My spiritual home.'

Angelina cringed. Just the sort of language she expected.

Ben pulled open one of the doors and made the sign of the cross over himself, then propped open the door with his foot and beckoned her forward.

'Are you ready to see? To truly see?'

She shot him a reprimanding look – *Don't try to sell your spiritual proselytism to me, Dr Verdyx* – yet she couldn't wholly conceal the fact that she did, in fact, want to see what was inside.

It took only a few steps for her to draw herself fully in, and realise it was nothing like any church service she'd seen before.

*　*　*

Angelina *felt* the service of charismatic prayer before she saw it. It came not as an interior, ethereal feeling, but a genuine pulsing of her senses. A drum beat filled the air, accompanied by guitar and other instruments, amplified to literally shake the flooring beneath her. For a moment she wasn't sure whether she'd walked into a rock concert or a church, and when she rounded the subdivision of the narthex and saw hundreds of hands raised in the air, swaying and pulsing to the rhythm, she was even less sure.

She turned to Ben, seeking some sort of explanation, but found him following the example of the others, his own hands raised high and his eyes closed.

The music thumped.

> *Sing praises to the Lord, with all your soul!*
> *Sing praises to the King, with all your heart!*

Spiritual words, perhaps, but the tune would almost qualify as pop.

Finally Angelina grabbed one of Ben's outstretched arms.

'Ben,' she tried not to yell, though the volume of the singing made it hard to do otherwise, 'what's going on?'

'It's the end of the morning Mass and praise,' he said. 'The last hymn. Something a little peppy to inspire people on to the day.'

Angelina's forehead creased. She remembered the sombre hymns that were always listed as 'Recessionals' on the bulletins for the Masses she'd been dragged to as a schoolgirl. They'd certainly never sounded anything like this.

A few seconds later the music reached a harmonious climax and then, to Angelina's complete shock, the whole congregation burst into cheering applause. It was only after the sustained cheering began to die down that a gentler voice, older, amplified over a sound system Angelina couldn't see, broke through the melee.

'The Lord is with us.'

'And will be forever!' the people cried back, as much a cheer as a communal response.

With that, the Mass had apparently ended. In front of them the crowd began to mill and move, gathering up handbags and hats, briefcases and babes-in-arms, and moving from the pews towards the exits. A whole sea of people swarmed past Angelina, the face of each one of them bright with radiant enthusiasm.

'If the service is over,' Angelina managed to say to Ben through the flurry of activity, 'does that mean we can speak to someone in charge?'

'There's only one person at the head of this congregation,' he answered. 'He doesn't normally speak with people after Mass, but I'll see if he'll make an exception. Give me a minute to have a few words.'

'And what am I supposed to do in the meantime?' Angelina asked, suddenly feeling out of place and exposed.

'Take a seat,' Ben replied, motioning to a recently emptied pew. 'You never know. The Spirit might just move you.'

Ben worked his way through the bodies, finally breaking out of the crush into an open space at the front of the sanctuary. He was sorry to have missed Mass, though it wasn't often he was able to arrange his work schedule to allow for a late arrival at the Archives on a Wednesday morning, so not being here this morning was hardly out of the ordinary. Ben was religious about his Saturday and Sunday attendance and took part in his local stake's morning prayers more or less daily, but being here at the tail end of a midweek Mass only served to remind him how much he wished he could be here even more often.

At the front of the room, a few volunteers were already beginning the normal motions of post-service clean-up, gathering leftover bulletins from pews and tidying the chairs that lined some of the side walls.

One was a fellow parishioner Ben recognised immediately.

'Thomás,' he said, walking up to the younger man, 'I need to see Father.'

Thomás smiled at him, more than a simple friendly greeting. He looked bemused.

'Is something funny?' Ben asked, confused.

'No,' though a laugh followed the word as Thomás extended a hand and embraced Ben by the shoulder. 'It's just that it's been less than twenty-four hours since I barrelled in here myself, saying just the same thing.'

His eyes were warm, energetic. He gazed into Ben's and sensed the seriousness behind them.

'You have someone with you?' Thomás asked, nodding towards Angelina, sitting in a pew at the far end of the church. Ben bobbed his head in affirmation.

'Okay,' Thomás added. 'Give me a minute. I'm absolutely certain Father Alberto will be willing to see you.'

56

The library
Church of St Paul of the Cross

Thomás led Ben and Angelina through a network of uninspiring corridors that led out of the side of the sanctuary, having returned to fetch them only a few minutes after leaving Ben. The priest had broken his usual regime of a period of reflection after Mass, and agreed to see them in the small library the parish operated within the environs.

The library surprised Angelina nearly as much as the church itself. There were no mahogany shelves here, no burled reading desks or calfskin armchairs. The room was a beige tiled cube lined with industrial-style shelving, perhaps three or four hundred books – no more than that – loosely arranged on dustless surfaces; fluorescent lights hung from drop-filled ceiling tiles drenching everything in blue-white light. There were three wooden chairs in the room, which Thomás immediately began arranging into a small triangle.

'Father should be here in just a moment,' he said. He motioned to Angelina to take a seat, but she continued to stand. Ben, however, smiled appreciatively.

'Thank you, Thomás.'

Angelina hadn't stopped glaring at the man since she'd caught her first sight of him. It had taken a few seconds to work out the recognition, but little more than that before she realised his was the face she'd seen on the computer monitor in the hotel lobby. This Thomás was the man who'd recorded the video streaming all across the Internet, speaking about prophecies and plagues and . . .

Christ, I can't believe I'm really here.

He beckoned once more towards the chair in front of her, and Angelina was about to decline a second time, perhaps a touch less politely than the first, when the door through which they'd entered swung open again.

Father Alberto Alvarez stepped into the room, and something changed in the air.

Angelina hadn't been able to see him as he'd concluded the Mass; the swell of bodies had been too dense. But she knew from the moment he passed through the door that he must be the church's priest. There was something – she couldn't put the right word to it – *different* about him. He wore the plain greyish-brown robe she associated with Franciscans and saw on a daily basis in Rome, but he carried himself entirely differently than most. He was slightly bent from age, though hardly a hunchback, his face grooved in wizened sobriety. Perhaps it was just the overpowering fluorescent lights, but his small eyes seemed to sparkle.

'Benedict,' he said warmly, stepping up to Ben and opening his arms. Ben embraced him like a child his father.

Benedict? Angelina mouthed the word as his glance caught hers on the way back to his chair. He smiled, almost deviously.

I guess 'Ben' had to be short for something.

'And whom do I have the honour of meeting here?' the priest asked, turning to face Angelina. *So much for prophetic vision*, she couldn't stop herself from thinking.

'My name is Dr Angelina Calla,' she answered, extending a formal hand. The priest took it graciously, though enveloped it in his rather than shook.

'And I am Alberto,' he answered. 'The "Father" is optional, since I suppose it makes you uncomfortable.'

Angelina balked. Was she so transparent? But then, she'd never made any effort at practising the art of concealing her thoughts about religion and clergy.

'Please, let us sit,' Father Alberto continued. He motioned to the chairs, and all three sat together, nearly knee to knee.

'Thomás said you wanted to speak with me urgently.'

'Yes, Father,' Ben answered. 'It's about . . . well, I think you know full well what it's about.'

Father Alberto merely smiled.

'It's about lies,' Angelina suddenly challenged, 'and the fact that I want to know who's telling them, and why.'

A corridor outside the library

Laurence watched the man and the woman follow Thomás into the library with absolute fury. When, a few moments later, Father Alberto joined them, his anger bordered on rage.

Laurence hadn't been a young man for a long time, and there were those in his current age bracket who would say that when plans wobble and go off kilter, it's best simply to let them falter. It wasn't that life was too short, just that they were too close to its inevitable terminus to waste time lamenting the plans that didn't go as intended. *Move on, live another day*. The usual tripe.

Laurence had always considered that kind of logic horse-shit. He didn't know whether he had another two years in him or twenty, but as far as he was concerned the question made no difference whatsoever. Even if it was only two months, he wanted them to be life on his terms. Life with all the frills and benefits he'd envisaged for himself.

With the extravagances this whole present work was meant to provide.

That meant not letting anyone screw it up, especially so close to the conclusion. He wasn't letting two academics and their intrusive interests ruin what he'd worked so hard for. Emil had promised him wealth beyond reason, and Laurence felt it entirely unreasonable to risk not receiving it.

Ridolfo and André might not have been capable of doing what had to be done, but Laurence was damned if he was going to prove himself so weak-willed.

Emil had given him an opportunity to end this threat. Laurence had every intention of taking it.

57

Via Tarsia
Listed residence of Ridolfo Passerini

Major Hans Heinrich adjusted the bulletproof vest around his chest and stood perched in the agreed location as the man to whom he'd given command of the incursion barked the go order. Till that moment they'd moved in silence, surprise a key. But the assault would be loud, and there was no point with whispers once it began.

'Go!' the commanding, shorter man shouted. Seven bodies burst into motion.

Heinrich's team had spent the whole of the night analysing the imagery gleaned from the CCTV footage of St Peter's Square during the gunfire and chase there. There had been two assailants, both male, and though the cameras hadn't clearly caught the faces of the two additional figures these men were after, it was clear that one of those was male and the other female – the latter appearing injured – and Heinrich was confident that it was Verdyx and Calla.

Told you you should have stayed with me, he'd muttered to himself as he'd watched the recordings.

The Swiss Guard had access to FRIS, the Facial Recognition and Identification Service database employed by all the branches of civil Italian law enforcement as well as its military, but, as with so much else, their ability to act on data retrieved from it was dependent on the treaties defining Vatican–Italian relations. When one of the two assailants' faces had, four and a half hours into refined digital comparisons, at last pinged a positive result, Heinrich knew the only way he could act to take the man would be to involve the Italian police. He could try to operate in secret again, as he'd done with the capture of Calla and Verdyx, but access to FRIS was always monitored, so the police would already know the Swiss Guard had been using it, and had located this man. It would be impossible to explain without involving them properly, so Heinrich had followed the route the law required.

The identification linked the face to the profile of a twenty-seven-year-old male named Ridolfo Passerini, a man with a brief and hardly jaw-dropping criminal record. He'd been photographed by the Polizia di Stato after an arrest on suspected breaking and entering charges four years ago, but there hadn't been sufficient evidence to indict him and Passerini had been released. The computer was able to match the image from the Vatican's cameras to that of his file with an unusually high 98.7809 percent accuracy, given the strange deformities that marked out Passerini's face and neck. He was not, to put it mildly, an attractive man.

But just as clearly, as the footage from St Peter's Square made obvious, he'd moved on to bigger things than breaking and entering.

The man running next to him on the recordings appeared of a similar age, perhaps a year or two younger, and of what most would consider a handsome appearance. Yet what makes a person 'handsome' in the conformity-minded consciousness of modern society tends to be his looking similar to a thousand other handsome people – and that meant the computer hadn't been able to pinpoint an identity. It had whittled a listing of possibilities down somewhat, but manually searching through 3,955 possible subjects was more than Heinrich had time for. He'd leave his men to that back in the office.

For now, the system had pinpointed Passerini's address as Via Tarsia, number 188. The street number linked to a small villa with a blue door.

The door shattered less than a second after Senior Officer Elia Biagi shouted 'go'.

A second later, a flash-bang grenade had been tossed inside, and a second after that their closed eyes and covered ears buffered the sound of its violent, debilitating but not deadly explosion.

Two seconds later, the incursion team was pouring through the shattered door, masks on and guns raised at eye level as they scoped out each and every room with practised efficiency.

Major Hans Heinrich stood outside, observing, leaving the work to the force whose territory it was. His tongue tingled with the adrenaline that came all the same, something within him craving being inside, in the action. But what he wanted most of all was the result. He wanted his man.

A minute later, Senior Officer Biagi stepped back through the smoky front door and on to the street.

'The house is clean,' he said, and Heinrich's heart sank.

'No one at all inside?' he asked.

'Whole place is empty. Looks like it's been that way a while, too. No signs of recent habitation.'

Heinrich considered what this implied, but the police officer grunted out his meaning as he turned and walked back towards his men on the scene.

'If your man was here, Major, he's been gone for a while.'

58

The library
Church of St Paul of the Cross

Ben's face betrayed the horror with which he absorbed Angelina's sudden, blatant accusation.

'Angelina!'

She kept her eyes glued on the priest, her visage fierce and unswayed.

Father Alberto, however, met Angelina's words with unshakeable calm.

'I am not sure what lies you're referring to, Dr Calla.'

'Or "prophecies", if you'd prefer to call them that,' she answered. She sat rigid, leaning forward in her chair. 'I most certainly do not. If you knew the river was going to change colour, if you knew the power was going to go out, and if you knew that the sewers were going to spew "fog" into the streets, I don't call that divine vision. I call it deception.'

'We have deceived no one,' the priest answered calmly.

'Your video.' Angelina wasn't willing to be dismissed so simply. She turned towards Thomás, standing behind the priest with his eyes wide, at least as shocked as Ben by her tone. 'The things you said on camera. You clearly knew what was coming.'

'We shared the truth with the world,' Father Alberto answered. 'Hasn't everything we said been proven true?'

'That it's "come true" is precisely the point! The only way you could know such things were going to happen is if you were behind them, or at least involved in them. What I want to know is, why? What's the game you're playing? Because I don't know if this is all just some religious spectacle you're trying to put on, but it's resulted in something a little different than awe and inspiration as far as I'm concerned. I had a bullet shot into my leg!'

Thomás gasped in a sudden intake of shocked breath. What surprised him, however, wasn't news of Angelina's injury.

'You . . . don't believe the prophecies are . . . real?'

Angelina spun her gaze at him, but couldn't find the words to reply.

Ben leaned forward, seeking a way to mediate the unpleasant air of the conversation. 'Reality, Thomás, can mean different things to different people.'

Father Alberto gazed at him silently, understanding on his face. Angelina, however, was incredulous.

'Different things? Different people?' Her face reddened. 'I can't believe what I'm hearing. You were shot at, too, Ben!'

'All I'm saying is that visions aren't always—'

'I don't want to hear another damned word about visions!' she shouted. 'Visions aren't what's firing guns, and *visions* aren't what lets people know when crimes are about to take place. This is deception, plain and simple!'

Finally, Father Alberto raised a hand. His palm was open, his face peaceful.

'Please, my friends, let's not proceed like this. It will get us nowhere.' He smiled gently to both of them in turn. Then, to Angelina, 'Yes, there is deception in the air today. And yesterday. And in the days before.'

Angelina froze. Her whole body pulsed with anger, but the last thing she'd expected had been an outright confession.

'And, no doubt, tomorrow,' Father Alberto continued.

'You admit it, then?' Angelina demanded, her tone half the volume it had been a moment before.

'I admit only the reality of man's foibles and propensities.' The priest's voice continued at the same calm pace. 'But we preach truth, here. Nothing more. And the tablet that's been discovered, the prophecies it contains, which Thomás read to the world on camera yesterday – they contain the truth. Of that I am certain.'

'But it's fraudulent,' Angelina persisted, 'it has to be. I don't know how, or by whom, or what for, but it's the only explanation.'

The voice in her head insisted firmly: *Authentic ancient texts don't predict modern phenomena.*

Then, a question Angelina hadn't yet thought to ask.

'How did you get it?'

The priest looked into her eyes, waiting for more.

'The text of the tablet. The Vatican told us the imagery was only released yesterday, but your group read out a translation of the whole thing. How did you get your hands on it?' Then, before he could start his answer, 'And don't tell me it was "prophetically revealed" to you.'

Father Alberto smiled. His eyes brimmed with compassion.

'No, my child. Nothing so supernal as that. The text was given to me.'

Angelina hesitated. 'Given?'

The priest's smile broadened, sensing her misgivings.

'By a friend. A very human friend.' Then the priest himself leaned forward. 'I can call him in here if you'd like.'

THE SEVENTH COMMANDMENT

The corridor

Laurence was still fuming, his sweeper in hand though he hadn't so much as moved an inch over the floor in minutes, as he pondered how he might get access to the two threats just beyond the door at the corridor's end. Beside him, his work trolley contained his usual array of tools.

Then, his only question was answered.

The door to the library opened and Thomás stepped out. Laurence realised he needed to look like he had a reason for being there, so he immediately set the sweeper into motion and lowered his eyes to the floor.

'Laurence,' Thomás's voice reverberated clearly through the narrow hallway, and he sounded pleased that he hadn't had to go searching for the janitor elsewhere in the building, 'do you have a moment?'

Laurence ensured his face was calm, expressionless, as he raised it towards the younger man.

'Of course, Thomás. What can I do for you? Something still to clean in the sanctuary?'

Thomás looked as if he wanted to smile, but the edges of his mouth wouldn't quite rise to the occasion.

'It's nothing like that. Father Alberto is here with Benedict and . . . a guest.' He paused. 'He'd like to see you.'

Inwardly, Laurence rejoiced. He was being beckoned to the very place he needed to be. It was almost enough to make him believe in divine providence after all.

Outwardly, he simply set aside his sweeper with a gentle nod.

'Of course, of course. What I'm doing can wait.'

He leaned the tall wooden handle against his cart, and his hands passed swiftly over his tools before he turned towards the far end of the corridor.

Laurence was not a man of any experience or skill with

weapons. God knew he'd never held a gun. But in this setting, in these quarters, he wouldn't need one.

He lowered his hands into his sides as he walked towards Thomás, a screwdriver dropping silently into his denim pocket as he moved.

59

The summoning of the man who had 'given' the text of the tablet to Father Alberto was an unexpected event that had both Angelina and Ben perched on the edges of their seats. Ben, wholly convinced of the divine element in all that had befallen them, was curious how such a human delivery might form a part of it; while Angelina, dismissive of anything paranormal in events she considered had to be entirely human, wanted to know who the next player was in the link of actors connecting everything going on around her.

Neither of them expected the figure of the man who entered the room a few seconds later.

'Benedict, I believe you know Laurence de Luca, who's been with us for the past seven months,' Father Alberto said calmly. Out of chairs, Thomás brought the elder custodian close to their trio of seats where the older man stood as upright as he was capable.

'Dr Calla,' the priest continued, 'I'd like to introduce you to a member of our parish community.'

Laurence nodded hesitantly, giving every appearance of having no idea why he'd been called into the room. He wore worker's denim coveralls over a white shirt, all of which hung loosely over a frame that had long ago lost the clearly defined solidity of youth. The man was skinny but not scrawny, his hair closer to white than grey, and though he kept himself shaved there was a thin fuzz across his face and neck that matched the colour atop his head. The whites of his eyes were dimly yellowed, but the blue orbs at their centres remained vivid.

And yet, Angelina noticed, there was something more to those eyes. Not simply age, nor surprise, nor pious devotion. There was . . . anger.

She was immediately suspicious. *Anger, even amidst venerable age and gentleness, reveals much.*

'Pleased to meet you,' Laurence said hesitantly, giving a courteous, quick nod to Angelina and then a more familiar nod to Ben, where his gaze lingered a moment longer.

'I was just getting to know Dr Calla,' Father Alberto continued, 'who rather insistently wishes to know how I received the full text of the tablet that was published online yesterday. The one you gave me last week.'

'Last week?' The exclamation burst out of Angelina's lips. 'You didn't tell me you had it so long ago!' The priest's story was becoming more incredible all the time.

Laurence's eyebrows, still surprisingly black given the grey-white tone of his hair and stubble, lifted high on his face.

'Father, are you sure? We don't normally speak about—'

'I'm sure, brother,' the priest gently cut him off. 'They wish to know. Please, don't be afraid. Tell them.'

The custodian looked increasingly uncomfortable with each passing second, though Angelina noticed that the mounting signs of anger within him appeared less feigned than the shows of embarrassment and hesitation.

It was these, however, that the man emphasised as he heeded his priest's instruction.

'I got the message from the only place such messages come.' His eyes focused on a spot on the floor midway between the chairs on which Angelina, Ben and Father Alberto sat. 'From God.'

Angelina wanted to snap. *More of this crap.* Her interior scepticism had long since reached its threshold for the day. But there was something about the way the man held himself. The way the words were forced through his teeth. Something wasn't right, beyond the obvious fact that, so far as Angelina knew, even amongst the most pious God wasn't known to make a habit of translating Akkadian tablets for elderly janitors.

'Angelina, please don't get upset,' Ben whispered, trying to use soft tones to calm what he knew was a line of discussion that would frustrate her. 'This is what we're all about, here. The reception of the working, and the words, of the Spirit.'

'How, precisely?' Angelina asked, keeping her eyes on Laurence. The question silenced Ben. It wasn't a challenge to the nature of revelation, or a denigration of religious 'superstition', as Angelina had so often called it. 'Tell me how God *revealed* this to you.'

Laurence didn't lift his eyes from the floor, but entered into what immediately felt to Angelina like a well-rehearsed speech on the nature of charismatic vision. Song and praise had lifted his soul out of the weighty shackles of worldly thoughts, prayer had opened his heart to the presence of God. In an ecstasy of devotion he had felt the Spirit pouring down on him like tongues of fire, speaking unknown words into the depths of his soul.

He recounted his experiences with surprisingly little emotion. It was meant to indicate a familiarity with this kind of phenomenon, Angelina surmised – a lack of surprise that God would and did act in such ways. But she felt something different in Laurence's emotionless delivery. She felt he was holding back a far heavier emotion that was barely caged inside him.

'This is how these things often come,' Father Alberto said peacefully. 'When our hearts are drawn up. When we don't expect them.'

'Though what came to Laurence was only the whole,' Ben added. 'Parts of the revelation had been emerging from different members of our group for weeks. A piece here, a piece there. Then Laurence delivered the whole.'

'And a week later, yesterday,' Laurence added, 'we saw news of a tablet having been discovered, and the imagery released on the web. An ancient relic, confirming everything we've been shown.'

Angelina could sense the breathing coming from Ben's direction had slowed. Reverence. The priest across from her looked serene, as if the will of God brought an extra peace to his soul and this whole situation confirmed the vibrancy of his faith.

But for Angelina . . .

'You're lying,' she suddenly declared. The words were shot directly at the janitor, whose eyes at last sprang up, wide. The skin at the sides of his neck began to turn a vivid red.

'You're lying, and you're a fraud,' Angelina repeated, more firmly.

'Angelina!' Ben cried again.

Laurence turned to Father Alberto, his whole face now reddened and indignant. 'Please, put a stop to this woman's accusations. Why did you call me in for this? She's not a believer. She knows nothing!'

'I know you're lying,' Angelina spat back.

'Stop this!' Ben cried out again.

'No!' The word thundered not out of Angelina's mouth, but Laurence's. The custodian had straightened himself as tall as his frame would allow, his breath heaving and his face a contorted mass of fury. His breaking point had been reached.

'I will be the one to stop this!' he rasped, spittle flying from his lips.

In his hand, he gripped a large screwdriver, his knuckles flexed white in pure rage.

60

Along the Piazza di Porta San Giovanni
Central Rome

Emil strode alongside Bartolomeo as they walked past the site of the next plague that would flare up in the Eternal City. Yiannis, the second person in Bartolomeo's team, walked a step behind.

It brought Emil a certain satisfaction to be so bold about it. He could be right here, in the public eye, surrounded by the tense tourists and frightened locals, seen by everyone – it made no difference. The art of prophecy was its origin; the whole reason it had been chosen.

With everyone's attention called towards God, no one was looking at him.

They moved past the spot, letting its ominous edifice recede behind them. The details were in place. Emil was confident it would come off as planned, tonight, just after sundown.

It would be so much more dramatic in darkness.

But his mind was already further afield.

'After this plague comes and goes, the fervour of fear and interest will be at its peak,' he said softly to Bartolomeo. A public transit bus drove past them, roaring diesel engines momentarily overpowering their conversation. 'Which means everyone will be glued on the one to come next. The fifth plague.'

Bartolomeo laughed. 'It'd be kind of hard for anyone not to have taken notice by then. The city's already an anxious mess.'

'And they'll have the hour, and the place.'

Another bus, and Emil let its blaring engine call their words to a halt. They kept walking, but he said nothing further.

The fifth plague had been 'prophesied' to take place tomorrow at daybreak. With such a specific time, and such a specific place, the eyes of the city would be glued there.

God, it was all so easy. By the morning he'd have everyone in Rome either believing, or at least questioning and curious enough about what the hell was going on, to be out, in the appointed place, watching. The spot foreordained by ancient words, confirmed by the voice of modern visionaries and seers, would be thronged with pilgrims, believers, sceptics and critics. With clergy. With reporters.

And, most importantly of all, with security. And Emil's men would already be moving.

'Your two threats,' Bartolomeo's voice suddenly cut through Emil's anticipatory reverie, 'they're not going to be a problem?'

Emil shook his head. 'Between now and then? No chance. Even if they were able, there wouldn't be time for debunking to stop curiosity from taking its natural hold.'

'But they're . . . not?' Bartolomeo persisted. 'Not "able"?'

Emil halted and turned to face Bartolomeo. He smiled at his diligent worker, discerning precisely what the other man meant.

'No, my friend. They're not. I suspect that at this very

moment, Rome is being relieved of two scholars whose presence was . . . no longer required.'

The smile lingered, was returned, and the men walked onward through the haze in silence.

61

The library
Church of St Paul of the Cross

Laurence snapped all at once. He was transformed from the figure of a meek and mild janitor he'd cultivated so well, into a figure of more power and strength than his age would suggest he could possibly hold. His breath rasped as it came in a frenetic, shallow pulse, and his eyes narrowed into slits. The muscles in his reddened neck contorted and the large screwdriver in his right hand was brought up to chest level as he stomped forward in fury.

'I've had enough of what this bitch has to say.' The words were poison as he shoved past Father Alberto's seat and lunged at Angelina.

The attack came quickly, but Angelina's suspicious focus on the man since he'd entered the room already had her on alert – perhaps not for this, but for something. When he pushed through the chairs and thrust the flat-head end of the screwdriver at her, she had just enough time to lunge to her right and avoid a blow that would have caused it to pierce through her lower neck. Instead, the flat blade rammed into the wooden backing of her chair and knocked it over as Angelina sprang to her feet.

Laurence's body followed the motion of his outstretched arm and he nearly toppled over the chair, but he caught himself and spun back at Angelina's new position. He was beyond words now, his anger vocalised only in bestial grunts that roared out of him, white spittle clinging to the corners of his lips.

He shot forward at Angelina in a second attempt, this time swiping the screwdriver in front of him in a face-level arc. It whipped the air with an audible *whoosh* each time he sliced it back and forth.

Angelina thrust herself backwards, a manoeuvre that slammed her spine against one of the metal bookcases, which in turn rattled vigorously as books leapt off its shelves and flew to the floor. The position was as far back as she could get, and she wasn't sure it would be enough. The blade of the screwdriver flashed by her face mere centimetres from her eyes, so close that the *whoosh* of air forced her to blink, and all at once she couldn't see what was in front of her.

For an instant, Angelina went blind.

Ben couldn't comprehend what had suddenly transformed the peaceful janitor he'd come to know over the past months into the raving madman attacking the woman next to him. But there was one thing Ben knew well: the servants of God didn't act like this. And though he wasn't sure whether at this point Angelina Calla counted as a colleague or friend, or perhaps, given her antipathy towards his faith, subtle enemy, he knew she was in danger and that he had to do something.

Ben burst out of his chair and ran at Laurence. The surprisingly vigorous old man had just attempted to slash his oversized screwdriver across Angelina's face and missed, but her slam into the bookshelf had winded her and she didn't appear to be in motion as Laurence drew back his elbow for a thrust straight into her stomach.

Ben didn't have time to say anything. He simply roared as Laurence's arm flexed and the screwdriver started to move directly forward.

Ben threw all his weight forward and ran at him.

Clarity returned to Angelina's watery eyes just in time to see Laurence's blurred form take shape in front of her. Her breath was hard to draw in, but she knew she had to move.

Then she glanced down. It was too late. Laurence's weapon was pointed directly at her stomach, his arm already in motion, less than a metre away. She pushed strength into her legs to sidestep the attack, but she knew she wouldn't be out of his reach in time. Sweat seemed instantaneously to form and go ice-cold across her entire body.

Then, without warning, Laurence lurched to the side, his arm still extending but suddenly out of her range. Ben had slammed his whole weight into the man, and with a deafening clank of metal the two men crashed into a bookshelf on the wall to Angelina's right.

She righted herself, took a deep breath in. By the time she'd swivelled towards their new position, both Ben and Laurence had recovered from the crash, Ben pulling himself quickly away to avoid a counter-swing from the older man. Laurence's rage had transferred, for the moment, to his new opponent, and there was bloodlust in his eyes as he sprang in Ben's direction.

Angelina realised they had to end this, and quickly, or this man would kill them both.

Ben could see Laurence preparing his next attack, lining up his position, massaging the shoulder where Ben had landed on him, then readying his makeshift weapon for the subsequent strike. Ben was near a corner of the small room and therefore at a decided disadvantage – something Laurence appeared to recognise.

'You fucking religious nut,' the old man fumed, the words as poisonous to Ben as the janitor's rage. 'I've had as much of your kind as I can tolerate.'

Laurence shot himself forward. He raised his arm high, already yanking the screwdriver downwards in a kill strike as he raced to Ben's position.

All Ben could do was duck. As Laurence threw himself at him, he dropped at the last instant to knee level and rolled forward.

Ben hit Laurence's left knee as the man's arm swooped down to end him, and the motion knocked him off trajectory. Laurence wobbled and spun, his arms instinctively rising to keep him from toppling over, but he couldn't completely control his motion. He swerved to his left, spinning, the screwdriver flailing.

That it landed in Father Alberto's chest had not been his intention.

The flat blade of the screwdriver tore effortlessly through the priest's woollen robe, given the mass of thrust behind it, and its eight-centimetre shaft sank into his flesh, colliding with ribs and ricocheting through his body.

For an instant, the world stopped. Motion stopped. Laurence's expression widened.

Surprise.

He hadn't intended the priest to be his victim here, and the blood that suddenly poured out of Father Alberto's chest on to Laurence's hand, still clenched around the screwdriver's handle, horrified him with its pulsing warmth.

Behind him, Angelina and Ben had frozen in their steps. In the far corner of the room, Thomás cried out in abject horror.

THE SEVENTH COMMANDMENT

A second later, Laurence's features hardened. The shock of stabbing the priest had halted him, but it wasn't enough to deter him from his course. All his anger and rage returned.

With a great yank he pulled the screwdriver out of the priest's chest, and with blood still dripping from his hand, he turned to face Angelina and Ben.

'Now, to be done with the two of you.'

62

The library
Church of St Paul of the Cross

The fight was one against two. The significantly smaller form of Thomás had stood in petrified stillness since the attack began, and once Laurence had ripped the screwdriver from the bleeding hole it had speared into Father Alberto's chest, Thomás had fallen to his knees and crawled over to the priest's side, tears streaming from his eyes, apparently oblivious to the battle going on around him and any threat it might pose to his own safety.

Laurence returned his focus to Ben. He was the larger of the two targets, a full head taller than the Calla woman. He'd also been the more aggressive of the two, attacking back while Angelina had thus far only been able to attempt self-defence. When Ben had slammed into Laurence's side, the impact had been with a mass of muscle and form. Verdyx might look a weakling academic type, but there was strength in his frame.

The screwdriver was slippery now in Laurence's hand, the priest's blood congealing around the handle, and he pulled back a thumb over the end to ensure it wouldn't simply slide through his grasp when he stabbed it into his next victim. It made for a more limited range of motion, but Laurence's rage was on full power and he knew it would suffice.

He sprang towards Ben in a surprise motion, instantly breaking the lingering stillness that had followed his inadvertent stabbing of the priest. Ben's eyes were on his pastor, and he didn't have time to react. Laurence was mid-stride, almost in the air, by the time Ben even saw him coming.

Angelina saw the muscles contract and flex through Laurence's blood-spattered white shirt, and knew he would be in motion in an instant. He was pointed at Ben, and as she turned to warn him, the attack happened. Ben's eyes were elsewhere, and she sensed his heart had all but stopped at the sight of the murder of the priest. Her mind cried out in instant realisation: *he isn't going to notice the attack in time*.

She threw herself at him, a cry erupting from her throat. With a clarity that could only come from adrenaline, she realised that if she simply slammed into him she'd replace her own body for his in Laurence's line of attack, and though she wanted to help, she didn't want to become a martyr. Instead, Angelina dove for Ben's legs, wrapping her arms around them and toppling him. She'd have to trust he'd manage to use his arms to stop his sudden fall from being as battering as the attack.

Ben's body tipped and rotated over his feet like an anchored lever, and Angelina grunted as she landed on her stomach, her arms still around his ankles. Above her, Laurence's lunge for his suddenly absent target caused him to trip over Angelina's back, the janitor toppling forward and landing a shoulder hard against the bookcase.

The bitch just wouldn't give up. Laurence's fury grew with each extra step he was forced to take, and he pushed himself back from the bookshelf and glowered at Angelina as she picked herself up from the floor. Maybe she wasn't the secondary of the duo, after all.

She was closer now, too. Laurence could take her.

And there was one easy way to do it.

Laurence was coming straight at Angelina with a look of final determination in his eyes. He had both hands wrapped around the screwdriver and held it at belly height. He ran wildly, as if aim were no longer important.

Angelina realised his goal. She'd risen by a corner, and Laurence was barrelling towards her in a way that would push her straight back into it. All he needed do was slam into her, body into body, and the screwdriver in his grip would pierce her like a javelin against the wall.

She could all but smell the panic rising off her skin, forcing her muscles to move her out of his path, when the explosive sound of cracking wood burst through the air. Laurence wobbled, a puzzled look suddenly on his face, and veered to her side, once again slamming into a bookshelf. Behind his former position, Ben stood with the fragmented remains of one of the wooden chairs in his hand.

In the midst of her panic, Angelina found the power to smile. Despite the awe-inspiring inner strength this man had demonstrated in his attack, an alternative thought had just flashed into her mind.

She knew a good idea when it came.

She sprinted forward and picked up the chair that had formerly been her own, grabbing it firmly by the back. She turned towards Laurence, who'd regained his balance and was now sighting up Ben as the nearest target. His bloodied right hand was high above his head, weapon in hand.

Angelina spun the chair in a broad arc from her right, slamming it across the janitor's back.

The crunching blow of wood against his spine knocked the wind from Laurence's lungs. His eyes widened as his throat locked and his balance faltered, but he sensed he couldn't stop his downward momentum. He flailed his hands towards a support position, but the floor was coming up too fast. There was a whirlwind vision of flesh and blood as his hands came into view in front of his chest.

And the heart-stopping realisation that it was all going to end in this instant.

His fingers instinctively widened in an attempt to brace his impact, and Laurence's grasp on the screwdriver faltered. The wide composite grip was heavier than the shaft – and once it was free of his grasp gravity did the rest. The screwdriver spun as it fell, the handled end pointing downward.

The flat end of the metal shaft slammed into Laurence's body as he collided with the floor. His momentum was so great that it not only pierced his solar plexus and drove its way into his heart, but Laurence's own body mass crushed down on the weapon so that even the handle pushed its way into the wound.

The top of the screwdriver emerged from his back, not quite enough length left to shred through his coveralls, leaving them tented in a grotesque triangle beneath his shoulder blades. A second later, the fabric started to go red.

He knew he was a dead man before the inevitable reality came. The position of the weapon in his flesh meant it came swiftly. He had only time to whisper out a single phrase before his life ebbed away.

'You'll never be able to stop them.'

63

The library
Church of St Paul of the Cross

The amount of blood spattered throughout the diminutive library of the Church of St Paul of the Cross was accentuated by the bright fluorescent glow of the lighting. A broadening pool expanded beneath the body of the deceased custodian, but in the attacks before he'd fallen he'd scattered the smears of Father Alberto's blood that clung to his tool and his hand in arcs around the room. The room looked like something out of a slasher film, chairs broken, books scattered on the floor.

The only person who had remained unscathed was Thomás. He continued to kneel at the priest's side, tears welling in his eyes and streaming down his face. He held one of the older man's hands in his own, his lips silently muttering prayers.

Once it was clear that Laurence was dead, Ben sprang over to join Thomás at Alvarez's side.

'Is he dead?' he asked. His own eyes began to go glassy.

'He's . . . barely breathing,' Thomás answered. Ben fell on to his knees and grasped the priest's other hand.

Angelina had kept her gaze on the fallen form of the janitor, still catching her breath. His resolve, his power, had been simply awesome.

In the sudden calm that followed the attack, her own leg had begun to throb.

'Bring . . . bring her . . . here.' The words unexpectedly rasped out of Father Alberto's throat. Ben and Thomás stared at his face, shocked to hear the priest speak.

'Her?'

Father Alberto wrenched his right hand out of Ben's grasp. With what little strength he had left, he pointed at Angelina.

She saw the gesture, and her pain seemed to vanish. *Religious or not, cleric or not, this is a man at the gateway of death.* His brownish robe bore the rosette of his wound at his stomach, the skin of his face a starkly contrasting white. Her heart filled with the compassion she would have for any human being in such a state.

She stepped around Laurence's corpse and walked to the small huddle of men. She stood in front of the priest, unsure why in his final moments he should beckon her.

'You . . . are wounded,' he managed.

Fear gripped her. Had he spotted an injury she hadn't realised? Angelina urgently scanned over her body for wounds, but there were none, just the swathes of blood that had come from contact with Laurence's body.

'No,' she answered, 'I'm okay,' and then, despite herself, 'Father.'

'No,' he gasped, 'there.' He motioned towards Angelina's left calf.

She looked down. The wound she'd suffered yesterday throbbed beneath her trousers, but nothing was visible beneath the bandages that Ben had carefully helped her apply.

'How do you—'

Father Alberto didn't give her time to finish the question. 'You need to . . . take care of that.' A slow breath. 'Don't let it get . . . infected. Still . . . work for you to do.'

Angelina was at a loss for words. *Poor man, so frail.*

Suddenly, Father Alberto clasped both hands together, a strength that hadn't been there a moment ago coursing through his body.

'The rest is coming,' he said, his eyes wide. He managed to turn his head from Angelina to Ben, then back again. 'The fire, and then the blotting out of the sun, and then the . . .'

His strength drained away as fast as it had come.

'Myths, Father,' Angelina said, shaking her head. Delusion was delusion, even in the throes of death. 'Deception.'

Father Alberto managed a soft smile.

'Maybe so, maybe so, professor.' His breath seeped slowly away.

'But God has worked in more mysterious ways than this before. Never . . . underestimate . . . his hand.'

With that, the light left Father Alberto's eyes, and the old priest's earthly words came to their end.

On the street outside the Church of St Paul of the Cross

The next four and a half hours were spent in the environs of the church, as an ambulance phoned by Thomás finally arrived, and then the police, and the ritualised procedure of interviews, questions, witness statements and all the other accoutrements of a crime-scene investigation were gone through. The scene was so bloody that the initial responders had handcuffed Ben, Angelina and Thomás as the medics huddled around Father Alberto's body, unsure who, or what, to believe about the gruesome scene around them. But Thomás had swiftly pointed out to the officers the presence of small security cameras everywhere in the church's property, including in an upper corner of the library. The scene recorded on digital tape matched the story each of the three told, and after extended additional questioning, the police eventually informed them they were free to go – though they were not to leave Rome.

'Our priest,' Ben asked, finally escaping the clutch of law enforcement and making his way to the medics. 'Is he . . .?'

'He's still alive,' an ambulance technician answered, slamming closed the vehicle's door behind him, 'but he's not conscious. It doesn't look good.'

He said no more, his professionalism apparently not extending to attempts at a gentle bedside manner.

The ambulance drove away in a whir of sirens and lights. Their beams seemed to dance in the remnants of the fog that still clung to the ground.

'What happened to the mist?' Angelina asked one of the officers, motioning towards the grey haze. It was noticeably less than when they'd entered the church an hour ago.

'Who the fuck knows?' a gruff, fat investigator answered. 'Stuff covered the whole city for about forty-five minutes. Came outta everywhere. Never seen anything like it. Scared the shit outta folk.'

'One of them signs of the, you know, apocalypse,' another officer answered, clucking in disapproval. 'That's what my wife says. Said she heard about it on the Internet, too, so you know it's got to be true.'

Dark laughter, and the officers went back to their chores.

Angelina and Ben did not laugh.

'What do we do from here?' Ben finally asked when they were left alone. He was coping with his shock better than Angelina had anticipated he would, especially given what had just befallen a priest he clearly loved.

But Angelina's mind couldn't stop replaying the scenes, and words, of the final moments of their struggles. She said nothing, leaning against the side of one of the patrol cars, pondering.

Suddenly, she stood bolt upright.

'He said "them".'

Ben looked at her quizzically.

'Laurence,' she continued, her words suddenly coming quickly, 'your janitor. As he was dying.'

'I don't see the meaning,' Ben said.

'His last words were, "You'll never be able to stop them." *Them*, Ben!'

He shook his head, still not grasping her point, and Angelina leaned forward to place a hand on his arm.

'He didn't say, "Stop what *I've* done," or even "what *we've* done". He said "them". Others. Someone outside your church.'

Ben's features started to pale.

'You think Laurence was tied up with someone else?'

Angelina nodded furiously, but she was already looking around them.

'Can we get out of here, Ben? Go somewhere else? Anywhere else?'

'You have a plan?'

'Of sorts. I want to get somewhere where we can sort out our next steps.'

Thomás, who had stood a few metres away during their discussion, stepped forward.

'I don't live far from here,' he said. 'If you want, you can come with me.'

For the first time since she'd met the young man whose face she'd seen on video, whose voice she'd heard proclaiming prophecy, Angelina smiled at him.

'That will do just fine.'

Thomás motioned in the direction of home, and a moment later the three marched away from the church into the remnants of the fog that dissipated around them.

64

Underground

The third plague was over. It had come and gone as it was supposed to. All the pyrotechnics had worked as intended, and the chemical mix had been just what was wanted. Annoying, but not poisonous.

Not pyrotechnics, jackass. Bartolomeo grinned as Yiannis's words replayed in his memory. He'd been scolded more than once for applying this term to the systems his partner had helped put in place to cause the spontaneous eruption of their makeshift fog throughout the city. *No fire's involved. Just 'technics'.*

Fire was for the fourth plague, not the third.

That would come soon enough. For the moment, Bartolomeo's focus was on the present.

'It's beyond this wall?' he asked. The long, vertical slab of concrete looked innocuous enough, with its strange, etched-out indentation that went past concrete and into metal. It was hard to believe that everything they were working for lay just beyond it.

'Yeah, but getting this close to it's been a bitch,' one of

their workers answered. A whole team had been labouring down here for months.

Bartolomeo nodded. Everything worth having required work to obtain it.

'The explosives we brought in, they'll be enough?'

'Ought to be,' the other man answered, then, seeing Bartolomeo's displeasure, 'yeah, it'll do. We've got far enough through already, the blast's just for the last few centimetres.' Then, hesitation. 'But, you know, it's still gonna make one big fucking boom.'

Bartolomeo smiled.

The other man did not. 'I mean, the kind that's gonna get noticed up at street level. Anyone around's definitely going to hear it.'

'There won't be anyone around,' Bartolomeo said with absolute conviction.

'But there always are,' the worker protested. 'People up on the streets, and the usual security over on the other side.'

'Tomorrow,' Bartolomeo answered, 'there won't be.'

'How can you possibly be certain of that?'

'Because,' he replied, 'they're all going to have their attention elsewhere.'

The worker fidgeted, uncomprehending. 'Where?'

Bartolomeo laughed. 'On heaven. Where else?'

65

The island of Pantelleria

On the island of Pantelleria, 305 nautical miles away in the midst of the blue waters of the Strait of Sicily in the Mediterranean Sea, nothing happened.

PART SEVEN

Destruction

66

Via Pausania
Home of Thomás Nascimbeni

It was late afternoon by the time Angelina, Ben and Thomás arrived at the unassuming entrance to Thomás's bedsit. With the Roman housing market as overpriced as every other major European city, the tiny space was all he could afford, and that only at a stretch. A narrow sitting room connected to a tiny kitchen, a double bed and bathroom squeezed into the space behind it. It was cramped when Thomás was alone, but with two other bodies inside the place felt restrictively small.

Thomás had decorated the apartment in simple, clean furnishings. The pale greens and off whites in most circumstances made the interior feel warm, but in the present the light colours only served to emphasise the haggard appearance of its new occupants. Thomás, the least dishevelled of the three, had blood on his hands and forearms from tending to the body of Father Alberto before the medics had arrived; but Angelina and Ben were in a far more dramatic state. Each had blood spattered and smeared across their clothes, arms, faces and into their hair. Angelina's blouse was torn near her right shoulder, and Ben's right trouser leg was one giant crimson smear – the remnants of the blood pouring out of Laurence's fatal chest wound, pooling on the floor as Ben had knelt down to check he was truly dead. As a result, Thomás had taken a somewhat circuitous route to get them from the church to his home, realising that as puzzled as the populace might be by the fog receding from the city, the sight of three blood-soaked stragglers would still raise alarms.

In the warm light of his flat, they all looked like visions out of a Wes Craven film.

'I think you could do with a change of clothes,' he said, directing his words to Ben. The latter peered down at himself. If at any other moment in his life he might have been shocked to see himself coated in another man's blood, at this particular instant he took the vision well. An eyebrow slowly rose as he scanned his chest, his arms, his legs.

'I think you might be right,' was all he said in the end. 'Unless you've got one hell of a good washing machine.'

'Only the launderette down the street,' Thomás answered, 'but I've got a few changes of clothes in the wardrobe. You're a little taller than me, but I think they should still fit.'

He disappeared through the kitchen into the back room, and for a moment Angelina and Ben were left alone to peer over the bloodstained apparitions they had become. Angelina looked as if she was on the verge of saying something, when suddenly Thomás re-emerged from his bedroom.

'These ought to do.' He handed Ben a folded set of khakis and a yellow top with open collar. A pair of boxers and a folded set of black socks were stacked on top of them. 'There's a shower back there, too.' He motioned beyond the kitchen.

'I'm not sure I want to stick around here long enough for all of us to bathe,' Ben answered, 'but I'll certainly take advantage of the chance to rinse off my face and hands.' His eyes fell down to his feet, his loafers caked in blood. 'And maybe my shoes.'

He took the new clothes from Thomás and walked into the back room. Angelina had already taken a step closer to the younger man.

'What about me?' she asked. 'I can't exactly go out like this.'

'Give me a minute to grab something for myself,' Thomás answered. 'I can change in the bedroom while Benedict is in the bathroom. It'll give you as much privacy as we can manage in here.'

Angelina straightened. Hearing Ben referred to as 'Benedict' still startled her – she'd assumed Ben was short for Benjamin, not something as overtly pious as the name of the founder of the Benedictine Order – but she was equally startled by the assertion that she needed pampering and privacy.

'It's not my privacy I'm worried about,' she answered back, too testily, 'it's what I'm supposed to put on.' She glanced at Thomás's attire, similar to what he'd just handed Ben and, Angelina could only assume, most of what remained in his wardrobe. To say his style wasn't hers wasn't so much the problem as the fact that they were nothing close to the same size.

Thomás smiled uncomfortably. 'I . . . my girlfriend . . . I think she left a few things in the chest of drawers beside my bed. They would probably fit you.'

He blushed, as if the words 'girlfriend' and 'bed' were unimaginable in the same sentence.

'Girlfriend?' Angelina asked, playing off his obvious embarrassment. 'What's a good religious boy like you doing with a woman over at his house, spending the night?' Thomás turned another shade of purple.

'Please, don't tell Ben,' he said timidly. Angelina caught

herself, recognising that his was a genuine embarrassment and wondering whether premarital cohabitation was a particularly nasty sin in their little community.

Religious people, the voice in her head sounded. *If it's not a revelation, it's a rule to inspire guilt.*

She shook her head, but calmed her features. 'Don't worry, Thomás. Your secret's safe with me.' She smiled. A moment later, Thomás re-emerged with a set of women's clothes in his hands: a pair of fashionably faded jeans and a snug top. Not exactly Angelina's style, but it would do.

Twenty minutes later, all three of them had had the chance to rinse the blood from the visible parts of their bodies, clothe themselves in Thomás's meagre offerings, and tidy themselves up as much as the situation would allow. As Angelina had rinsed her hair under the sink's tap and brushed it out with Thomás's hairbrush – a kind of intimate sharing she'd never expected to undertake with a man who until a few hours ago had been a perfect stranger – Thomás had switched on the kettle and extracted a few tins of biscuits from a cupboard. By the time she re-entered the front room, three mugs of strong tea were waiting.

Ben and Thomás were mid-conversation as she rejoined them, reaching out for one of the mugs and lifting it to her lips. *God, my eternal soul for a cup of coffee.* Though an interior scolding followed. *The tea's not that bad. Your eternal soul might be a bit of a high bid.*

Ben laughed mildly at something Thomás had said – the first time Angelina could think of him laughing since before they'd entered the Archives together. It seemed like a lifetime ago, though in reality it had been fewer than twenty-four hours.

'We need to figure out what he meant by "them",' she suddenly said, ignoring their conversation and simply butting in with what was important. 'It's why we came here, and we need to get down to it.'

Ben's smile broadened. 'Why don't you take a seat, Dr Calla.' He motioned to the space next to him on the two-seater sofa, the use of her title an obvious josh. 'Thomás and I have just been discussing that.'

Angelina felt a blush emerge on her cheeks. *Ever the rash one*. But she sat as instructed and took another sip of her tea before asking, 'So, any thoughts?'

'Could be another religious group,' Thomás said. 'I just said to Benedict, Laurence only joined up with us six or seven months ago. Maybe a few more, I don't quite remember. Came without much of a background story, but then, most of us do. Nobody's going to make you reveal your past unless you want to.'

'He always seemed so gentle,' Ben said. 'Devoted.'

'But that's what I mean,' Thomás countered. 'He was *very* devoted, right from the beginning. Were you like that?'

The question seemed to catch Ben off guard. He didn't answer, screwing his face up into a puzzle.

'I mean, I wasn't,' Thomás went on. 'I was totally amazed when I first walked into the church, don't get me wrong. Its effect on me was almost instantaneous. Mama is Portuguese and Papa is Venetian, which are cultures worlds away from this, so when I walked through those doors the first time it was like nothing I'd ever seen before. Nothing I'd ever *felt* before.'

Ben's head slowly rose and fell, eyes growing distant, recalling memories that apparently mirrored Thomás's experience.

'But actually getting *into* it,' Thomás continued, 'I mean, the whole praying in tongues, opening up your heart to hearing God's voice, all that – it took me a while. It was, well . . .'

'Awkward.' Ben found the word for which Thomás was groping. 'For me, too. My family were strongly conservative when it came to religion. Getting near this kind of thing first-hand was an entirely new world to me. I had to adapt.'

'That's my point!' Thomás sat straighter in the lounge chair opposite the sofa. 'Laurence never seemed to need to. He showed up, quiet and kind, and seemed to be open to the voice of God almost immediately. I remember him joining me in a rapture session just two days after he arrived.'

'Excuse me,' Angelina interrupted, 'a rapture session?'

'It's the name we use for a certain kind of prayer . . . experience,' Thomás answered. 'When you're really caught up in the Holy Spirit. Like being raptured up into heaven. You feel like you're outside yourself.'

A decent dose of LSD will do the same thing, came an automatic retort. Angelina kept it to herself, out of respect for Ben more than the religion. She still couldn't bring herself to understand how a rational man like him could be into this religion at all, much less a *rapture session*.

'It usually takes newcomers a long time before they reach that level of prayer,' Thomás continued, 'but Laurence was right there beside me, speaking in the Spirit, after just a couple of days.' He shook his head, disappointed. 'Maybe that should have been a sign that something wasn't right. It could mean he was with some other group. Maybe out to discredit us? Plenty of people are.'

'But to what end?' Ben asked. 'He wasn't mocking us, he became one of our most devoted members. Father Alberto held him close.'

'Maybe that's . . . maybe that's a sign, too. Maybe Father Alberto was taken in by him.' Thomás paled at his own words. Angelina wondered whether the younger man considered this the worst realisation of all: that the priest he admired might have been duped.

Ben shook his head energetically. 'I can't believe that. Father Alberto is a visionary. He would have seen through a lie.'

Now Angelina's head was shaking. 'No one's infallible, Ben.' *What a comment to make, to two Catholics.* 'What Thomás is saying isn't impossible. Maybe Laurence was out to discredit your church by tying it to a bunch of fraudulent miracles. Shame and disgrace, that sort of thing. It's not like it hasn't been done before.'

'It seems like a long way to go,' Ben answered. His emotions told him this wasn't the right path, but even his analytical mind had its own justifications. 'There would be far easier ways to accomplish that. To cut the power to a whole city? To mess with the sewer system and fumigate an entire population? I'm sorry, it seems like overkill.'

Angelina wasn't ready to dismiss Laurence's potential religious motivations, but she had to admit Ben had a point. 'What, then, if not another religious group trying to discredit yours; what would an outside motivation be? Terrorism? Some power-hungry sectarians?' The words sounded strange on her tongue, but Angelina was groping for answers.

'I was thinking of those options as well,' Thomás answered, 'but I can't figure out how these particular plagues work as terrorist acts. Okay, they're obviously disruptive, but they haven't actually hurt anyone.'

Angelina's stomach rumbled. She took a bite out of a biscuit to try to calm it.

'The river water wasn't poisonous when it went red,' Thomás continued, 'at least that's what they told us on the news. And a power outage across the whole city is dramatic, but most places where it could result in killing people – hospitals, that kind of thing – have generators for back-up. So again, not deadly. And the fog . . . I've never heard of a group of terrorists hell-bent on making the whole world cough a bit and rub its mildly itchy eyes.'

Angelina couldn't stifle a laugh, which she managed to snort around a mouthful of biscuit and tea. *Good lad. Some wit behind that zeal.*

'So all the "plagues", as you call them,' she finally said, wiping the residue of her laughter from her lips, 'have been symbolic. They've grabbed attention, but nothing else. What's the point?'

'It all comes back to the prophecy,' Thomás answered, automatically. 'We must be interpreting it wrong. Missing something important.'

'Enough with the prophecy!' Angelina barked. Her humour left her swiftly, annoyance quick to take its place. 'Haven't the two of you figured out yet that the whole "prophecy" is a fraud? Christ's sakes, by now we all have to acknowledge that that tablet is obviously a fake. How, and who, I don't know, but *someone* faked it, and your former custodian obviously had something to do with whoever they were. This "revelation" you say you all received – he could easily have drip-fed it to you. A whisper to one woman in the right context, and *voilà*, the next day she has a vision about a river. Talk to a man in just the right voice and spirit a day or two later and *surprise*, he has a vision about fog. Christ! Even your priest said it was Laurence who "received the vision as a whole". What more evidence is really necessary? The two of you need to wake the hell up!'

She could feel the flush in her face and knew she'd gone red. *Do you always have to be so harsh, woman?* she scolded herself, and she could see from Thomás's pained expression that her words had hurt him.

Ben, however, didn't look wounded. He looked focused.

'I think Thomás is right,' he finally said.

'Oh, hell, Ben I'm too tired to—'

'Fraud, no fraud, that's up in the air, I'll acknowledge

that,' he countered abruptly, 'but right now, it's not the most important question.'

Angelina pinched her eyebrows together. 'It isn't?'

'Do we have a translation here?' Ben asked. He edged forward in his seat, a transformation of enthusiasm firing through his body. 'Of the whole text?'

'Hold on,' Thomás answered. Without saying more, he rose and walked to the back room, reaching into the pocket of the trousers he'd been wearing earlier in the day. He re-emerged with a sheet of paper held between three fingers of his right hand.

'We got copies this morning at stake prayers.' He passed the folded page to Ben, who promptly opened it and scanned over the printed lines. He nodded, as if what he was reading confirmed the idea forming in his mind.

A moment later he shoved the tray of biscuits to the edge of the small coffee table between them and laid the page down flat.

'We all know the opening words,' he said, sliding his finger past the first lines, 'that the discoverer will die, which he did. That the river will turn to blood, which it did – figuratively.' His finger kept moving. 'The darkness . . . the fog . . .'

Angelina edged closer, gazing over the translation as Ben spoke.

'But here, these latter revelations,' he continued. 'We haven't been paying close enough attention to these.'

Leaning down towards the page, Ben read aloud.

'And in the fourth place, a cross of fire shall consume their holy things, the seat of the Mighty See at its head.

'And then shall come the moment, at the hour of first light on the third day after these things have begun, when above the resting place of the Rock dawn itself shall be stopped and the sun shall be blotted out of the sky.'

After reading the final words aloud, Ben looked up and peered slowly at Thomás, then at Angelina.

'Whether this is a fake or not, we've been overlooking the fact that it is definitely one thing, with absolute certainty.'

His eyes widened as he kept them drilled into Angelina's.

'And what's that?' she asked.

'A map.'

67

Underground

The schematics the insertion crew had drawn up had proven remarkably accurate. Given that this was a place about which almost no one knew, secure in large part by that very fact, they hadn't exactly been able to run to the public records bureau for blueprints. The details they'd pieced together had been gleaned from Emil's memory, augmented with surveillance and months of technical investigation.

Pretending to be plumbers at a site across the street had provided southerly access to the underground infrastructure, and the plumbing charts for surrounding buildings themselves revealed the size and general shape of the space in which they were interested.

Pretending to be electricians at the store two doors to the east had provided rooftop access to one member of their crew and subterranean access to another; and again, the wiring of the public buildings had been revealing in the gaps that it showed between known structures.

Pretending to be sewer workers . . .

Pretending to be telephone repairmen . . .

Pretending to be drunk tourists, passed out on the kerb until late at night when few would take notice of their snooping about, for all visible purposes to find a place to take a piss . . .

Lots of subterfuge, combined with lots of technical know-how. Ground-penetrating sonar had helped ascertain the precise dimensions of the space, and refined calculations on its readings had assisted in verifying both the thickness and construction of its three-layered walls.

Searching easily hacked computerised city records had also provided them with schematics of nearby underground tunnels, which were essential in getting in – and out – unnoticed.

It had involved drilling a bit of extra tunnel themselves, of course, but they'd had plenty of time to do it. Emil had reflected in everyone's company that the problem with so many incursion plans was that they relied on everything being done at the eleventh hour. Blow a door off a vault with two kilos of TNT seconds before you want to enter and it's going to cause one hellfuck of a blast. Only the senseless and the dead aren't going to notice it.

Far better to start etching your way through before. Not days, not weeks – but months before. A little scratch here, another there, no one notices those things. Let concrete barrier walls flake away a few teaspoonfuls of grit at a time. A metre may take four months to get through, but what the hell is the rush? And eight centimetres of steel? Different tools, but same story. Iron was more of the same.

Little by little. Flake by flake. Chemical etch by chemical etch. Micrometre by micrometre.

Until the day came when it was time to enter, and all a man would have to do was tap through the wall.

68

Thomás's apartment

Angelina's brain was working furiously, trying to understand what Ben meant by referring to the text of the fraudulent tablet as a 'map'.

'Don't you see?' he persisted, sitting back while they continued to search over the page. 'It doesn't just tell us *what's* going to happen, it tells us *where*.'

'The river,' Angelina said, the first light of understanding starting to dawn, 'that was obviously the Tiber.' A connection of event and place, but hardly anything significant. 'It runs the whole length of the city. It's not one place but hundreds of them.'

'And darkness, and fog,' Thomás added. 'They happened everywhere. The whole of Rome.'

'Yes, but,' Ben said, leaning forward and dropping a thumb on to the line that began the prophecy of the fourth plague, 'that's not the case with this one.'

Angelina looked once again at the words he indicated. *In the fourth place, a cross of fire shall consume their holy things, the seat of the Mighty See at its head.*

'I don't know what "a cross of fire" is supposed to mean,' Ben continued. 'I can't imagine it's just a flaming crucifix – such a thing might be offensive, but it's hardly a plague.' His voice went level, stern. 'But the second part, that sounds like a place to me.'

Angelina bolted upright. At last, Ben's meaning was clear to her.

'It's a specific spot in Rome,' she said. 'One we can identify!'

His warm smile resurfaced. 'Exactly. So long as we know what it's pointing to, we can figure out where the "cross of fire" is going to emerge – whatever it might actually be.' He paused, then added dramatically, 'And when.'

'When?' Thomás queried. His face had been a portrait of confusion since Ben had begun this line of discussion, and was newly scrunched up at his latest words.

Angelina was a step ahead of him. 'To get that answer you have to look at the next plague. The one to come after the fire.' She placed her own finger on the page, two lines below where Ben had positioned his. She read aloud, aiming her words at Thomás: *Then shall come the moment, at the hour of first light on the third day after these things have begun, when above the resting place of the Rock dawn itself shall be stopped and the sun shall be blotted out of the sky . . .*'

Thomás seemed to swell at the sound of prophetic utterance, the question of its origins still an open one in his mind, but for Angelina the words had become revelatory for entirely different reasons.

'"The third day after these things have begun,"' she repeated. '"These things" has to refer to the plagues the text is describing, and "the hour of first light" is straightforward.'

'This all started yesterday,' Thomás replied, his own realisation dawning. 'Yesterday morning.'

'Which means tomorrow is the third day,' Angelina added.

She looked squarely at Ben. 'The fifth plague is predicted for tomorrow morning at dawn.'

'That means the fourth has to happen between now and then,' he answered.

'But when?' Thomás asked. 'There's no "at the hour of first light", or any other indicator of time, attached to the fourth prediction.'

'But it talks about fire,' Ben answered. 'You tell me, Thomás, what time of day is it easiest to spot fire?'

The young man didn't need to answer. There was no such time of day. As was clear to all three of them, fire was most visible at night.

Ben's insights into the text fuelled a new fire of enthusiasm in each of them. Night was fast approaching; the next plague was coming. All they had to do was figure out precisely where it was they needed to go to witness it.

And stop whoever's doing all this, Angelina's thoughts reminded her. *Or at the very least, figure out who they are.*

'Whatever the "cross of fire" will be,' Thomás said, 'the text says it'll have its head at the "seat of the Mighty See".' He looked into the two faces opposite him on the sofa, shrugging his shoulders. 'That doesn't exactly seem like rocket science.'

'St Peter's,' Ben said, affirming the obvious solution to what was hardly a riddle at all. 'There's only one church at the head of Catholicism as a whole, and since all these prophecies have been centred here in Rome, I can't imagine this one relating to any other church.'

'Exactly,' Thomás agreed. 'The "Mighty See" has a mighty basilica at its head.'

The two men were certain, but Angelina's head was shaking.

'You're wrong,' she announced starkly. 'St Peter's won't be the target.'

'What are you talking about?' Thomás questioned. 'The symbolism seems clear.'

Angelina found the composure to take another draw of the tea, noticing for the first time that Thomás had left the bag in the mug. *Chew yourself through this mouthful, then answer.*

'Are you really both such devout Catholics,' she finally asked, setting down the mug, 'charismatic in variety or otherwise, and you don't realise that St Peter's isn't actually the see of Rome?'

Ben and Thomás simply stared at her.

'Everyone assumes it is,' she continued, 'because it's grown to a place of such significance over the past five hundred years, and because of its position as the focal point of Vatican City.'

Ben's features began to change, as if he could sense where she was leading, but Thomás's expression remained blank.

'The Pope,' Angelina continued, 'is head of the Catholic Church throughout the world, which is administered from Vatican City. But first and foremost he is the Bishop of Rome, his own diocese. And the cathedral of Rome isn't St Peter's.'

'It's St John's,' Ben said suddenly.

'St John's,' Angelina repeated, nodding.

'Excuse me,' Thomás interjected, 'I've lived here my whole life. This is the first I've heard of this. Which St John's?'

'Lateran,' Angelina answered. 'Technically, the Papal Archbasilica of St John in Lateran. It stands atop an old Roman fort dating back to the second century AD. And it's just . . . stunning.'

'Then,' Ben said, rising from the sofa and reaching down to fold up the paper and hand it back to Thomás, 'that's precisely where we have to go.'

69

Headquarters of the Swiss Guard
Vatican City

The incursion into the home of Ridolfo Passerini had not led Hans Heinrich to an automatic trove of new information. He'd been so sure of success, following their solid ping on his identity from the CCTV footage, the failure to find him at home – or indeed, any signs of him having been there in weeks – had proven a confidence-fracturing frustration. Their first solid lead, cut short and dead.

Though obstacles were never to be accepted as the end of an inquiry. It was something Heinrich had learned early on as he'd ascended the ranks of the Guard, and it was a principle he held to closely.

For the past few hours, his investigations team had been engaged in what they innocuously referred to simply as 'networking'. It was in-house lingo for tracing out connections on suspects of interest – figuring out who they knew, who they called, where they went; everything they could find, seize or hack their way into.

Ridolfo might not have been home to capture and interrogate, but that didn't mean there wasn't a whole lot more they could know about him.

'We're not exactly the NSA here, as you know,' one of Heinrich's team reported as the Major loomed over him at his desk, 'but we've got a few tricks in our arsenal.'

On the screen before them, as on multiple screens around the open-plan office space, data was being traced out and accumulated. Passerini's physical address had been tied into phone records, which had themselves been linked to national identity numbers. Those opened the gateways to mobile and financial records, travel documents and a host of additional personal information.

More importantly, interpersonal.

Ridolfo Passerini's email and phone records revealed a connection to an individual called André Durré that went back years. The two men were obviously long acquaintances, and the content of their correspondence revealed that the two had in fact become personal friends. André's emails were often reflective, even emotional, and Passerini's replies, if less emotive, were nevertheless the fruit of an intimate closeness. And never had their digital interactions been more active than over the past eighteen months.

Just who was this André Durré?

A search paralleling that undertaken on Ridolfo was begun on him as a new person of interest, and before long André's own record of networking had linked him to a name of an altogether different calibre in Heinrich's mind. André's father. Emil Durré.

The dossier that they began to assemble on Emil registered red flags from almost its first moments. The first, the most compelling, was a single fact: Durré had once worked for the Vatican. He'd been an employee of the Secret Archives, sacked four years back for 'gross ethical and professional violations'.

Red flag number two.

The more details that emerged on the monitors, the more Heinrich felt the hairs on his neck stand at attention. Inwardly, with a rapidly increasing confidence, he felt he'd found his man. The man at the heart of all this.

'I want to know everything there is to know about Emil Durré,' he announced in a loud voice to the whole room. 'Focus your energies on him. I want his full employment portfolio and personnel record from his time at the Archives, and everything you can get about what he's been doing since. Liaise with the Polizia di Stato. Get them to trace out whatever connections you can't get on your own.' Then, firmly, 'Find me *everything*.'

He walked through a glass dividing wall into his small office and picked up his phone.

Cardinal Giotto Forte answered two rings later. Within a few minutes, Heinrich had brought him up to speed on what they'd discovered.

'Do you remember this man at all, Excellency?' he asked the Cardinal. 'Did you ever have any dealings with him?'

'Only when he was sacked,' Forte answered. 'His work at the Archives wasn't anything to do with me, but a firing from a Vatican post always gets reviewed by the Curia.'

'What kind of man is he?' Heinrich questioned. 'I know his formal details, but I need to know what kind of personality we're dealing with. A religious zealot? A fanatic?'

'If anything, I remember him being exactly the opposite,' Cardinal Forte replied. 'When he came before us for the tribunal hearing, he struck me as a man who believed in nothing at all.'

Heinrich tried to absorb what this meant for his profile.

'If he's your man, Major,' Forte continued, 'then it's not the Church's power or spirituality he's out to attack. He'll want something else entirely.'

70

The courtyard before the Papal Archbasilica of St John Lateran

The late light of afternoon was already fading as Angelina, Ben and Thomás stepped off a city bus at a stop near the end of the tree-lined Viale Carlo Felice. A few paces from the stop no fewer than nine streets converged in a complex interchange of lanes and lights that managed, by the happenstance of city planning over a span of millennia, to create the uniquely triangular courtyard in front of the Archbasilica of St John. The street lamps were already coming to life, though they were hardly necessary yet, and the shadows of an orange sky ahead of them and a purple sky behind cast an unusual, spectral light on the enormous facade of the ancient church.

The structure was stunning. Even though Angelina had never harboured warm thoughts for religion, she'd always been awed by the architecture the faiths of the world could inspire. In this city, Christianity had mounted its finest monuments. St John Lateran gazed solemnly westward with a vast white edifice of enormous pillars in offset spacing, those lining the face an uncommon square style while those at its centre were more typically cylindrical, all capped in ornate Corinthian capitals. Destroyed by earthquakes and rebuilt several times over its nearly two-millennia-long history, the current building looked more like a palace than a church, but was eminently impressive. High atop the structure stood twelve monumental statues of the apostles, added in the eighteenth century at the instruction of Pope Clement XI, and perfectly centred at ground level was the Holy Door, depicting the crucified Christ surmounted over the image of his mother and disciples, all cast out of solid bronze.

'So, that's the actual centre of the Catholic Church?' Thomás asked. He still seemed unable to accept that St Peter's wasn't the heart of things as he'd always believed.

'It's the cathedral of the Bishop of Rome,' Angelina answered as they walked closer, 'and since the Pope is Pope by virtue of being Rome's pontiff, it's ultimately from here that his papal authority has its origins.'

'From the . . .' Thomás struggled to remember the word Angelina had used when speaking with him earlier about it, 'the . . . *cathedra* . . . inside?'

'Most people aren't aware,' Ben offered his own answer into the conversation, 'that the term "cathedral" technically refers to a church in which there is a throne, or chair, which in Latin is *cathedra*, on which the reigning bishop sits. The presence of a *cathedra* in a church – technically it doesn't matter if the building is immense or tiny – is what makes it a cathedral.'

Thomás shook his head, gazing up at the awesome structure in front of them. 'This certainly isn't tiny. You're saying the actual papal throne is in there?'

'A version of it,' Angelina answered. 'The original is thought to be in the Vatican Museums, though it isn't shown to the public. But we're not here for the history.' She was going against her natural impulse, but necessity demanded it. 'Night's falling, which means that if we're right about all this, something is going to happen here. Soon.' She glanced meaningfully at both men. 'Keep your eyes open.'

The triangular courtyard before the basilica was, uncharacteristically, not filled with crowds of tourists. The frightening events of the past two days had Rome's citizens hunkered down, locked into their homes, and Angelina couldn't help but notice that even most of the curtains on the neighbouring buildings were drawn, as if their inhabitants simply didn't want to see whatever was coming next. There were a few brave ones out in the square, determined not to be ruled by the fear that had gripped the city expecting another 'plague', but even these appeared tense, sticking together, looking entirely ill at ease.

At the edges of the courtyard, beyond the lanes of depleted traffic, the traditional array of religious stores, coffee shops and *tabacchi* were scattered on the ground level of old buildings. Ben gazed at the tobacco shops with a longing that couldn't quite be concealed, but once again Angelina noticed the unusual absence of activity. Shops that never closed, day or night, had blackened fronts and bolted doors. The one food shop whose glass windows she could see through appeared to have its shelves almost entirely depleted, as if the local neighbourhood had panic-bought supplies in anticipation of being holed up for an indeterminate period ahead.

The evening sky was normal, but nothing else was. The city was tense. For a moment, Angelina thought she could still catch a whiff of the fog's strange scent in the air, left over from the morning. And she remembered the river, as they all did. And the darkness. And their terror started to creep into her bones – bones she could not, however, allow to be governed by that fear. She marched forward with Ben and Thomás in tow.

The church was locked, of course. Six p.m. was its standard

closing time, like most major churches in the city, after which only the exterior of edifices could be enjoyed, not the glories contained within. So she and Ben surveyed the structure, Thomás following them and doing his best to join in the work. But beyond its overwhelming proportions and beauty, there was little that appeared to relate to the purpose of their search. There were no crosses to set alight. No cauldrons or fonts or foundations that might suddenly burst into flame. There were no monuments at all outside St John's, apart from an obelisk that was off to its side at the rear of the connecting palace. Hardly a focal point for a plague.

Angelina was beginning to wonder if their interpretation had been wrong. They had come to it so surely, so quickly – perhaps too quickly. Perhaps this wasn't where fire would consume—

It was then that Angelina caught the first, and the only, thing that seemed unusual in her whole survey of the space around the basilica.

Across the Piazza di Porta San Giovanni, a car was parked in front of a closed magazine shop. Within it, Angelina could just make out the figures of two men.

Of itself the sight shouldn't have startled her, yet something tugged at the nerves in Angelina's neck as she watched them. They were not getting into the car, nor getting out. Neither appeared to be talking on a phone. They weren't passing the time reading the paper. They sat in their car, statuesque, motionless.

Increased nervousness pulsed through Angelina's skin. *Two men . . . two men . . .*

Could these be the two from before? *Could these be—*

But the question was never completed. Angelina's words faltered in her head as the massive structure of the Archbasilica of St John Lateran burst into a ball of fire.

71

Rome

The enormous basilica exploded in flame, the sudden bright-ness like a new sun replacing the one that had set behind it only minutes before.

Though 'exploded' was not quite the right word. There was no roiling *boom*, no shaking of the earth or the structure of the building itself. No walls rattled or fell, and no windows shattered, launching stained-glass particles out over the surrounding streets. There was no whoosh, no bang – the church was simply, suddenly, alight in a strange, ethereally blue fire.

For twenty seconds the fire glowed that strange, supernal colour. The whole basilica was enveloped in the blue tongues of its surprising appearance. But then flame did what flame always does: it consumed. Its heat grew and the unnatural blue turned a more earthly orange and began to char its way through wooden rafters, to melt leaden window casings, and to splinter and crack windows which at last fractured and fell. Sixty seconds after it had spontaneously begun, the Archbasilica of St John in Lateran was an enormous tower of fire.

Not far away, across the city, the same thing happened to the ancient, though significantly smaller, edifice of Chiesa del Domine Quo Vadis – the famed church built on the spot where Christ had caught Peter fleeing persecution, querying his cowardice and turning him back towards the swords and crosses. The flames appeared suddenly over the whole structure which stood at the gateway to the ancient Appian Way, glowed an unearthly blue, then consumed it.

And it happened, too, at the famed ruins of the Terme di Caracalla, the ancient baths that had been in use up until the nineteenth century. And at the convent of Suore Dorotee, with its orange chapel standing cosily beyond low stone walls. All four revered structures, all simultaneously. In the twinkling of a single eye.

It would take some time for a news helicopter flying high above to provide the images to confirm it, but somehow the whole populace seemed to know, even before the photographs came, that these four sites were not random. Some felt the warnings they had received had come by a supernatural power; others that they were a hoax. But they were all convinced that it was part of a plan – *somebody*'s plan. That the events around them, including this one, were happening with purpose.

From above, the lines between them traced the shape of a perfect cross, laid out over the city, with St John Lateran at the top of the central line.

Just as they knew it would.

Just as the prophecy had said it would.

'And in the fourth place, a cross of fire shall consume their holy things, the seat of the Mighty See at its head.'

72

In front of St John Lateran

The flames leaping from the edifice of St John's Basilica sent the sparse crowds outside into a panic. River, darkness, fog: but a massive cathedral consumed in flames was another kind of shock altogether. The plagues befalling Rome were becoming more aggressive. More . . . destructive.

Bodies ran from the triangular courtyard towards each of the streets that served as outlets from the church. Thomás felt the impulse to follow them. His eyes had taken in the catastrophe in awe, the words 'the fourth plague' on his lips amidst the roaring noise of the flames, but his demeanour quickly changed from awe to fear. He turned towards Ben and the two began retracing their path away from the cathedral at a sprint.

Ben grabbed Angelina's shoulder as he drew closer to her, pulling her along with them, but she kept her feet planted solidly on the pavement. He noticed her intensity, stopped, and followed the line of her eyes across the street.

'That car,' Angelina yelled, straining to be heard over the noise of the fire and the screams of panicked bystanders running from the scene, 'it's been there since before the fire started . . . and the two men in it haven't moved.'

It's more than that. They hadn't so much as flinched.

She'd strained to see their faces, but the distance didn't allow for identification. 'I don't know who they are,' she shouted to Ben, whose own eyes were now glued on the car and its unmoving occupants, 'but I'm pretty sure they're the "them" of your janitor's last words. Nobody just sits and watches something like this that calmly.'

But even as her words came, so did the first motion from the car. The front wheels turned outward and it began to move slowly away from the kerb.

'Shit!' Angelina cried. 'They're leaving!'

She made to bolt after them, but Ben reached out a strong hand and grabbed her by the back of her top. They had no way to stop them, much less catch them.

'Ben!' she shouted, spinning on him, an arm extended in the car's direction. 'They're our only connection! We can't lose them!'

But Ben didn't answer. He simply held her firmly and stared past her fingertips as the car drove slowly off, his eyes bearing down on its number plate and his lips reciting the numbers and letters over and over again as he strove to commit them to memory.

In the car

Bartolomeo kept both hands firmly on the leatherette steering wheel and his eyes straight forward on the road. People were running in panic, other cars were jolting out of parking spaces, and he didn't want to hit anyone. He kept his speed slow, just under the limit, and drove carefully.

But his focus didn't prevent him from speaking to the man in the passenger seat.

'The others have all gone off?' he asked.

Yiannis was on his phone, nodding and muttering 'okays' and 'mm-hmms' into the device as he received a report over the line. A moment later he flipped the old phone closed and turned towards Bartolomeo in the driver's seat.

'Each one. Right on time, like clockwork!' Bartolomeo didn't move his eyes to look at him, but he knew there would be a smile beaming from Yiannis's features. 'The cross, as the prophecy predicts, is burning.'

Yiannis deserved his evident satisfaction. Coming up with the method to effect this particular plague had been a stroke of genius on his part. Taking advantage of the thick fog they'd produced for the third plague, they'd ensured it was especially concentrated around the sites of the four buildings they would employ for the fourth. The cover of the nearly opaque mist had been ample for four teams with high-pressure hoses to draw close to each structure and spray a coating of clear solvent over their stone surfaces, wooden awnings, everything they could reach. The pressure allowed them to get the solvent up from ground level to about five metres high on walls, doors and windows – and that, Yiannis had assured Bartolomeo and Emil, would be enough. It was a particularly syrupy, thick substance that had a slow evaporation rate, which meant it would still be more than potent enough by the time nightfall came, when electronic triggers – remotely controlled devices barely the size of a packet of cigarettes, which the teams had placed in position after concluding the spraying – could be fired by wireless signal. They would ignite the concentrate, which had a near-instantaneous flash rate, meaning the structures would be surrounded by flame almost instantly. The chemical burned at a low temperature for the first thirty or forty seconds, meaning that it wouldn't consume the buildings immediately; and, as the pièce de résistance, Yiannis had instructed their chemists to include a mineral that would ensure the initial flame was an impossible, other-worldly blue.

'About as plague-y as you can get, I think,' he'd described it during the planning phases. The line had made even Bartolomeo smile.

Though at the moment, he wasn't smiling. He was pleased the plague had come off as planned, but he was disturbed. As they'd waited for the exact moment to press their remote trigger from the side of the road, Bartolomeo had watched three people emerge from a bus and make their way into the courtyard in front of the basilica.

One was a young man whose face Bartolomeo had seen on a video recording last night. Part of the PR manoeuvre Laurence had been so critical in setting up. And the taller one – Bartolomeo recognised him immediately as the man he and Yiannis had been tasked to kill alongside the river yesterday morning. The one who'd got away.

'Those three people in the square,' Bartolomeo finally said, 'just now. I know who they are.' The third had to be the woman that Ridolfo and André had been meant to take out. They'd failed as well.

'Yeah,' Yiannis answered, his voice suddenly serious. 'I saw 'em too.' He fidgeted beneath his seatbelt. 'Should we turn around? Go back and take them out? I mean, how many fucking tries does it take?'

Bartolomeo shook his head. He had the same impulse, of course. He didn't like leaving any job unfinished. But Emil had been clear: the moment the flames were lit, all hands were to be on deck for the final push.

'They're no longer important,' Bartolomeo said, keeping the wheel steadily pointed forward. 'This will all be over by morning.'

73

Outside the Lateran Basilica

The one thing that was absolutely clear as Angelina, Ben and Thomás backed away from the flaming hulk of St John's Basilica, was that Ben had been right. The Akkadian text found on the tablet near San Clemente, however it may have come to be there, whoever may have forged it, was not only tied to a group that was bringing its 'prophecies' to reality, but it had also served as an effective map, once their trio had understood what it meant. It had led them to this spot.

And it would also lead them to the next. Ironically, it would do so even more clearly. If the details that had pointed towards St John Lateran had been somewhat specialised allusions, the details for the fifth plague were not.

They knew the place, and even the time.

'Shouldn't we, er, tell someone about this?' Thomás asked as Ben guided them away from the flaming cathedral. 'I don't know, the police?'

'You don't think someone's already called the fire brigade?' Ben answered, shaking his head. 'I don't think we have to make that our responsibility.'

'But we do need to tell someone,' Angelina said. 'Especially as we know details about where we need to be next.'

'*We* need to be?' Thomás repeated. 'I'm not sure I want to be anywhere near whatever comes after . . . this.'

Ben faced Angelina. 'If we go to the police, we'll have to start at the very beginning. Explain everything, convince them of everything.'

Angelina understood. 'We don't have that kind of time.' Not with the next prophecy so precisely scheduled.

'But,' Ben continued, 'there's another option. This is church property, after all.'

Angelina's face brightened. 'It so happens, you and I had the chance to make the acquaintance of a certain member of the Swiss Guard yesterday.'

Thomás screwed up his brow. 'You two hang out with the Swiss Guard?'

'Let's just say they had a way of capturing our attention when they wanted to speak to us,' Angelina answered, and there was a wry smile on her face. She turned towards Ben. 'Can you call them?'

Ben had already dialled.

'Hello,' he said once the line had connected. 'I'd be grateful if you could connect me to the central office of the Swiss Guard in Vatican City. Yes, I'll accept the connection charge.' He paused while the operator carried out the request.

'Good evening,' Ben said calmly a moment later. 'Would you be so kind as to connect me to Major Hans Heinrich. Tell him it's Ben Verdyx and Angelina Calla. And tell him it's urgent.'

74

Headquarters of the Swiss Guard
Apostolic Palace, Vatican City

This time, when Angelina and Ben walked into the offices of the Papal Swiss Guard, they did so without their hands cuffed behind their backs or hoods over their eyes. They had made their appointment with Major Heinrich, who had instructed them to arrive as soon as they could. Darkness was once again covering the Vatican as Angelina and Ben approached, though this time the lights were lit and the domes and colonnades glowed in their brilliant splendour. They were met by guards who recognised them on sight, and escorted them together with Thomás into the belly of the Palace.

'I've never been here before,' Thomás confessed as they moved through the venerable space. His eyes were wide. 'It always seemed so . . . worldly.' But worldly apparently didn't exclude captivating, and he soaked in the surroundings with visible awe.

When at last they reached the underground level that housed the Guard's central command station, the trio passed through two security checkpoints and were led into Heinrich's office. A fogged glass door drew silently closed behind them.

'I sure as hell hope you're over any thoughts of us being involved in any of this,' were the first words out of Angelina's mouth. Her eyes lasered into the Guardsman's.

If Heinrich was surprised by the accusatory greeting, he didn't let it show. 'No, Dr Calla, we are not.'

She huffed.

'In fact, we know precisely who is,' Heinrich continued. He reached to a flat screen display on his desk and swivelled it to face his three guests.

'Do any of you recognise this face?'

Angelina stared at the screen. A man's shoulders and head were captured there: gaunt, though not sickly. Well groomed, but not overtly handsome. His eyes seemed to bear the lines of experience, and while he didn't look particularly sage or motivated, there was something unsettling in his stare.

Angelina had never seen him before.

'Me neither,' Thomás added as Angelina shook her head in the negative.

Ben's reaction, however, was altogether different.

'That's . . . Dr Durré. Right? I remember the face.' Heinrich nodded. Ben continued, 'We worked together at the Archives for a few months. Back before he was . . .'

'Sacked,' Heinrich said sternly. 'For gross violations of professional ethics and misconduct.'

Ben merely nodded again. From the look on his face, Durré was the last person he'd expected to have brought to his attention here.

'Since that time,' Heinrich continued, 'let's just say that he's collected a rather different assortment of colleagues. He appears to have been royally pissed off at having been kicked out of the establishment, and his new companions all have that trait in common. None of them quite fits in with a wholly above-board outlook on life.'

Major Heinrich reached down to his keyboard and entered a few commands, then used the arrow keys to cycle through a series of additional photographs. He announced the names as the images came up on the screen facing Angelina, Ben and Thomás.

'Ridolfo Passerini, age twenty-seven, a man with an unimpressive background and a few tags from his juvenile record, mostly relating to retaliatory acts against those who mocked him for his facial deformities.' The headshot was from a CCTV camera, grainy and black-and-white, but the deformities were still evident.

'André Durré, age twenty-four, and Emil's son,' Heinrich continued as the next image flashed on to the display. A young man, slender and well dressed, with magazine-worthy good looks. 'An intimate friend of Mr Passerini. Never seems to have excelled at much. Lived with his mother in Belgium until a few years ago. Came under his father's wing, and since then has been picked up on a string of petty crimes. No charges that stuck.'

Angelina was frozen in place. 'It's them,' she said, her left hand reaching out of its own accord and grabbing Ben's. 'Those are the two men who shot at us in St Peter's Square. I recognise the one with the deformed face.'

Whether in conformation or solace, Ben squeezed her hand back.

'Indeed,' Heinrich confirmed. 'We caught that bit on video. Ironically, in a way it was your choosing to leave our custody and getting yourselves shot at a second time that helped us determine these men's identities and forge links back to Durré.' He permitted a moment of silence.

'There are others,' he eventually continued. A finger hit the keyboard and a new face appeared on the monitor. 'Bartolomeo

Scarsi, a man with a background in civic engineering who went into civic thievery instead.' Another finger press, and another headshot. 'Yiannis Nikolaidis. We just managed to get his identity secured a few minutes ago. No details yet, but I'm quite sure it will fit within the general profile of all these men with whom Emil Durré has been surrounding himself.'

'This is amazing work,' Ben said, his eyes still fixed on the screen and his hand still encapsulating Angelina's. 'You've found all these men so quickly.'

'Except we haven't actually *found* them,' Heinrich answered. 'Any of them. All we've been able to do is link them together. The homes of each have been checked out by the Polizia di Stato, but all of them have been empty. Look like they haven't been lived in for months.' Heinrich stood a centimetre taller. 'It appears for all the world like the whole lot of them have gone underground. Getting ready for something.'

Suddenly Angelina felt the temperature of Ben's hand drop. In an instant it was cold and clammy.

'CE 937 LK.' Ben spouted out the numbers and letters robotically.

Major Heinrich peered into his suddenly distant eyes. 'Excuse me, Dr Verdyx?'

'CE 937 LK,' Ben repeated again, then, after squeezing Angelina's hand, let it go. He leaned over Heinrich's desk and grabbed a pen, jotting the number down on to the edge of a piece of paper next to the computer. 'This may help you to find them. It's the number plate of the car that two of these men,' he pointed to the monitor, 'were sitting in when St John's burst into flame. We spotted them there, and saw them drive away.'

Heinrich picked up the page on which Ben had written the number, looked it over, then passed it silently to a nearby officer who was close enough to have been in earshot and clearly knew what to do with it.

'We'll check it out,' Heinrich said as the other Guardsman walked away, 'but they'll surely have ditched the car by now. What's most important is that we figure out exactly what it is they're planning to do next. This all may not have started as terrorism, but they've just set fire to four of the most magnificent structures in Rome. We don't know yet if anyone was inside, but we've escalated from dyeing a river to shooting at citizens and burning down cathedrals. Whatever's next, wherever it takes place, could be a lot worse.'

Angelina took a step closer to his desk. 'We may not know the what,' she said boldly, 'but we definitely know the where. And what's more, we know the when.'

Heinrich stiffened, his eyes an urgent question mark.

Angelina turned to Thomás. The folded page containing the full text of the prophecy was still in his pocket.

'Show him.'

PART EIGHT

Dawn

75

St Peter's Square
Ninety minutes before daybreak

The circular piazza of St Peter was, for the second time in as many days, closed. The vast public space Bernini had designed to represent the two arms of Mother Church reaching out to embrace all who would draw near, was broadcasting a different message in these hours before dawn broke. *Stay away.*

The whole square had been cordoned off by the Swiss Guard after Major Hans Heinrich had spent most of the night with Angelina, Ben and their companion, discussing all they had to offer on the situation facing them. Far more unanswered questions remained than Heinrich could ever feel comfortable with, but he was suitably convinced that the piazza was to be the locus of whatever the fifth plague turned out to be. He'd ordered the whole space to be made inaccessible, reallocating the Guard's operational teams to vastly increase their presence on the square, and employing movable metal fencing to block off the interconnecting open spaces that normally made St Peter's so freely accessible to all who wished to enter.

Beyond the barricades and posted Guardsmen, however, a crowd was already growing. Throngs of people, in a city with more than an average sprinkling of religious conscious-ness, had also interpreted 'the resting place of the Rock' as meaning the resting place of St Peter – the apostle whom Jesus Christ had called 'the rock on which I will build my church', just as Ben Verdyx had reminded Heinrich during their discussions. These throngs were drawn, even in the pre-morning darkness and despite the terror that had now well and truly seized the city, towards the massive structure built atop Peter's tomb. The Guard stood firm, holding them at bay, but the size of the crowd was swelling. They breathed out anxiety to see what was next in store for their city, for them, and for those who were religious, perhaps for their faith.

What was next in store . . .

That was the question Heinrich still couldn't answer. As far as he could see it, there were two realistic possibilities. Either the next 'plague' was going to bring danger, or dese-cration. The pattern thus far had followed those patterns. The river had been a desecration of the memory of Old Testament history, which billions held as sacred. The darkness had followed the same course. But with the fog that had emerged from the manipulated sewer system, the pattern had shifted from desecration to danger. There was no history of fog as a miracle or plague that Heinrich could think of. It appeared to have been designed to cause disarray and fear, which it had successfully done. And then the burning of the four structures – that act had endangered many. Destruction, fully embraced.

As for what was to come here at St Peter's, Heinrich could only assume it would be worse.

The thought was sufficient to cause a shudder even in the Major's sturdy frame. St John Lateran and the other buildings that had gone up in flames at sundown were treasures, and contained further treasures within, but nothing compared to the wealth of history and sanctity nestled within a half-kilometre radius of the obelisk at the centre of St Peter's Square. There was the basilica itself, one of the greatest architectural works of all time, filled with relics of the saints and the capital monument of a faith that had spanned the globe for the whole of modern history. The Sistine Chapel was mere metres away, containing some of the most recognisable art in the world. Then there were the cavernous museums with their manuscripts, sculptures and treasures that amounted to one of the most important collections on earth, alongside libraries, archives, and . . .

The list was too long, and the thought of an act of destruction here almost incomprehensible. It could not be allowed.

And all that, without even mentioning that Vatican City was home to the Supreme Pontiff himself. Of course, Heinrich had already liaised with the Pope's personal detail, and the Pontiff himself had been secreted away from Vatican City hours ago, placed in a helicopter and flown to Castel Gandolfo – a more isolated site, where security had nevertheless been doubled.

Now, Heinrich was left in a position to do what he loathed more than almost anything else: wait. He did not know what to expect. Only that it was coming, soon, and that his men needed to be at the ready for anything.

76

At the edge of St Peter's Square

Angelina, Ben and Thomás had spent the darkest hours of the night with Heinrich and his team. They'd gone through the prophecy till they could go through it no more, dissecting every potential meaning they could discern. There was certainly more there, they could feel it; but they had reached their limits. Exhausted minds were not clear minds, and what they hadn't determined yet would have to wait.

Now, as morning drew near, they had become more a hindrance to Heinrich than a help. It was time for him to put teams in motion, to order men to new locations, and prepare for the eventualities ahead. The theories were going to come to life and response was necessary, and there was nothing Angelina or Ben could do to assist with that.

Heinrich had given them a radio as he'd beckoned a junior Guardsman to see them out. 'Keep it with you, out there.' He'd surmised, correctly, that they had no intention of going farther from the piazza than the barriers his men had erected. 'And keep your eyes open. If you see anything suspicious, anything at all, radio it through. That broadcasts straight to me.' He'd given all three of them an intent, still look before they'd left – silent thanks for their assistance from a man who was still coming to grips with the weight of just what might lie ahead.

Now, they wandered the periphery of the square, milling amongst a crowd that multiplied in size with the passing minutes. It was already enormous, the crush multiplied by the fact that St Peter's Square was designed to hold rallies of people inside it, not outside. Space there was more limited, and people were already flooding over streets and pavements.

Angelina walked at the front of their trio, Ben and Thomás a few paces behind. They'd been talking for so many hours, it felt good to all of them to have the opportunity not to speak – just to observe the crowd, to 'keep their eyes open' as Heinrich had instructed, and to gather their own thoughts.

Angelina kept them close to the pillars of the colonnades. Gooseflesh momentarily re-emerged when she took notice of the view through them, into the square, and remembered that the last time she'd seen this view she was running at full bore from two men with guns, a fresh bullet wound in her leg, wondering if she would make it out of the piazza alive. The bandaged wound beneath her borrowed jeans throbbed anew, joining in the memory.

She forced her thoughts away from that encounter, lest emotion and fear come back to inhibit her. *There are more important things to worry about in the present.*

She swept her gaze across the scene as a whole. The Guard, as Major Heinrich had indicated, was out in full force. In fact, it was more force than Angelina had ever seen before, even for major papal addresses. Even, if her memory served her well, for the election of the current Pontiff, at which she'd been present 'for reasons of historical and cultural interest'. Today the Guardsmen were there in their blue-and-yellow billows, halberds in hand, at every pillar and post.

Then there were rows in fatigues, armed with far more modern weapons, and she knew that many of the suit-clad men milling about in the square were Guardsmen in plainclothes, and that others would be out amongst the crowd behind her. It was as large a team as Angelina imagined the Swiss Guard could assemble. She didn't know how many men actually served in the papal force, but this had to be close to the majority of them. Heinrich was clearly taking no chances.

Not that Angelina could fault him. The unknown was the worst kind of opponent, and what they'd witnessed over the past two days gave no reason for confidence or calm.

She turned to face the crowd. *A sea of bodies, arriving when they should be fleeing.* Yet amongst them Angelina saw nothing out of the ordinary. No one looked fiendish or conspiratorial, as if she would be able to spot such things on sight. Nothing sent her into alert mode.

Which meant she was left to dwell on the one question that ate at her. *What are we all here for?*

They'd worked out the place, the time. The flow of the 'plagues' had led them to what she was confident was the right spot and moment. But the *what* . . . she couldn't find an answer.

What could possibly block out the sun and stop the dawn from coming?

77

Balcony of the Hotel Palazzo Cardinal Cesi
Across the street from St Peter's Square

Emil had hired the shockingly overpriced hotel room in the Palazzo Cardinal Cesi for the solitary reason that the establishment's 'Luxury King Suites' had small balconies that offered one thing almost no others in the world could: balcony viewing of St Peter's Square, from as close to 'across the street' as the urban geography allowed. The view was, exactly as the reception manager had said it would be, 'breathtaking'. Emil drew back two heavy burgundy curtains and pulled open the double doors, immediately inundated with the sounds of crowds and traffic, and overwhelmed by the vast, illuminated dome that appeared to rise out of the earth so close in front of him that he felt he could reach out and touch it.

Three storeys below, between the hotel and the dome, was the Piazza San Pietro, its colonnades framing it with perfect symmetry. He could make out the crest of the obelisk at its centre.

And the fact that it was empty.

Emil smiled and looked more directly down. The crowd outside the perimeter of the square was massive, gathered all around its edges in expectation, illuminated by morning street lamps and the headlights of passing cars. God, he would love to be down there, to take in their mystified chatter and the fearful, tense atmosphere. He was as excited as they were – more so, because he, alone among the thousands crushed shoulder to shoulder below, knew what was coming next.

But of course he couldn't join them. He couldn't take the chance that his identity might have become known through the events of the past two days. Calla and Verdyx had evaded killing and capture, and had managed to off Laurence in the process. Emil felt bad at the old man's departure. That wasn't a noble way to go. But Laurence had served his purpose, as far as Emil's work was concerned, and at the end of it all his death meant one less claim on what they would take.

So, no going down to taste the air of anticipation in the crowd. But the view from the balcony was an excellent second choice option. Emil could see them perfectly, and found himself equally disgusted and thrilled by the sight. The people were behaving just as he'd known they would behave: like sheep, flocking, bleating.

Blind, and fools, the lot of them.

Gathered to behold what could never happen, fervently believing in the impossibility Emil had so creatively sold them. If the fact that they were here wasn't proof of humanity's fallibility and idiocy, he didn't know what else possibly could be. It had taken him some significant work, yes, but he had managed to convince masses of a modern populace to abandon their morning plans, leave their homes and postpone their travels to work, to assemble in a spot he'd chosen, to gape expectantly after something that the rational among them couldn't possibly believe would actually happen. And yet, they were here.

Sheep.

And around the sheep, holding them at bay, security. *So much security!* As Emil had hoped, the number of Guardsmen shifted from their usual posts to supplement control of the square was significant. They stood in their new positions, armed, and so very focused.

Though, in reality, what they all really were was *distracted*.

It was absolutely, gloriously perfect. Emil sighed a breath of relief mingled with anticipation, then walked back through the double doors into the opulent suite he'd occupied for all of fifteen minutes.

As he approached its exit, he retrieved his mobile from his breast pocket. The line connected after only two rings.

'It's time,' he said calmly. 'Move.'

78

Eighteen hours earlier
The island of Pantelleria
305 nautical miles south of Rome

It came as a rumbling that disturbed the quiet of afternoon. A vibration in floors throughout the village, and then throughout the island as a whole. Cups rattled in cupboards and a few plates fell from lintels and shattered on wooden floors.

A lull followed, and the people collectively breathed their relief. This happened, now and then. Always a touch nerveracking, but part of life on the island. The fragments of shattered dishes began to be swept up, life moved again towards normal.

Moments later, the world exploded.

For the first time in more than 150 years, Montagna Grande, the dormant volcano at the island's heart, blew apart at its seams. Impossible depths of topsoil, stone and ancient rock burst away from the mountain's peak and flew into the sky with a force far greater than most nuclear blasts. The orange lava that propelled it came like a geyser from the heart of the earth and rose like a pillar to heaven. As the column spread, streams of molten, fiery rock arced away from its core and began to fall back to the ground with the speed of rain and the weight of stone.

The mountain lashed its tongue of fire into the sky without cessation, molten lava pouring down its slopes as great belches of gas and ash were blasted upwards at well over a hundred and eighty kilometres per hour. The small island itself was transformed from green pastures to a great red, flowing mass that consumed livestock, homes, villages. Even the small airport disappeared under the deadly flow of new rock.

And the geyser of fire and ash came. And it came. And it came.

79

Underground, roughly centred beneath the picturesque three-tiered fountain that stood at the centre of the small piazza two storeys above, Emil's men received their order.

'Positions,' the foreman said softly to another member of his crew, who went and whispered the same to others gathered in the dark subterranean space.

The foreman turned to the two men behind him.

'The call just came in,' he said to Ridolfo. The ugly man nodded, then swivelled to face André. They had one job left to do, and it had to be done now.

And it had to be done right. For an instant Ridolfo was worried whether his friend might cause them to fail again, but he shook away the worry.

Even André wouldn't be able to miss a man at point-blank range.

Once Ridolfo and André had scuttled through the side tunnel his men had dug over the past months, connected to the

376

legitimate access corridor that led to the surface, the foreman turned back to his men. They were, one by one, moving to the positions determined beforehand for each of them.

Efficiently, they each reached down to small packs stashed in those spots and extracted goggles, earplugs and breathers. Soon, the faces of each were covered, their ears protected, and they were ready.

He pulled on his own mask, excited for this moment. They had worked so hard for so many months. Etching through concrete, then through metal with layer after layer of acid applied with rollers. What was left of the wall they needed to get through was only a few centimetres thick, and had been brittled.

The small explosion would make quick work of it.

Ensuring his earplugs were snugly in, the foreman reached down and picked up the firing trigger. He unspooled the remaining wire as he walked to his protective position and awaited the final go.

The various tunnels and hollowed-out work areas dug over the past months provided access to the site from the eastern side – exactly the opposite of the vertical access corridor that ran from its west edge up to the surface by three flights of steep metal stairs. At the top of them was the guard station, with its three-inch steel security door surfaced and painted on its exterior side to match the brickwork of the buildings surrounding it.

Two plainclothes members of the Swiss Guard were always at post in the station, just inside the door. They operated on six-hour shifts, twenty-four hours a day. They were highly trained, diligent and devoted to their charge.

But one fact, Ridolfo knew, was the most pertinent for him. They were always looking in the other direction.

The steel security door was normally the only access point

to what was below. The Guardsmen monitored cameras that scanned the piazza outside, the streets nearby, even the air above. The aim was to keep anyone, everyone, out.

Because it wasn't possible for anyone to be inside.

The thought brought particular satisfaction to Ridolfo as he and André silently crested the final steps, wearing specially soled shoes which had been chosen in order to render them soundless on the metal stairs.

The two guards were at the posts, watching their monitors. Facing the other way.

Ridolfo lifted his right hand and held the tip of the barrel mere centimetres from the back of one guard's head. To his left, André did the same with the other. Two friends, about to be bound together in an act that would change both their lives forever.

The simultaneous firing of their Glocks resonated like cannon fire in the enclosed space.

The guards had no chance to respond. The monitors in front of them were painted red with their blood, and their bodies slouched to the floor.

80

St Peter's Square

Above the piazza, the sky began to brighten. Dawn had arrived. The appointed hour.

Still prevented from entering the square proper, the crowd outside its barriers – now swollen to maximum capacity and filling the connecting streets like a great, unmoving parade – could almost be heard to whisper amongst itself: 'It's now . . . this moment. This place.'

The Swiss Guard continued to keep them at bay as thousands upon thousands of necks craned upwards with the fading of the darkness, but even a few of their highly trained members couldn't resist the urge to lift their eyes a little higher than surveying the crowd required, captivated in their own right and wondering just what the changing colours above them would bring.

The sky grew a shade brighter.

The mess of humanity was a mixture of expectation and doubt. The prophecy that had drawn them here claimed that dawn would be stopped. Yet dawn was breaking, *as it always does*. But, as they all seemed to feel, *something was coming*.

Could the two things be true together? Or was their expectation failing here, finally, as the sky brightened over them?

Minutes passed, the air above the rooftops becoming shades lighter with each one. The murmurings of the crowd gradually went soft, then silent. The whole world seemed to be staring up into heaven, waiting.

But nothing happened.

Angelina stood next to Ben, frantically surveying the crowd, trying to spot someone out of place – but everyone was frozen, heads tilted back. Was she wrong? Had they all been wrong?

Finally, a single ray of sunshine crested the roof of a building. As if aimed by some mocking version of providence destined to disappoint the thousands who had gathered, the ray pointed straight into the heart of St Peter's Square, illumining the cross atop the great obelisk at its centre.

The sun was shining.

Of course the sun is shining, Angelina spoke inwardly. *It always does*.

Then, a singular voice from somewhere in the thick of the crowd. 'Look, over there!'

It was followed by the sound of countless bodies in motion, trying to locate the 'there', scanning the sky above them.

Then, another voice. 'There!'

Arms flew upwards, pointing to the sky.

The voice became three, and a hundred, and then thousands.

As they cried out, a wall of black cloud billowed over the rooftops with shocking speed. It was not the grey of a rain-cloud but a black like slate, specked with flashes of orange, and it spread over the square like a blanket.

The cries went silent, awed. Then they returned as screams of terror and confusion.

The black cloud overtook the sky, blotting out the singular ray of the rising sun, and pushing away the dawn that did not come.

81

St Peter's Square

Angelina and Ben stared at the black sky in utter incomprehension. Thomás's jaw hung open, his eyes wide, watering. Around them were cries of praise and shouts of terror in a jumbled cacophony. A group had started singing a hymn. Another had begun to shout angrily, crying foul, and others were screaming, 'It's an attack!', and running from what they assumed was a terrorist activity.

Whatever it was, one thing only was certain. The sun was black, and morning was gone – just as they had been promised it would be. Even Angelina could not deny the correlation of what she was seeing to the prophecies of the text she knew – she *knew* – had to be a forgery. She could not deny it, but she could not understand it.

How could this possibly be accomplished? *There is only so much human ingenuity can do.*

If such questions ate at Angelina inwardly, they had a more external effect on the crowd around her. Beholding the obvious miracle, or plague, or whatever each wanted to call it, the mass was no longer willing to be held back. It burst through the barriers erected by the Guard and flooded into the square to behold the sight more clearly.

The Guard tried to stop them, but even in all their array there was only so much force they could marshal. That limit was passed, and the sea of humanity flooded into St Peter's Square like an unstoppable tide.

Heinrich could barely form his words as he depressed the button at his shoulder and shouted into his microphone, 'All hands, all hands! Into the piazza!'

The sky was black. Heinrich was shocked, terrified and dumbfounded. But he was here for a purpose, however incomprehensible the circumstances. He frantically surveyed the flood of bodies as they came into the square, but he couldn't identify anyone that looked out of place.

Everyone looked out of place. The whole scene was a shambles, a chaos.

And he sensed that it was only going to get worse.

82

In car, en route to Piazza Mastai

Emil had just stepped into the car when it had happened. He was now halfway to the incursion site, a short trip of only a few minutes, but he hadn't spoken since the man behind the wheel had pulled away from the kerb.

He was absolutely dumbstruck.

It was all happening, actually happening, exactly as he'd said it would.

As I said! his thoughts roared, baffled. *As I determined!*

Emil had chosen the place for its grandeur. Of course a pinnacle moment should take place in a locale of power and mystique. The timing he'd chosen for dramatic effect, as well as practical reasons. 'On the third day' would resonate with even the most nominally religious, and it gave him the time he needed to get the city distracted and prep the final stages of his other manoeuvres.

He hadn't anticipated that the Guard would block off St Peter's Square in quite the way they had, but that had only rendered his choice of the spot all the better. At the end of the day, it hadn't really mattered what location Emil chose for his 'fifth plague'. It could have been at the Colosseum, or the Forum. Or a glacier in the Antarctic. Or on the moon. *Because it isn't possible to stop the dawn and blot out the sun!*

His fist slammed down on the leather seat at his side as confusion clenched his muscles. Outside the windows, the streets of central Rome were blacker than they had been at midnight. Behind him, the square at St Peter's was a mayhem of cries and shouts, but outside his windows the rest of the city seemed to have gone silent in shock. In the strange blackness, the thick clouds cutting out the light, even the morning birds had stopped singing. Cars halted at the sides of roads. Pedestrians stood rooted to the ground, staring at the sky, jaws open. The more religious made the sign of the cross, eyes wide in wonder. And there were tears.

But Emil Durré had only one question in his heart.

What the fuck is going on?

From his breast pocket, Emil's phone suddenly chirped him out of his mental shock. He recognised the number on the screen immediately. His hands, however, were so clammy that he had to swipe his finger across the screen three times before he finally gained the traction to answer it.

'What!' The word flew out of his mouth at twice the volume necessary.

The voice that answered came from the man Emil had assigned as foreman for the incursion itself.

'Boss, the guys up top say something's happened,' the man said gravely. 'We're all set down here, everything's in position. But I just got a radio chirp – something about the sky going black? The fuck's that about?'

Emil bristled. None of this had been part of his plan. How could it have been? What he was seeing was simply impossible.

But he couldn't allow even the impossible to stop him.

'It doesn't matter,' he answered. 'Not important.' Outside his windows, the world seemed to broadcast a different message. But the foreman was underground.

'What's going on up here doesn't change anything,' Emil barked again. 'Your men are ready?'

'The trigger's in my hand. But, boss, we weren't expecting this. Everything's been so tightly planned. Synchronised. Do we abort?' There was obvious nervousness in his voice.

For an instant, Emil considered the request. It was sensible. This whole venture had been orchestrated down to its finest minutiae, planned to hour-by-hour execution over the span of more than a year and a half. An unknown fact at this stage, of this magnitude – who knew what it meant for their success?

But a second later, Emil's resolve firmed. He wasn't having his whole project go awry now.

He pressed the phone close to his face.

'Pull the trigger. Do it now.'

83

St Peter's Square

The noble piazza had been transformed into a mass of uncontrolled human emotion. Its bright lights had snapped off a minute ago, on timers that expected this morning hour to be flooded by the natural light of day. Instead, it rendered the darkness yet thicker than it had been the moment the cloud swept over the Vatican.

Ben's neck had barely craned downward since the event had begun, his eyes straining to take in every inch of the strange cloud above them. As if vision would enable comprehension.

Angelina, however, had given up on trying to understand. Whatever was actually happening in the sky was something she was sure would be explained eventually, but the scenario of what was taking place with the event as a whole was something she was increasingly convinced was . . . wrong. The tablet's prophecies were fakes, of course. No one could deny that now. But it was the same set of prophecies that had predicted this morning – down to the place and time. And now . . .

No one could do this, her inner voice said on repeat. *No one can change the sky, not to this extent.*

It was the collision of these two realisations that finally led her to a conclusion.

A person couldn't do this; *but a person could get everyone to come and see it.*

Something clenched within her as the conclusion hit. Freak accident, coincidence – hell, Angelina had no idea how to characterise the actual arrival of the darkness above her. But the fact that they were all here, that someone had concocted a way – a convincing, and clearly effective way – to amass this crowd here, now. A crowd that numbered in the thousands, opposed by nearly the whole force of the Guard . . .

The whole force of the Guard.

Suddenly Angelina spun towards Ben. 'Quit looking up and give me the radio.' He'd shoved it in a pocket after Heinrich had given it to them, and with his look of bafflement remaining plastered on his face he extracted the small radio and handed it to her.

Angelina clicked the call button a few times, shouting Heinrich's name into its microphone. It took longer than she would have liked for any sound to emerge in response, but after nearly thirty seconds of trying, the box finally chirped to life.

'Heinrich.' His response was yelled, just as Angelina's call had been. 'I can barely hear you!'

Angelina knew he must be somewhere in the midst of the fray of the square, those Guardsmen who'd been posted on its periphery having moved in when the crowds burst the perimeter.

'Listen,' she shouted into the radio, 'this isn't the spot! Whatever Durré and his men are planning, it's not taking place here.'

There was barely a pause before Heinrich's answer came back.

'Bullshit!' Frustration tore through his roaring shout. 'Look up, woman! Look around you!'

In all directions the scene was pure chaos.

'I see it,' Angelina replied, 'but all this, this . . . this isn't *it*.' She didn't have further details. She just knew. 'Somewhere else, something is happening. Not here.'

Heinrich's voice snapped something back over the radio waves, but Angelina's attention was overtaken by the sight of the man himself. Heinrich stood on the massive staircase in front of St Peter's, his radio at his face, a sinister-looking weapon strung over his shoulder.

'Hold on,' Angelina shouted, clipping off his broadcast. 'I see you. We'll be right there.'

A second later the radio was in her pocket, her hands grabbing at the wrists of Ben and Thomás, and the three ran towards the Major of the Swiss Guard.

84

Two streets away from the Piazza Mastai

Emil's driver slammed on the brakes harder than was necessary as they arrived at their destination, his nerves tense from the inexplicable environment, and Emil was out of the car almost instantly. The access route his men had created over the past months had its entrance in the back room of a flower shop off the Via della Luce, a panel in the floor pulled back to reveal a vertical shaft that led down into the sewer system. Emil knew the entrance well, having observed the process of its excavation at numerous stages along its development.

He climbed down the ladder, grime and dust staining his suit, and dropped to the cement floor of a tunnel that ran the length of the street and provided sewer drainage as well as a conduit for water and electrical pipes feeding the buildings above. Emil was nearly at a jog as he traversed the required length of the city tunnel, finally arriving at a large metal electrical box that stood as tall as the walls themselves. The box had been a plant, fabricated by Yiannis's crew, and as Emil tugged on its right side it swivelled on concealed hinges, revealing the entirely illegitimate tunnel they'd dug behind it.

He had to crouch as he walked through the narrow corridor that connected the sewer to the precise incursion point, beneath the piazza above them.

The entire journey from his car to the spot took Emil just a tense ninety seconds. When he arrived, though, his tension slipped away. It was replaced, instantaneously, by awe.

And envy.

And joy.

He'd been here many times before, had seen the protective concrete wall and watched the painstakingly slow process of scraping it away – undertaken at a pace that wouldn't risk triggering the motion sensors contained within, configured to overlook minor trembles, such as those caused by buses and trams above, but which would certainly notice anything more violent. The chemical etching away of the metal layers beyond the concrete had been even slower. Progress, milli-metre by millimetre.

Today, it was entirely different.

The foreman handed him a paper mask without saying anything, knowing Emil would not want to pollute his moment of triumph with words. He took the mask and held it over his mouth and nose, keeping out the dust that still filled the air from the explosives the team had set off a few minutes before.

The result was visible directly before him, the perfect result of his perfect dream.

The blast hole was large, the height of a man. Its bottom edge was flat, flush to the floor, shaped charges having done their work precisely. Just as he'd instructed.

Emil took a deep breath through the mask, grabbed a torch from the foreman's outstretched hand, then stepped forward through the hole in the wall.

THE SEVENTH COMMANDMENT

The space into which he entered was everything he'd hoped for. *Not just hoped, known.* There was no light except for the torch he held, but it was enough to make the interior sparkle and glow, Emil's face turning a glittering gold in the reflection.

It was here. And now, it was his.

85

St Peter's Square

Heinrich's eyes were wild as Angelina, Ben and Thomás approached him on the steps of the basilica. The scene beneath them was the worst scenario a man in his position could contemplate. Chaos, right in the heart of the Vatican.

Angelina's arrival only seemed to flare his temper.

'If this isn't *it*,' he shouted, waving an arm over the crowd and repeating her words, 'then what is it?' A question, technically, but it was clear that Heinrich didn't expect an answer. His frustration simply required an outlet.

'A distraction,' Angelina answered, nonetheless.

The Major stared at her blankly for a full second. Then, 'This is one hell of a *distraction*!'

'I can't explain it,' she continued, shifting to keep herself in his line of sight and prevent him from gazing back at the crowd or up at the sky, losing the attention she momentarily had, 'but it's the only thing that makes sense. We were brought here.'

'*Brought* here?'

'The whole city, us, you.' Angelina motioned towards the

ranks of the Swiss Guard. They tried to attend to their duty, but their faces were white and the sky above them kept attracting their attention. 'So many of you.' Her eyes locked into Heinrich's. 'Almost all of you.'

He steadied himself, Angelina's words sinking in.

'And we were brought here for a reason,' she continued.

'What sort of reason?' A coldness, dry from an emerging understanding, entered into Heinrich's words.

'Presumably, to keep us from being somewhere else.'

The Major paled. He looked out over the square, where Angelina's summary of the situation suddenly hit home. Almost the whole of the Swiss Guard was here. Even city and state police were in the square.

All . . . right here.

He spun back to Angelina. 'If not here, then where? The sun's been bloody well blocked out. Look above your head, woman!'

His radio chirped to life, however, before she had a chance to answer. A voice crackled through the small unit Velcroed on to his shoulder.

'Is that Major Heinrich?' a male voice asked.

He batted at the radio irritably. This was not the moment for interruption.

'Yes, but this isn't a good—'

'Agent Como here, from the Polizia di Stato,' the man's voice cut across Heinrich's protest. 'That number plate your men asked us to run last night, you remember that?'

Heinrich stiffened. 'Yes, I remember.'

'Well, we just got a hit on it. A stoplight camera caught it a few minutes ago, and we've got a present location from CCTV footage. Assuming you're in the Vatican now, it's only about three kilometres away from you.'

*   *   *

393

The officer read the address aloud over the radio a moment later. *Via della Luce 46, near the Piazza Mastai.* Heinrich thanked him abruptly, his features stony, and the transmission ended.

Angelina's rising curiosity, however, sank as the address was read. She knew this city too well not to know the address, at least in terms of its general location, and she knew there was nothing there. Piazza Mastai was pretty but insignificant, a fountain in a paved square bordered by an eye-catching but inconsequential building that used to be the headquarters of a tobacco company. Hardly a site of religious significance, or political – or anything else.

'There's nothing at that spot,' she announced once the radio call was over. 'I take tour groups past the square occasionally, simply as a way from getting from point A to point B, nothing more. The two men in the car must have simply ditched it there, like you said.' Defeat sagged in her shoulders.

But Major Heinrich's face was white, his eyes wide. His gaze was locked with Ben's, and as Angelina turned to face him, she could see his features were just as tense.

'Ben, what is it? What's going on?'

'The Piazza Mastai,' he said, his voice lowered. His eyes lifted up again to stare at the black sky above them, his face filled with wonder. Could there possibly be a connection between what he was seeing here, and what he knew was there?

She shook her head. 'Like I said, there's nothing at the Piazza Mastai. I've walked over that square a hundred times.'

'Over it, exactly,' Heinrich interjected. He was already starting to move. 'But given what you've said, that's precisely the point.'

86

In car, en route to the Piazza Mastai

The swirling blue lights of the unmarked Swiss Guard sedan into which Heinrich had directed Ben, Angelina and Thomás, together with himself and a driver, glowed brightly against the foreign darkness of the black sky. Behind them, three SUVs filled with armed Special Activities Teams – the Swiss Guard's equivalent of SWAT – had their lights and sirens blaring and the whole enclave raced towards what Heinrich had assured them was the site that needed to be their point of immediate and complete focus.

They had taken little convincing.

'The reason you've never heard of anything significant at the Piazza Mastai,' he explained to Angelina and Thomás as the car rounded a corner, 'is that what's there is not meant to be known about. Lack of knowledge is a significant portion of its secure status.'

'But it's an empty square,' Angelina protested, still baffled as to why they were speeding towards a location that, as far as she knew, was of no significance whatsoever.

'Precisely. Nothing to see. Nothing to tempt you.' Heinrich's eyes were forward as he spoke from the passenger seat. 'It's what's underneath that has value.'

'Underneath?'

'A vault,' Ben said. He sat at Angelina's left, Thomás at her right, on the bench seat in the back of the car. 'A secure vault that's been buried under the Piazza Mastai for over sixty-five years.'

Angelina stared at him with incredulity. 'A vault? I've never heard about this.'

'That's not a surprise,' Heinrich muttered.

Angelina was still staring at Ben. 'But . . . you have?' He nodded. 'How, Ben?'

'Presumably, the same way Emil Durré learned about it,' he answered.

'They both had the same access,' Heinrich said from the front.

Angelina was getting irritated by how little she understood of what these two men were saying.

'Ben, what the hell are you talking about?'

'The records of the vault's existence are kept in the Vatican Secret Archives,' he answered. 'There's a lot in our collections that's ancient, and a lot that's considered "secret" in the modern sense, even though we make almost all of it available to researchers who have a legitimate interest.'

'Almost,' Angelina repeated the key word.

Ben nodded. 'People always assume it's the most ancient things that we keep restricted, but in fact it's precisely the opposite. The only section of the Archives that is entirely forbidden for access, except by staff or members of the Curia, is the post-1945 collection.'

'After 'forty-five?' Angelina asked in surprise. 'The modern stuff?'

'Right. Modern records, details, plans.'

'Such as plans for the bullion reserve,' Heinrich interjected.

He twisted round to face his three passengers. 'It was a project created after the war, when the Vatican realised the political turmoil in Europe was significant enough that keeping its raw wealth in public banks was a risk no longer worth taking. Vatican City may be eternal, but it's a few city blocks in the heart of a nation that rises and falls with Fascists, Communists, Nazis, Socialists. Too much risk.'

'Hold on,' Angelina interjected, raising a palm. 'Bullion reserve? What are we talking about here?'

'It's a vault to hold the non-religious physical wealth of the Vatican,' Ben said.

'Non-religious?' The question came from Thomás.

'In the cathedrals and churches we have wealth of every kind,' Heinrich answered. 'There's two hundred million euros worth of bronze and gold dangling above the altar in St Peter's alone. The Vatican Museums house billions in artefacts. But most of that is potential value. Historical. Hard to convert into hard cash for thieves, which is why it's relatively safe – though we guard it with absolute diligence.'

Angelina understood Heinrich's meaning. The papal throne might be worth millions for its historical value and the inherent worth of its materials, but it wasn't exactly something you could sell on eBay.

'So the vault was conceived, and constructed, to house the bulk of the raw wealth that's actually . . . usable,' Ben said. 'Nothing of historical or religious significance. Just raw gold, silver, cash.'

'Shit,' Angelina said. 'I had no idea such a thing was under there.'

'No one does,' Heinrich said. 'The vault isn't a major target for crime precisely because there is so much more visible wealth above, and because almost no one knows it exists. We have hundreds of attempts every year at thefts from our churches and museums, but in all the years since it was completed we've never had a single attempted incursion into the vault.'

'Durré must have learned about it during his period of work in the Archives,' Ben added. 'It's the only way. And that would have included details on the construction, as well as its location and its contents.'

Heinrich said nothing, but Angelina could see his shoulders tense.

'But obviously it has to be guarded?' she asked. 'The Swiss Guard presumably keep it protected.'

'Of course,' Heinrich snapped. 'We have a presence there at all times. There's only a single access point, guarded around the clock, and the vault itself is equipped with all the security features of a modern bank system.'

The car banked as the driver swerved around another corner, tyres squealing against the tarmac. In front of it, its two headlight beams were cones of light in the uncommon darkness.

'We pay attention to it, just like we pay attention to everything else in our care,' Heinrich said once they'd straightened out again.

But to Angelina, to whom their circumstances now made sense, he'd left off an important detail.

'You pay attention to it,' she said, 'unless your attention is elsewhere.'

She could almost feel Heinrich's skin go cold.

87

Inside the Vatican Bullion Vault

At Emil's instruction, his men were packing his longed-for prize into thick vinyl bags that had been precisely chosen both for their sturdiness and for holding almost exactly the quantity of gold bullion bricks that a single strong man could realistically manoeuvre on his own. The density of gold meant the bags were small, but could be stacked neatly as bricks on the carts they would use to remove them from the site.

The carts themselves were also custom-designed creations that Yiannis had crafted for the incursion. They were two-layer units of reinforced steel, allowing them to support the weight of two dozen bricked-bags of bullion each, and the wheels were oversized to what appeared an almost comical degree – but one which made it possible to roll in and out of the vault over the rough edging of the blasted hole in its side. The shaping of charges to ensure the bottom of that hole ran flush to the floor had been precise. The carts moved easily over the unusual terrain.

Emil was thrilled with everything he saw. He couldn't, of course, shake the tension that had jolted through his nerves since the moment the sky had gone dark over St Peter's, but hell, he'd take a freak accident that worked in his favour any time. It didn't matter, at the end of the day. *No, screw it*, it actually made things better. Within minutes he and his men would be out of here, with more wealth than the entire troop of them could ever spend in their collective lifetimes, and the whole city would still be staring up at the clouds.

Maybe God was smiling on him, after all. The thought brought a smile to Emil's lips. The divine favour of heaven, showering grace upon his brilliance and granting him success.

It would be a pleasant thought, if Emil Durré believed in any of that crap. As it was, and as the whole affair had made eminently clear, he was perfectly capable of taking what he wanted, all on his own.

Piazza Mastai

The motorcade of Swiss Guard vehicles swept into the piazza and halted in positions that all pointed towards an innocuous section of brick wall that only they knew was the false-facade entrance to the bullion vault beneath. At Heinrich's instruction, their sirens had been muted and lights switched off as they neared, which had made the final seconds of their drive eerily black and silent. But the instant they were in position, doors flew open in unison and men started to pour out on to the square.

The three Special Activities Teams emerged in full incursion kit. Bullet-resistant vests shielded their torsos and slender, visored helmets covered their heads. They were armed with SIG 552s and MP7s, all with laser sights and enlarged magazines, and within their helmets night-vision capabilities allowed them to move in the blackness as if it were the brightness of day. They also allowed their microphoned communications to be carried out in such low tones that they spoke in what outwardly was complete silence.

Angelina emerged from the sedan after Ben, Heinrich having already rushed over to one of the SUVs to get a suit for himself.

'There's nothing there,' Angelina whispered to Ben as she saw the whole entourage of men moving towards a section of brickwork on one of the buildings that surrounded the piazza.

'You can't open a door you don't see,' Ben whispered back, and then Angelina watched as a metal wand was waved by one of the Guardsmen over the wall. It looked like the kind of handheld metal detector used for body searches in airports, but this one wasn't searching for metal. It was beaming an encrypted access code to a receiver embedded deep within the wall. The instant the signal was received and decoded, the wall began to move. Angelina watched in wonder as a door-sized section of brickwork protruded out from the edifice more than an arm's length, then swivelled silently open. At its new angle, she could see that only the exterior surface was brick. Behind, the door was solid metal.

'The control room is just inside,' Ben whispered, but Angelina was already walking towards the opened door.

She was four metres away when she heard Heinrich question a man at his side, 'What do you mean, there was no response chirp from the guards inside?'

Angelina felt dread lump concretely into her stomach. She didn't know the details, but his demeanour made it clear that Major Heinrich had expected the electronic beacon would not only open the door but also notify the guards posted inside, alerting them to new entrants and drawing some sort of verification.

That none was coming put everyone on edge.

A second later, they saw why.

*   *   *

It took Angelina's eyes a few seconds longer to see the corpses of the fallen Guardsmen inside the entrance than it did the teams equipped with night-vision helmets. By the time her brain had made sense of the sight – two slumped bodies surrounded by congealing pools of their own blood, heads reduced to masses of gore and scalp – Heinrich was already shouting.

'Full incursion! Go now!'

The Special Activities Teams rushed through the entrance and bounded down the metal stairway that led to the vault.

Though his men had felt no need to work in perfect silence, both the awe of their take and the strenuous physical effort required to move so much heavy bullion had kept Emil's teams operating in a natural, efficient quiet.

Which made the sudden thumping of boots on metal staircases boom like thunder through the subterranean space.

When, three seconds after it began, the boom was superseded by the explosion of gunfire, the blood iced in Emil's veins.

With all the confusion already present over the mystery of what had taken place above ground, it took Emil's mind fractionally longer than usual to cope with the new questions that burst into it. How could anyone have found them? How could anyone have got inside? Ridolfo and André had executed the two guards at the top of the stairs, and the external door was sealed. The only other way in or out of the vault was through the tunnel Emil's own men had dug – but these noises were coming from its other side.

The thoughts wrestled and battled in his brain for a few seconds before the only available conclusion smacked at him like a fist. He had been found out, despite all his best efforts.

His fury was overwhelming.

Another round of gunfire from the access shaft on the far side of the vault.

Emil spun on his men. Like him, they'd frozen in place the moment the noise had sliced through the silence, bullion and bags in hand.

'Pick up your fucking guns!' he shouted to everyone on his left, and to those on his right, 'Get everything out of here!' The carts were already heavy. They weren't full, but it was still more than enough wealth to luxuriate a lifetime for all of them.

He turned back to his other men, now scrambling after their weapons.

'Shoot on sight,' he commanded. 'Shoot everyone. Anyone. Just keep them away.'

88

Piazza Mastai

Heinrich had not, of course, allowed Angelina, Ben or Thomás to get a step closer to the vault's ground-level entrance than the distance Angelina had crossed as the door opened. After barking his commands to the special forces teams he'd spun to face them.

'Get back in the car,' he ordered, his voice stern and his motions already marked by the swift strokes of military efficiency. 'You've done enough. Stay put, and stay out of the way until this is over.'

He'd said no more. The Major was a man in command and he'd spun back to his teams and his task, disappearing into the dark entrance.

Angelina, Ben and Thomás were left on the square in what quickly became silence, as the last of the teams followed their colleagues inward and vanished.

They were alone.

The situation appeared to suit Ben and Thomás just fine, both men tense but clearly relieved that troops of agents with large guns were buffering them from Durré's men underground. Men who had already left behind corpses.

But her inner voice seemed to scream at Angelina. *You have to go in! You can't just stand here. You have to act!*

And Angelina decided to obey.

Without saying a word, she simply turned towards the entrance, raced inside and began to run down the stairs.

Ben's horror at the sight of Angelina running into the vault's entrance was immediate. If there had ever been an order he was willing to heed, it was the one to stay put and out of the way.

'Angelina, stop!' he shouted, but he knew the words were in vain even as they came from his mouth. 'What are you doing?'

She didn't answer, and didn't slow. And somehow, it didn't come as a surprise to Ben that his own feet were beginning to move as his next words fell from his lips. 'Oh, hell.' He drew together his strength – and followed.

Not wanting to be left entirely alone on the piazza, Thomás was in motion an instant later, following Ben into the vault.

Ahead of them, Angelina had already descended a second flight of stairs and was rounding a final corner when a man in black, barely visible in the darkness, shot out of a concealed space in front of her. He swivelled deftly on his feet, and before Angelina could register anything else, the barrel of his gun was held at the level of her face. He was close enough for her to see his eyes on the other end of the weapon.

His helmet! her thoughts barked. *Helmet!* It was the only fact she needed in order to react.

'Stop!' she shouted. 'It's me! I'm with you!'

The Swiss Guardsman dressed in his Special Activities Teams kit didn't lower his gun, but registered her words and held back from firing.

Then, behind her, two more bodies became visible in his range of sight. Ben and Thomás descended in a flurry from the steps above.

'It's *us*,' Ben corrected, his breath heavy, 'all three of us.'

Despite the gun still held at her face, Angelina turned around at the sound of his voice. She smiled, surprisingly happy to see him, and even the sight of Thomás's young features encouraged her.

When she turned back again, the Guardsman had been replaced by the commanding figure of Hans Heinrich.

'What the hell are you doing down here?' he shouted. 'I told you all to stay put!'

The opportunity to defend their infraction of his rules was, however, cut short by a barrage of small-arms fire that suddenly boomed through the access corridor.

Heinrich's men were in action without needing any additional command, their weapons levelled and brilliant flashes of light marking the explosions of return fire unleashed at targets Angelina couldn't yet see.

The sound of exploding stone, though, was one she knew well. Centimetres from her head, a bullet slammed into the rock wall and blew it apart. Shards of stone ricocheted into her face, and Angelina could feel blood start to pour from a dozen tiny wounds in her cheek.

'You're exposed!' Heinrich cried out, reaching out towards her and her friends. 'Quick, down, and over here!'

He motioned towards a control box on the far side of the landing at the bottom of the stairs. 'I'll cover you, just get your asses over there and behind that, all three of you!'

None of them argued. Crouching as low as they could, Angelina, Ben and Thomás dodged across the small open landing as Heinrich fired a barrage of bullets into the space beyond.

Seconds later, they were protected – as much as they could be – behind a large metal electronics control box, as the gun battle between Heinrich's men and Emil's played itself out around them.

Beyond the box, as she peered around its edges, was a sight Angelina Calla never in her life thought she would see.

The enormous door of the Vatican Bullion Vault stood open in the centre of the subterranean chamber that had been excavated for it a few years after the conclusion of World War Two. The vault itself was a massive concrete cube, built up right to the edges of the purpose-dug chamber, and its opened door revealing that its thick concrete exterior was only the external of a three-layer construction that made for more than a metre of solid wall on all sides, most of it metal.

Inside, the vault shone with a radiant sparkle of more gold and silver than Angelina had ever seen.

The light that illuminated it came from the far side of the vault, which was also open. There was no door there, Angelina realised as she looked at the scene more closely through the gunfire. It was an immense hole, obviously blown through the encasement by brute force. Beyond it, another excavated landing, more rugged than this.

Angelina sprang back as a bullet slammed into the other side of the control box that was her only shield. Another flew into the stone wall above them, and Angelina, Ben and Thomás were showered in a rain of dust and debris.

The gunfire sounded everywhere, reports echoing over the top of each other, the noise deafening.

Until one noise rose above it.

'ENOUGH!'

The voice took advantage of a hesitation in the firing and

boomed out with feral strength. 'ENOUGH!' it thundered again.

As if controlled by the command, the firing ceased. The echoes wore away, an eerie silence replacing them.

It took Angelina a few seconds to muster her courage, but she leaned sideways and tilted past the edge of the control box, looking again towards the vault.

On its far side, a bank of men had their slew of firearms aimed in her direction. On her side of the space, Heinrich's men had theirs raised back. Face to face, barrel to barrel, across an expanse interrupted by the tunnel-like structure of the vault in its centre.

From the midst of the men on the far side, a single figure emerged. He stood among his weaponised companions, wearing a suit though covered by a protective bulletproof vest – the only one on his side of the vault that was. As if he'd been prepared for anything, at least for himself.

Angelina heard Ben flinch, his breath drawing in sharply over his teeth as he leaned out behind her and took in the same scene.

The identity of the man was clear to her from the headshot she'd seen in Heinrich's office.

'We seem to be at something of an impasse,' Emil Durré announced, his voice tense but controlled. He directed his sardonic expression towards Heinrich, who was crouched in the midst of his men. Recognising he was being addressed, the Major rose slightly, signalling his troops to keep low and cover him.

Emil had identified the man in charge.

'I think we both know,' he continued, 'that there are only a few ways this can end.'

Angelina was shocked by the man's confidence. It was true that he had a sizeable group of men around him, all armed and clearly willing to kill, but Emil Durré was standing with more than a dozen Swiss Guard elites pointing guns at his head, and yet he spoke with an almost preternatural calm.

Preternatural. Was it that thought that caused her to take notice of Thomás, huddled at her left?

He was still crouched down, his back to the metal control box, knees in front of his chest, rocking on his ankles and muttering.

For the briefest instant, his behaviour distracted Angelina from the drama playing itself out a few metres away.

Because, she realised, Thomás wasn't muttering. He was whispering a single phrase, over and over again.

'The prophecies aren't over yet. The prophecies aren't over yet. The prophecies aren't over yet.'

It was at precisely that moment that the world began to shake.

89

The Vatican Bullion Vault

The shaking began as a rumble, but in a heartbeat became something more. Deep underground, massed beneath three storeys of stone, concrete, tarmac and the buildings of the city above, everyone in the vault chamber felt a sudden, new terror as the earth unleashed its own violence to overtake their own.

The movement was erratic, thrashing. Emil lost his footing and toppled on to the man next to him, and behind her Angelina could feel Ben's crouch give way as his body fell against hers. She reached forward to grab the control box for support, but as the earth itself shook and vibrated, there was nothing that felt stable. Beneath her feet the ground moved one way, above her it moved another.

Cement, stone and dirt burst their way through the crumbling support structure above the chamber, and started to fall down on them all in thumps and crashes. The vault itself, already weakened by the chemical treatments and explosives Emil's men had used to infiltrate it, not to mention the massive hole they'd blown through one of its sides, could no longer withstand the earthquake's violent vibrations. It split across a seam that ran ceiling to floor, the force of the moving earth tearing apart the 'indestructible' treasury of human wealth.

Unsure, at first, what was happening, men on both sides of the splitting vault squeezed down on their triggers, gunfire spraying into an air already filled with falling debris. But at some point survival instincts overtake command instructions even in the most well-trained of people, and as the world bellowed and collapsed around them, both Heinrich's men and Emil's simply reached after something, anything, to support them.

The shaking went on for what seemed an impossibly long time, but then, as swiftly as it came, it ceased.

The room went from explosive noise to dead silence in an instant, punctuated only by the intermittent thud and clunk of stones dropping from above.

That, and just to her left, the dust-covered frame of Thomás, still huddled, eyes pinched closed in terror, but whose lips were still moving.

'And then the earth shall quake,' he whispered, quoting from the prophecies that had so transfixed him. He repeated the phrase over and over again.

'The earth shall quake. The earth shall quake.'

And the lull came to an end.

With a thunderous boom louder than anything a storm could produce, the earth lurched into motion again – a singular jolt that knocked over half the men still standing.

As its sound faded, it was replaced by another as the earth between the opposing groups trembled, then simply fell away.

An enormous sinkhole had been opened up by the quake, and as its upper surface gave way, the flooring of the vault tore from its moorings and ripped itself from the walls.

With a sickening slowness, a chasm emerged beneath the

vault, growing deeper and deeper. What little of the flooring hadn't already fallen in, now slanted at straining angles, the remaining contents of the vault sliding off their shelves and falling with golden shimmers into the emerging darkness below.

'Grab what we've got!' Emil's voice suddenly boomed out again. 'Everything you can, and get out of here!'

Whatever the scenarios for victory might have been before, all that was left now was to survive, and to make it out with whatever they'd already extracted and got to a distance far enough away that it wasn't being pulled down into the massive hole.

Emil's men scrambled into motion, grabbing bags and packs while trying to keep their weapons trained on Heinrich's team across the chasm. But the ground still rumbled, the flooring lurching into unexpected motion, the danger unpredictable and violent.

It was a danger one man didn't adapt to quickly enough.

A heavy bag in one hand and his Glock in the other, his balance faltered as a new vibration shook the earth. He spread his feet on instinct, trying to adapt, but the ground beneath him angled too steeply. The weight of the gold in his hand pulled him towards the hole in the earth, and even after he released his grasp and let the bag go, gravity had already pulled him too far off his footing. The only way his body was going was down, and as he reached the ledge the speed of his descent increased as his scream began.

'Ridolfo!' another man cried out, reaching forth a hand to try to grab him by the pack on his back, but the man's tumble couldn't be stopped. He cried out as his footing met open air, his eyes growing wide on a disfigured face as the inevitability of what was coming registered. A second later, he fell over the edge of what had formerly been the vault's floor, his scream fading as he disappeared into the darkness.

THE SEVENTH COMMANDMENT

The man who had tried to save him remained rooted to his spot, one arm angled around a beam to support himself while his other was still reached out in the failed effort at rescue.

As other men grabbed what they could and fled in retreat, this man stayed motionless, his eyes on the spot where his friend had fallen out of his sight.

And then they turned with fury to face across the vault. Angelina recognised his face.

90

André felt an emotion within him he'd rarely experienced in his life. In front of him, so close that his fingertips had brushed against the man's pack as he'd reached out for him, Ridolfo had simply slipped away. His one true friend. A man he'd known for years, with whom he'd been partnered for almost as long. The one man who was always at his side, and who never would be again.

The pain of genuine loss emerged from somewhere deep within him, a recess André didn't know was there, and tore its way through all his senses. His fingers trembled, his sight blurred. He could taste the emotion on the buds of his tongue and smell the rage through his flared nostrils. He could still hear Ridolfo's cry, though in reality it had already faded to silence, as if it would forever remain in his ears.

In that stark, unexpected instant, André's whole world changed.

They – he and Ridolfo – had been fighting for his father before. For the vision his father had, for a future filled with extravagance and ease. They'd worked side by side for a cause, selfish though it may have been. Now he, alone, felt that cause evaporate – not from his grasp, but from his desire.

His father and the rest of the team were evacuating enough wealth from the crumbling room to see them all set for life, but all at once the thought lost its appeal to André. He wasn't interested. Not any more. Not without his friend.

His blurring eyes telegraphed all his rage and anguish across the pit at the centre of the vault. They fell on Heinrich and his men. His arm was still outstretched, though now it had become an extended finger, pointing. Accusing.

'You!' he shouted, his voice tortured, at no one in particular and at everyone in general – everyone opposite him who represented the source and cause of his loss. 'You did this!'

And his eyes were transformed into an unspoken threat.

Angelina recognised André from her perch at the edge of the control box. His voice was unfamiliar and his face was contorted in emotion, but the features were unmistakable. The man had high, well-defined cheekbones. Artfully arched eyebrows. A sturdy jawline. *Magazine good looks*.

He was the one Heinrich had identified as André Durré, and he was one of the men who had tried to kill her. *Twice*.

It didn't take Angelina long to sort out that the man who'd fallen to his death had been his partner and, through the rage that loss was evoking in him, a close friend to André. He'd been the second man who'd chased after her.

As she watched, the furious man slowly reached his free arm to his back while his other remained held outward in accusation. She knew a gun would appear from behind his belt before the gesture was complete.

Angelina couldn't escape the sudden thought that her part in this whole affair was running full circle. It had begun with this man firing a gun at her as she stared down at the river. Now, a gun in his hand again, he was in a position to bring it to an end.

* * *

As the small Glock 25 appeared from behind his son's back, Emil saw the immediate future in vivid detail. Ridolfo was gone, and André was overcome – a fact that surprised Emil only in its extremity of emotion. His son had always been too thick to make a host of friends on his own. Thrusting the two of them together had provided André with his only close friendship in years, and all at once it had been taken away from him, with an emotional impact André wasn't prepared to handle.

His son was going to take matters into his own hands, and it was going to end badly. Emil saw the scene unfold in his head: André would fire, likely at whichever Swiss Guardsman was closest. He'd fire, and they would all fire back. In under a second the vault would fill with a new rain of bullets, and with protective cover reduced by the crumbling of the room, the chances of any of Emil's men making it out alive were slim.

The whole scene played out in his mind in an instant, and Emil knew he had to prevent it becoming reality.

He took two massive steps forward, arms outstretched for balance on the sloping floor, then used one to gently push down André's gun.

'It's not worth it, son,' he said flatly. 'We have plenty.' The riches were the point of this, after all. The whole reason they'd committed themselves to his visionary project. 'We'll live a good life. You'll never have to work another day.'

Spittle shot from André's lips as he answered. 'It doesn't matter, any of that.' An enraged sob burst its way out of his throat. 'I had a friend!'

'Stop this,' his father insisted, disgusted by the overt emotion. 'Accept the hits you have to take, André. This is over. It's time for us to go.'

The tension in the room had brought everyone else to silence. A dozen guns were trained on André, but none of

Heinrich's men wanted to open fire and initiate another wave of the battle they'd had before. They were more exposed now, too. There was no way a renewed assault ended well for anyone.

Emil's hand continued to press down on André's arm, his eyes pleading for him to obey. His son's breath came in rapid bursts.

Then, to everyone's utter surprise, Thomás burst upright from his huddle behind the electrical box. All the timidity that Angelina had witnessed in him before was gone. The young man was a vision of power and determination, his eyes red – from the dust in the air or from some interior possession Angelina could not tell. He bolted over her and marched to the front of Heinrich's men, standing at full height less than a metre from the edge that broke abruptly into the sinkhole.

'Nothing is over!' he shouted, his voice like thunder. In a gesture that strangely mimicked André's accusing posture of a moment before, Thomás held out an arm and pointed an accusing finger squarely at Emil. 'Not for you!' he spat.

It took a moment, but across the vault Emil recognised him. 'You're that kid,' the words came out contemptuously, 'the one from the video. From the Church. Well, shit!'

Thomás's chest appeared to expand with a flux of new strength. 'The prophecies have all come true!' he bellowed.

Emil responded with a peal of laughter. 'The prophecies! I *wrote* those prophecies, you dumb fuck! Christ, fools come in all sizes.' The laugh, again, redolent of even more spite than before. 'Every plague, crafted in my sitting room with a pencil and a few swills of Scotch, you idiot little shit.'

Thomás's gaze was unnervingly steady.

'There's one more left,' he said in a monotone.

The comment gave pause to Emil's laughter, not because he was affected by Thomás's show of resolve or belief, but because for an instant he couldn't actually remember what the next plague was supposed to have been. Only the first four were ever going to amount to anything, that had always been the plan. The fifth was the distraction at the heart of his whole smoke-and-mirrors campaign. The sixth and seventh had been added only for show. He and Laurence had thought them up over drinks and a hearty dish of pasta.

But Emil's body started to stiffen.

The fifth plague, the blotting out of the sun that no man could accomplish, had happened.

The prophecies have all come true. Thomás's words echoed in Emil's mind.

The sixth plague had been . . .

Christ. The sixth plague had been an earthquake.

The ground trembled again beneath Emil's feet.

The prophecies have all come true.

The seventh plague had been . . .

Emil's head snapped up and his eyes locked into Thomás's.

'No,' the word fell from his lips. It was absurd. It couldn't possibly be.

Thomás raised his arms wide and looked upwards, heaven still above him even if there were layers of earth and construction in the way. He took a deep breath, then returned his eyes to Emil's.

'Then shall come the seventh plague,' he pronounced solemnly. 'The firstborn son shall die as he stands, and all the world shall know the power of the Lord.'

Emil felt the blood drain from his extremities as he heard the words, words he and Laurence had penned and provided to a translator in a hoax that was supposed to have ended in wealth and luxury. Instead they came to him as a . . .

A curse. The word was sick in its irony, but Emil was overtaken with only one emotion. He had to protect his son.

418

Across the void between them, he saw Thomás reaching to his waist, his fingers pushing into a pocket.

The little fucker's going to kill André. The thought was a clear vision. The religious zealot was going to make Emil's final 'prophecy' come true, and his son was going to pay the price.

Emil moved with surprising speed. Spinning his left hand around André's wrist, where he'd been pushing the boy to lower his weapon, he drew it up and grabbed it from him with his right. The Glock was already sliding snugly into his grip as Emil swivelled back towards Thomás. He was no practised shot, but at this range, no one could miss.

He fired without hesitation. Three shots.

Each hit their mark. A trio of red rosettes appeared almost simultaneously at Thomás's chest, while sprays of red mist and gore flew out his back.

Thomás faltered only a second, then fell to his knees. He seemed to hover there an instant, frozen in time. Then, motion. His last act was to draw his hand out of his pocket, where he'd been reaching when the gunshots came. What emerged, clutched between his fingers, was not the weapon Emil had feared, but a single sheet of paper, folded into a small rectangle. Angelina recognised it immediately for what it was: the translation of the prophecies which had led them to the churches, to St Peter's, and ultimately, here.

Thomás's eyes looked up once more. For reasons Angelina would never comprehend, they looked neither shocked nor saddened. They simply looked content.

Then the light of life went out of them. As his body started to tilt forward off his knees and into the pit, Heinrich shot upright and lunged forward to catch him. His muscular arm forced itself around the young man's waist in time to prevent the fall, but Thomás's life was already gone.

Heinrich's nostrils flared, his skin flushing red. His neck craned up across the pit. His gun rose.

He fired back with the same speed Emil had evinced a moment before, but Heinrich didn't need three bullets to take out his man. He had trained with a weapon his whole life. He knew his shot would be true. He squeezed down on his trigger the moment the barrel was aimed at Emil's head.

But at the precise instant Heinrich fired, the earth jolted once again. Not a violent thunder as before, but simply a small vibration. A lurch. Just enough to shift Heinrich's balance.

The bullet that torpedoed its way out of the end of his gun flew wide of its mark.

Directly into the chest of André Durré.

Emil stared in horror as his son's torso was transformed into a mess of red. He didn't even have the time to react, to reach out to him. He only saw the eyes of his firstborn son, his only son, go round as orbs as his eviscerated body fell backwards and disappeared into the pit below. Emil's cry tore through the air.

Though Thomás was no longer alive to say it, Angelina could hear his words echo from somewhere beyond.

'The firstborn son shall die as he stands . . .'

The final prophecy had been fulfilled. Just as they all had, one by one, to this very moment. This impossible moment of forgery and hoax that had culminated in the inexplicable blackness of the sky, the impossible shaking of the earth, and this strange moment of death.

'They shall come, one by one,' Thomás had said.

'Until all the world shall know the power of the Lord.'

PART NINE

Aftershock

91

The next day

The sun did not rise on Rome the following day. At least, not in a way visible to any of its inhabitants. The dense black clouds that unusually strong prevailing winds from the Strait of Sicily had blown over it at daybreak the day before had yet to depart, though they were thinning slightly. Beneath them they left a layer of grey-white ash that coated the Eternal City in a blanket of what could have been snow, rendering it ghostly in the limited light.

The City of Seven Hills lay dormant beneath the remains of Pantelleria's Montagna Grande volcano, whose sudden eruption more than three hundred nautical kilometres to the south had been a surprise to geologists the world over. The cloud of ash and gas that it belched into the air now covered a massive section of southern Italy, and already there were questions about what its long-term environ-mental impact might be on the region, not to mention what the unpredicted eruption meant for the renewed activity of the other supposedly dormant behemoths in the Strait of Sicily.

The violent earthquakes that had shaken the Italian peninsula as far north as Bologna were after-effects of the eruption on Pantelleria, and it was another mystery that would consume the attention of geologists for years, how the shocks could have been felt so forcefully in Rome. Thirteen buildings had suffered what the city would formally call 'significant or complete structural collapse', while hundreds met the far end of the quake with fractures running through foundations and facades crumbled. Monuments had toppled and sinkholes had opened in numerous locations throughout the city. Even the obelisk at the centre of the Piazza San Pietro had suffered – not a complete collapse, to the relief of millions who cherished the Egyptian monument that had stood in the heart of Rome since the time of Caligula, but it no longer pointed up into the sky. It lay at an odd angle, the earth beneath it newly recessed, its red granite tip now aimed awkwardly at the dome of St Peter's Basilica behind it.

What struck Angelina Calla as particularly strange, in light of all the bizarre events that had taken place around her and the whole of Rome over the past seventy-two hours, was that as they had all ended, it was not these details that most consumed her.

It was not even the details of the fate that ultimately would befall Emil Durré and his men. The fate they had hoped for – escape with the stolen wealth of the Vatican's raw riches – was not to be. The drawn-out confrontation at the edges of the underground chasm had given the men of Heinrich's rearguard Special Action Team time to work their way back up the access shaft and out on to the piazza. Having discovered that Emil's crews had worked their way into the vault from its southern side, it didn't take long to determine that it must have been via a connecting tunnel dug out from the sewer system. By the time André's body had followed Ridolfo's into the pit and his distraught father had darted into retreat, running with his remaining men towards what they thought was safety, the Swiss Guard was already waiting for them where their tunnel joined the sewer.

Emil Durré was in custody, and Heinrich's forces would not be the only ones questioning him and his accomplices over the coming days and weeks. The Polizia di Stato wanted their share of him, as did the Italian government. They would track down his friends, his companions, and there would be trials and prison terms to last out the years these men had thought they would spend in luxury. All those trials would be held behind closed doors, of course, and without press awareness. The Vatican still didn't want the world knowing about the secrets, and the wealth, it hid beneath ground.

'But the vault was destroyed,' Ben had protested as Heinrich had told them this. The Major of the Swiss Guard had simply placed a hand on his shoulder and smiled.

'Did you ever stop to think, Dr Verdyx, that it might not have been the only one?'

So there were still secrets, and buried realities, and truths not to be publicly known.

But, again, even these details were not what consumed Angelina the day after everything had concluded. She had more questions than she might ever be able to ask, much less answer, and more emotion pent up, seeking escape, than she knew what to do with. She'd been chased, shot at, and nearly buried alive. She'd met new faces, and watched too many of them killed in front of her.

At the end of it all, however, there was one face she felt herself strangely compelled to see again.

'Is he in there?' she asked, motioning towards an antiseptically blue door.

The duty nurse nodded. 'But you can only have a few minutes with him. He's still extremely weak.'

But alive, Angelina muttered to herself. Relief filled her with spirit. She turned to Ben and, despite herself, reached out to take his hand.

'I'm glad you let me come with you,' she said.

'I'm glad you wanted to come,' he answered softly.

Beyond the door, Father Alberto Alvarez was wrapped tightly in hospital blankets, an outline of his bandaged chest traced in contour and IV drips hosed into both arms. He was gaunt, pale, but his face brightened as he recognised the identity of his two visitors.

'Benedict,' he said with muted energy, 'and Dr Calla.' The priest smiled. Ben walked to his bedside and gently wrapped a hand around his fingers.

'So,' Father Alberto said, after a moment of silence that Angelina presumed was dedicated to an interior prayer, 'it's all over.'

'It seems to be,' she replied, drawing closer to him, standing beside Ben.

'All God's predictions have been fulfilled,' he added.

Angelina felt herself clench. *At the end of the day, it always comes down to this*, pronounced the familiar voice in her head.

'I'm not sure God was as involved with these things as you suspected,' she answered, trying to keep any trace of bitterness or sarcasm out of her voice. 'These were the workings of men,' a pause, 'plus a few additions from the natural world.'

Ben's face remained stoic, but Father Alberto smiled knowingly in Angelina's direction.

'Ah yes, of course. The doubter must always doubt.'

She flushed, but the priest's expression was too kind to have meant her any injury.

'In the end, the Lord's commandment was heeded,' he added.

A brow rose involuntarily on Angelina's face. 'His commandment?' She knew of ten of them.

'I'm speaking of the seventh, of course,' answered the priest.

Angelina tried for the numeration in her head, but she didn't know them well enough.

'"Thou shalt not steal",' Ben recited from memory, lifting her out of her predicament.

Angelina huffed. 'I'm not sure all this was worth keeping a group of thieves from stealing a bit of gold. There have been far bigger heists in history.'

Father Alberto sighed, then lifted a weak hand and beckoned Angelina closer.

'Have you ever thought,' he said as she drew near, 'that the Lord might not be overly concerned with money, stolen or not?'

Her eyes were a puzzle, mirroring her thoughts. 'I'm sorry, Father. I don't understand.'

'That maybe,' the priest continued, 'the commandment is about stealing something else?'

Angelina tried to interpret his meaning, but her emotions, her weariness, her confusion – they all warred against her.

'Plagues, revelations, prophecies,' Father Alberto finally said, 'that's pretty heady stuff. Holy, some would say.'

She gazed into his eyes. Ben had said he found peace when he looked into them, and for a moment she wondered if she felt the same.

'That kind of glory,' the priest said, 'should be reserved for God alone. It shouldn't be taken into man's hands. It shouldn't be—'

'Stolen,' Ben said. His face was filled with sudden contentment.

'I'm sorry,' Angelina said, 'I still don't understand.'

Father Alberto tapped a hand over hers. 'I know,' he said. 'And that's okay. Understanding doesn't always come in an instant. Tomorrow, my child, is another day.'

*   *   *

Outside the hospital, Angelina walked alongside Ben in silence. She'd found the encounter with the priest oddly emotional. She had wanted, for reasons she didn't fully comprehend, to know he was okay, that he'd survived the attack in his church which she had been powerless to prevent. But his words only evoked new emotions and frustrations.

'I know you think this was all part of some divine plan,' she said to Ben as they walked along the ash-covered street, 'but I just can't accept that.'

'Nobody's asking you to,' he said calmly. 'We each have to believe what we believe. These things can't be forced.'

'I just can't bring myself to believe that God acts like this,' she said. She caught herself. 'That God exists at all, but that he would act like this in particular. That he would control events. Talk to people.'

Ben slowed and turned to face her. 'You're telling me that never, not once in your life, have you heard God talking to you?'

She shook her head. 'I'm not the superstitious kind, Ben,' she answered. 'I have my own inner voice, my thoughts, my conscience. They speak to me, urge me along.'

'And you've never thought that voice might be . . . something more?' Ben asked.

Angelina peered into his eyes. *No*, she thought, *I never have*, but she was tired. Too tired to have this conversation today, now.

Instead, she did the very last thing either of them expected. She leaned forward and kissed Ben on the lips, slow, but firm and with passion. As she drew away her face, she smiled, and he smiled back.

The loner finds a companion, pronounced her familiar inner voice, *and after the plagues are done, a new life begins*.

Author's Note

While this book is obviously a work of the imagination, I have tried to incorporate as much historical fact into its pages as I could. A few of the historical details contained within these chapters may be of interest to readers in their own right.

The *Archivum Secretum Apostolicum Vaticanum*, or 'Vatican Secret Archives', are of course real and as misunderstood as they are well known. Despite the implication of the name (the real meaning of which Ben Verdyx explains in the book), the Archives are open to scholars year round, and thousands have access to their extraordinary contents. They contain over eighty-five linear kilometres of shelving, a significant bulk of which is contained in a reinforced chamber that actually is called 'the bunker', sunk beneath the Cortile della Pigna of the Vatican Museums and opened by Pope John Paul II in 1980. The items mentioned in the novel as being in the Archives (with the exception of our invented tablet, which while invented is, in its opening lines, a literary play on Exodus 7:3–5, the preface to the ten plagues of Egypt) really are there – for example, the handwritten documentation of the trial of Galileo Galilei, the founding documents of the Curia – and the rule that no one may photograph or reproduce the contents of the indices remains in effect to this day. Nevertheless, even the oldest and most fragile of items are available to scholars for research; the only restriction is on modern stock. With the exception of three folios of specially released materials, no contents dating after February 1939 are available for review.

The culture and language of the tablet in this book, Akkadian, is an extinct East Semitic cuneiform language tied to the cultures of the Ancient Near East – linked with the locales of Sumer, Mesopotamia, Babylon and the surrounding areas. The language flourished from the mid-third millennium BC up until about the fourth century BC. After that, its runic-like forms were known mostly only to ancient scholars and historians, with the last-known document in Akkadian dating from the first century AD. It is a captivating language in its visual form: triangular, conical and slashed indentations (a few of which can be seen on the cover of this book), normally impressed into clay or carved into stone, and it was used to transcribe both histories and the extraordinary mythologies of the Ancient Near East, which included such famous epics as Gilgamesh, the Enuma Elish (with strong parallels to the accounts of Noah and the flood of the Old Testament), and a host of others. Anyone who spends time with these myths, cultures and the language itself can easily see why a character such as Angelina would find it sufficient to captivate her curiosity for life.

The idea of a forged document was fresh in my mind while writing this book due to a significant case of apparent document forgery having been in the news over the past year. The so-called 'Gospel of Jesus's Wife Fragment', a scrap of papyrus supposedly 1,300 years old, written in ancient Coptic and containing 'the only known reference to Jesus Christ being married', was initially presented at a conference in Rome in 2012 after its apparent discovery had ultimately led to its arriving in the hands of an eminent and well-known scholar, hailing from one of the most eminent universities in the United States (and the world). The impact that this tiny fragment of ancient paper – a tattered rectangle of just a few centimetres – had on historical and religious discussions over the coming years was extraordinary. However, its origins and provenance had not been sufficiently studied, leading to serious questions and suspicions that culminated in the summer of 2016 with the publication of an article in *The Atlantic* (called 'The Unbelievable Tale of Jesus's Wife', written by Ariel Sabar, which I highly encourage readers to locate online – it reads with as much suspense and action as any fiction) which provided compelling evidence that the 'ancient' fragment was a forgery and a hoax. The fact that a reporter at a popular magazine had discovered what scholars and university departments had not, is still causing waves in the academic community; but more importantly, the whole matter showed that even in our modern world, with all our technology and acumen, forgery is still possible, and still happens – and can have widespread effects. It was the unfolding of this real-life drama of deception that inspired me with the idea of creating a tablet in another ancient tongue, to speak to another kind of deceit.

The volcanic explosion that features in the book is something I hope will never befall the good people of Pantelleria (a real island which genuinely is the cone of a dormant volcano, as described in the story); but the details of how dramatic such an explosion can be – including the production of thick black clouds that can travel in excess of 180 kilometres an hour – are genuine. I was 'inspired' (if that word can be used of such destruction) by watching Werner Herzog's *Into the Inferno* (2016), which features video documentation

431

of explosions similar to the one I fictionalised here, and with consequences that are not at all dissimilar.

Finally, a brief word on the Charismatic Catholic Church. While the community and clergy featured in this book are fictional, the movement itself is not. Its origins are complex, as with most movements, but it had a significant starting point in 1966 when the book *The Cross and the Switchblade* (1962), authored by a non-denominational American evangelist, was read by a group of Catholics and began a movement emphasising the role of Pentecostal experience, charisms, healings and similar revelations within a Roman Catholic framework. Usually known as the 'Catholic Charismatic Renewal Movement', it has grown ever since, and today claims some 160 million members worldwide. It is officially a movement within Catholicism, though since its beginnings has had a tenuous relationship with the broader Catholic Church, often being held in suspicion. Yet its members are deeply devoted, officially in good standing with the Catholic Church as a whole, and committed to the life of their communities with intense devotion. I am grateful for the experience of getting to know several of them.

Acknowledgements

I want to thank the readers of *Dominus*, together with its novella companions *Genesis* and *Exodus*, for the extraordinary response their publication met last year. It was an absolute thrill for me to see *Dominus* climb through the charts in so many countries, to see its covers on the sides of buses and on trains throughout Europe, and to receive such a wonderful response from readers and reviewers. It was this reaction, above all else, that inspired me to push forward with the present book, and I can only hope that those of you who enjoyed the previous will enjoy this one as well.

To my friend, masterful literary agent and ever-willing lunch companion, Luigi Bonomi, my sincerest thanks, as ever. He, together with Alison, Dani and the rest of the crew at LBA Books, put such effort and enthusiasm into my work, and it is a joy to have them behind (and beside, and in front of) me in this wonderful literary world. There simply isn't a better agent out there.

Emily Griffin has always been such a tremendous believer in my writing, and working with her at Headline was a genuine treat. I miss her now that she's moved on to other roles, but am absolutely delighted to be surrounded by the enthusiastic likes of Frankie Edwards, Kitty Stogdon and the whole, energetic team at Headline in the UK. In the USA, my Quercus team continue to pour their hearts and souls into the amazing American editions of my books; and all the international editors, translators and publishers do jobs that simply amaze me. I am fortunate to be surrounded by as superlative a set of publishers as an author could hope to work with, and my thanks are due to them all, both for the great success of *Dominus* as well as the enthusiastic labours poured into this book and future projects.

As with the writing of *Dominus*, I had access to a collection of priests who provided extraordinary insider knowledge on both the operations of the Curia in Rome, as well as an induction into the extraordinary communities of the Catholic Charismatic Renewal. All, as before, wish to remain anonymous, but my profound 'surreptitious' thanks to Fr A—, Fr I—, Fr J— and the young monk Br D— who became as much a friend as a resource.

Finally, to all the reviewers who take the time to transfer their enthusiasm for a good book into a review, whether in the national papers, on the radio, on blogs, on Goodreads or Amazon or elsewhere: thank you! You're such an integral part of this beautiful, book-minded world, and as an author I am far from alone in being truly, deeply appreciative of the time you take on our behalf.

Here's to what's ahead!

**If you enjoyed *The Seventh Commandment*
you will love Tom Fox's first novel**

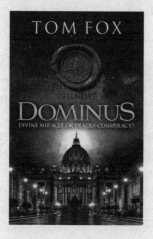

The Vatican Cathedral is packed to the rafters as Pope
Gregory XVII leads the congregation in mass. A cloaked
stranger steps suddenly and fearlessly towards the altar and
commands the wheelchair-bound Pope to stand.

He does.

The miracle stops the world in its tracks. Who is this stranger?

More miraculous events follow and as the Vatican retreats and
closes its doors to the world, journalist Alexander Trecchio
and police officer Gabriella Fierro set out to find an explanation
that might calm an increasingly hysterical nation.

Because the question on everyone's lips is what the stranger's
arrival might mean . . . and whether it finally heralds the
End of Days.

Available in paperback and ebook now.

The world of DOMINUS doesn't end there.

Read the action-packed prequel . . .

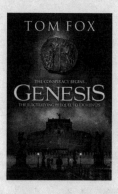

and the electrifying sequel.

Both short-stories are available exclusively in ebook.

THRILLINGLY GOOD BOOKS
FROM CRIMINALLY
GOOD WRITERS

CRIME FILES BRINGS YOU THE LATEST RELEASES FROM TOP CRIME AND THRILLER AUTHORS.

SIGN UP ONLINE FOR OUR MONTHLY NEWSLETTER AND BE THE FIRST TO KNOW ABOUT OUR COMPETITIONS, NEW BOOKS AND MORE.